RUN SILENT, RUN DEEP

Illustrated with line drawings

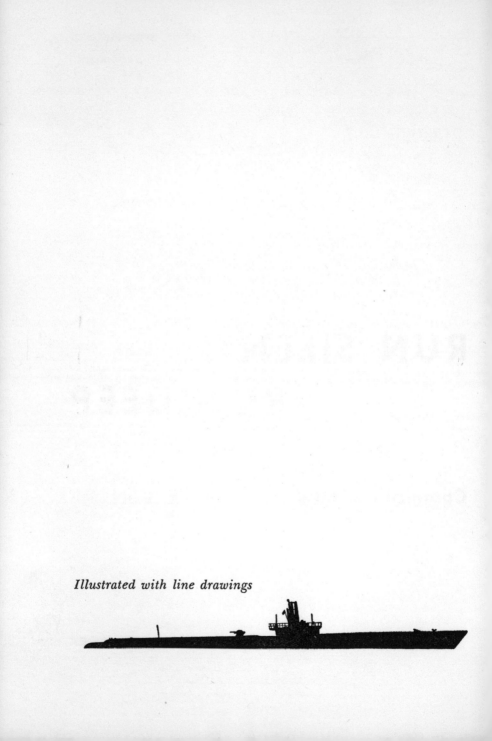

RUN SILENT,
RUN DEEP

Commander Edward L. Beach, USN

HENRY HOLT AND COMPANY · NEW YORK

80850-0215

Printed in the United States of America

To the men of our submarine forces
in the Atlantic and the Pacific who are today
driving their boats down under the sea

ACKNOWLEDGMENT

The author makes the following grateful acknowledgments to:

Ingrid, my wife, for her encouragement and thoughtful criticism;

Katie Finley, for giving so generously of her own free time to assist in the preparation of the manuscript;

Charley Langello, for his help on week ends and late at night;

Theresa Leone, who also put in late hours and in addition gave her name to one of the characters; and

Vernie M. Locke, for keeping me from forgetting the proper use of the English language.

1941 and 1945 when many of us unwittingly realized our highest purpose in life. To that extent, and with these qualifications, this book, though fiction, is true.

Edward L. Beach

Falls Church, Virginia
January 26, 1955

Deep in the sea there is no motion, no sound, save that put there by the insane humors of man. The slow, smooth stirring of the deep ocean currents, the high-frequency snapping or popping of ocean life, even the occasional snort or burble of a porpoise are all in low key, subdued, responsive to the primordial quietness of the deep. Of life there is, of course, plenty, and of death too, for neither is strange to the ocean. But even life and death, though violent, make little or no noise in the deep sea.

RUN SILENT, RUN DEEP

U. S. NAVY DEPARTMENT
Washington, D. C.

In reply refer
to number
N/P16/2117

August 31, 1945

From: The Director, Broadcast and Recording
           Division
To: The Officer-in-Charge, Security and
           Public Information

Subject: Commander E. J. RICHARDSON, U. S. Navy;
           tape recording by

Reference: (a) Article 1074(b) BuPers Manual
           (b) SecNav Memo of 11 Aug. 1945

Enclosure: (A) Transcript of subject recording

    1.   A transcript of a tape recording made by Commander E. J. Richardson, U. S. Navy, who was awarded the Congressional Medal of Honor on August 30, is forwarded herewith as enclosure (A).

    2.   It is not believed that subject recording can be of use during the forthcoming Victory War Bond Drive mentioned in reference (b) without severe condensation of the material. Subject failed to confine himself to pertinent elements of the broad strategy of the war, and devoted entirely too much time to personal trivia.

    3.   Subject to the foregoing comments, a verbatim transcript is forwarded for review. In accordance with provisions of reference (a), subject tape will be retained for such future disposition as may be directed.

                            S. V. MATTHEWS

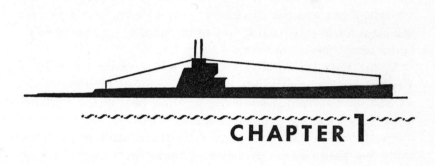

CHAPTER 1

MY NAME IS EDWARD G. RICH-
ardson and I am a Commander in the Navy, skipper of the submarine *Eel.* They said to tell the whole story from the beginning—about the Medal of Honor and what led up to it, I
mean—and that's a big order. The story is as much about Jim
Bledsoe and the *Walrus* as it is about me—but it starts long before the *Walrus* left New London. It properly begins on the old
S-16, one frigid day right after Christmas, 1941, and it includes
Laura Elwood, Jim's fiancée, and Bungo Pete, a Jap destroyer
skipper.

We were out in Long Island Sound making practice approaches in the freezing weather for Jim's qualification for com-

— 3

mand of submarines. The war had begun nearly three weeks before. When Jim's qualification came up, the *S-16* had just started her first refit since going back in commission the previous summer.

Jim was Executive Officer of the *S-16* and I was her skipper. She was a World War I "S-boat"—though not completed until 1919—and had seen only five years' service until we came along. She had been laid up in "red-lead row" (for the red preservative paint) ever since 1924. Her main trouble had been her engines, which had been copied from German designs but which could never be made to run properly. The Navy had had enough of her and her mechanical troubles by 1924 and gave her up as a bad job, putting her in mothballs and hoping to do better next time.

At the time I'm talking about, I was a senior Lieutenant. *S-16* was my first command. Jim was also a full Lieutenant and we had served together since the broiling heat of the Philadelphia Navy Yard the previous summer when, at the urgent request of the Navy, we had dragged the rusted hulk of *S-16* from the Navy Yard's back channel and began to put her back together.

Jim Bledsoe was tall, bronzed, and good-looking; two inches taller than my five-feet-eleven. He was a product of Yale's NROTC and had been in the Navy two and a half years— practically all of it in the Submarine Service. I had graduated from the Naval Academy six years before and had nearly three years more than Jim in submarines.

Jim was of inestimable help in turning the old rust bucket we found in the Navy Yard back into the submarine she once had been. With Keith Leone, an Ensign just out of the submarine school, and old Tom Schultz, a one-time Machinist's Mate, USN, now a Lieutenant (jg), the officer complement of the *S-16* was complete—and busy. With the accent on "busy," for the ship, when we took her out of the mud, was a gutted shell. All spring and summer we worked on her madly, sweating all the time, crawling about in the filthy bilges, racing against we knew not what, for the increasing tension in the world had its effect on us, too. There was an unmistakable urgency in the air— every particle of dirt which ground its way into our sweat pores carried its quota of haste and importance with it. There was also a pointed urgency in my orders as "prospective Commanding Officer," which said, among other things, "Report earliest when ready for sea." We did our best.

I didn't meet Laura until later, on reporting to New London, but I don't want to explain about her yet, although you will have to understand about her to know about Jim and me.

In the spring of 1941, when the Navy Department decided to shake up *S-16's* old bones after all, it was with something like despair that I made my first inspection of her innards. She had been labeled "junk" for fifteen years.

Jim and I were the first to arrive at Philadelphia; Keith and Tom came a few weeks later. We were all new at our jobs. Tom, with his sixteen years of enlisted service as a Machinist's Mate, had just received his commission. We practically lived in the bilges and engines of our old pig of a submarine. Jim took to the job of getting our gradually accumulated crew organized as though he had been an Exec all his life. Keith, fresh from Reserve Midshipman School and submarine school, otherwise a simon-pure product of Northwestern University, became Torpedo Officer. Tom, of course, became Engineer. My last job had been Engineering Officer of the *Octopus,* the boat I had reported to upon graduation from the submarine school, and so I concentrated my spare time on finding out what the basic design trouble with the engines had been—and, with a little good luck and the assistance of the Engineering Design Department of the Navy Yard, arrived at some sort of an answer. As a result, *S-16* ran better after we got her back together than she had ever run before. And she had been on the run ever since, logging more miles, more dives, and more hours submerged in the ensuing six months than in her whole previous five years' commission. You would have thought she was the only submarine in New London, the way the submarine school, to which we had been assigned, kept us going. We were not even allotted normal upkeep time, on the theory that having just come from the Navy Yard we needed none. So, when the accumulated list of urgently needed repairs began to approach the danger point, I protested to Captain Blunt, our Squadron Commander, with the result that the school at last grudgingly allotted us two weeks of "upkeep"—to our disgust over Christmas and New Year's. Even this had now been interrupted for Jim's qualification.

Jim, eager, alert, and ambitious, had earned a reputation as a "natural" submariner. Normally an officer with only two years of total submarine service would not have been considered for a command billet or even for qualification for command, but the war had already changed a lot of things.

It had taken me a full year to complete my submarine notebook and qualify in submarines, and gruff old Joe Blunt, my skipper in *Octopus* at the time, had pinned his own dolphins on my shirt. Jim had needed no notebook, had put on his dolphins within six months of graduating from the submarine school. Three years I served in *Octopus,* fourteen months as Engineer, before the man who had relieved Blunt, Jerry Watson, judged me worthy of his recommendation for "Qualification for Command of Submarines." That had happened only last spring, and I had received my orders to the *S-16* within two weeks. The *Octopus* had sailed for Manila the same day I had taken off in the Pan-American Clipper, bound in the other direction.

And here was Jim going through the same thing after only half the time in subs. This seemed contrary to the conservative submarine instinct—contrary to my reservations, too; and yet the whole thing, in this instance at least, had been my own doing.

An interview with our Squadron Commander, Joe Blunt

himself, now older-looking and gruffer than ever, had kicked the whole thing off nearly a week before.

Captain Joseph Blunt was short and spare, and he looked and acted his name. Everyone in the submarine force knew that diesel fuel ran in his veins instead of blood. He was hard-boiled, but his weakness was "the boats"—and he had no use for any man who did not feel the same way. When he sent for me that Tuesday morning, I knew him well enough to climb right out of *S-16's* superstructure and run over in my dirty khaki. True to form, he started shouting questions at me the moment I opened the door to his office.

"Richardson," he barked, "what about your Exec? Do you think he's ready for command yet?"

The question caught me by surprise. "Why, I haven't thought much about it, Commodore," I answered. "He's an excellent officer, but still very junior——"

"He's a Lieutenant, too, isn't he? Anyway, his rank makes no difference if he knows his business. I've a particular reason for asking you. He's your responsibility, you know."

I could think of nothing more intelligent to say than a non-committal "Yes, sir!"

The Squadron Commander waited a moment, clamped a well-chewed pipe between his teeth and sucked moistly—and futilely—on it. "Did you know that our submarine production target has been tripled for next year? Does that mean anything to you?"

I waited in my turn. This was the first time I had heard this particular piece of news, though I suppose I should have anticipated something of the sort on account of the war. "We'll need more qualified submarine personnel," I ventured.

"Do I have to draw you a diagram, Richardson?" Blunt cracked out. "Just where do you expect we're going to find the skippers for these new boats?"

"You mean me?" I stuttered, feeling as though a cold blast of air had suddenly blown on the back of my neck.

"Precisely. I've received a request from the submarine detail desk—and this is all private information, understand—to nominate officers from my squadron for the new boats under construction at the Electric Boat Company here and in the Navy Yards at Portsmouth and Mare Island." Old Joe Blunt was looking me right in the eyes, the way he did when he was really putting a man on the spot. "But also I've got to keep this training squadron going. Now do you see why I asked you about Bledsoe?"

"You mean," I said, "if Jim can take over the *S-16*, I can be nominated for one of the new submarines?"

"That's about right, Rich. Of course, you'll get one anyhow eventually—that is, if you want one"—here old Blunt looked suddenly sardonic—"but you've been doing well with the *S-16*, and I think you should have your chance now. There are a number of skippers senior to you, however, who will have to take priority over you for the available replacements; so the way it stacks up, unless Bledsoe can take over the *S-16*, I'm going to have to hang on to you for a while longer."

This was the first time since he had left *Octopus* that Captain Blunt had called me by my nickname, and obviously it was not accidental. He was telling me, as clearly as he knew how, that he would back me up in giving the *S-16* to Jim, but that doing so was my responsibility. That was the whole crux of the matter. I was morally sure that Jim, despite his good qualities, was not yet ready for an independent command of his own. There was a certain flippancy—a sort of devil-may-care attitude—almost recklessness, about him. And yet Jim had shown extraordinary aptitude in certain phases of the *S-16's* work. He certainly knew the ship, mechanically, as well or better than anyone on board. It was just a hunch, more than anything else on my part, that somehow there was a degree of immaturity about him which needed more seasoning before he was turned loose with the responsibility of a ship and crew on his back. He had been commissioned in the Navy only slightly more than three years. His

— 8

total submarine service was less than three years. This was reflected in the fact that he was not yet "qualified for command of submarines," a designation requiring proof of one's ability before a board of skippers and written certification of acceptance by them, ordinarily earned some time prior to actually getting your first boat. Subconsciously, without giving the subject open thought, I had not yet been ready to recommend him.

"Bledsoe is not yet qualified for command, Commodore," I began slowly. "As a matter of fact, I had not intended to put him up for a while——"

Captain Blunt slid himself forward on the edge of his chair, hands placed on its arms as though he were about to rise from it. "That's really up to you, too, isn't it?" he said. "Why don't you talk it over with him and think about it for a while. Let me know tomorrow."

I rose, beating him to it. "Aye, aye, sir," I answered, and turned to go out.

"By the way, Rich," Captain Blunt called after me, "keep all this confidential for the moment."

This was the second time he had cautioned me. I gave him another "Aye, aye, sir" and beat my retreat. There were entirely too many things to think about. Undeniably, the idea of having command of one of the newest and most powerful submarines our Navy could build, one of the new *Gato* class, even better than the recently completed *Tambor* and her sisters—and far improved over the old *Octopus*—was tantalizingly attractive. The new boats carried ten torpedo tubes and a total of twenty-four torpedoes, as compared to only six tubes and sixteen fish in the *Octopus*. They were bigger, built to dive deeper, and had a considerably longer cruising range. Their fire-control system had been improved and streamlined so that it was both easier to operate and simpler than any I'd been used to. By comparison even to the *Octopus,* poor old *S-16* was nothing but antiquated scrap iron, kept in operation for training duties only so that the fleet boats could be released for other more valuable service.

The skippers of the fleet boats were the elite of the submarine force. When they spoke up in the squadron or division councils, or before the Admiral, their words carried weight and they were listened to. Someday, naturally, I had hoped to join their number. Now, because of the war, the dream of a submariner's career was suddenly practically at hand—all I had to do was to turn the S-16 over to Jim.

By the time I got back aboard I had gone over all the arguments at least three times. The chance of getting a first-line command early was too much to pass up lightly, even though I could be practically assured of being given one later on. But there was also the fact that I owed something to the S-16 and her crew. It would be unthinkable to leave them in charge of anyone not fully ready and competent to be in command of a submarine.

All the way back to the refit pier alongside which S-16 was moored I wrestled with the pros and cons, and as I felt the wooden planks of the dock under my feet I was no closer to a decision than before. Stepping close to the edge of the dock, I looked over the short, angular profile of the ship to which, until an hour ago, I had felt virtually wedded. Now she looked small, puny, and tired. The only mission she would ever have in the war would be to train submarine-school students. She could never expect to go anywhere nor do anything worthwhile; just spend the war going in and out of port, carrying trainees into Long Island Sound for a day's operations.

Then the deciding argument flooded my brain. The fleet boats by contrast were going into war and danger. Suppose Captain Blunt were to misunderstand my motives for choosing to stay with the S-16 instead of eagerly taking a far-ranging fleet boat? For that matter, how could I be sure myself: Could that have been the thought prompting the peculiar expression on his

— 10

face when he said I could get one, eventually, if I really wanted one?

My head was spinning as I climbed down into *S-16's* torpedo room and made my way aft to where Jim was working in the wardroom. He was deep in sorting out work requests and job orders; comparing one against the other and making three piles which he had labeled "Will be Done," "Fight For," and "Next Time." No doubt about it, he knew how to be an effective Executive Officer. But at this moment the consideration of what was to be accomplished during our refit, ordinarily of consuming interest to all of us, had suddenly lost all fascination for me. I interrupted Jim, beckoned him into the tiny stateroom which he and I shared.

"Jim," I said, "have you thought much about qualification for command?"

Jim looked startled. "Of course. You have to be qualified before you can have your own boat."

I grinned at him, but inside I was in a turmoil. This was casting the die. Jim's face still held the surprised question as I took the plunge. "Well, I'm recommending you today."

A succession of emotions crossed his face. "You're kidding! I thought I was too junior——"

"Not any more." Jim's bunk was folded up against the curved side of the ship, leaving room above mine so that a person could sit upright upon it. I sank into it, leaned back.

Jim looked down at the deck, shifted his weight uneasily. "What's happened?" he asked.

"Nothing, old man. I just thought it was time to put you up——"

"I mean when the Commodore sent for you. Is this what you talked about?"

"Nope." I forced another smile.

"I'll bet it was though." Jim seemed lost in thought. He kicked the side of my bunk impatiently, jackknifed his length into the chair in front of our desk. He reached for a cigarette. "Know what I heard yesterday?" He paused, the lighted match in front of it, then sucked the flame into its tip.

"What did you hear yesterday." I made it a statement instead of a question.

"That we're going to start a big submarine campaign against the Japs." He puffed moodily.

I put both hands behind my head. "What's so surprising about that? It's what the submarine force was built for."

"I mean against the Japanese merchant marine. We've been training to fight warships and to act as fleet advance scouts and all like that. That's why the big boats are even called 'fleet submarines.' Now they're going to send us against the merchant ships, just like the Germans have been doing."

"Maybe so. What's that got to do with your qualification?"

More quick puffs. "Don't you see? We'll have to build a lot more boats—the dope is that E.B. tripled their order for steel plate already. Everybody who has a training boat now will get one of the new fleet boats. All the fleet-boat skippers who have made a few war patrols will become Division Commanders, and all the Execs of these river boats will move up to skipper!"

I snapped to attention, immediately on guard. "Where did you hear that?"

"Oh, it's around. All over the base, in fact. They say all the skippers around here will receive orders in a couple of weeks. I'll bet"—here Jim took a deep drag—"old Blunt told you to qualify me, didn't he?"

"No such thing, Jim." I hoped the lie sounded convincing. "A Squadron Commander can't do that anyway. You know that."

"Sure, but he can make some pretty strong suggestions. I'll bet he told you to get me qualified so I could take over somebody's boat when he leaves—come on now, didn't he?" Jim's face lighted with pleasure. He rushed right by my beginning remonstrance. "Say—that would be pretty good! Skipper of my own boat! They'd probably even give me the *S-16*—you'll be leaving pretty soon, you know!"

"Listen, Jim," I began again uneasily. "You can think what you want. It doesn't make any difference. Maybe you're right and there will be a lot of moves. Eventually it's bound to happen, but it can't all take place in an instant. After all, it takes over a year to build a fleet-type submarine."

But Jim's enthusiasm was not to be dampened. He probably didn't even hear me. "Everybody knows they're setting up a pool of Execs qualified to take over these river boats when the skippers leave, but I didn't think I was eligible. If I get the *S-16*, or some boat like her, they won't want to send me back to being Exec again; so they'll just have to leave me here until they get far enough down the list to give me one of the big ones. That will take a long time." Excitedly he stubbed out his smoke, jumped to his feet.

"What do I have to do?"

"Well," I hesitated, "I imagine the Squadron Commander will appoint a Qualification Board on you."

Jim's face fell. "You mean I'll have to make a submerged approach with this old tub? Why, she's so out of date it would be just a waste of time!"

"That's where you're wrong, Jim," I said, a bit sententiously, startled by his sudden vehemence. "Even if the *S-16* is not very modern, for all you know you might have to command this ship or one like it in action. After all, there is a squadron of S-boats out in the Philippines right now. Besides, what about the training exercises for the sub school?"

"They ought to have their heads examined," said Jim, reaching into the desk for another cigarette. "That's just plain crazy, keeping those S-boats out there. They ought to be brought back as quickly as they can."

Jim and I had argued this point before, although he had never expressed himself so directly regarding the fighting prowess of the *S-16*.

"Easy, old boy, you may be right, but there is nothing you can do about it. The Examining Board will expect to see you make a submerged approach in this boat, using the equipment she's got—so you may as well figure on it."

Jim lighted off and took a petulant puff.

"I haven't had a chance to do any approach work since reporting to Philadelphia."

As skipper, it was, of course, my responsibility that my officers have adequate opportunity for their own training, and I had to admit the justice of this. The demands of the sub school had taken priority, and I had not insisted on saving adequate time for either Jim or Keith. Keith, of course, would soon be up for his dolphins.

"Look, Jim," I said, "after we get the *S-16* back together and this refit finished, we'll take time out of our post refit trials to give you a couple of practice runs. That's all you need. Just enough to get your hand back in."

Jim's brow cleared, somewhat indecisively. Then he leaped to his feet, crushing out the hardly tasted cigarette as he rose. "I want to run up the dock and phone Laura. Okay?"

"Sure!" I rose too. "Give her my best."

"You bet I will!" He turned at the stateroom entrance. "This is a terrific break, you know! This is just what we've been waiting for. You'll be our best man, won't you?"

He turned and dashed away, leaving me virtually thunderstruck. I had, of course—as we all had—realized that Jim and Laura were as good as engaged. But I didn't expect their marriage to hinge upon his qualification for command of submarines.

The upshot was another unforeseen complication, too. Upon receipt of my recommendation for Jim's qualification for command of submarines, Captain Blunt immediately ordered three other skippers in our squadron to form an Examining Board, and he furthermore directed them to meet on Jim at once.

With Christmas almost upon us, this was not a popular order. The conversation with Blunt had taken place on Tuesday; Thursday was Christmas; Friday, Saturday, and Sunday the Examining Board worked Jim over on his knowledge of Submarine theory, tactics, strategy, logistics, and even history. Furthermore, our two weeks' refit was summarily cut in half and the following Monday found *S-16* getting under way again.

Cutting short our repair and upkeep period was hard on the ship and crew. Jobs which had long wanted doing had to be again postponed; some of the very urgent ones had to be hastily rushed to completion. Our topside paint job had to be foregone, the rust spots merely scraped and daubed with red lead. Nor was this all, for the members of the Examining Board also had to give up what plans they might have made. One, Roy Savage, had already received his orders to the *Needlefish,* soon to be launched at Mare Island. Carl Miller was awaiting his orders any day. Only the third, Stocker Kane, was like myself apparently fated to stay in his old R-boat a while longer.

After thinking over the prospect of leaving my ship to Jim, I was not too happy either. Against my better instincts I had pushed him into a situation for which I knew he was not yet ready. I had officially signed my name that, in my opinion, he was ready for the examination, when in my bones I felt this not to be the case. True, Jim could handle the ship well, and he had studied and therefore presumably knew—the submerged-attack doctrine. But now that the question had come to issue I was convinced that, so far as Jim Bledsoe was concerned, it was much too soon. His judgment under pressure or in emergency situations was still an unknown quantity. Somehow I felt unsure of him. Under these circumstances how could I, seeking my own advantage, blithely leave *S-16* and her crew of forty men to him? And yet, having started the train of events, I was powerless to stop it.

Qualification for command of a submarine is probably the toughest formal test of a submarine officer's career, and it is almost equally tough on the Examining Board and his own skipper. Successful qualification usually does not carry with it an immediate command assignment—though in Jim's case it would, and somehow he had guessed it. No special insignia exists for it like the gold dolphin pin for qualification in submarine duty. A mark is merely placed opposite your name in the submarine force roster—but no man can be ordered to submarine command without that mark.

A submarine is a demanding command in peace or war, probably more so than any other ship. The submarine skipper personally fights his ship, giving all the commands and making all the decisions. During war his is the responsibility for success or failure; his the praise for sinking the enemy, the blame for being sunk himself. In peacetime there are still the hazards of the malevolent sea—ever-ready, with its sequence of inevitable consequences, to pounce mercilessly upon momentary disregard for its laws.

Appearance before a Qualification Board, a serious matter for the candidate, is thus equally serious for the members of the board themselves. On the one hand, they hold the career of a brother officer in their hands, but on the other, and much more important, they must consider the lives and well-being of his future ship's company as well. And it is serious, also, for the person or persons recommending him, whose own judgment in so doing is under inspection.

On Monday we were—somehow—ready. The disassembled pieces of machinery had been put back together, mostly unrepaired, and great patches of red preservative on our decks and sides betrayed the areas we had been scraping free of rust and loose paint. Prior to the arrival of the Qualification Board, Jim, at their dictum, had made all preparations for getting under way; this was something he normally did every third day anyway, when he had the duty—though not, of course, under quite the same degree of pressure. The engines were warmed up and primed, the batteries fully charged, the crew at stations. All lines to the dock had been "singled up," which means that the usual three strands of mooring line to each of our four cleats had been reduced to one, ready for immediate release. I waited on the forecastle, swathed in muffler, foul-weather jacket, and sea boots, turning my back to the freezing wind sweeping the river. Jim, of course, was on the bridge.

Three figures suddenly appeared from behind the parked cars at the head of the dock, marched toward us. I recognized them immediately: Carl Miller, skipper of the *R-4*, Roy Savage of the *S-48*, and Stocker Kane of the *R-12*. Savage was the senior in rank, a Lieutenant Commander of several years, and had been designated "Senior Member" of the Qualification Board. He was a stocky, taciturn individual, whose usual imperturbability seemed only intensified by this assignment. Bluff Carl Miller, also a Lieutenant Commander, had gone through submarine school with me several years before. Stocker Kane, junior member of the board, and my closest friend of the three, was another hard-to-know person, though one soon learned to like and respect his careful thinking.

Jim hurriedly climbed down on deck and stood with me to welcome the three other skippers aboard. Gravely we acknowledged their salutes. "Good morning, sir," I said to Savage. "Morning, Carl. Morning, Stocker."

Roy Savage didn't believe in wasting time. "Take her on out as soon as you're ready," he said to Jim. "Rich"—turning to me —"Bledsoe is skipper of this ship today. You and I are just passengers. You're only to take her over to avoid danger of casualty, and you know the consequences, of course, if you do."

This was customary for the under-way qualification, and Roy Savage knew I knew it. His care to spell it out for me, therefore, somehow tinkled a warning note in my mind. Savage, I had heard, had been indignant at Blunt's sudden directive to head the board on Jim. He was the senior skipper in our squadron, and had already received his official orders of detachment from the *S-48*, though there was as yet no sign of his relief. Perhaps he felt that his pending detachment should have absolved him from the duty. Perhaps this was an inkling of the attitude we might expect from him throughout the day.

Stocker Kane now spoke, handing me a typewritten sheet of official stationery. "This will save your Yeoman a little trouble. I've got a copy for the Quartermaster, too." He smiled faintly as I reached for it.

S-16's Yeoman, Quin, a young, eager-faced lad, stepped forward and took the piece of paper from me, attaching it to another sheet he carried in his hand. The papers constituted our "sailing list"—a list, corrected as of the last possible moment, containing the names, addresses, next-of-kin, and other pertinent information on all persons embarked, which is sent ashore whenever a submarine gets under way. This was an outgrowth of one of the early accidents wherein difficulty was encountered in determining exactly who had been aboard the ill-fated craft and how to reach their relatives.

Rubinoffski, our Quartermaster, who had been loitering near the conning tower, also received a list of our passengers and forthwith disappeared to enter their names in the log. Noticing the unobtrusive efficiency of these two, I felt a glow of pride at the fact that they so obviously knew exactly what they were doing.

Jim had returned to the bridge and was waiting. I could well appreciate how he must have felt, remembering how I had sweated under the eyes of my Qualification Board on *Octopus'* bridge. But I had never really given thought until this moment to the feeling my skipper must have experienced.

Despite the qualification gimmick, nothing relieved me of responsibility for *S-16*. And yet I had to stand idly on her red-lead-spotted deck, too far from the bridge to take corrective action should anything go wrong, while one of my own officers, as a result of my recommendation, held my career as well as his own in his nervous hands.

There was reason for Jim to sweat. There was a strong ebb

tide, aided by a north wind, in the Thames River that morning. The signs in the river were obvious—heavy current making around the buoys and a slight chop in the channel. One of the ways to handle this situation is to back out rapidly, getting the whole ship in the body of the current as quickly as possible, thus allowing the vessel to drift bodily downstream while maneuvering to turn. Backing slowly would result in our stern being caught by the current first, thus getting the ship awkwardly backward in the river.

Jim surveyed the situation, then cupped his hands and bellowed to the dock: "Take in the brow!" Quin bounded over the gangway, handed an envelope to the petty officer who had appeared to superintend casting off our lines, sprang light-footedly back. Kohler, our Chief of the Boat who was in charge topside, waved to the same man, and two dungareed sailors on the dock pulled the gangway up and pushed it out of the way. Jim leaned over the hatch on the bridge—"Stand by to answer bells on the battery," he ordered. Then to the men on deck—"take in Two and Three." Our two middle lines to the dock were lifted off their cleats by the line handlers on the docks and tossed to us. Our men quickly snaked them aboard and passed them into the stowage bins under the deck.

"Take in Four," Jim called to the stern.

As Number Four, our stern line, came in, *S-16* remained moored only by Number One line from our bow to a corresponding cleat on the dock. We were on the downstream side of the dock, the current tending to push us away. This was a favorable effect, in a light current; one to watch in a heavy ebb on the Thames. Jim, correctly anxious to back away smartly, did not wait for the current to be felt.

"Slack One!" he shouted to the bow detail; then nearly as loudly to the helmsman on the bridge, "All back full!" and a moment later, again to the bow, "Take in One!"

He might have given some additional order to the helmsman standing on the bridge as he turned around to face our direction of motion, but of this I could not be sure. In a moment *S-16* commenced to gather sternway and to my horror her stern commenced to move to port, toward the dock. Jim, standing facing the stern beside the periscope standards, saw it, too.

"Left full rudder," he yelled, with urgency in his voice. If the shear to port did not stop, our port propeller would hit the pilings of the dock, probably necessitating a dry-docking to repair it or replace it. This time I heard the helmsman's reply as he raised his voice in response to Jim's, and I thought I detected an unusual note of apprehension.

"Rudder *is* left full, sir!"

That was enough for me.

I took the first running step toward the bridge, cursing Jim's confusion with the rudder—facing aft, he must have confused port and starboard—and the traditional requirement which had put me on deck instead of on the bridge at this moment as well. But Jim had realized the error, too. He turned around.

"All stop!" he bellowed. "Starboard ahead full." The orders came in time. The slant to port was arrested and the ship halted her sternway. In a moment, the danger past, Jim was again in command of the situation.

"All stop!" again. Then, looking over his shoulder, this time, "Rudder amidships—all back full." The *S-16* backed this time straight as an arrow. As her stern cleared the dock Jim put the rudder full left once more, and she neatly curved around, backing smartly upstream against the current and squaring away for the downstream passage. As she did so, three little black notebooks unobtrusively slid back into the hip pockets of the three alien skippers, bearing their quota of newly penciled comments.

By the time we had reached our assigned exercise area, Jim was sweating freely for a different reason. The board had made him turn the deck over to Keith and take all three members through the ship while he laboriously rigged her for dive. Normally, on rigging a submarine for dive—which means lining up all the valves and machinery in readiness for diving as differentiated from the "Rigged for Surface" condition in which she cannot dive at all—the enlisted men in each compartment actually do the work in accordance with a very thorough check-off list, and then all officers not on watch, each taking a couple of compartments, carefully check each item. Rigging a submarine for dive, though obviously of major importance, is considered so basic that it is invariably demanded of a candidate for qualification in submarines, but rarely of a candidate for qualification for command. The members of the board might have been hazing Jim a little, for all I knew, but of course he had to go through with whatever they asked.

The *Falcon* was right behind us as we proceeded down the Thames River, a little later than usual because a full day of training submarine-school students was not before us. We passed Southwest Ledge in column and then angled slightly to starboard, heading for the area just to the south of New London Light. Having the Examining Board with us at least had given us the pick of the operating areas. With Sarah's Ledge abeam to starboard we angled more to the right to head for our point to begin the exercises, while *Falcon* held her original course and commenced to diverge from us as she bore up for her own initial point.

Jim was back on the bridge and had resumed the conn by the time our divergent courses had separated the two vessels by the desired distance. Besides myself, there were only the members of the regular watch—two lookouts—on the bridge with him.

"Take it easy, old man," I said. "I think they may be hazing you a little, so don't let it throw you. Everything is okay so far."

Jim commenced to shiver, the perspiration rapidly congealing on his drawn face. The air on the exposed bridge was biting cold, whirring our antenna wires and sucking the air out of our lungs as it whistled against our unprotected faces. *S-16* pitched jerkily in the gray waters of the Sound, water slapping heavily against her superstructure and once in a while splashing on her angular, red-splotched bow. Where it hit our superstructure a film of milky-colored ice began to form, blurring her outlines. In the distance the hazy shape of the *Falcon* could be distinguished, still heading away from us. In a few moments she would turn and run toward us at an unknown speed using an unknown course and zigzag plan. Jim's problem, after diving, would be to determine her speed and base course, get in front of her, and then outmaneuver her zigzag so as to shoot a practice torpedo beneath her keel.

It was something we had all done many times on the "attack teacher," beginning in our earliest submarine-school days. The attack teacher is a device which simulates the submarine periscope station. The trainee can peer through a dummy periscope which goes up through the ceiling to the room above, where he sees a model ship, in the size and perspective of a real one, as though it were an actual target some miles away at sea. He then "maneuvers" his dry-land submarine, makes his approach on the target, and goes through the procedure of firing torpedoes just as he would in actuality. Dozens of approaches can be made, and any number of targets, from aircraft carriers to tugboats, can be sunk—or missed—in one day. If he makes a poor approach, for instance is rammed by the target or an escort, the instructors in great glee drop a cloth over the top of the "periscope," stamp heavily on the floor above, make banging noises with anything handy, and in general let it be known that the submarine—not to mention the embarrassed approach officer—is having a bad time.

Having learned the technique, the student is permitted to try it with a real submarine on a real target, shooting a real torpedo—with exercise head instead of warhead, set to pass under instead of to hit. Graduation exercise in the submarine school wraps everything up in one bundle; the student is required to make his own torpedo ready for firing, superintend hoisting it into the submarine assigned, load it into the torpedo tube and make the final adjustments himself, then go up into the control room, make the approach, fire the torpedo, and write the report resulting. And woe betide the student whose torpedo fails to run properly, who does not conduct the approach and attack effectively, or whose report does not measure up to Navy standards of thoroughness, accuracy, and brevity!

After graduation every submarine officer is required to make several approaches to the satisfaction of his skipper before being put up for qualification in submarines—and the Examining Board requires here again that he conduct a satisfactory submerged attack. And the same procedure is required for qualification for command. The degree of technical expertness demanded is of course greater as the level of qualification increases, and of Jim, this day, the board expected nothing short of perfection befitting the commanding officer of a U. S. submarine.

In the distance *Falcon's* hull lengthened. She had begun to turn around, preparatory to starting her target run.

Jim leaned toward the open hatch, cupped his hands: "Rig out the bow planes!" he ordered between chattering teeth. Immediately the bow planes, heretofore housed flat against the *S-16's* bow like elephant's ears, commenced to rotate and fan out, stopping when they were extended perpendicular to her hull and slanted slightly downward, their forward edges digging deeply into the shallow seas.

This was the final act in the preparation for diving. As I stepped toward the hatch the *Falcon's* hull commenced to shorten again, indicating that she had nearly completed her turn, and at that moment a small spot of intensely brilliant light appeared at the base of her foremast.

"There's the light, Jim," I said. He had seen it too, and was extracting a stop watch from his pocket. When the searchlight was extinguished, after having been pointed in our direction for several seconds, this would be the official moment of the commencement of the exercise. A stop watch would be started on the *Falcon's* bridge, matching the one Jim would start at the same instant. The two watches would be kept running throughout, and the watch time of each maneuver recorded. Stopped by simultaneous signal after the run, they would provide Jim with the essential time comparison he would need when later he had to draw the tracks of target and submarine on the same chart and explain the maneuvers of both.

The light must have lasted only a few seconds. I was only halfway down the ladder into the control room when I heard Jim order, "Clear the bridge," and a moment later the diving alarm sounded. There was just time to step off the ladder onto the tiny conning tower space to get out of the way of the first lookout scuttling by. Immediately after him came the second one, and then Jim, holding the wire hatch lanyard in his hand. Bowing his back, he pulled the hatch home with a satisfying click as the latch engaged. Then, straightening up, he swiftly whirled the steel wheel in the center of the circular hatch, dogging it tightly on its seat.

The next second he was below in the control room, superintending the operation of diving—something else the qualification committee had insisted on observing.

Up from the control room came the familiar noises. The venting of air, the slight additional pressure on my ears, and the quiet report, usually directed at me: "Pressure in the boat, Green Board, sir!" The noise of the bow and stern planes operating, and the calm voice of the diving officer—Jim—giving instructions to their operators. The blowing of air as regulator tank, which we used as a negative tank or a "Down-Express," was blown nearly dry and the inboard vent opened to release the pressure in it, thus, incidentally, further increasing the notice my ears were taking of the operation. The tilt of the deck, down by the bow ever so slightly, and the subsequent return to an even keel. The gurgle of water, hurly-burlying up the sides of the bridge and conning tower, the sudden darkness as the tiny glass "eye-ports" went under, and the quietness when fully submerged. Swiftly the graceless surfaced submarine, uneasily breasting the waves, became a poised, confident fish, moving with ease and certitude in her element.

In a moment came another signal: the clanging of the general alarm bell. Most of the crew, anticipating it, had already gone to their stations, but there was a last-minute movement of a few of them below me. Then came a sharp "Klack!" as the electric brake on the periscope hoist motor released, and the whirring of the hoist cable and sheaves as Jim, relieved of the diving duties by Tom Schultz, ordered the periscope raised for his first look at the target.

Quietly I descended the ladder and took station beside the helmsman in the forward part of our crowded, dimly lighted control room. During maneuvering watches his station was on the bridge, where there was a duplicate set of steering controls, but during surface cruising, and of course when submerged, his station was in the control room. Today there seemed hardly room for him, so crowded was the tiny compartment. The ship's company were at their stations, ready to execute Jim's orders upon the multiplicity of equipment located here. The members of the qualification committee were here, too, having taken up positions from which the progress of not only the submerged approach but also of everything else in the control room could be observed. I was only an extra number, an observer. It had been cold topside; here it was already stifling hot, men packed closely together, body against body, breathing each other's body smells. I could feel every move of the helmsman as I stood, facing the other way, jammed hip to hip against him.

The base of the periscope came up. Jim stooped on the deck of the control room—what extra space there was, naturally, went to him—captured the handles as they came out of the well, extended them as the base of the periscope came clear, applied his right eye to the eye-piece, and rose smoothly with it to a standing position. Once the 'scope was fully elevated, he spun it around twice rapidly, then ordered, "Down periscope!" step-

— 25

ping away slightly as the shiny tube started down into its tubular well in the deck. All three black notebooks came out of their hiding places, received comments, and disappeared.

Jim gave me a bleak look. For three days the little black notebooks had been in and out of sight. They had got on my nerves too; it is never pleasant for a skipper of a ship to have what amounts to an inspection party making notes about his ship. The most serious effect by far, of course, was on Jim, for whom they constituted an unexpected mental hazard.

The Qualification Board was looking expectantly at Jim. Every move of a submarine making an approach is at the sole behest of the Approach Officer; it was up to Jim to make the correct observations and give the right orders.

"Nothing in sight," Jim said. Out came the notebooks for another moment.

Jim waited nearly a full minute, then "Up periscope!" he ordered. The 'scope slithered out of its well, Jim fixing on the eye-piece, as before, the moment it appeared.

He twirled it around, stopped suddenly slightly on our starboard bow. "Bearing—Mark!" he said.

A disc-shaped celluloid "Is-Was," used for matching target bearing with target course, was hanging from around Keith's neck on a string. He was standing on the other side of the periscope from Jim, watching the spot where the vertical cross hair on its barrel matched against the bearing circle on the overhead around it. "Zero-one-six," he announced.

Jim's right hand had shifted to a small hand wheel on the side of the periscope. He turned it, first rapidly, then slowly and carefully. "Range—Mark!" he finally said.

"Six-seven-double-oh!" said Keith, who had shifted his attention to a dial at the base of his side of the instrument.

"Down periscope!" barked Jim, and the 'scope slid smoothly down. "Angle on the bow—hard to tell—looks like port thirty."

"Port thirty," muttered Keith, spinning two of the concentric celluloid discs carefully with his thumb. As Assistant Approach

Officer, or "Yes-Man," Leone was responsible for keeping the picture of the developing problem up to date on his Is-Was, for informing the Approach Officer—Jim—of the progress of the problem, the condition of readiness of the ship and torpedo battery, and in general anything else he wanted to know. Hence the term "Yes-Man," as well as the unusual title of the gadget he used to keep track of the relative positions of target and submarine.

"What's the distance to the track?"

This was an easy one. At the instant the target has a thirty-degree angle on the bow—is thirty degrees away from heading right at you—the distance from the submarine to the target's projected track is equal to half the range. "Three-four-double-oh!" returned Keith, after a moment's pause—close enough. Keith was all right.

"Left full rudder!" Jim had taken a little time to make the obvious move, and the three little black notebooks were half-way out of their hiding places before he gave the order. Crowded against the helmsman, I could feel his right fanny muscle harden as he threw his weight into the wheel.

"All ahead three thousand a side!"

S-16 leaped ahead with the suddenly increased thrust of her propellers, curved to the left in obedience to the helm—and three black notebooks leaped also into the hands of their own-ers.

CHAPTER 2

THREE THOUSAND AMPERES TO
each of *S-16's* two propeller shafts, six thousand total out of the
main storage batteries, is a high rate of discharge in any league.
For slow speeds the two main storage batteries are normally
connected in parallel, and for high speed switched to series—
thus doubling the voltage and halving the current for any
given power requirement. In neglecting to shift to series Jim
was failing to get the maximum speed possible for the discharge
rate and, in addition, was to no purpose risking damage to power
cables and main motor armatures from the high current and
the resulting heat. Our ship's procedure was specified in the
Engineering Orders: shift to series for everything over two
thousand amperes per motor, and start with half the current.

Vainly I tried to catch his eye. He knew the score as well as I, as did everyone in S-boats for that matter, but somehow, in the stress of the moment he had completely forgotten. What was even harder to understand was the fact that he had, nevertheless, ordered a discharge rate far in excess of the allowable limit. An easy thing to correct, ordinarily, but now, in the midst of his qualification approach, he was unreachable.

Tom Schultz turned solemnly toward me from his position directly behind the two enlisted men stationed at the bow and stern-plane controls. In the after part of the control room First Class Electrician's Mate John Larto also fixed his eyes in my direction, after a quick look at Jim. No words were necessary. Both men knew that I was not permitted to interfere in any way with the approach, that if I did so because of some emergency I automatically resumed command of the ship.

Imperceptibly the lights began to grow dimmer as *S-16* picked up speed. We accelerated slowly—much more slowly than if we had been in series. Larto shot me an agonized look, reached with both hands toward the electric control board at which he was stationed. I shifted my gaze to the three other skippers, found all still deep in their notebooks, went back to Larto, and nodded ever so slightly.

The battery circuit breakers in *S-16* were in the forward starboard corner of the control room. To shift them involved pulling all power off, kicking out the parallel breakers, and putting in the series breakers—all to the accompaniment of a snapping symphony of electrical disconnects. But Larto was equal to the occasion.

"Series, aye, aye! Fifteen hundred a side!" He vectored the response directly at Jim. The lights, which had been dim, suddenly grew bright again, and a cackling cacophony of noise arose from the deck plates in our starboard corner. Jim apparently took no notice. All three board members looked up at me quickly. But I was scrutinizing the back of Tom's head and could offer no enlightenment.

Jim had been deep in consultation with Keith, and now he spoke. "Target looks like a man-of-war," he stated. "Possibly a small cruiser or large destroyer. Set torpedo depth twelve feet. I'm going to try for a straight bow shot with a port-ninety track."

Well and good. This was more like it. Getting the target description out of the way and telling your fire-control party what you want to do were both doctrine requirements.

For several more minutes S-16 rocketed along, her superstructure vibrating and her antennas and lifelines singing, her thrashing propellers communicating a drumming note to the body of the ship. On and on we went. Jim, deep in consultation with Keith, seemed perfectly satisfied. One minute passed—then two—then five. Still nothing from Jim.

My anxiety mounted once more. Jim had made only one observation; as a result we had been racing at top submerged speed for several minutes, heading for a mythical point near where the target would be if it, likewise, kept steady on its course. This is the essence of the submerged approach—except that if the target zigged, Jim's tactic of running blindly would almost certainly put him out in left field. This is exactly what the zigzag system was designed to achieve. The counter to it is to make sufficient periscope observations to detect the zigs, and to govern your approach course and speed accordingly.

But Jim had only seen the target once and as a result of that had been running for it as though no change whatever could take place in the Falcon's course. True, with such a large initial angle on the bow we had a long distance to cover—and each observation required slowing down to avoid a big periscope feather. The problem is always to outguess the enemy, but the sub skipper has no occult powers to help him guess. He has to compromise with speed, and look at the target every one or two minutes.

But not Jim this day. One would have thought he knew exactly what to expect, judging by his lack of concern, and by the time he made up his mind to take another observation I was nearly beside myself. The *Falcon* might have zigged sharply just after Jim had last seen her, and the whole distance we had covered since, at the expense of around half of our total battery capacity, might have been in exactly the wrong direction.

I tried to project my thought waves at him, to catch his eye, lift an eyebrow, somehow make him realize he could not keep on blindly, but Jim did not even look in my direction. Nor was Keith any better, huddled with him beside the periscope in the dimmed light of the control room. Minute after minute dragged by. By the time the order came I was sweating—and I noticed that Messrs. Savage, Miller, and Kane were watching gravely.

"All stop! Parallel!" The drumming stopped precipitantly, and you could feel the boat slow down.

"Parallel, sir!" from Larto an instant later, as his eyes caught mine. Jim had either never realized that he had failed to shift to series, or was not going to let on.

"All ahead three hundred a side!" He turned to Tom. "Make your depth four-six feet," he ordered.

Schultz had been keeping the depth gauges rigidly at four-five feet. Jim's order would bring the boat down one foot deeper in the water, resulting in one foot less of the periscope sticking out of water when fully raised.

Tom had been handling depth controls for years and he knew his job. He gave a few quiet instructions to the planesmen. After a few moments the depth gauge needles gently moved from the four-five to the four-six-foot markers and remained there.

Jim turned to Larto. "Speed through water?"

Larto, expecting the question, had been consulting the ammeters and voltmeters as well as the shaft-revolution indicators. He shot back the answer immediately, "Four-and-a-half, sir."

Still too fast. Jim waited.

Keith brought up the Is-Was, showed him the relative positions of submarine and target. Propped in a corner was another device, shaped roughly like a banjo, which Keith, at Jim's indicated request, now picked up. The purpose of the Banjo was to give the firing bearing, or lead angle, for shooting torpedoes. The two discussed for a moment the various solutions which might be arrived at with the problem as it stood.

Jim turned back to Larto. "What speed we making now?"

"Three and a half knots, sir!"

Jim motioned the Banjo back into its corner, turned toward the periscope.

Keith ranged himself on its opposite side, facing Jim, reached for the control knob, or "pickle," hanging on its wire nearby.

There had not been much conversation among the other members of the control party, but now the control room seemed to grow even quieter as men stood stolidly to their stations waiting for the periscope observation.

Larto broke the silence. "Three knots, sir!"

Jim motioned with his thumbs upward, and Keith squeezed the pickle.

The hoist motor brake clacked open again. Accompanied by sounds of spinning sheaves and the squeak of flexible steel cables, the periscope started up from its well.

Jim and Keith stood there motionless. Except for the movement of the hoist cables from out of the well as they brought the periscope up, the shining steel barrel, wet and oily, might as well have been motionless too. Then suddenly the periscope yoke appeared, bolted to the ends of the hoist cables. Immediately below it was the base of the periscope with eye-piece, range dials, and two handles folded up at its sides.

Jim was ready for it, stooping as before. The handles rose into his outstretched hands, were snapped down. He rose up with the periscope, before it was all the way up suddenly motioned to Keith. Keith released the button on the pickle and the periscope stopped, not quite fully raised.

Jim was looking through it now, stooped over in an unnatural position, swinging it first one way and then the other.

"Can't see him," he muttered. "I'm under now—now I'm up again—" as a wave on the surface of the sea passed over the periscope.

This was good technique: minimum practicable exposure.

"Where should he bear, Keith?"

"We should have been gaining bearing on him," answered Keith, consulting the Is-Was. "He should be on the starboard beam. Swing more to the right." So saying, Keith placed his hands over Jim's on the periscope's handle, and forcibly turned it until Jim's stance showed he was looking on our starboard beam.

Jim suddenly pushed the periscope back a trifle the other way. "There he is!" unnaturally loudly, "it's a zig! Bearing—Mark! Down 'scope!"

"Zero-eight-seven," answered Keith, as the scope went sliding down. "What's the angle on the bow, sir?"

"Starboard thirty," from Jim. "Didn't get a range, about four thousand."

Keith was spinning the Is-Was when Jim motioned for the periscope to be raised again. "Stand by for a quick range," he said. As the periscope broke water he had his hand on the range dial, adjusted the bearing slightly as he turned it.

"Bearing—Mark! Range—Mark! Down 'scope!"

"Zero-nine-zero"—"Three-eight-zero-zero," answered Keith, shifting his attention rapidly from azimuth ring to range dial.

"Right full rudder! All ahead two thousand a side!"

The ship surged ahead again as Larto twisted his rheostats.

"What's distance to the track?"

"Nineteen hundred yards!"

Jim seemed to be in complete command of the situation. "Target has zigged to his left. We'll swing around and get him with a straight bow shot starboard ninety track as he goes by."

— 33

In nonsubmarine parlance this meant that although the target had changed course, thus putting us on his other side, Jim was coming around toward him and would try to hit him squarely on the new side. As before, he hoped to do it with a torpedo with zero gyro angle—set to run straight ahead. The whole submarine would have to be aimed at an angle ahead of the target in somewhat the same manner as a duck hunter leads his birds.

Jim was doing very well, aside from his initial error in running too fast and too far in one direction before taking a second look through the periscope, and fortunately *Falcon's* zig had taken place late enough so as not to be particularly damaging. I was particularly warmed, also, by Keith's steady behavior as assistant.

Jim spoke again. "What course do I come to for a straight bow shot?"

Keith didn't answer immediately as he studied the figures on the face of the Is-Was. In a moment he said, "One-three-four," holding out the Is-Was to Jim as he did so.

Jim consulted it briefly. "Steady on one-three-four," he directed the helmsman, and the latter called back just past my ear, "Steady on one-three-four, aye, aye!—passing zero-one-zero, sir!"

We had to wait until the boat came around to the new course. I could not help noticing how luck had played into Jim's hands. He had actually overshot the target, but *Falcon's* zig had come so late that he was still in an excellent attack position from the opposite side—a bit long-range, but nice.

Another thirty seconds passed. *S-16,* like most S-boats, turned on a dime once you got her going, and we were nearly around to the intended firing course.

"All ahead two hundred a side!" Another periscope look coming. At least Jim was not forgetting all he had learned about periscope technique. That is one of the items most closely observed in a submarine officer, and one of those most freely criticized—especially by one's Qualification Board. Every skipper counts himself an expert and has strong opinions about how the 'scope should be handled.

One thing Jim had not yet done; at no time had he looked all around with the periscope, turned it through a full 360 degrees. Doctrine as well as technique called for this as assurance against being caught unawares by another ship or a screening vessel.

Jim waited for our speed to come off; then directed the periscope to be raised.

As before, he rode it up, with Keith swinging it around to the port bow as the Is-Was had predicted.

"Bearing—Mark!"

"Three-one-seven!" Keith was quick with his answers.

"Range—Mark!"

"Two-three-double-oh!"

"Down periscope!" Jim was still looking through it as Keith squeezed the pickle button and the handles and eye-piece fell away. Eleven seconds the observation had taken. I pursed my lips approvingly, held out my stop watch to Stocker Kane, hoping no one had noticed the failure to look all around.

"Angle on the bow, starboard forty-five!"

"Starboard forty-five," muttered Keith, spinning his Is-Was. "Distance to the track is sixteen hundred," he went on, a moment later, anticipating Jim's next question.

"What's the firing bearing for this setup?"

Keith dropped the Is-Was on its cord, reached swiftly for the Banjo, squatted down on his haunches with it on his knees. "Target speed, sir?" he said.

"Use twelve knots," returned Jim.

Keith nodded, bent over the instrument and began carefully setting up the computing arms in accordance with the tactical situation. It took a little time—Keith, though he had learned at submarine school how to use it, was not the expert on the Banjo that Jim was. It was Jim's normal battle station as Assistant

Approach Officer for me, and I could sense his impatience to get the answer. The target was moving toward the firing point; there was not much time to go.

Jim watched, irresolute. Then he turned to Tom at the diving station to his left. "Four-six and a half feet!" he rasped.

Tom nodded, obediently began to ease the boat six inches deeper in the water. This also took its quota of time, for the bow and stern planes had less effect at low speeds and he was anxious not to drop below the ordered depth. Since the tip of the periscope when fully extended reached only to forty-seven feet two inches above the keel, it would be very easy for a momentary loss of only a few inches in depth to drag it entirely under and thus blind the approach officer at the instant he might most need to see.

For an appreciable period, during which Jim tensely waited, the depth gauges did not budge. He turned to Keith, still sliding the computing arms on the face of the Banjo, and then back again to Tom—whose depth-gauge needles had not wavered from the forty-six-foot mark.

It had all taken only a dozen seconds or so, but Jim's temper, already strained to the flash point, steamed over.

"Goddamit!" he shouted at Tom, "I said four-six and a half feet! When are you going to get there?"

Tom's neck settled imperceptibly into the open collar of his shirt, but he made no reply. In the next instant the gauges quivered and, by the barest perceptible movement, crept down to a point midway between the forty-six- and forty-seven-feet marks.

Jim's attention swung across the control room to Keith, now patiently recording on a piece of paper the answers he had picked off the curved lines on the face of the Banjo. "I haven't got all day," he snarled. "What's holding you up, Leone?"

Keith looked as if he had been struck, but his voice betrayed no emotion as he answered: "Firing bearings, four fish; three-four-three, three-four-four, three-four-four-a-half, three-four-five-a-half. Set gyros one-and-a-half right, one-half right, one-half left, and one-and-a-half left. Firing bearing for the exercise torpedo, zero gyro angle, three-four-five."

"Firing order normal order! Set depths twelve feet, speed high! Set gyros one-and-a-half right, one-half right, one-half left, one-and-a-half left!" Jim was all business again. As he gave the order he made a sign of negation to Quin, who functioned as telephone talker during battle stations.

"Torpedo room! Firing order, normal order," repeated Quin, making not the slightest move toward the telephone mouthpiece mounted on a breastplate attached around his neck. "Set depths twelve feet. Set gyros one-and-a-half right, one-half right, one-half left, and one-and-a-half left."

A second later Quin spoke again: "Torpedo room has the word, sir! Gyros set! Depth set!" He still made no indication that he had transmitted or received one iota of information or instruction.

Jim now spoke again. "Set depth on the exercise torpedo thirty feet! Set torpedo gyro on zero!" There was a shade of greater urgency in his voice, and he pointed with emphasis at Quin.

This time Quin picked up the mouthpiece, pressed the button on its top, and spoke into it. "Torpedo room," he said, "set depth on the exercise fish thirty feet. Set gyro on zero."

The exercise torpedo was the real torpedo, the one on which depended Jim's qualification. In a moment the answer came back from the torpedo room; was relayed by the yeoman: "Torpedo ready, sir! Depth set thirty feet—gyro set on zero. Gyro spindles are still in, sir!"

"Stand by!" snapped Jim and, seconds later, "Up periscope!"

The 'scope whirred upward, broke surface. I could see the shaft of light from the eye-piece shining out and striking Jim on the face just as he got his eye fixed to it.

"It's a zig away!" he shouted. "Bearing—Mark!"

"Three-three-eight!"

"Range—Mark!"

"One-five-double-oh!"

"Down periscope!" As the periscope went down into its well, Jim spoke in violent tones of bitter disappointment. "The bastard has zigged away! Right at the firing point, the son-of-a-bitch has zigged away! The angle on the bow is ninety right now!" He raised his clenched fist above his head. "Goddamit!" he swore.

At this Keith broke in rapidly. "That's no zig, Jim! The angle on the bow should be ninety! He's right on the firing point! Put up the 'scope and shoot him . . . Look!" And Keith excitedly held out the Is-Was so that Jim could see its face.

"It's no good, I tell you! He's zigged away! We can't get him!"

"Dammit, the hell we can't! Take another look!" I was surprised at Keith's vehemence. With his right hand he pressed the pickle to raise the periscope again—unbidden—and with his left he pushed Jim toward it for another observation.

"Out gyro spindles!" shouted Keith, as the 'scope came up. "Stand by!"

"Gyro spindles are out, sir!" Quin's answer came within a second.

"There he is, sir! Right there!" Keith had pushed the periscope around another few degrees, was intently looking at the azimuth ring and the periscope hairline mark against it.

Almost unwillingly, Jim permitted himself to be pushed into position for another look through the periscope. He grasped the handles, moved them slightly.

"Bearing—Mark!" he said, still unconvinced.

"Three-four-three—*simulate* fire ONE!" called Keith.

"Fire ONE," repeated Quin quietly. "ONE's fired. Standing by TWO!"

"What's the angle on the bow, now, Jim?" Keith had picked up the Banjo again, spoke insistently in a low but carrying tone.

"Starboard one hundred!" answered Jim, without taking his eyes from the rubber guard around the eye-piece.

"Okay!" said Keith, laying down the Banjo. "Stay on him!"

"I'm on him," growled Jim.

"Three-four-four! Simulate fire TWO!" Keith was back at the azimuth ring.

"Fire TWO! TWO's away!" from Quin.

"Stand by!"

Quin picked up his telephone microphone for the first time in minutes. "Stand by forward," he said. "Gyro spindle out?" The answer seemed to satisfy him, for his report, rendered almost instantly, was simply, "Standing by forward, sir!"

Keith's eyes were riveted on the hairline on the forward edge of the periscope barrel, where it went through the azimuth ring. Only Jim could see the vertical cross hair in the periscope field of view, but the thin line etched on the barrel of the instrument indicated the direction he was looking. When that line matched the predetermined firing bearing for the torpedo —three-four-five in this instance, or fifteen degrees on our port bow—the torpedo would be fired. The moment was a tense one. A lot more than most of us realized depended on it; how much, only I could have told.

Jim had lost his temporary disappointment. He now carefully kept trained on the target, slowly rotating the periscope to keep up with it. With the slow, precise movement of a watch, the two marks closed together. You could hear men breathing in the compartment. Keith's mouth hung partly open. His eyes elevated, right hand holding the pickle, he waited.

"Bearing, three-four-five! FIRE!" Keith let this one out with a bellow, as though he personally could shout the torpedo out the tube.

"FIRE!" shouted Quin into the telephone, a split second behind. There was a rumble from somewhere forward, and a hiss of air. *S-16* quivered as her hull took up the jolt. In the immediate stillness I thought I could hear the whine of propellers starting.

All thought of continuing with the fictitious salvo was forgotten as Jim watched the progress of his torpedo through the periscope. I wanted to crowd up to him, take a look myself—decided not to.

Jim suddenly spoke. "He's seen the torpedo. There goes the flag hoist."

The instructions for torpedo exercises called for the target to hoist a flag signal upon sighting a torpedo or its wake. This the *Falcon* had evidently done, thus signifying that she would assume the responsibility for retrieving our fish. The rules, however, did not permit *Falcon* to deviate from her course or otherwise attempt evasion until after the torpedo had crossed. She would later report her best estimate of where it intersected her track. A perfect shot would be signaled as M.O.T., or Middle of Target.

Jim still stared fascinatedly through the periscope. "Looks good! Looks perfect! I'll hit him right in the M.O.T.! He's sunk, as sure as God made little green apples!"

I could sympathize with Jim's exuberance. I had felt the same way after my qualification approach and in fact still did whenever I had a chance to shoot a torpedo.

"There! It's crossed the track. It's a hit! Right under the M.O.T.!" Recollecting himself, Jim barked, "Secure from battle stations! Stand by to surface!"

This was Tom's cue to swing into action. He gave several low-voiced rapid orders, then turned to Jim and announced: "Ship is ready to surface, sir!"

Jim reached forward to the vicinity of the ladder to the conning tower, grasped the diving alarm handle and jerked it three times. Three raucous blasts resounded through the boat.

"Blow safety!" ordered Tom. Air whistled into the tanks, was shut off at his signal. The bow planesman at Tom's direction ran his bow plane up to the "full rise" position. *S-16* tilted slightly up by the bow and the depth-gauge needles began to drop.

At the first note of the surface alarm Rubinoffski swung his lanky legs up the ladder into the conning tower. Larto turned his rheostats, increased the speed of the motors. An intermittent, low-pitched hiss of air—back aft in the engine room they were turning over the engines, clearing any water out. Jim was going around and around with the periscope, at last.

"Eye-ports awash!" The call came down from Rubinoffski. You could feel the surge toward the surface suddenly stop as *S-16* broached. The little glass portholes in the conning tower, other than our periscopes the only means of seeing out of the ship, let a stream of light into the tiny compartment as they popped out of the water. The reflected rays danced in the open hatch and glittered on the steel rungs of the ladder below.

Jim left the periscope, motioning to Keith to lower it, and leaped for the ladder, climbing rapidly up. Surfacing is not quite as critical an evolution as diving, but during the period that the boat is barely awash all hands must stand fast to their stations. Only the skipper and the Quartermaster go to the bridge, and the ship remains ready for instant diving.

"Eighteen feet, sir, holding steady," Tom Schultz passed the word up the hatch.

"Crack the hatch!" I could hear Jim's command to Rubinoffski.

The Quartermaster grasped the handle of the hatch, turned it rapidly several times. I heard the familiar whistling sound as the slightly increased air pressure in the submarine commenced to vent out.

"Put the low-pressure pump on the main drain—shut the Kingstons. Line up ballast tanks for pumping!" The routine orders from Tom were a backdrop to the sudden rush of air past me as Jim ordered the bridge hatch flung open. In a moment came the call: "Lookouts to the bridge."

The two planesmen, no longer needed at the bow and stern

planes, had hastily donned submarine jackets upon surfacing, buttoning them over the binoculars which they had also slung about their necks. Now they raced up the ladder to join Jim.

In a little more than a minute the submerged routine had been terminated and surface condition established; *S-16* plowed through the choppy waters of the Sound along the track which Jim's torpedo had taken, and as the engines were started, a frozen blast of air poured into the control room from the now-open passage to the bridge. When Jim sent for Keith to take over the bridge watch, I followed him up, the vague feeling of uneasiness which had grown during the previous hour still permeating me.

The Quartermaster was just receiving the tail end of a semaphore message from *Falcon* when I arrived topside. "HIT TEN YARDS FORWARD MOT X TORPEDO IN SIGHT BT."

Jim was delighted. He slapped Keith on the back. "What do you think of that, hey? I knew that was a hit the minute I let her go! That old *Falcon* out there is sunk colder than hell. I guess that's all, hey? I guess that showed the Board—turn her around and head for the barn."

Keith seemed as happy over the successful shot as Jim, but at the latter's last words I could sense his question. It was hard to tell whether Jim meant it as a command or was merely expressing his feelings.

"Easy, old man," I said. "The rules don't let you go back to port until *Falcon* picks up your fish."

"Ah, hell, skipper," Jim grinned unabashed, "they're practically alongside of it already. Let's at least start back."

It was true. The *Falcon* had turned as soon as the torpedo passed under her and had followed its wake. *S-16,* not having changed course since firing, had been proceeding all this time in the same direction, gradually increasing her speed as her ballast tanks went dry. Up ahead the *Falcon* still had the two flag hoists signifying "torpedo in sight" at her yardarm, and several ship lengths ahead of her we could see the splashes as the torpedo, its exercise head having blown dry, expended its last few ounces of fuel and air before coming to a stop.

I knew what Keith was thinking. Our squadron orders required that the Torpedo Officer of the firing submarine see the torpedo out of the water before departing the area. Later, after our return to New London, Keith would likewise have to inspect the torpedo with the *Falcon's* Torpedo Officer and sign the torpedo record book.

"We'd better stick around just a bit longer, Jim," I said easily. "Might as well do it right, you know. Besides, don't forget the Board down there is watching everything you do. They might not agree with your shoving off so soon."

Jim shot me a startled look for a split second, then relaxed with a short laugh.

"Guess you're right at that." Then he turned to Keith. "Close on in to the *Falcon* until you can see them hoist the fish out of the water."

"Aye, aye, sir," answered Keith, taking the measure of the *Falcon* through his binoculars.

Strangely enough, I had begun to notice that not once on this day's operations had Jim called me "Captain" or used the word "Sir" in our conversations. A little friendly colloquialism is not unexpected in submarines, and it was not anything definite that one could lay a finger on. It was, however, almost always customary to call one's skipper, "Sir" or "Captain." Nobody else in the ship used titles in normal address, nor was it customary for the skipper to do so in speaking to officers or crew. It was noticeable also that apparently by tacit understanding both Keith and Tom had on this day, contrary to their normal habit, used the word "Sir" in official conversation with Jim. Perhaps I was imagining things, but I could not quite decide whether Jim's omission had any significance.

It was now nearing noon. We had been under way since shortly after eight o'clock. The day, instead of warming with the sun, had turned even more chilly during our short submergence. I buttoned the top button on my coat and turned the collar up to protect my ears. A few moments ago I had been too hot and had been perspiring. Now I was shivering. Jim and Keith, too, had already buttoned themselves up. They had put their hands in their pockets and were shielding themselves as well as they could from the biting wind whistling over the bridge. Occasionally severe health problems resulted from the rapid changes of temperature and pressure experienced by submariners, but they certainly made for a maximum of discomfort all the time, I reflected, as I sought the leeward side of the periscope standards.

Falcon now slowed down and we gained on her rapidly. We could see the torpedo, its yellow head bobbing in the water a few yards on her port beam. Keith gave the order to decrease our speed.

Men were leaning over *Falcon's* rail with pieces of line in their hands, one man in particular with a grapnel or hook on the end of a pole. Her long hoisting boom on the afterdeck was swung over to the port side, and you could see that hooking the torpedo would be a mighty tricky business, even with the relatively small sea that was running. With no way on, *Falcon* rolled mightily; every time she rolled to port the end of the boom splashed in the water. In calmer days they would have put a man on the boom, or even lowered him to pass a line through the ring on the nose of the torpedo. Today it would have been suicide.

With the *Falcon* rolling violently and the torpedo bobbing up and down, they had their work cut out for them. As I watched, the man with the grapnel leaned way out over the rail, made a stab—and was drenched from head to foot with solid green water which suddenly rose up under *Falcon's* counter just as he was reaching. For a moment I thought he must have gone overboard, but the wave receded and he was still there, doubled over the bulwark and clutching it with both hands, a heretofore unnoticed line leading from his waist inboard.

There was no sign of his pole, and I thought it gone until I noticed another man hauling in on another line trailing astern, and in a moment he had returned the first man's equipment.

He made several more stabs, each ineffectual, until Jim directed Keith to bring us close aboard on the other side of the torpedo so as to make a lee for it. For fear of drifting down upon it, the *Falcon* had had to come up to leeward of the torpedo, leaving it to windward and thus making it most difficult to lasso. The interposition of the lower-lying and slower-drifting *S-16* to windward created a lee of comparatively smooth water and made the difference. Within minutes after we had moved up we saw the torpedo in the air being hoisted onto *Falcon's* capacious afterdeck.

"Good thing we waited, hey, Keith," said Jim.

Keith had no opportunity for reply, for at this moment a voice beneath us spoke up.

"Permission to come on the bridge?" It was Roy Savage.

"Permission granted," rejoined Jim, with a glance at me.

It had been crowded before on *S-16's* cramped little bridge, bundled as we all were against the cold, and the addition of a seventh person made it a very tight squeeze indeed.

"How'd the torpedo look?" asked Savage.

"Fine, sir," replied Jim. "Hit ten yards forward of the M.O.T."

"I mean the torpedo itself, when they picked it up," insisted Savage.

Keith, who had been inspecting the *Falcon* through his binoculars, spoke up. "It looked all right, Captain. No dents that we could see. Propellers and rudders looked okay. They got it aboard without hitting the side."

"Good," rejoined Savage. Then he turned to Jim. "Signal the *Falcon* to return to base."

Rubinoffski, being not more than two feet away, had heard also. Jim nodded to him and the Quartermaster leaped lightly on top of the periscope supports, bracing himself with one foot on the bridge rail against the wind, as he unfurled his semaphore flags.

Savage was talking to Jim: "We want to go through a few emergency drills before returning to port. After you get the message off to *Falcon* get clear of her and dive. We'll spring the emergencies on you after you get her down."

"Aye, aye, sir," answered Jim, and Roy Savage disappeared below again. As he did so, Jim turned to me, his face contorted, "Good God! What more can they want? They saw me hit with the torpedo, didn't they? And they've worked me over for three days besides——"

The feeling of uneasiness with which I had come on the bridge, and which had remained and intensified during the minutes prior to the recovery of the torpedo, became stronger yet. I beckoned to Jim—crowded over with him in the after corner of the bridge.

"Jim, old man," I said in a low tone. "That wasn't a very good approach."

"What do you mean?"

"Look, Jim, you were just plain lucky. You ran for over five minutes at high speed without making a single observation. If the *Falcon* had zigged during that time instead of at the end, you would never have got close enough to shoot."

"Nothing so lucky about that: when she flashed the light she was on one course, and when I finally got a look at her through the periscope she was on another one. So I knew she had already zigged, and wouldn't zig again for a while!"

"Well, okay," I said, "though that's not a very realistic way of doing it. Another thing: not once during the entire approach did you look around with the periscope. If there had been another ship in the area, or if the target had been escorted, you might have got us in serious trouble."

"But there weren't any other ships anywhere around! I knew that. I took a good look all around before we dived."

"That's not the point, Jim. There are plenty of unrealities in

— 46

the whole thing, among them that the target flashes a light at us and runs toward us. What if the *Falcon* had gone the other way—headed out through the Race toward Montauk Point? Then you'd not have had an approach at all. But the worst thing was that at the very end of the approach, at the firing point, you obviously lost the picture. Keith saved the approach for you——"

Jim's face became a mottled red. "The hell he did!" he almost shouted. "Who put the ship in firing position? Who aimed the torpedo? He was my assistant, wasn't he—it's his job to back me up!"

I still spoke in a placating tone. "I know you did, Jim, but remember when you said he had zigged away? Keith knew he had not zigged. You announced the angle on the bow as ninety, which is about what it should have been. Frequently when the target passes at close range just at the time of firing, it looks like a zig, and you fell for it. You wouldn't have fired at all if Keith hadn't made you."

Jim's jaw muscles bulged. "What are you telling me all this for? Don't you want me to be qualified? Are you for me or against me?"

"I want you to be qualified just as much as you do, Jim," I said steadily, "but what I am trying to say is that the Qualification Board has probably picked up these same points I'm telling you about."

Jim muttered an obscenity. "Damn this whole thing, anyway," he mumbled.

We would have talked further but there came a voice from the conning tower.

"Commander Savage wants Mr. Bledsoe in the control room!"

Jim swung away abruptly without another word and went below.

The *Falcon,* with our torpedo secured on deck, had already started on her way back to port. Keith in the meantime had turned the ship around and was heading back toward the point where we had previously dived. He looked at me inquiringly, bowing his head against the stiff breeze which on this new course whipped straight across our bridge. There was nothing I could tell him about what had just gone on.

"Keith," I said, "you know what you're supposed to do. As soon as Jim passes up the word, go ahead and dive."

"Aye, aye, sir," answered Keith. "We're still rigged for dive, but the hatch has not been checked yet."

"Hasn't it?" I asked, surprised.

"No, sir. We were crowded up here, and Jim said not to bother because we weren't going to dive again." Our ship's orders required that the bridge hatch be inspected while rigging the ship for dive, and again after every surfacing. This involved closing it, and if we were under way the skipper's assent was therefore required. "I'll ask Jim for permission to check it as soon as you get below," said Keith. Ordinarily, of course, I would have given the authority, but today was Jim's show. Even with Jim and Roy Savage below, however, there was hardly any room to spare on the bridge, and Keith evidently wanted to spare me the contortions necessary to allow him room to shut it.

"Very well," I answered, and dropped down the hatch into what passed for a conning tower in an S-boat, hardly more than an enlargement of the hatch trunk down to the control room. It contained a built-in desk, used by Jim and the Quartermaster for some of their navigational work, and some signaling equipment. It was not like a fleet boat's conning tower, however, nor really a "conning tower" at all, in the strict sense, for the ship could by no means be conned from there.

Set into the steel walls on either side were two tiny round windows, or eye-ports made of thick glass. Occasionally some member of the crew would watch a dive from there or seek some of the mysteries of the undersea from this vantage point.

In the floor was a hatch identical to the bridge hatch, thus permitting complete isolation of the compartment should it become necessary. Like the bridge hatch, its weight was counter-balanced by a large coil spring—too much so, as a matter of fact, and now that it had become "worn in" a bit the hatch, during the last few days, had developed an unpleasant tendency to resist being closed or to fling itself open when undogged.

As I reached for the hand rail preparatory to continuing below, Jim appeared, standing on the control-room deck, framed in the open hatchway.

"Bridge!" he shouted.

"Bridge, aye, aye!" answered Keith from above.

"Take her down!" Jim shouted. "Course two-seven-oh!"

Looking upward, I could see Keith's face as he leaned over the hatch opening, cupped his left hand to his mouth. "Permission to check the hatch first, sir!" he answered.

The light from the hatchway was in Jim's face and I knew he could not see me. Keith already had hold of the hatch, had swung it part-way shut. "It'll just take a minute, Jim," he yelled. "—okay?"

The past four days had been hell for Jim, and I could most strongly sympathize with his feelings at this point. Even so, his next action was unwarranted.

He shook his head in an impatient negative. Hands gripping the ladder rails and head thrown back, he shouted imperatively up the opening, "Take her down, I said!"

Keith had no further choice. "Clear the bridge!" he called in answer. A moment later came the two blasts of the diving alarm.

I stepped clear of the lower hatch, drew back into the recess of the conning tower near the eye-ports. Watching through them as our narrow slotted deck went under and the sea rose up to meet us had always been irresistibly fascinating to me, and I was never tired of an excuse to do so.

With the diving alarm still reverberating, one lookout and then the other appeared, scurrying down the ladder. Both continued straight on through the lower hatch to the control room below. Next came Rubinoffski, and then Keith. In the meantime from the control room there were sounds of air escaping as the vents went open.

The first intimation of something wrong was the noise made by the hatch as Keith pulled it to. Instead of the satisfying thud of the latch snapping home and the gasket seating on the rim, there was a peculiar, arresting clank to it.

Keith's face went dead-white. I leaped to his side as he struggled with the hatch dogging mechanism. A glance disclosed the trouble. Somehow the dogs had not been fully retracted when the hatch had been opened the last time, and now, by the narrowest fraction of an inch, one of them was caught between the hatch and its seat!

Nor was this all. The latch, having enough slack in it to latch easily, had entered its slot and engaged. Try as we could, Keith and I could not push it free, nor could we budge the dogging mechanism. The hatch was locked in its present position, with daylight showing all around the edge by a matter of an inch or so. Jammed as it was, the only way of clearing it was with a maul and a heavy screw-driver or chisel.

I could sense, rather than feel, *S-16* settling beneath us as my mind encompassed the significance of our situation. There was no maul to be had in the conning tower, nor any time to work on the hatch if there were. Our only hope lay in stopping the boat from diving.

"Stop the dive!" I yelled down the hatch at my feet. "Hatch jammed!"—in an effort to let the control room know what was wrong. Our "hull openings" indicator, or "Christmas Tree," might still be showing red for the bridge hatch, though there was a strong possibility that since the hatch was nearly shut, it might have gone green.

In answer there came a whistling noise from below, and air commenced to escape through the partly open hatch. With a groan I realized the control room had not heard my order and was carrying out standard diving procedure—admitting high pressure air into the boat as a test for tightness. If the barometer went up and then held steady after the air was shut off, it indicated that the hull was airtight, hence watertight. A good test under leisurely circumstances—but worse than useless in this instance because the boat was not watertight, and it was already diving. Not until the control room shut the air valve in order to check the barometer would the ship's inability to hold air become evident. In addition, until then the noise made its personnel unable to hear anything we might shout down the hatch from the conning tower above.

In the meantime I could feel *S-16* tilting her nose down. It was still only about twenty seconds since the diving alarm had been sounded, but we had only about the same number of seconds left.

"Leone," I snapped. "Get below and surface the boat."

Keith gave me a scared look and bolted below.

Undecided as to my next move, I stood there, feeling far from heroic, half standing on the ladder and hanging on to the hatch wheel with both hands. I looked it over carefully. The latch, the immediate cause of the jamming, was partly home under the rim of the hatch seat. Made of a piece of steel about a quarter of an inch in thickness, it offered only a relatively sharp edge to push or hammer on. Attached by a linkage to the latch, so that it would retract when the latch engaged, was a short bolt supposed to intersect the spokes of the hatch hand wheel when the hatch was fully open to keep the hand wheel from turning. The bolt was retracted, all right, as it should be, but the hand wheel still would not turn in either direction. Three of the four hatch dogs had slipped past the inside edge of the hatch seat, but one was clearly caught on top, jammed between the seat and the hatch itself. With one dog jammed one way and three the other, the hand wheel was effectively prevented from any movement whatsoever.

The only way to clear the jam was to push back the latch, open the hatch, reverse the hand wheel so as to take up the lost motion, retract the dogs, and haul it shut again. Standing on the second rung of the ladder to reach it, bracing myself and wrapping my left arm around the rail, I pushed on the latch with all my might with my right hand. Nothing happened. I tried hammering it with my clenched fist, bruising the fleshy part of the hand in the process. Still no luck, though my hand ached.

Suddenly the noise of air blowing stopped from the control room, though air still hissed out the open ring around the hatch. In a second I heard the noise of the main vents shutting and more air blowing, a different note, as high-pressure air whistled into the main ballast tanks. Keith had gotten through and surfacing procedures had been started.

But there could be no stopping the downward momentum of a thousand tons of steel. Suddenly I heard a gurgling sound. A quick look through the nearest eye-port was rewarded with a splash of sudsy foam; then another and then suddenly there was green water and the daylight in the conning tower grew dimmer.

Air continued to hiss out above me, as the slightly increased pressure in the reservoir of *S-16's* hull equalized to atmosphere. I could hear water climbing quickly up the watertight structure. Obviously the boat would not stop before the open hatch went under. There was no telling, in fact, how far she might go down, and maybe the sudden inrush of tons of water into the ship would overbalance the slight amount of positive buoyancy we were gaining by the air going into her tanks.

At this point I don't remember any further conscious thought about it. Once the hatch went under, water would rush into the control room, sweeping people away from their stations, shorting the electrical equipment—generally making a mess of things and possibly knocking out the bow and stern planes, the main motor control, and the high-pressure air manifold on which our safety now depended. If the control room were flooded, nothing could keep the ship from sinking to the bottom of Long Island Sound. Perhaps some of the crew would be able to shut watertight doors leading forward or aft, but men trapped in the control room would certainly be drowned, while those who managed to save themselves from that fate would be faced with the prospect of slow suffocation if for any reason the rescue bell or the Momsen lung device could not be used.

It is said that a drowning man sees his whole life flash before him. Perhaps my sensation at that moment was somewhat the same. Certainly it could have taken me no more than a second to race through all these possibilities.

Water, which had been gurgling up the sides of the conning tower, now reached the hatch—there, meeting the gush of air still streaming out, it blew idiotically backward, and only a few drops fell inside.

From my position on the ladder I could see into the control room through the still-open lower hatch. I leaned toward it and roared, "Shut the hatch!" Just below it stood Tom Schultz, and I caught a glimpse of his twisted face as, without a word, he reached up, grabbed the hand wheel, and tried to pull it down. It was awkward for him and the spring resisted movement. He had the hatch almost closed when it swung partly open again. I sprang off the ladder and landed on the top of the hatch, holding it shut with my weight while Tom spun the hand wheel between my feet from below, sealing it tight.

Instantly a deluge of cold sea water hit me in the back, knocking me to my hands and knees. I struggled to my feet in a veritable Niagara of angry ocean pouring into the conning tower. I still remember a moment of wonder at the tremendous amount of water that came in despite the fact that the hatch was actually ninety per cent closed. It rose rapidly in the tiny compartment, and I could feel the pressure on my ears as the air was compressed. Ultimately, of course, a condition of equilibrium would be reached and the air would commence to bubble out through the hole at the top. Frantically I searched the overhead for some high protected corner where I might be able to find a few gulps of precious air when the compartment became entirely flooded.

S-16 now commenced to right herself, her bow slowly coming up. With the flooding confined to the conning tower, there was no doubt that she would get back to the surface all right. The question was whether I could manage to avoid drowning until someone was able to come out through another hatch and rescue me. With that weight of water in the conning tower there would be no hope of pushing open the lower hatch and draining it through there. Besides, with the difficulties they were facing below they might not even think of me for a few minutes.

I climbed up on the tiny chart desk, bumping my head against the overhead, but the water had reached my waist and was rising rapidly when it stopped coming in as though a hydrant had been shut off. I can remember the instantaneous relief. The ship was safe, and so, in a few moments, would I be.

It was several minutes in fact before anything else happened. I found out later that, unable to open the lower conning-tower hatch, Keith and Kohler had come up through the forward torpedo room, rushed over the slippery deck, and climbed up on the bridge. With a large open-end wrench which Keith had snatched up, they began battering at the latching mechanism from above. I shouted to them to stop for fear of breaking it, had them slide the wrench through the opening to me down below. Sloshing backward away from the hatch I measured the distance, swung gently and fair, and tapped the latch free on the first blow. The hatch instantly swung open under the combined heave of the two anxious men above.

After dogging the hatch properly from topside, the three of us made our way forward and below via the torpedo-room hatch. Jim was waiting at the foot of the ladder.

"You fool," he hissed at Keith. "Do you realize what you almost did?" His face was livid with emotion and his lips quivered with the fury of his voice. I could see Keith wilt.

"That will be all for you, Leone," Jim raged, "this will be

your last day in submarines. You ought to be court-martialed!"

I was amazed at Jim's outburst. Kohler and three or four other members of the crew who happened to be in the forward torpedo room stared their shocked surprise.

"Cut it out," I told Jim. "It wasn't that bad. It wasn't Keith's fault." Then I tried to relieve the tension a little. "So what if I did get a little soaking? I needed a bath anyway!" The joke fell flat. I motioned Keith up ahead of me through the water-tight door into the forward battery compartment and followed him, dripping a trail behind.

A difficult decision confronted me, and I had to make it immediately. Roy Savage, Carl Miller, and Stocker Kane might—just possibly—still qualify Jim, particularly if I made excuses for him and pressed his case. Captain Blunt would of course take their word for it. The question which weighted me, as I sloshed my way aft to change clothes, was the same one with which I had got Jim—and myself—into the present impasse.

Except that the last four days had been an eye-opener. I knew, now, that I could never turn the *S-16* over to Jim, at least not until he had amassed considerably more experience and steadiness under stress. And I also knew that the whole situation had really been my own fault. I might have been blind, might have temporarily been tempted, but I could never face myself if anything later happened to *S-16* under Jim's command. Everything he had done these last several days, every thought he had had, every word he had said, clearly demonstrated his unreadiness for that type of added responsibility. And yet, there was no denying that he was a fine submariner, all-in-all an asset to the Navy, and that he would not be in this situation had I not, for my own advantage, put him in it.

No matter how I argued it, it all came back to the same thing. I had to choose between sacrificing the *S-16* or Jim. In either case, I was really the one to blame and there was not a thing in the world that anyone could do about that. As our sorry little procession wound its way between the bunks in the forward end of the battery compartment toward the wardroom and Jim's and my stateroom, I went over and over the situation in my mind. There was only one thing to do, and it was up to me.

When we reached the curtain in the doorway I turned to Jim. "Come in a minute, will you, Jim?" I said. The others, sensing their dismissal, went on. Jim stepped with me into our little room, automatically reached for a cigarette. He avoided my eyes as he offered me one. I ignored it. This was going to be tough.

"Jim," I said, "I'm more sorry than I can possibly tell you. I'll take over. I want you to start us back for New London. I'll explain to the board."

Jim had just taken a deep drag. With his lungs full of to-bacco smoke he at first seemed not to hear, and then as it sank home he choked. "Why, you—you—" he gobbled for a moment, unable to speak. He threw the cigarette on the floor, stamped it furiously, opened and shut his mouth twice without a word. When he finally found his voice, his words were in direct contradiction of every naval tradition, everything he had learned, all the indoctrination the Navy had exposed him to. He spoke in a manner which no self-respecting person could forgive or forget, no commander of a United States man-of-war could condone. And yet I couldn't do any more to him after what I had already done. I had to take it, had to let him get away with it, had to swallow the sudden sick indignation.

"You Goddamed son-of-a-bitch," he said.

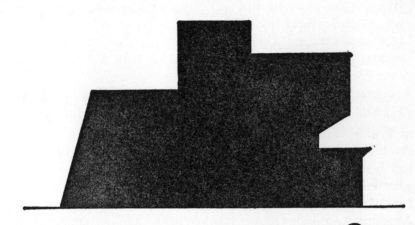

CHAPTER 3

LAURA ELWOOD ENTERED MY
life at the tag end of a nerve-shattering day in mid-August,
shortly after the *S-16* arrived in New London from the Philadelphia Navy Yard. One of old Joe Blunt's maxims had always
been that no officer of the Navy worth his salt ever needed a
drink to settle his problems—but this was one time that I did,
and I didn't care who knew it. An hour before I had supervised the final operations in tying the boat up to her usual dock
in the river, and as soon as I could get rid of a few essential
items of paperwork I headed for our tiny shower. Jim, from the
appearance of our stateroom, had preceded me; we passed each
other, draped in towels, as I headed forward. He halted, made

— **57**

a tremendous pretense of clicking his bare heels together, and raised his right hand in a caricature of a Nazi salute.

"Heil, Führer! I took a good look and there's not a scratch on me, so can I have permission to go ashore?"

Jim was obviously trying a little, but the absurdity of his salutation could not help but make me chuckle. "Sure," I said. "After today I think I'll do the same." He strutted down the passageway between the bunks, teetering from one side to another. When I got back he was already dressed and gone.

Along with several other boats, S-16 had gone out into Long Island Sound for the so-called "graduation approach" of a group of Ensign students then nearing the end of their accelerated three months' course at the submarine school. Five torpedoes had been loaded aboard, each one made ready by the Ensign who was to fire it. While he was doing so, the other four members of the party would take over the supporting assignments: Assistant Approach Officer, Banjo Officer, Diving Officer, and in nominal charge at the tubes. Our own crew, of course, would be standing by at the remaining stations necessary to operate the ship, and I, as skipper, held the responsibility of "Safety Officer."

Approximately fifty per cent of the grade the trainee would receive for the course depended upon the proper functioning of his torpedo, his conduct of the submerged approach leading up to firing it, and, most importantly, where that torpedo passed with relation to the target. It was a crucial test for each trainee and it was important to the S-16, too, since it was to be our first "shoot" for the school. Jim and Keith had labored most of the previous day and far into the night with our torpedo gang, checking our tubes and associated equipment.

As far as the first four fish were concerned, we need not have worried. Two of them passed under the target and the other two, though wide misses, were the results of poor approach technique. When our fifth and last approach began, however, it was late in the day. Considerable time had been lost with both of the bad shots, since each had to be pursued and hauled aboard the converted motor launch acting as retriever before the approach following could begin. And if one could judge by the length of time required to locate them, Roy Savage in *S-48*, with whom we shared the target's services, must have had one or two bad ones himself.

Our target was the old four-stack destroyer *Semmes,* and her job was simple; merely run back and forth between two submarines five miles apart, and help chase the torpedoes at each end. Since Roy was senior, the odd-numbered runs were his, and, of course, he had chosen for his initial point the one nearer the entrance of the Thames River channel. When the *Semmes* squared away for the tenth and last run, our fifth, *S-48* was already well on her way back to port and every minute she ran for us carried her double that time directly away from her own comfortable dock in the submarine base. I think we all expected the target to crank up the maximum speed permitted and to make the run as short as she could. Everyone, that is, except the tensely anxious officer student waiting to shoot his torpedo.

His approach was doctrinaire; he looked through the periscope every three minutes regardless of when the target's zigs took place, and we ran first one way and then the other—and succeeded in remaining practically stationary near the spot at which we had originally dived. Even so, it looked as though he might attain a favorable firing position no matter what he did, for *Semmes* was coming right down the initial bearing line, zigzagging regularly an equal amount to either side. It would be difficult not to get in a shot, in fact, and this was doubtless what the skipper of the *Semmes* had in mind.

The school instructor, a Lieutenant named Hansen who had recently come from being Exec of the *Barracuda* in Coco Solo, looked my way and shrugged. He pointed with a grin to the sweat-streaming face of the toiling student, made as if to wipe off his own, looked at his wrist watch, shrugged again. We were all anxious to get it over with, for it was hot in the control room. All of us were perspiring freely, moving about in a fetid atmosphere which reminded me of nothing so much as the fogged interior of the glass jar in which as a child I had once sealed a half-dozen inoffensive bugs.

The periscope rose out of its well, reached the top of its travel, and stopped. Standing bolt upright before it, the Approach Officer reached for the handles, folded them down into operating position, then gingerly applied his eye to the guard.

"Bearing—Mark," he said.

The acting Assistant Approach Officer read it for him, then turned back to fiddling with the Is-Was.

The Approach Officer jiggled the periscope back and forth with little taps with the heel of his left hand, his right hand cranking the range crank back and forth. "Range—Mark," he finally said.

"Two-four-double-oh!" read the yes-man, breaking away from the Is-Was and searching the range dial with his finger.

The Approach Officer was named Blockman, and so far as I could tell the name suited him. Rivulets of sweat running down his face and into the open neck of his sodden uniform shirt, he put up the handles of the 'scope and turned away. The yes-man fumbled for the pickle button hanging nearby on its wire, pressed it, started the periscope back into its well. It had been up nearly a full minute.

Hansen and I exchanged glances. Nearly at the firing point, the supposed enemy hardly more than a mile way, the surface of the sea smooth and calm—and the periscope up in full view for a minute! On the other side of the control room Jim winked as I looked at him.

"Angle on the bow is zero." The words cut across the compartment, perhaps from Blockman or his apparently equally stolid assistant. All three of them were now huddled with the Banjo operator in an oblivious group.

Even assuming a fairly large range error, there should be several minutes before he would be upon us. Fifteen knots equaled five hundred yards a minute. Divide that into the range for the time—nearly five minutes. Nevertheless I had not made an observation myself for some while, and there was just enough of uncertainty in the air, something which did not quite fall easily into place as it should have, which impelled me to do so now.

"I'll take a look," I said. I gave the order to the yes-man: "Up periscope!"

The 'scope whirred up. I stooped by force of habit, captured its handles as they came out of the well, folded them down—and as I did so a suddenly cold feeling gripped me in the middle of the belly. The right handle, the one governing the magnification power of the periscope's optical system, was in low power instead of high!

This meant that the range, instead of being twenty-four hundred yards at the last observation, had been roughly one fourth of that, six hundred yards. Some time had passed since, the *Semmes* was running right at us, and the range might have been inaccurate at that! I flipped the handle to high power, rose with my eye to the eye-piece. Lightning thoughts flooded into my brain.

"Jim!"

"Right here, Captain!" Jim's voice was close. He might have noticed the hand motion with which I discovered the position of the control handle, had in any event come over to the periscope in case I needed him.

Perhaps Blockman had for some reason turned the handle to the low power position after his last observation, actually had accomplished the range-finding operation in high power after all. In this case everything was all right . . .

The periscope popped out of water, stopped its upward travel with a familiar jolt. And there it was. Catastrophe. I took it all in. Solid. My head nearly burst with the shock of it. Chill all over my body. Prickling sensation at the ends of my fingers. "Take her down!" I shouted. It was nearly a scream. *"Take her down emergency!* Series! Two thousand a side! Sound the collision alarm!" Hastily I flipped the handle to low power and back to high power again.

I was looking at the most fearsome sight any submarine commanding officer can ever be given to look at. Just such a sight must have greeted poor Jones, skipper of the *S-4*, years ago off Provincetown. When his boat was finally raised, after all the heartbreaking failures, there was, of course, no one left alive to tell, but they found the periscope half-down, bent over at a sharp angle and stopped in mid-travel, its steel cables spewed forth by the unhalted hoist motors in strangling loops all over the control room. Jones must have given these same identical orders, in this same identical situation, fourteen years before. But the *Paulding* had been too close and going too fast, and the *S-4* couldn't make it.

And now we were in the same spot. In high power, equivalent to a six-power telescope, which is exactly what it is, all the periscope could show me was a huge gray-painted steel bow, oddly broad because seen from right ahead, not slender and lean as a destroyer's bow commonly looks, but deadly. In the center stood the sharp stem to which the bow plates were riveted—the rivets stood out plainly—and some distance to either side I could see the outlines of numbers, too foreshortened to read the "189" which I knew them to be.

In low power, one and a half magnification instead of six, I could see part of the mast and all of the bridge, and the curling bone in her teeth as she sliced swiftly through the smooth waves toward us. No time to take a range. No time, nor need, to do anything! Can't take a range this close anyway—just look at it, let your eyes bug out, this is the look of death coming at you—at least you'll have had a privilege few people get—*leave the 'scope up and pray they'll see it . . .*

There was suddenly a lot going on. I could feel the frantic hurry throughout the ship. The watertight doors slammed shut. Feet scurried into desperate action. Air whooshed out of regulator tank. There came the murmur of the diving planes suddenly jammed over into the full dive position, the heartening tilt of the deck as it inclined downward, and the sustained push of our now racing propellers. The range must be about two hundred yards now. Maybe *Semmes* will see the periscope and put her rudder over to avoid it—not much chance any more. They'd be looking out to the side, expecting to see the torpedo coming their way, ready to spot where it passed under their keel, and follow its track to where it surfaced . . .

Water closed over the end of the 'scope. No further purpose it could serve. No chance they might see it, nor of seeing through it—"Down periscope!" I barked. Instantly it whistled into the well.

"Depth!"

"Five-oh feet!" Tom had taken over the dive from the trainee. "Going down now, sir!" That situation was under as good control as it could be.

The periscope motors automatically stopped when the periscope bottomed, and Jim released the pickle. We could hear the destroyer coming now, a drumming-thumming, steadily-growing-louder sound. Great bronze propellers thrashing the water, shoving it astern, driving the ship ahead, dispassionately and unconsciously—nonetheless inevitably—bringing doom our way. Gigantic bright bronze choppers flailing, slashing, projecting downward a good two feet below the *Semmes'* keel. One bite from a single blade would be instantly followed by dozens of others, would open our pressure hull like a sardine tin. One blade already had a nick, for we clearly heard the swish-swish-swish of it going around. We must be sure to tell the skipper of the *Semmes* of it, if we get back.

Strange. If we get back. It's about time we'll know; it's about to pass overhead! If it's going to hit us, now's the time . . .

"Depth!" I snapped out the word question for the second

time within a quarter of a minute. Tom was only six feet away but Jim was between us, and so were several others.

"Five-eight feet!" Tom snapped the answer back. There was a roar of cacophonic sound, a sudden dropping of pitch, a thumping-banging-clanking of all sorts of miscellaneous machinery, and then the *Semmes* was past. I looked around, weak from the reaction, mopped my face. She hadn't hit us, but we had to make sure. "All compartments report!" I ordered. Jim, with white set face, moved with alacrity.

Hansen hadn't budged from the spot where he had been standing during our silent interchange only a few seconds earlier, but his face showed the strain it must have cost him to hold himself rigidly in check while others took care of the emergency which might cost him his life.

Blockman's round countenance was no longer stolid. It looked scared, in fact, but this was as nothing compared to the look that would be there after Hansen and the submarine-school authorities got through with him. Now the danger was past, I derived grim pleasure from the thought, and an insane urge to batter in that wet, stupid face shook my self-possession.

All the way back to our dock in New London my nerves were as tight as a violin string, and about as ready to screech if anything scratched across them. It was dark when we got alongside—luckily the tide was with us and the landing was easy —and as soon as the boat was safely snugged down for the night I went below. I needed something to sooth my jumpy nerves, to relieve the tension which had grown worse instead of relaxing. The muscles in my arms and neck were jumping spasmodically.

An hour later, in seldom-used civilian dress, I stood at the bar in the club, with my second drink as yet untasted in my hand. The first had not helped a bit, for suddenly I knew what the real trouble was. The old naval saying that an emergency properly prevented never becomes one was ringing loudly in my ears. Had we become a casualty this afternoon—joined the *S-51* and the *S-4*—or even merely suffered superficial damage, I knew that it would have been my fault more than Blockman's. I should never have permitted our safety to rest upon such a narrow margin. I had waited too long to take over the periscope; I had let the situation develop too far before asserting myself. My job was to help protect the trainees from their inexperience —it had been MY fault, not Blockman's.

I hadn't decided whether my drink was shaking because my taut nerves had not yet unwound or because of the sudden realization of my own shortcomings, when Jim's familiar voice interrupted.

"Captain, we were hoping we'd run into you here. This is Laura Elwood."

Jim's arm through hers drew her gently forward. His voice ran on, receding into the general background hum around us. Laura was tall and slender, erect of carriage, and her hand felt cool as she placed it in mine. I remember looking straight into gray-green eyes, wide-spaced in a soft golden tan. Everything in the room dropped away.

Jim was still talking, but it didn't register. The smooth line of her throat vanished in the suggestion of gently rounded fullness. Her blonde slimness was set off by a soft green jersey dress which left her arms and throat bare and gave her an elusive air of feminine innocence.

"You're going to have a hard time living up to the buildup Jim's been giving you, Captain," she said.

"Call me Rich," I said.

"That's right, Laura." Jim grinned in high good spirits. "Don't pay any attention to me because I'll still have to call him 'Captain'—it's that good old Navy Tradition I've been pumped full of."

"That suits me fine, Rich," Laura said. Then, turning to Jim with mock concern, "Will you look this serious when you get to be a Captain, too?"

Jim hesitated. Laura's eyes flicked to me with sudden apprehension. "I'm sorry, Rich. Did I say something wrong?"

"Of course not," I told her. I made room for both of them at the bar.

"We almost had a little trouble today, but it came out all right," Jim told her. "It was just one of those things that could have happened to any sub in this training racket. It was over so fast that nobody had any time to get really scared except the skipper."

The light from the candles above the bar wavered in the depths of Laura's eyes. As she waited I thought quickly for the right words to get it over to her without becoming too technical.

"One of the officer students was making his graduation approach," I said, "and he got us right in front of the target at close range. So there was just enough time to pull the plug and go deep to clear before the other ship passed overhead. It didn't actually hit us, but I guess it passed pretty close." As I said the words I could again see the huge white numbers on the *Semmes'* bow, the geometric furrows turned on either side of the steel stem of the destroyer as it rushed directly toward us, the rows of rivets I could practically have counted, the fact that had the two ships struck, even very slightly, we might have been dragged, or knocked, upward enough to permit the old destroyer's heavy low-slung propellers to rip into our hull.

The strain of the scare must have communicated itself to my voice in spite of all I could do, for Laura's face filled with sympathy. But she said nothing, for which I mentally thanked her. The nerves were jumping steadily in my right arm.

"I don't blame you for feeling a little rugged about it, skipper," said Jim, "but, after all, we got away with it so why worry. A lot of boats have had close shaves that we never heard about."

Laura turned to him, "Jim, can't we take Rich in with us to dinner? He needs cheering up."

I thought Jim seemed just a trifle taken aback, but he grinned quickly at her. "Sure," he said. "Why don't you ask him?"

She had already turned back to me, slipped her arm impulsively through mine, hugged it to her. "You will, won't you, Rich?"

Emotions submerged for four and a half years flooded to the surface. Had the events of the afternoon and then this meeting with Laura opened me up emotionally? Had they taken me back to those firmly forgotten days when I had decided that a career was more important than marriage? I had been very young and noble about it—too dumb to realize that I could have had both.

I could see now where I had been wrong. This was one of those decisions which need not have been made. Marriage or a career—you couldn't launch them both at the same time. But other men had, and successfully, too. The day that Stocker Kane married Hurry and I was best man, I knew then I'd been a fool. But Sally had gone away with the wound I had dealt her. Later I heard she had married.

And now, here was Laura, and what was I going to do about it?

Laura, I soon learned, had come down from New Haven, where she had been working since the death of her father as combination secretary and assistant to the head of a small accounting firm. Professor Elwood, a widower of many years, had taught economics at Yale, and it was there that she had first met Jim. She wrinkled her nose impishly at him when they got on the subject—it was a straight nose, slightly aquiline, with delicately chiseled nostrils and barely the suggestion of an upturned tip.

I needed to know more about her, searched desperately for a suitable conversational gambit. "Laura," I finally lamely asked her, "are you one of those whizzes at balancing books?"

She made a gesture of deprecation. "It's surprising what a mess the average storekeeper will make of his accounting," she answered, "and that's what gives us our business. For a small fee we'll come in and straighten things out for him. Otherwise,

— 67

some of them never would know from one year to the next whether or not they're making money."

"You mean you're one of those stony-hearted business women like in the movies?" I teased.

"I'm not, but my boss can be pretty hard-boiled," she smiled, "especially when it comes to cheating, which we find now and then."

"You don't look tough enough for that kind of a job."

She laughed outright. "You'd be surprised to see what an efficient little accountant Katherine Gibbs turned out. I majored in accounting and business administration—you don't have to be a man to add two and two." She grew a little more serious. "Of course, being a girl sometimes helps you to find out things, too."

There was a trace of thoughtfulness in her voice and a hint of a wiry core to her character.

But she was changing the subject, asking me about life in the submarine service, and I found myself telling her all about it and about my most terrifying experience on board the *Octopus* —when the carrier *Yorktown* rammed us during a fleet problem. The *Octopus'* welded hull shuddered violently under the impact of the *Yorktown's* speeding bow, recoiled drunkenly into the depths. Tons of foaming sea water, backed up by rapidly increasing pressure as the boat careened downward, roared through the hole.

Laura listened with rapt attention, her face reacting to the different aspects of the crisis as I recounted them. The tips of her fingers rested on my arm as I told her about our struggle in the control room—the absolute blackness, the ship almost on her beam ends, sinking rapidly by the bow. Frantically working with the lights of battle lanterns and flashlights, we split our high-pressure air manifold so as to concentrate all the air remaining in our air bottles into the forward tanks. Thus we gained the precious air volume necessary to blow our forward tanks completely dry against the compressive force of the sea and start the ship back up to the surface before it was irrevocably too late.

"Is that why you're so disturbed over this afternoon?" she breathed.

I was startled. I had to think this one over. "Why, yes. I guess subconsciously it is," I responded slowly, feeling for the solid ground. It had not yet occurred to me to make the comparison, but Laura had hit it unerringly. This was undoubtedly the core of it, the background reason for my distraught nerves, the subconscious reason why our own near-disaster had hit so hard and had stayed with me. But now that it was out in the open, there was a sensation of a knot slipping at the base of my brain, the pressure in my temples that was almost a headache beginning to disappear. I could feel myself, for the first time, slowing down.

Dinner passed in a haze of delight. Not for years had I so enjoyed merely being with a girl. I had almost forgotten the completeness the right girl can bring in life. Laura's eyes, now gay, now thoughtful, now sober, contained enough promise to drown in. I began to wonder whether I would have a chance to dance with her after dinner, when a bustle in the lounge heralded the arrival of the orchestra. Jim was on his feet in a moment. They were the first couple on the floor.

I waited a respectable time and then cut in on them. One of the arresting things about Laura was the steady straightforwardness of her personality. It was typical of her, I realized immediately, to come simply and directly into my arms from Jim's without self-consciousness. Nor was she unaware, and in my heightened sensitivity I appreciated the compliment.

All my senses responded to hers. She moved when I moved, stayed when I stayed, and in a little while the side of her forehead rested against my cheek, and I felt the brush of an eyelash. I couldn't tell whether we were dancing or drifting on a cloud, and I fiercely willed the music to play on and on and on—but after a while it stopped and Jim was standing there with his hand outstretched to claim her.

I have no further specific recollection of the rest of that Saturday night. I danced with Laura once more, then said good-by. Back on the *S-16*, I turned in to a deep, thankful slumber, punctuated by a recurring dream of having Laura for my very own for ever and ever down a long, white, slick marble stairway.

A feeling of well-being possessed me the next morning. For the first time in months, ever since leaving the *Octopus*, I felt completely relaxed. This was Laura's doing.

And then the reasoning part of my brain took charge. I had seen her only once. I had met her at a moment when mental and physical tension had been high and were yet to unwind themselves. She had unwound them, true, but I should not try to infer too much from that. As far as I was concerned, she belonged to Jim. Sternly I concentrated on that salient fact.

During the following months I came to see more and more of Laura. She came to New London nearly every week end when Jim and she could be together. The hectic training schedule and the fact that the 16-boat had only three watch-standing officers did not allow them much time.

I had to admit that I welcomed every opportunity chance threw my way to see her or dance with her. Though there were no further moments of strain comparable to the one which she had banished on our first meeting, the heightened awareness remained with me, and she reciprocated with a generousness and basic good will which warmed me every time we met and I resolved that if Jim ever dated another girl that would be my chance. But he never did.

Jim and Laura made a handsome couple, and little by little, as the months drifted by, it came to be accepted that some sort of understanding had been arrived at between them. It was on December 7, a cold, rainy Sunday in New London, that I, for one, knew it must be so.

I had gone to the Club for lunch, and finding Laura and Jim

there, accepted their promptly wigwagged invitation to join them. Afterward we settled on one of the deep-cushioned divans in the sitting room. It was about 2 P.M., there was a crackling fire in the fireplace, and someone at the bar had turned on a radio. We could hear music playing and occasionally the strident voice of an announcer touting something or other. And then we sensed an electric change in the program. A new voice was talking on the radio; the excitement he conveyed was real, altogether different from the synthetic sales talk of a moment before.

There was a sudden tenseness in Laura as she looked quickly from Jim to me, and a studied casualness as her hand sought his. I stood up.

"Guess I'd better go find out who robbed what bank," I said, and marched into the next room feeling a little heroic and a little foolish.

I'll never forget the look on Laura's face, and the round horror in her eyes, when I came back. "I'll have to go right back to the ship," I said. "Jim, there's really not much either of us can do, but you know what the regulations say. You'd better take Laura back to her hotel and help her get the next train."

Jim nodded without speaking, but Laura interposed quickly, taking his arm in an unconsciously revealing gesture as she did so. "I'd appreciate help finding the nearest bus from the submarine base, but I can certainly catch a train in town by myself. The place for Jim is right back on the *S-16* with you, Rich, and the quicker he gets there the better. Why, you might get orders to go to sea right away—and—never come back!"

For all her brave words, Laura's chin trembled as she finished, and the last words were uttered in a sob. She hid her face on Jim's shoulder. Awkwardly he patted her, put his arm around her, and suddenly her shoulders shook with deep, uncontrolled sobs, as she clung to him.

"Stow it, Laury," Jim gently whispered. "It's a bad break

for a lot of people—a lot of them must have been killed this morning. It just can't be helped what it does to us." He pulled a handkerchief out of a pocket, handed it to her.

Controlling herself, Laura pushed herself away from Jim, sat upright. "I'm all right. I'm sorry, Jim—it's just—just—so horrible. Everything's so terribly mixed up—nothing will ever be right again!"

They had completely forgotten my presence, and somehow I felt myself an intruder. "Excuse me a minute," I mumbled. "I'll be right back."

At the bar old Homer was talking into a telephone. "Yessir! Right away, sir!" he was saying as I arrived. Then he picked up a microphone beside it.

"There will be a bus leaving the front of the Club for New London in ten minutes," he announced. "All visitors are requested please to leave the base, by order of the Base Commander." Homer had a melodious Negro voice just suited to the announcing system speakers, and I could hear it resounding through the building. In a few minutes there was a small exodus taking place.

Laura was completely herself again as Jim put her on the bus. It was a sober crowd, and sober good-byes were said. I shook hands quickly so as to get out of their way, waited quietly a few feet distant. When Jim approached he said nothing, but his mouth showed a trace of lipstick, and his face was grim and downcast.

Tom was waiting for us on deck near the gangway as we approached the *S-16*. He wore a heavy overcoat against the frigid wind sweeping the river, had buckled a service forty-five automatic around his ample middle, and the gangway watch was similarly armed. I noticed with approval, also, that he had stationed two additional men on watch, one on the bow and another on the stern, likewise wearing pistols.

"Are those guns loaded?" I asked him.

"Yes, sir!" said Tom. "A full clip in each gun but none in the chamber. I've instructed the sentries they have to pull the slide back before the first shot. Besides that, each man has two loaded clips in his belt."

I nodded approval. "What instructions have you given them?"

"Remain on their feet and alert for sabotage or other unusual incidents in the river or on the beach," he answered. "Be particularly alert for any unusual movement in the water at night. Challenge anything suspicious immediately in a loud voice. If no answer, or not satisfactory, draw gun and fire one shot in the air. If still not satisfactory, shoot to hit. By that time the rest of us will be up here."

"Good man!" I said. "Where did you pick up all these ideas so quickly?"

Tom looked pleased. "I was in the old *S-31* in China when the Japs sunk the *Panay*," he said. "The place was swarming with bumboats, and we expected any minute that a whole gang of Japs would come jumping out of one of them."

I looked up and down the river, and at the other submarines peacefully tied up to their docks. It was hard to imagine that, for all we knew, at that very moment sabotage attempts were being planned against them, perhaps actually being carried out.

My watch said two-thirty when Captain Blunt showed up. His manner was incisive and to the point. What additional security measures had we taken? What percentage of our crew was aboard? How much fuel and provisions did we have on hand, and how many warshots were there in the torpedo rooms? He made notes quickly in a battered notebook and departed as abruptly as he had come, en route to the next boat of his squadron.

I was grateful to Tom for having enabled *S-16* to come through from the inquisition with credit. Some of the other submarines, I could see, were still getting men topside, and I was morally certain that some of them had few, if any, officers on board in addition to the duty officer. Not that we would have been much better off ourselves, had Jim and I not happened to sit within earshot of a radio after lunch.

I looked at my watch again. Two-forty. It had taken us just forty minutes to go to war.

But neither the Japanese nor the Germans attacked us, and after a few days, with the imposition of additional security patrols on the base and in the river, and more men on watch at a time in the submarines, life was permitted to resume much of its former habits. Except that the frenetic pace of our underway operations had virtually doubled.

So far as Jim and Laura were concerned, it had not been good-by after all. We received no orders to leave New London, continued doing exactly what we had been doing, with less time off than ever. And next week Laura resumed her weekly visits to New London.

By Christmas time, when the matter of Jim's qualification for command came up, I should not have been surprised at learning that as a contingent plan, he and Laura would very shortly thereafter be married. Before the beginning of the war a more leisurely and considered approach, with announcements, parties, and the like, would naturally have been in order. But now all such plans had to go into the discard. Many couples were marrying with only a few weeks in prospect during which they could be together. I should have realized what the prospect of an assured year in New London would mean to two people in love.

Jim had figured it out pretty accurately. He had correctly guessed the reason behind my sudden decision to recommend him, and his analysis of its effect was equally correct. There was not much the Bureau of Naval Personnel could do except let him stay in New London, while he waited until it was willing to give him a fleet boat of his own. Lucky was the couple, during these tortured times, who had this indefinitely long prospect to look forward to!

But I couldn't prevent a twinge of jealousy, or envy, when Jim gave me the news of his and Laura's plans. And then when I had to destroy it all, there came the strangest feeling of nakedness, as though for an instant he had looked right into my innermost soul—had seen there things I hadn't even admitted to myself, or suspected until that moment—which he hated me for.

CHAPTER 4

THE WEEK IMMEDIATELY FOL-
lowing Jim's failure to qualify for submarine command was an
extremely uncomfortable one for everybody in the S-16. He fell
into a cold sullenness which included everyone in the ship, and
he spoke to no one except when absolutely required to. When on
watch his orders were given in loud, defiant tones as if daring
anyone to question them. There was no more of the cheerful
banter which had been his habit, and I don't think he addressed
ten words to me during the whole time.

We were back at the refit pier to complete what we could of
our interrupted repairs—hence both Saturday and Sunday, for
the second time since our arrival in New London, were sched-

uled "alongside." Friday afternoon at the close of working hours
—still saying not a word to anyone—Jim dressed in civilian
clothes and disappeared. The customary "Permission to go
ashore, sir" was conspicuously absent, and we did not see him
again until Monday morning when he arrived precisely fifteen
minutes prior to our scheduled time for getting under way.

Next week, amid the rain and sleet of the winter's first storm,
was no better. He took his turn on the bridge without a word,
did what was required of him, and no more. When it was his
turn to get the ship under way or bring her in at night, I had to
spend long, uncomfortable, silent periods on the bridge with
him, and twice when, following our long-standing custom, I
went up to relieve him for a few minutes during long stretches
of watch, he refused me with a curt "No, thank you." Keith and
Tom, of course, also felt the strain keenly, though we did not
discuss it, and the rest of the crew's unwonted quietness showed
they felt it too. Jim had been popular with them.

Miller and Kane had accepted my dictum regarding Jim without question or comment. Roy Savage, though he also said
nothing, showed signs of irritation; but I made no explanation.
There was really not much to say.

The Squadron Commander's initial comment, delivered in the
process of lighting his pipe, was generous. "You've got to do
what your conscience tells you, Rich. I wouldn't want you to
recommend someone you don't believe in." That much of it was
easy. Then the conversation took an unexpected turn.

"Do you want to disqualify Bledsoe for submarine service?"
he asked abruptly, palming the glowing pipe bowl and pointing
the stem at me. "If he's not qualified to take command, he has
no right to be an Exec. He's supposed to step into your shoes,
you know, if anything happens to you."

I suppose it should have been predictable. I could have fore-
seen this reaction, should have expected it. I could feel panic
growing in me as he waited for my answer. After what I had
already done to Jim—now this. All I could think of was one of

Blunt's own aphorisms to the effect that there are times for caution, and times to stand up and be counted. This was one of the latter. I drew a deep breath and shot the works:

"Listen, Commodore. It was my fault for recommending Jim Bledsoe prematurely and for not having him ready—not his. There is nothing wrong with him that a little time won't fix. He is an excellent, fully qualified submarine officer, and he will be a credit to the submarine force and to the Navy. He should not be disqualified for submarine duty." I paused worriedly, searching for the clincher. "I'm satisfied with him. I would be willing to have him as my Exec anywhere," I ended uncomfortably.

Blunt remained silent for several seconds, tapping the desk with his finger and drawing on the pipe. "Well, you're Bledsoe's skipper and you ought to know, but it is damned near unprecedented for a man's C.O. to withdraw his qualification in the midst of his test. If he can't take responsibility when it comes his way, we don't want him around."

Blunt was known for his you're-on-the-spot way of looking at people and he bent such a gaze on me now. "You should not have recommended him if you did not think him ready for qualification, Richardson," he said slowly. My heart sank to my shoe tops. "We'll look at it your way and give Bledsoe the benefit of the doubt—but this is going to prevent you from getting the boat I promised you. I'm sorry."

"I'm sorry, too, sir," I replied, but this I had been expecting, and my heart was pounds lighter as I closed the door of his office behind me.

Life went on in its new groove for several weeks with no appreciable change. Our operations were routine. Jim was efficient, precise, thorough, and unapproachable. He went to New Haven every chance he got. Then the whirlwind hit us.

Captain Blunt was waiting on the dock with a group of three other Captains and three civilians as we pulled in one rainy, cold Thursday evening.

"We want to see you right away, Rich," he shouted as Tom Schultz, whose turn it happened to be, was nosing alongside our dock. "Turn your ship over to your Exec and hop ashore."

This was indeed unusual. I swung over the edge of the bridge and hurried down the ladder rungs welded to its side, scissored across the wire lifeline on deck, clung to it for a second, measuring the slowly closing intervening distance, then leaped to the dock.

"Lieutenant Commander Richardson, this is Captain Shonard of the Bureau of Ships," said Captain Blunt. I stared at the Commodore, my tarnished Lieutenant's bars only too evident on my shirt collar. "This is Captain Smyth, and Captain Weatherwax"—bringing forward the other two naval officers—"and this is Commander Radwanski, Lieutenant Sprawny, and Lieutenant Dombrowski." The Commodore struggled over the names of the civilians. I shook hands gravely, wondering what this was all about.

"We have to talk. Come up to my office." So saying, the Commodore strode toward the two cars waiting at the head of the dock and there was nothing to do but follow him. I shouted over to Jim, standing sullenly on deck, "Take over, Jim. I'll be back as soon as I can."

Once up in Captain Blunt's office, he as usual got right down to cases and confused me even more.

"Gentlemen," he said, addressing the civilians, "Lieutenant Commander Richardson is the skipper of your new ship." I almost choked.

The tall civilian, Radwanski, now turned to me and spoke hesitatingly. "We-are-pleased-to-make-your-acquain-tance." He accented all syllables with equal emphasis. "We-hear-you-have-a-fine-sub-marine. We-shall-call-it-*Light-ning-Swift*." I still had not the vaguest idea what he was talking about.

One of the other civilians came forward, the one introduced as Sprawny. He could hardly speak English at all but managed to get out something sounding like, "I am Meckaneeshun of the

Blinks-a-Wink." Lieutenant Dombrowski merely grinned and nodded his head.

The Squadron Commander took pity on my evident confusion.

"Rich," he said, "these gentlemen are officers in the Free Polish Navy—the Navy Department has sent them up here with instructions to take over the *S-16*. Their crew will arrive by train in a couple of days. You'll probably get your orders by dispatch tomorrow, but you might as well start thinking about turning her over immediately."

I stared my consternation. Captain Blunt went on: "They won't even need much training in your ship. This is the same crew which has been operating the *S-17* since we turned her over to them six months ago. The Germans bombed her in dry dock in England and I understand there's little hope of getting her back in commission. They're going to take over your ship as replacement for her. Since the two boats are identical, the *S-17*— or what's left of her—will be an excellent source of spare parts."

Radwanski, Dombrowski, and Sprawny all nodded their heads vigorously.

I pulled myself together as well as I could. "How soon do you want us to turn over?" I asked. "There are quite a few outstanding repair and alteration items, and some modifications we've made in the ship . . ."

"That's what we're here for, Richardson," said the Captain who had been introduced as Shonard. "I'm from BuShips, so is Smyth—and Weatherwax here is from the Bureau of Ordnance. We're going to accomplish your complete list of outstanding repairs, as well as several items we have in mind on our own. This is what we've had in mind for the *S-16* all along. You've done a nice job on her."

So this was to be the result of all our work! We had been getting *S-16* ready for war, all right—for somebody else to have the fruit of our labor!

"When is all of this supposed to happen?" I asked, trying to keep the bitterness out of my voice. "What about my crew?"

"Immediately," said Shonard, "that is, as soon as possible."

Messrs. Radwanski, Dombrowski, and Sprawny grinned and nodded.

Captain Blunt broke in: "I don't blame you for feeling a bit rushed, Rich, but we must cooperate to the best of our ability. Their crew will get here this week end. The three officers will go down to your ship tomorrow to look her over and start making plans. We will terminate your assignment to the submarine school as of now and your only duty will be to assist Commander Radwanski in whatever he needs. You can understand they are anxious to get the S-16—I mean Lightning-Swift—into action, and the Navy Department has agreed to turn her over all standing."

I nodded my comprehension, too miserable to do more.

Captain Blunt went on. "Commander Radwanski and his friends have an appointment with the Admiral. Rich, will you wait here for about three minutes—while I show them to his office—I've got one more thing I want to talk to you about." He indicated the chair by his desk, led the three Poles to the door, and closed it behind him.

For twice three minutes I sat there, staring at the wall. Events, or luck, had conspired against me. In my eagerness for a new ship I had put Jim Bledsoe up for his command qualification prematurely. As a direct result his reputation had been damaged, his marriage plans spoiled, and deservedly I had lost his regard. I had made my choice between Jim and the S-16, chosen the latter's welfare as the more important—and now she too, was gone.

My despondency deepened as Blunt's footsteps came back down the hall and the door opened. He smiled.

"You've probably been wondering why I addressed you as Lieutenant Commander. Well, here it is. Your promotion arrived by AlNav this morning." He handed me a sheet of closely printed mimeograph paper which had the words *AlNav #12* across the top. "You're listed there. About halfway down."

Then he smiled even more broadly—an unusual look, for him. "That's not the best of it, either. You're getting the *Walrus*—she's just been launched at Electric Boat. Furthermore, the Admiral has decided that the simplest way to put a crew aboard is to transfer the whole *S-16* outfit to her with you."

My jaw hung open. My heart bounded as the import of it sank home. But old Blunt wasn't quite done yet: "You don't have to take them all—just those who want to go. Of course, those who don't——" His smile, for the second time in my immediate recollection, took on a sardonic glitter.

I don't know how I found my way back to the *S-16*. Three body blows like these, all made known to me within an hour, were a little out of the ordinary at the very least. I called Jim, Tom, and Keith together in the wardroom and they were as flabbergasted as I. The four of us went together to the control room, where I broke the news to the crew.

Turning *S-16* over to the Poles was an unmitigated headache. Few of them understood English and explaining things was not merely difficult, it was a problem of extraordinary magnitude. Had not most of the Poles already been familiar with the *S-17*, it would have been impossible.

We glued strips of paper with Polish writing on all our gauges and dials, and we made dive after dive with each of our men instructing his Polish relief. When we turned the boat over to them for their first dive we thought them fairly well indoctrinated—but even so they made my hair literally stand on end.

There was apparently no preparatory command, no "Clear the Bridge" or its equivalent in Polish; merely two blasts on the diving alarm. Everyone dashed below; all vents were pulled wide open and the motors put ahead full speed. Somehow the bridge hatch was shut. No one paid any attention to the Christmas Tree or bothered to bleed air into the boat to test for tightness. The bow planes were not rigged out until she was thirty feet under and no one paid any attention to the bow and stern plane controls until we passed thirty-five feet on the way down. Our bow went down at an ever-increasing angle, steeper than I had ever experienced, and I began to have the sensation of going into an outside loop. We could never complete a loop, of course, but we might ram her nose into the bottom of Long Island Sound with enough force to break something.

Commander Radwanski shouted in Polish. Nobody moved. Dombrowski, in charge of the dive, had yet to utter a word. I could see Larto standing by the main power control beside his replacement in the Polish Navy. He looked at me beseechingly, imploring me with his large, expressive Italian eyes. I was about to shout "All back emergency" when Radwanski yelled several more Polish words. We were by this time passing ninety feet and the *S-16* had assumed a fifteen-degree down angle. The little bench which was the station of the Chief of the Watch began to skid on the slick linoleum deck; a couple of wrenches located by the trim manifold slid from their accustomed location and fell on the deck with a clatter; someone had parked an empty coffee mug in an unnoticed corner and now it burst forth, making its presence known with a shattering of crockery.

The two Polish sailors detailed under the silent Dombrowski's supervision now ran both planes to "full rise." The Polish Chief Electrician's Mate impassively leaned over his rheostats and, to my amazement, increased the speed. Suddenly, alarmingly, *S-16* swooped out of her dive, reversing her down angle and reaching ten degrees rise. We had climbed back to sixty-five feet before the sweating planesmen could level her off.

More shouted commands: The Polish Electrician's Mate reduced speed and *S-16* settled out into some sort of submerged control. Radwanski, standing in the center of the control room and maintaining balance by holding on to one of the periscope hoist wires, leaned his sweaty, whisker-stubbled jaw toward me and hissed into my ear with a nod toward Dombrowski, who so far as I could see had still not opened his mouth.

"That-is-al-ways-his-way. Beau-ti-ful-sub-mer-gence, not-so?" he said.

From that moment on the *S-16* under Polish hands acquired an entirely new personality. I saw her for the first time in a detached, unemotional state of mind, and was even able, without a twinge, to watch them paint her new name, *Blyskawica,* meaning *Lightning-Swift,* on her stern and replace our numbers on the side of the bridge with a large white B. It was not until we all stood on her deck, seeing the United States ensign hauled down for the last time, that a pang of regret suddenly registered. She had been a good ship—we had made her into one— and now she was going to war without us. We wished her luck.

Walrus was already in the water, much nearer to completion than we had had any idea, when we reported to Electric Boat. The yard workers were knocking themselves out—had been ever since Pearl Harbor—and she would make her first dive within two months. Twenty-four hours a day a veritable army of overalled workmen were in her, on her, and about her. The acrid smell of welding, the din of power tools, and the clatter of workmen never ceased. Every day we went down to her and looked her over, trying ineffectually to stay out of the way and yet get some idea of what was going on, and every day something new had been added, some new piece of equipment installed, some additional step taken toward getting her ready.

In our office on the second floor of a temporary wooden building erected at the head of the dock at which *Walrus* lay, Jim, Keith, and Tom wrestled with the problems of preparing the ship's organization and orders and making duty assignments for the crew.

Jim was doing his usual good work, but there had been one bad moment. Shortly before the final transfer ceremony of the *S-16* he had come up to me with a sheet of official ship's stationery in his hand. I had been going over the spare-parts inventory in our tiny, soon-to-be-relinquished wardroom, preparatory to having a joint inventory with the *S-16's* Polish skipper, Radwanski. "Captain," Jim said—it was the first time he had thus addressed me since the qualification fiasco—"I have been thinking it over for a long time. I would like a transfer." The paper was an official request from Jim addressed to the Chief of the Bureau of Naval Personnel, via the Commanding officer of *S-16* and the Commander, Submarine Squadron Two, requesting a change of duty from *S-16* to "any other vessel of Squadron Two."

"What's this for, Jim?" I asked.

Some of Jim's sulky look had returned, and he fidgeted uncomfortably.

"How do you think I'd feel going on the *Walrus* and knowing that I can never get any place in submarines?" he asked petulantly, all in a rush, as though in a hurry to get it out. "I've got feelings and ambitions, too. I want to make something out of myself. After what you did to me—putting me up for qualification for command and then bilging me—can't you see I'm all through—shot? With another ship maybe I can qualify to be skipper."

I had expected that Jim might feel this way, and had my answer ready, or thought I did. Quixotically my mind spun sixty miles to the westward and I found myself wondering what he had told Laura. I had not seen her since that day.

"Listen, Jim, you've got this all wrong. I've no prejudice against you. I want you in *Walrus* because I like you and because you're a good Exec. Someday you will be skipper of your own boat."

There was a plaintive note in Jim's voice. "That's what I want, too, but I'll never get it with you."

"That's exactly where you're wrong, Jim. There's a lot more to submarining than running a boat up and down the Thames River. The future of the submarine force is in boats like the *Walrus*, not in old antiquated ones like this one."

"But don't you see? I don't want to go with you. I want to stay where I can do some good. Where people respect me."

"What can you do here that you can't in a fleet sub?"

"I might be able to take over one of the school boats, if I can get with a skipper who'll recommend me."

"What about the war. Don't you propose to get in that?" Jim looked away. His voice was strained, as though it might be a struggle for him to speak.

"I'm looking out for Number One from here on. Nobody else will—not you! To hell with the *Walrus* and to hell with the war, too!"

I couldn't tell Jim of my conversation of a few weeks ago with Captain Blunt, but there was another way. Heretofore I had used the friendly approach, had stood for his silence and sullen bad temper. Maybe this was the time to change, though it would give Jim cause to hate me all the more. I stood up from the wardroom table in *S-16*, picked up his neatly typed request, and held it in my hand. I made my voice emotionless.

"Listen, Bledsoe, what you've just said is disloyal and disrespectful. The Bureau of Naval Personnel has ordered this whole ship's company to the *Walrus*. That was your chance to register an objection, but you didn't. I was asked if I wanted you for my Exec—and I said I did. You have already received official orders to that effect. It's too late to change your mind now. Furthermore, I've stood for your bad temper long enough. It's time you stopped acting like a spoiled child. If you deserve command, you'll get it."

Navy regulations specifically forbade my doing so—but as I finished I ripped the paper in half twice and threw it back on the table. Jim had half-opened his mouth to speak, closed it uncertainly as I tore up his request. For a moment he stood, irresolute, and then, muttering something under his breath, he turned and stalked away.

Jim knew the regulations as well as I did but the bluff worked nevertheless. There grew a new wariness about him and we concentrated on our job: organizing *Walrus*. There was a lot to do, and the burden, of course, fell primarily on Jim. We ate, slept, and breathed the *Walrus*. We lived in a little world of our own, sometimes not even recognizing the fact that other submarines, some more nearly completed than *Walrus* and others not so far along, also were going through the same processes alongside us.

And then one day I realized that Jim's sulkiness had been gone for some time. He was not the same as before, of course, and there was this new contemplative awareness. He did his job as usual, organizing not only the official watch sections and administering responsibilities of the ship but also the extracurricular activities such as baseball teams, bowling leagues, and the like. It was not a complete about-face, but distinctly an improvement. At times I thought he might have finally understood. They were followed by moments when it seemed more probable that he was only submerging what feelings he might have, perhaps awaiting more appropriate expression. Whatever it was, I was too grateful for the improvement in our relations to want to question it even had I been able to do so.

And I realized another thing, too. When I finally saw Laura, there was no longer the warm friendliness I had once felt so strongly. We got up a ship's party as a parting gesture for the *S-16*. It was almost a command performance for all of us, enlisted and officers, to attend. I wondered whether Jim would bring Laura, and when he was late, for a few uneasy moments it looked as though he might have decided to ignore the party after all.

When the door to our hall opened and he and Laura stood there, I had the sudden feeling of cold ice on my backbone. She was as beautiful as ever, and they made a pleasing picture as Jim, with a solicitous, possessive air, led her through the crowd to the table set aside for us.

"Here comes Mr. Bledsoe!" Kohler spoke in a loud, carrying voice. "Now the party can begin!" Jim turned and waved to him, then acknowledged with a grin Larto's violently gesticulated, white-toothed greeting.

Somebody let out a low-pitched whistle from the middle of the crowd, and the irrepressible Russo stood up on a chair to get a better look. "When you going to let me bake you that cake, Mr. Bledsoe?" he yelled at him. Jim grinned and shook his head slightly.

Laura's cheeks were flushed and her eyes were dancing as she sat down. She nodded hello to Tom and Cynthia Schultz, greeted Keith warmly, and tossed me a curt, cool hello. Throughout the evening she avoided my glance, applied herself assiduously to gay repartee with the other members of our party, answered my attempts at conversation in monosyllables. I couldn't avoid asking her to dance, and it was as I had feared, like holding a faultless dummy in my arms. Jim claimed her as soon as he decently could.

The party, as far as I was concerned, was a flop. I had expected some such reaction from Laura, especially after realizing the store she and Jim had set by Jim's qualification for submarine command. Someday, perhaps, after Jim had become a skipper, she might understand why I had had to do it. But it was hopeless to try to explain. The hurt was deep, and I had to let it go in silence.

The Poles stayed in New London for several weeks after we turned *S-16* over to them and then one day, as I was sitting in our second-floor office poring over *Walrus'* fire-control setup, I saw her heading downriver on her final departure from New London. The *Blyskawica*, or *Blinks-a-Wink* as we called her, was low in the water and down by the stern, loaded with fuel in her after main ballast tank for the long voyage. She looked tiny and bold and a little forlorn, standing bravely down the Thames River with the white ensign of Poland fluttering from her flagstaff. Her crew was at quarters on deck as she passed under the bridges, and as she came by the dock where the *Walrus* lay I saw them stiffen to attention. The notes of a bugle wafted across the muddy waters of the river.

I had not known the Poles carried a bugler and I don't think anyone else saw her, but I stood up and returned the salute, bare-headed and indoors at that, feeling all choked up inside and just a little ashamed at the sentimental feelings suddenly evoked. I knew I would never see her again.

Walrus was half again as long as *S-16*, and she was at least twice as much submarine. She had four huge diesel engines of the latest type, the same as in our latest diesel railroad tractors, in two engine compartments. There were ten torpedo tubes—six in the bow and four in the stern—and of course two torpedo rooms. Her battery was more than twice as large as *S-16's*, also located in two compartments, one just forward and the other just aft of the control room. Her control room was commodious compared with that of the *S-16*, and crammed with new equipment. Best of all was the conning tower, consisting of an eight-foot-diameter horizontal cylinder above the control room—in *Walrus* a real fire-control station—from which the periscopes could be operated, the ship maneuvered, and torpedoes fired.

In the after end of the conning tower, curved to fit against its shell, was installed the computing machine by which we would solve for enemy course and speed and automatically send the proper torpedo gyro angles to the torpedoes. Its official designation was "Torpedo Data Computer," and it was known by its initials as the TDC. I had become acquainted with an earlier version of it in the *Octopus* and therefore, fortunately, had some understanding of how it could be used. The whole ship, for that matter, reminded me greatly of an improved *Octopus*, and I was soon grateful for my three years' service in that vessel.

We had only a short time, two months, to get the *Walrus*

ready to go to sea, and only four weeks after that to prepare for our voyage to the war. The emergency of the war had affected the shipyard workers, planners, and supervisors alike; they did their jobs with certitude and speed as though every welding bead they ran, every bolt they tightened down, were a personal attack on the enemy. We had our hands full keeping up with them, so that we would be ready for our new ship when it was delivered to us. All the new boats at Electric Boat had the same problem.

Most of the crew of S-16 had volunteered to come along to the *Walrus*. Kohler, Chief of the Boat and now additionally in charge of two torpedo rooms instead of only one, was in his element. He had long envied the fortunate submariners serving in the new "gold-platers," as he termed the fleet boats, and his pleasure in ours was good to behold. Larto, First Class Electrician's Mate in S-16, was notified of his appointment to Chief at the same time he was assigned to the electrical control station or "Maneuvering room" of *Walrus*. Quin happily took charge of a "really commodious"—as he termed it—little office all his own about four feet by three feet by five and a half feet high. It was, indeed, much bigger than the part-time corner he had been assigned before. Rubinoffski took over the conning tower, the bridge above, and a whole series of chart drawers located in the wardroom. Our cook on S-16, Russo, couldn't spend enough time in his new galley. He had never seen anything so beautiful, he said, watching with delight as two new electric stoves were lowered into his new domain.

Jim, Keith, and Tom as a matter of course kept their original assignments as Exec, Gunnery-and-Torpedo, and Engineer. In addition we were informed that two more officers, junior to Keith, might be expected before the ship went into commission. They would become our Communications Officer and Assistant Engineer, we decided.

Getting a new ship organized and supervising her construction is in many respects a time-consuming and seemingly thankless chore. The prospective skipper and crew never quite see eye to eye with the builder regarding just how the ship is to be built, just where each incidental piece of equipment is to be installed. Likewise, personnel requirements regarding the assignment of the crew and officers are bound to create problems needing solution. There is plenty to do from the beginning, especially when you start with only two months to go; and then gradually, as the commissioning date nears, you find that those were the easy days. Long hours become ordinary, late nights the rule rather than the exception. A Watch Quarter and Station Bill has to be worked up. The men have to be given battle stations, cleaning stations, watch stations. The crew must be divided into three sections, approximately equally spaced as to ranks and abilities, and given such training ashore as is possible. Certain men had to be sent away to school to acquire basic knowledge about some of our new equipment. We all, at Tom's insistence, attended diving drill on the diving trainer at the submarine school—with the equipment set up to simulate fleet-boat conditions—and Jim arranged for special time in the Attack Teacher's crowded schedule so that our embryonic fire-control party would have a few opportunities to work together as a team before we went to sea.

It was late in March, during this preparatory phase prior to getting *Walrus* to sea, that Jim sought me out. Something was bothering him and he hemmed and hawed before beginning.

"Skipper," he finally said, "the others thought I should bring this to you right away. It's bad news."

"What?" I asked.

"It's about the *Octopus*. She's gone."

I stood up, feeling a peculiar dullness in the front of my head. "Gone?" I repeated stupidly.

"Yes, sir, the announcement came in by dispatch about an hour ago. We just got it."

"Let me see it."

Jim silently handed me a pink sheet of tissue paper.

THE NAVY DEPARTMENT REGRETS TO ANNOUNCE THAT THE USS OCTO-
PUS IS OVERDUE FROM PATROL STATION AND PRESUMED LOST DUE TO
ENEMY ACTION X THE OCTOPUS ASSIGNED TO THE PACIFIC FLEET WAS
FIRST COMMISSIONED AT NEW LONDON IN 1936 X HER COMMANDING
OFFICER WAS COMMANDER GERALD M WATSON OF CHICAGO X THERE
ARE NO OTHER DETAILS AVAILABLE X

It had had to come, of course; losses in war had to be expected, but who could have foretold that when I departed to
take command of *S-16,* then in the back channel at the Philadelphia Navy Yard, I was saying good-by to my shipmates for the
last time; that my orders to that "old, broken-down tub" would
spell the difference between life and death between me and my
old friends. I read the dispatch over several times. When I
looked up Jim was gone.

Getting *Walrus* ready now took on a new meaning. The war
had come home in a particularly personal way. I fretted under
the delays and redoubled our efforts at training and preparation.
March drew to a close; April came and went and our commissioning date grew nearer. I was wrapped up all day long with
Walrus, all night studying her plans and specifications and the
way we had to fit ourselves into them. The weeks passed on
winged feet.

Jim still made his week-end pilgrimages to New Haven, and
once in a while probably had Laura with him at the Club at
the submarine base or elsewhere in New London. With the ship
under construction there were no watches to stand or to prevent
his having every week end to himself if he could arrange his
work and responsibilities accordingly.

Hugh Adams and Dave Freeman reported fresh out of the
submarine school the first week in April. Adams was tall and
gangling, nearly as tall as Jim, with an unruly thatch of reddish
hair and a heavy crop of freckles. He could have passed for a
high-school senior anywhere. Freeman, a small, intense youth,
contrasted violently with Adams in appearance and personality.
It was hard to conceive of these two having been roommates

and best friends in Quarters "D" at the submarine school or even having anything at all in common. I felt immediately drawn to Hugh Adams. Freeman with his reserved, less colorful personality, would take more developing, but seemed to have a certain seriousness of purpose about him. The meticulously careful handling required for codes, ciphers, and classified documents would be his dish, I thought, as I made the assignments designating him Communications Officer. Adams could be understudy to Daddy Schultz as Assistant Engineer.

We got *Walrus* to sea for the first time the last week in April, or rather Electric Boat did. By the terms of their contract the boat company's trial crew had to take all newly constructed submarines out in the Sound for proof dives and operation of equipment before turning them over to the Navy. It felt odd to be a guest in my own ship, and stranger yet to see a submarine being expertly operated by a bunch of Yard workmen clad in various assorted pieces of civilian work clothes.

The ship was mechanically complete, though hardly a thing of beauty. Yellow chromate paint was everywhere inside. Her steel decks were covered with heavy cardboard rather than the prescribed linoleum. Discarded pieces of cable were lying about and large chunks of cork, rags, dirt of all kinds were in the corners and underfoot. She presented an unkempt appearance, but I had to admire the way the trial crew went about their business. There were only fifteen of them, just enough to operate the ship—no more.

Half our crew had to remain ashore to make room for official observers, and the resulting ship's company—if you could term it that for this first trip—was a strange one, with divergent interests all over the place. The Trial Captain, Captain Morgan, rode serenely above it all. He was at least sixty years old, had been with submarines all his life, and his handling of *Walrus* was finesse itself. Disdaining the proffered assistance of two tugs standing by off the end of the pier, he backed her smartly out into the Thames River, turned her on her keel with one propeller going ahead, the other backing, and headed her swiftly downstream. The unused tugs followed to act as safety observers when we submerged.

Our first dive was in great contrast to the first dive of the Poles in *S-16*. Captain Morgan's objective was to test *Walrus* for the tightness of her welded seams. First came a thorough air-pressure test; satisfied, he eased her down gently, testing her balance as he did so and letting water into her variable water tanks a little at a time until finally he had both submerged and obtained a perfect initial trim. "None of these slide-rule calculations for me!" he told us. Then two more dives, a few rapid surface tests including hard-over rudder with the ship going full speed astern, and he was satisfied for the first day.

"We used to try a boat for a week before turning her over to the Navy," he told me, "but they are rolling so many off the lines these days, all exactly alike, that all we need to do now is test the hull for tightness and the systems to see if they work. You've got a good ship here, boy."

I could not object to his calling me "boy," for he had retired from the Navy before I had even entered the First Grade. Most of his crew likewise were retired Navy personnel, nearly all Chief Petty Officers, each an expert in his own line or trade.

Twice more the trial crew took *Walrus* out in the Sound, until the inspectors and supervisors were satisfied. A few more days of cleaning her up, laying the linoleum, scraping off excess paint, and then Captain Morgan delivered her to one of the piers at the submarine base, upriver. I read my orders to the assembled crew in the presence of a small group of visitors and we all stood rigidly at salute as the United States flag was hoisted on her stern. *Walrus* was ours, the newest unit of the fleet.

Our work had just started. Now it was drilling the crew aboard ship, over and over again going through the myriads of details necessary to the effective operation of a fleet-type submarine. We were assigned an area in Long Island Sound and every day, Sunday included, we took *Walrus* out and went through our paces. The only days we stayed in port were when we had to provision ship, take on fuel, or make some small repair.

At first there was simply the matter of being able to dive. Time after time we went through the motions. Time after time we dived, got the boat trimmed to a hair of submerged balance, made a few simple submerged maneuvers, and surfaced again. Each of the three sections into which the crew was divided was required to be able to dive, get a trim, and operate the ship independently. Each of the officers, Hugh Adams and Dave Freeman as well as the rest, had to take his turn handling a dive, handling the main engines, working out on the levers in the maneuvering room, firing torpedoes, getting under way, and making landings.

There was no denying that it was a tough grind, and it gradually became tougher as the tempo of our days' operations speeded up. We were not weighted with a class of trainees from the submarine school, required to do the same thing with a different group time after time, and we progressed steadily to high-speed maneuvers, quick dives, in which the diving alarm is sounded without warning of any kind, and simulated casualties of all sorts. The section on watch got so they could man their posts with instant alertness, ready at any second to send *Walrus* below into the sheltering depths, or to handle any emergency, submerged or on the surface.

A lot of our work was on attack procedures. First we went to Newport, Rhode Island, took on a load of exercise fish, and fired them in Narragansett Bay, one after the other, to determine that the torpedo tubes were properly bore-sighted and that the torpedoes would go where aimed. Then we began to carry out approaches using the *Falcon, Vixen,* or sometimes another submarine—anything that came handy. Every time we could get more than two targets at once we pretended some were escort vessels. Torpedo after torpedo we shot in the safe waters of Long Island Sound, learning the fundamentals of our new fire-control equipment.

Keith, the TDC operator, was a very real help during an approach. He had never seen a TDC before but its functions were obvious and well laid out, and he showed himself, as usual, quick to learn.

Jim, so burdened with work that he seemed by this time to have forgotten his original bad feeling, was also a tower of strength as Assistant Approach Officer.

Tom Schultz, of course, was back at his old stand, either in the engine rooms or handling the dive during battle stations submerged.

After a month of practice we were ready for our final operational inspection at the hands of Captain Blunt. We were assigned the deepest area in Long Island Sound—not very deep at that for a boat like *Walrus*. To the westward the *Falcon, Vixen,* and *Semmes* formed the "convoy" we were to attack. Blunt, Jim, and I, and Hugh Adams as Officer of the Deck, were on the bridge; above us on the upper level of the periscope supports stood four lookouts with binoculars; on the "cigarette deck" Rubinoffski, Quartermaster of the Watch, also simulated aircraft watch with binoculars.

The *Vixen,* playing the part of a Jap troop transport, had not yet turned around to head for us. I was watching her idly, my binoculars scanning the horizon, when suddenly I heard a stentorian bellow:

"Plane on the starboard quarter!" Captain Blunt was shouting at the top of his lungs and pointing off our stern. Involuntarily I swung my binoculars to see it. The Squadron Commander shouted again, pointed violently. "Plane coming in on our starboard quarter!" He pointed again.

Hugh looked back uncertainly, then made up his mind and reached for the diving alarm. "Clear the bridge!" he shouted as he pressed the diving alarm twice. There was a pop from forward as Number One main ballast tank vent went open. Then another pop as Number Two did likewise. Three and Five had fuel in them, but within less than a second, Four, Six, and Seven popped in their turn and little geysers of spray blew up through our slotted deck. The lookouts came tumbling down from their upper platform, protecting their binoculars with their arms across their chests, diving for the hatch. Back aft I could see the wake of water thrown astern by the suddenly speeded-up propellers, and up forward the bow commenced to settle in the water. Captain Blunt was grinning at me and he had a stop watch in his hand. It had already traveled a quarter of the way around the dial.

"Didn't you see the plane, Rich?" he chuckled.

There was no time to engage in conversation, even if Captain Blunt would have liked to, for *Walrus* was already on her way down. Jim, the Squadron Commander, and I ran to the hatch. I motioned Jim down ahead of me and then Blunt. Hugh Adams was right behind us—as Officer of the Deck he would be last man below on a dive. I jumped down the hatch, stood clear for Hugh. He came down, slammed the hatch shut, and leaned back on the wire toggle holding it in place. Rubinoffski, having preceded us, was standing by the helmsman; now he jumped up on the ladder rungs, grasped the hatch wheel, and locked it firmly. Adams released the wire lanyard and dashed below.

Walrus' deck tilted forward a little more, and I could hear water gurgling up the sides of the conning tower. The needle on the conning-tower depth gauge wavered off its peg, commenced to climb.

"Depth, Captain?" came floating up the hatch from Hugh.

"One hundred feet," I called in return. I turned to Captain Blunt. "If it were a plane we should go deeper but we'd better not here; the sound is too shallow for a big boat like this."

He nodded.

"Sixty feet," said Rubinoffski, as the depth gauge reached that point.

The Squadron Commander looked at his stop watch. "Sixty-one seconds. That's only fair. Won't she dive any faster?"

"I think you caught Adams a little by surprise, sir."

"*Walrus* has got to stay on her toes, Rich. You'd be surprised how many boats don't even think of diving out from under attacking planes until they get to Pearl Harbor and talk to some of their buddies."

We could hear the bustle below, the slamming of watertight doors, the securing of ventilation pipe bulkhead valves. The conning tower commenced to warm up rapidly with the air supply cut off.

"One hundred feet, Captain! The ship is rigged for depth charge!" Hugh Adams' voice came easily up the open hatchway from the control room below.

"Very well," I answered. I leaned over the hatch, raised my voice to make sure of being heard: "Secure from depth charge! Sixty feet!" *Walrus* inclined upward. Again the banging of bulkhead doors and ventilation valves as they were opened. The depth gauge at my elbow slowly recorded the decrease in depth. When it touched seventy feet I started the periscope on its way up. Rubinoffski leaped forward and relieved me of the pickle control button.

I was looking through the periscope when it broke the surface, spun it around three times swiftly.

"Down 'scope!" The sheaves creaked and the periscope bottom disappeared. "Three ships in sight, Commodore. Looks like our target group with a large angle on the bow."

"Y'don't say!"

I waited. Old Blunt was giving me that shaggy-eyebrow look and suddenly the light dawned. "Enemy in sight!" I rapped out. "Sound the general alarm!"

Walrus' general alarm sounded like a musical doorbell, except that it kept going for eleven seconds after you let go the knob. The musical "Bong, bong, bong, bong, bong" reverberated through the ship, and I heard men dashing about below. Jim,

Keith, Hugh Adams, Quin, and several others climbed swiftly up the nearly vertical ladder and joined us in the conning tower.

"Conning tower manned and ready, skipper!" reported Jim.

Within a few moments—less than a minute—Quin had received the telephone reports: "The ship is at battle stations, sir," he said.

Keith was spinning the dials of his TDC. It gave forth a low-pitched sirenlike whine as the motors came up to speed.

"Initial bearing of target?" he said to me.

Rubinoffski sang out the answer: "Two-six-six!"

"Angle on the bow?"

This was mine. "About port forty." Keith gave a low whistle.

"Give them an initial range of ten thousand—that puts us nearly seven thousands yards off the track!"

This meant that unless the target group zigged toward us we would have to go three and a half miles to reach a firing position, and during the time this would take a submarine the target would have to travel only about a mile farther. Barring unusually slow enemy speed or a radical zig toward, this meant there could be no hope whatsoever of our catching up.

"Up periscope," I ordered. Maybe another look would give us more specific information, show the situation less unfavorable. The 'scope slithered up. Rubinoffski swung it to the bearing on which I had seen the targets.

In *Walrus* we had decided that Rubinoffski, instead of Jim, would be "periscope jockey," thus leaving Jim free to ride herd on Keith and the other conning-tower personnel, insure that things progressed as they ought, and back me up as Assistant Approach Officer.

"Bearing—Mark!" as I laid the vertical cross hair on *Vixen's* mast. "Range—" my right hand fell to the range crank. I only saw the tops of *Vixen*—the ends of her masts and a broad structure that was probably her bridge. Two other masts—other ships —one to left and one to right. They would be *Falcon* and

Semmes. Vixen had two masts about equal in height; that was how I knew it was she.

"Use masthead height thirty feet," I snapped, then repeated, "Range—Mark." At the word "Mark" I had cranked the range knob around so that the target divided itself in two, and I laid the tip of the mast in one image alongside the squat structure which I took to be *Vixen's* bridge in the other. The total height from the tip of the mast to the waterline would be about sixty feet. Thirty feet would be a good guess for the height of the mast above the bridge.

Rubinoffski was studying the range dial on his side of the periscope. As I gave the "Mark" he swiftly read off the range opposite the thirty-foot masthead height marker.

"Eight-eight-double-oh," he said.

"Down periscope." I turned to the rear of the conning tower where Keith was still twisting dials on the TDC, inserting the latest bearing and range information.

Jim, on the other side of the compartment, somewhat closer to me, was setting up the Is-Was.

"Angle on the bow port forty," I said.

Jim twisted the Is-Was dials. Keith gave one last turn to the range knob of the TDC, adjusted the "Target Course" knob, leaned back a few inches. Jim and I crowded in to look at it.

"Not so good, skipper," said Jim. "We'll have to run like a rabbit to get over there."

Keith nodded. "Distance to the track is five thousand yards."

"What's the normal approach course?" I asked. The "normal approach course" steers the submarine toward an imaginary point ahead of the target such that the submarine will have the shortest possible distance to run—and the target the longest.

Jim spun the dials of the Is-Was, looked at it searchingly. "One-seven-zero," he said.

"One-seven-zero, sir!" Keith corroborated from the TDC.

"Left to one-seven-zero," I called to the helmsman at the other end of the conning tower. "All ahead full."

The clink of the annunciators. "Left to one-seven-zero. Answered all ahead full, sir!" The battle-stations helmsman was a new man, a Quartermaster third by the name of Oregon who had been added to the old *S-16* complement to build *Walrus* up to the seventy men required for her crew.

I waited half a minute, until the ship was swinging nicely. "All ahead one third!" I ordered. We should not get too much way on the ship quite yet.

Another half-minute. "Steady on one-seven-oh!" Oregon's nasal twang.

It was what I had been waiting for. "Up periscope!" I swung it to the bearing. "Bearing—Mark!"

"Zero-eight-two!" There was hardly a pause between my "Mark" and Rubinoffski's reading of the azimuth circle.

"Range—Mark!"

"Eight-four-double-oh!"

"Down 'scope! All ahead full—control, one hundred feet!" I turned to Jim and Keith. No zig yet. Angle on the bow about forty-five port."

Crossing to the hatch leading below, I looked down on the top of Tom Schultz' balding head. "We'll try her this way for another minute, Tom," I told him. "He's got to zig sometime!"

Tom looked up and nodded. "One hundred feet, aye, aye!" We could sense the increased throb of *Walrus'* propellers, and her deck inclined down by the bow.

Walrus could make nearly nine knots at full speed—though not for long, of course, because even her huge battery could only last about an hour at the high discharge rate required. The question was how long to run before taking another look; and every look required slowing down, planing back up to periscope depth.

At nine knots the periscope would throw up a spray visible for miles. If we slowed down to make a periscope observation we would lose ground in our race to catch the *Vixen*. If we didn't look, a big zig might leave us in an even worse position.

I leaned over Keith's shoulder, watched the dials going around on the face of the TDC. One of the two biggest dials indicated our own ship's course, the other that of the target. The six-inch line between their centers represented the line of sight down which I looked every time we used the periscope. Other smaller dials, placed symmetrically, showed target speed, our own speed, gyro angles, time elapsed, and various other bits of pertinent information. Beneath the face of the instrument were two rows of cranks by which data could be inserted or changed.

One minute since the last observation. Perhaps a zig toward will have taken place since we last looked.

"Control, six-oh feet!"—"All ahead one third!" Almost a minute to wait, while Tom planed up and the ship slowed down. Finally . . .

"Up periscope!" The handles gently rose into my waiting hands. "Bearing—Mark! Range—Mark! Down 'scope!"

"He's zigged, all right!" I spoke with feeling. "Zigged away, that's what. Angle on the bow is port seventy!"

Keith spun the new data into the TDC. Jim, with a single twist of his right hand, reoriented the Is-Was.

"Control! One hundred feet! All ahead full!" We felt the ship dip once again, and the communicated throb of our screws.

Jim stood behind me, studying the face of the TDC and occasionally glancing at his Is-Was. Captain Blunt, in deference to the crowded conditions in the conning tower, was making himself as small as possible in a corner of space between the two periscope hoist motors. Crowded in behind us, Hugh Adams bent over the track chart he had started on a tiny table top nestled into the after part of the conning tower.

Time moved with lead shoes while I looked at the slowly creeping "own ship" and "target" dials, and the speedometer-type distance counter ticking off the reduction in range as target and submarine ran for the same imaginary point.

"Dammit!" I muttered, under my breath. "Where does he think he's going anyway!"

The timer on the TDC indicated two minutes since I had last looked through the periscope. We could hear a throbbing, almost a musical note, as *Walrus* tore through the water. A lifeline perhaps, or some excessive vibration in a stanchion or hand rail. I made a mental note to look into it and see if we could stop the noise. Jap sonar, so the first reports had commented, was better than we had anticipated, and it would be well not to make any avoidable noise.

Two and a half minutes. Jim broke the silence. "Captain, do you think he knows where we are? He never got a chance to shine the light on us . . ."

It was true, and I had been thinking along the same lines. The procedure for practice approaches specified that the target's initial base course should be the direction of the submarine from the target at the time the searchlight was extinguished. If *Vixen* had not happened to see us dive or had failed to make note of our true bearing during the moments just before we dived, it was quite possible that her skipper was actually in doubt as to what his base course ought to be.

"Dammit, anyway!" I said again.

Three minutes came up. We could not wait any longer. "All ahead one third!" I ordered the helmsman.

Answered "One third, sir" from Oregon after the annunciators clinked.

Quin was watching me gravely. "Control—six-two feet," I told him. Quin relayed the word and in a moment I heard Tom acknowledge by calling up through the open hatch.

It would take us a minute to slow down and there was nothing to do but chew our fingernails until Tom got us near enough to the surface and our speed had reduced enough that we could use the periscope.

Captain Blunt was looking at me as if about to say something.

"Anything wrong up there, Rich?" The drawl in his voice was out of character for him.

"Yes, there is, sir," I snapped, somehow irritated by his lack of concern. "I don't know where this fool is going. Maybe he is running target for another submarine somewhere else."

Blunt's drawl was even deeper. "What d'ya expect? Are the Japs going to run right at you and make it easy?" Suddenly the familiar incisive note was back in his voice. "Listen, Richardson, that is one of the things wrong around here. The big problem is to get in front of the target. Anybody ought to be able to hit him with a torpedo after that. Getting into attack position is ninety per cent of the job. Too many of our people seem to think the Japs are going to shine a searchlight at them and zigzag happily down to where the submarine has been waiting." Again that sardonic glitter. "Nuts!" he said.

There was no contesting his point.

The ship's speed indicator located on the bulkhead near Oregon's steering wheel showed three and a fraction knots, giving me an opportunity to break away gracefully from Captain Blunt. The depth gauge showed sixty-two feet keel depth.

"Up periscope," I ordered. A quick one this time: "Bearing—Mark! Range—Mark! Down 'scope!" I turned back to the TDC where Keith was inserting the information as relayed by Rubinoffski. "Target's angle on the bow, port ninety," I said sarcastically. "He zigged away again."

Keith changed the target course by the requisite amount. Jim did likewise with the Is-Was, then both turned to me.

"This is no good, skipper," Jim said. "He's not playing the same game we are."

I wavered in indecision. Maybe we ought to abandon the approach and surface, signaling *Vixen* to start over again. It had been done before . . .

"Don't forget this fellow's a Jap," I found myself saying. Then to Oregon at the other end of the conning tower, "All ahead, flank!" and to Tom, "One hundred feet!"

At flank speed the Electrician's Mates poured everything the battery could give into the motors and the whole frame of the ship trembled with the added power. You could feel her accelerate like a living thing as she drove forward. She couldn't last long, not over a half-hour more at this speed.

This was all we could do—our maximum effort. But indecision still gripped me. What if *Vixen* zigged even farther away? What if we used up the whole battery in a fruitless chase? We might very well do this, all to no purpose. The dials on the TDC gave no comfort, either, for they now showed *Walrus* and *Vixen* running on parallel courses about five thousand yards apart. This could go on indefinitely, or until our battery gave out. If we turned toward the "enemy," *Vixen* would swiftly pass ahead, never once having come close to torpedo range, and we would be left with a hopeless stern chase. The only thing to do was to keep going and hope the next zig of the target would be in our direction.

The timer ticked off another minute and I bent over Hugh Adams' plotting sheet, shooting a fleeting look at old Blunt as I did so, hardly hoping for a suggestion and finding none in his customarily grim visage. Hugh's chart contained a paucity of information; merely the location of the two ships and lines showing their respective movements. I studied it carefully. Somewhere in the back of my mind a forgotten idea was stirring. I tried to wrest it from Hugh's plot without success. A look at the TDC, nearly blocked by Jim and Keith's shoulders. Nothing unusual there. Back to the chart.

"What was the initial bearing of the target when we dived?" I asked Hugh.

He silently indicated a lightly penciled line near the right-hand edge of the paper. "This is about what it was, sir. I had to work backward a little after we figured out which way he was going . . ."

"Is this north?" I indicated the head of the paper.

Adams nodded.

Still the idea wouldn't come, and then suddenly it stood there, full grown. I looked for the Squadron Commander; he was studying the dials and instruments alongside Oregon, our helmsman.

"Rubinoffski," I muttered under my breath, "where's the area chart?"

The Quartermaster reached under Adams' desk and pulled out a rolled up navigational chart of Long Island Sound.

"Didn't I see something about net-testing operations?" I asked him.

"Yes sir." Rubinoffski's tapering forefinger indicated a freshly inked line about one inch long on the chart.

Another observation was due. "All ahead, one third." The singing note changed as the boat began to slow down.

"Hugh!" I said, pointing to the net-testing area on Rubinoffski's chart, "transfer this line to your plotting sheet. Also draw in the location of Little Gull Island, the mid-channel whistle buoy, and that danger buoy we received notice of last week."

I went back to the TDC and drew Jim aside to give him a few last-minute instructions. Jim was, among other things, in charge of our firing check-off list pasted in the overhead of the conning tower. We had so far accomplished only two of the half-dozen or so items listed thereon.

Walrus slowed and at the same time neared the newly ordered depth for the next periscope look. I had told Tom to bring her only to sixty-three feet—a foot deeper than the previous observation. This meant that with the periscope fully extended, only three and a half feet of it would project above the surface of the water. It was desirable to have less and less periscope visible, of course, during the latter stages of an approach.

The speed was just on three knots as the periscope came up. I grasped the handles, started going around with it before it had stopped its upward motion, completed a full circle before it was fully raised.

"Down 'scope," and the periscope dropped away. I turned to

the TDC. "Angle on the bow, port one hundred. Stand by for an observation."

Keith pursed his lips, turned the target course knob slightly. Jim, fiddling with the Is-Was, looked unhappy.

Hugh Adams in his corner was still busy, and Captain Blunt was watching gravely.

I motioned with my thumbs for the periscope. It slithered up into my hands.

"Bearing—Mark! Range—Mark! Down 'scope."

Jim held up a stop watch with a sidelong approving look for me to see as I turned toward him. It indicated seven and a half seconds—the time the periscope had been out of water.

As soon as Keith had finished setting in Rubinoffski's readings I gave him the angle on the bow. "No change," I said.

Adams stepped back from his table and I crowded over beside him.

My hunch had been correct. The danger buoy, the whistle buoy, the net emplacement, and Little Gull Island all lay approximately in a row athwart our target's course. He had to come toward us. He could not go through them, and there was no other way for him to turn.

"We'll be shooting in a few minutes. Make the tubes ready forward, Jim," I said.

Jim motioned to Quin. "Tubes forward, flood tubes. Set depth thirty feet. Speed high." He reached up with the pencil, marked off an item on his check-off list.

"Right full rudder," I told Oregon.

I could see the Squadron Commander lean forward taking it all in with a confused frown. This time he was going to get some of his own medicine.

Keith looked up at me puzzled. "Did you say angle on the bow was port *one hundred?*"

"A little more if anything. Give him one-oh-five, port."

With a look of disbelief Keith made the adjustment.

"What's the course to head for him?" I asked.

Keith reached up with his finger to aid in measuring the angle. Jim beat him to it from the Is-Was. "Two-two-six!"

"Two-two-eight." Keith's answer differed slightly from Jim's.

I raised my voice for Oregon to hear. "Steady on course one-nine-zero!" This would lead the target by a few degrees as he came toward us.

Nearly a minute passed. I was aware of a worried frown on the Commodore's face from where he stood between the periscope hoist motors.

"Steady on one-nine-zero, sir!" from Oregon.

I motioned for the periscope, took another look. Range and bearing were fed into the TDC. "No change on angle on the bow," I said. I caught Captain Blunt's increasingly puzzled expression; Keith also glanced at me uneasily. I would have informed Jim and Keith but could not; catching old Joe Blunt by surprise just once was too good to risk losing. I could see him itching to question me, and finally it was too much for him to stand.

"Good God, Rich! What in hell are you trying to do?"

"Nothing special, sir." A look of bland innocence. "We are getting near the firing point and I'm getting ready to fire our salvo."

"Tubes forward flooded. Depth set thirty feet. Speed high," from Quin.

Jim made another check on the overhead, as I nodded to him.

"Open the outer doors forward," he said.

Quin repeated the command over the telephone.

Captain Blunt seemed about to leap out from between the periscope motors.

"What did you say the angle on the bow was?" he growled.

"Port one-one-five, sir."

"Range?"

"About four thousand."

"Richardson, if you're playing games with me . . ."

"No, sir," I said as blandly as I could, "we will probably be shooting in around three minutes on this course."

The puzzled look increased on Blunt's face. He was famed for his uncanny ability to retain the picture of a submarine approach and do practically all the calculations in his head without mechanical assistance. He had, of course, missed my low-voiced interchange with Hugh.

"Observation!" I rapped out, motioning with my thumbs to Rubinoffski to start the 'scope up as I squatted before it. "Be ready to stop it short," I told him. He nodded. The periscope handles hit my outstretched hands. I snapped them down. Rubinoffski put the 'scope on the target bearing, different now because of our course change.

". . . Mark!"

"Zero-five-eight!"

"Range—Mark!"

"Three-oh-five-oh!"

I spun the periscope in a complete circle before letting it dart back into its well, lingered for barely an instant on the other two ships. We were well clear of both, and neither, so far as I could see, had seen us.

"Angle on the bow, port thirty."

Keith leaped at the handles of the TDC, commenced cranking them energetically with both hands.

Jim was hurriedly twisting the dials of his Is-Was. I waited, shot the periscope up and down once more. "Zero-two-five . . . one-eight-five-oh!" said Rubinoffski.

"Port sixty . . . stand by forward," I barked.

Jim followed me up. "Stand by forward."

Quin picked up the phone. "Stand by forward."

"This is a shooting observation," I tried to make my voice dry and unemotional. "We will shoot three exercise torpedoes, set to pass beneath the target's keel. We are inside the screen. *Semmes* will pass astern of us immediately after we shoot. *Falcon* is on the far side and will be no trouble. Up 'scope!"

I had studiously avoided the use of the word "Fire." The handles of the periscope came into my palms. I went up with it, setting it on the target.

Rubinoffski was watching the azimuth just as Keith had done for Jim several months earlier. The situation, in many respects, was very similar. A lot depended on *Walrus'* being found ready.

"Mark!"

"Zero-one-two!"

"Set!"

This was Keith, indicating that the bearing from the periscope had been set into the TDC.

"Shoot!" I said.

Jim was watching the angle-solver part of the TDC where a red "F" was plainly to be seen.

"Fire!" he shouted.

Quin had turned around, was now facing the firing panel, an elongated metal box with a series of glass windows in the cover through three of which red lights glowed, and below the lights a group of switches. Beneath the firing panel was the firing key, a plunger topped with a round brass plate curved to fit the palm of one's hand. At the word "Fire" Quin reached up to the firing panel, turned the first of the line of switches with his left hand, pressed the firing key with his right.

"Fire One!" he said into the phone. He held the firing key down for a perceptible instant, then released it, flipped the first switch upright, and turned the second switch to the horizontal position. He waited another instant and then pressed the firing key once more.

"Fire Two!" he announced into the phone. ". . . Fire Three!" The same process was repeated.

We could feel three solid jolts as our three torpedoes went on their way.

I motioned for the periscope, swung it around. *Semmes* was still clear. Three torpedo tracks diverging slightly were fan-ning out toward *Vixen's* bow. It looked as though they would pass ahead.

"Down 'scope!" I turned to Jim. "Have we fired the flare?"

"Yessir!" Tom Schultz shot the flare as soon as Quin fired the first torpedo.

Our instructions were to fire a submarine flare from the signal ejector in the control room at the instant of firing topedoes. This would aid in marking the original point of release and assist in their recovery.

I kept Captain Blunt in his niche a little longer by motioning for the periscope again and taking another sweep around. I had Rubinoffski stop a bit short of full extension and because of my bent-over position Blunt had to suck in his breath to allow my posterior to pass clear. I swung around twice and then fixed on the *Vixen* just in time to see our torpedo spread intersect her hull.

"A hit," I announced calmly, collecting myself in time to avoid shouting. "I think all three torpedoes passed under the target. . . . Range—Mark!"

"One-three-five-oh!" from Rubinoffski.

"That checks TDC!" from Keith.

I felt myself rudely shouldered aside. "Let me see, damn you!"

Captain Blunt had pushed his cap on the back of his head so that its bill would not get in the way of the periscope eye-piece. He planted himself firmly in front of it, stared through it.

"This is the first time I have ever seen this kind of an approach, but there he is all right. Did you pull this one out of your hat?" His eyes remained at the 'scope.

"It was nothing at all, Commodore," I said at his side. "I just did what you said a while ago—pretended we were patroling off the coast of Japan."

Blunt gave forth with an unintelligible grunt.

"And of course," I went on, "I naturally took a good look at the chart of the Jap coast."

The Squadron Commander jerked away from the periscope, glaring.

I pulled Hugh Adams aside to show his track chart. "Here's the convoy's track and here's the coast," pointing to the line made up of Little Gull Island, the buoys, and the nets. "I knew they'd have to come around this way, so we just waited for them."

Blunt stomped over to the chart to get a closer look, and as he moved his cap fell off. Clumsily, I nearly stepped on it.

"Rich, you're a bastard," he said.

CHAPTER 5

The operational readiness inspection by Captain Blunt was the last item prior to our departure for the Pacific Ocean and Pearl Harbor. Ahead of us lay the necessary chores of fueling ship, cramming her with provisions, taking a full load of torpedoes and spares aboard—and saying good-by to families and friends.

We had a week to get ready. Five days before our scheduled departure Jim came to me with a rather unusual request. He wanted three days' leave.

I couldn't help showing a little surprise. "What's up, Jim?" I asked. "This is a pretty busy time."

Jim looked uncomfortable. "I know it, sir, but this is one of those things. . . ." His voice trailed off and an intuitive flash told me that it concerned Laura.

It was true that *Walrus* had been under a steady grind for the past several weeks. Jim had borne the brunt of it and had done an excellent job.

"Jim," I said slowly, "I don't see how we can spare you just now—there is all the work you have been supervising . . ."

Jim was ready for that one. "I've got everything all set, sir. Everybody has his instructions and all the officers know their own jobs better than I do anyway. Things can get along pretty well without me for the next few days."

This wasn't quite true because an Executive Officer's work is never done so long as his skipper has things on his mind. But since we were leaving to go to war and would be gone a long time, perhaps we could make a special arrangement for him.

"OK, old man," I agreed, "figure to be back a couple of days before our scheduled departure."

Jim's countenance brightened. "Thanks, skipper." He bounded away almost with his old lightheartedness.

I mentally made a note to take over the supervisory functions of Jim's job during his absence, but found this unnecessary. They were indeed, as he had said, well organized. My own duties I found to be rather more complicated, however, mainly because of a series of briefing and study sessions which apparently all departing skippers had to undergo. The most impressive of these to me was the one given two days before we were to leave, in which the full extent of the damage at Pearl Harbor on December seventh was made known. The briefing was specified as "Secret" and Captain Blunt warned me about it before taking me in to see the Admiral commanding the Atlantic submarine force.

"ComSubLant" was standing in a room fitted with a long table and several chairs, obviously used mainly for conferences. On the table was a stack of papers and charts. His name was Smathers and he had been a submariner of repute years before.

"Richardson," said Admiral Smathers, greeting me, "I suppose you've heard most of the details of the Jap attack at Pearl Harbor?"

"I've heard a lot of stories about it . . ."

"Well, that's the reason we've called you up here. We want you to know exactly the situation, not only in Pearl Harbor but also in the Philippines and in Malaya. This first pamphlet"—he picked up a loose-leaf bound portfolio of photographs—"is a set of pictures taken immediately after the Pearl Harbor attack. And here"—he picked up another pamphlet—"is a list of our forces in the Pacific and their general location. The rest of this will also be of interest. When you get through you will see why we've had to accelerate submarine construction so drastically—and why every boat we can fit out is going to the Pacific right away. Also you will appreciate why it has been imperative to keep word of the true conditions out there from getting back home or to the enemy. Come to my office if you have any questions." With that the Admiral shook hands again, strode to the door, and departed. Captain Blunt went with him.

I spent three hours alone going through the papers with growing consternation. We all knew things were tough in the Pacific, but I had not known they were this bad. Fighting a naval war in both oceans at the same time automatically reduced our available forces to shoestring size when it came to operations, and the losses we had suffered right at the outset made the situation look downright desperate.

The Admiral was wrong in one thing. There was another mimeographed pamphlet which was to me of even greater interest than the ones he had singled out. It listed our submarine forces to date and the losses we had sustained. I found the *Octopus* listed there, the *Sea Lion* at Cavite, the *Shark,* overdue in the Philippines, and the *S-26,* rammed and sunk by her own escorts off Panama. There were also two other losses I had not known about as yet, *S-36,* which had run aground in the Malay Archipelago, and *Perch,* overdue from patrol since March. In the section devoted to Dutch submarines the casualties were even higher.

When I had finished reading every word and looking at every chart and every photograph, I silently reassembled all the papers, said good-by to the Admiral's aide, and thoughtfully made my way back to the *Walrus*.

She was lying at the berth in which all boats about to leave for the war zone were placed—the pier directly in front of the Submarine Base Commander's office, and she had it all to herself. On either side of her, nested two to a pier, were other fleet boats, looking as much alike as so many peas in a pod, the only difference between them being that those built in the Navy Yard at Portsmouth, New Hampshire, had a slightly more angular silhouette than the Electric Boat Company version. Electric Boat's schedule, I understood, called for twenty-eight to be delivered by the end of the year. Portsmouth was building almost as many, and, out in California, Mare Island Navy Yard also had a greatly increased quota. Alongside these sleek, streamlined monsters the older boats occupying the other docks looked like antiquated toys. Somehow there was a studied deadliness about the smooth black shapes of these new ocean cruisers. They were built for war and they looked it. All other considerations had been subordinated to the requirements of war under the sea.

The bridge, set well forward of amidships because of the space taken by the two engine rooms and the four great engines in the after part, was slightly swept back and smoothly rounded, with glassed portholes in its forward covered section. In its center rose the towerlike periscope-support structure built of heavy steel framing and plated over for a sleek appearance. In its after part was the "cigarette deck," deriving its name from the now-outmoded requirement that men come topside if they wanted a smoke.

Directly beneath the bridge was the horizontal cylinder, eight feet in diameter and about fifteen feet long, which constituted the conning tower. When the ship was under way, access below decks could only be obtained by going from the bridge through the heavy bronze hatch and down a ladder into the conning tower, then climbing through another hatch and down another ladder into the control room.

On the main deck abaft the bridge *Walrus* and all her sisters carried a three-inch antiaircraft gun with waterproofed mechanisms, designed for rapid fire. Gun action, which required an ammunition supply from below, constituted one of the few occasions when a main deck hatch would be opened while under way. Otherwise, the only hatch ever opened—the only one needing to be closed for a quick dive—was the bridge hatch.

The boats on either side of *Walrus* bore numbers on their conning towers, and salt-streaked sides showed signs of their rugged training regimes. Our numbers had already been painted out along with the new paint job we had received, and the somber black exterior of the ship was now unrelieved by markings of any kind.

A provisions truck was leaving the dock as I walked up. The pile of crated and canned foodstuffs it had left was already melting away under the attentions of the working party Kohler had detailed to help Russo get the food stored below.

A feeling of tension ran through the ship. I could sense it—perhaps it must always be thus when ships and men go to war. It is the realization of what is faced, the risks one is going to run, and it is the gnawing thought, felt in the pit of your stomach, that maybe this is it—maybe this is the last time you will see this particular place again.

The other boats in various stages of incomplete readiness at the other docks, or those in from training periods under way, would not have quite the same atmosphere. But I had invariably sensed when a ship was going to war and I sensed it now from *Walrus* as she lay there quietly moored to the dock. Her silent bulk seemed about to tremble at some secret fear, and as I stepped over the brow and returned the salute of the gangway watch I was struck by a sudden thought: "This ship will not survive the war."

Jim got back the next morning. We were at breakfast in the wardroom when he came aboard and sat down to join us. He had some sort of news, I could tell, and Keith broke the ice for him. Keith had an amusing name for each of us. It was he who had dubbed Tom Schultz "Father" or "Dad." Jim he occasionally called "Cobber"—probably because of a secret yearning Jim had once expressed to go to Australia. So far as I could discern I had yet to be honored by his attention in this regard. But, of course, a skipper could never be sure.

"Father, Oh, Father," said Keith in mock plea to Tom, "Cobber's home with us at last and going to help us with the war after all. Dost thee think thou couldst make our gallant Executive tell us where he's been?" Keith pronounced the last word as though it were spelled b-e-a-n.

Jim chuckled. "Hold it, Sonny boy. If you'll give me a chance, I'll tell you where I've *bean*." He drew a deep breath. "Two days ago Laura and I were married. She came back with me to New London and is at the Mohican Hotel right now." We all stared at him.

I could not begin to explain the peculiar sensation the news evoked in me. Certainly I had no right to be interested in Laura for myself. There was just that odd yearning for an indefinable something that never could have been that she—or the mention of her—always brought out. I forced a congratulatory smile.

"That's grand, Jim. We all hope you'll both be very happy —but what a shame you have so little time together!"

Jim smiled ruefully. "Thanks," he said, "but it can't be helped. We might have had more time if certain things had worked out better, but we'll make out. We'll even send all of you an announcement—after the war's over."

The deep-seated resentment was still there all right.

Two days later was Memorial Day, the day we were scheduled to leave New London en route to the Panama Canal. We were to get under way at 1430—2:30 P.M.—and the morning was filled with last-minute preparations which belied the status of that day as a holiday. We started cleaning up the ship at ten-thirty and at eleven-thirty piped down dinner for the crew. At one-thirty we would have open gangway for relatives and friends of our ship's company. Certain critical pieces of equipment had been covered over with paper or canvas so that our visitors could be permitted to go below in order actually to see and feel the places where their sons and husbands would be fighting the enemy.

At noon we had lunch in the wardroom. Tom brought his wife Cynthia; Dave Freeman his mother, a large matriarchal-looking woman who had journeyed up from Washington to see him off; and Jim, of course, was with Laura. It was a bit crowded with three extra people in the tiny eight-by-six-foot room, and the conversation ran in uneasy fits, with long lapses of silence.

Cynthia Schultz was a sweet-faced, pleasant woman about Tom's age. In their life together, no doubt, they had had many separations for various lengths of time, but this was a special one and no one knew how long it would last or what the outcome would be. She sat very close to him during the whole meal and hardly touched her food.

Mrs. Freeman, on the other hand, chatted gaily as though there was nothing whatsoever on her mind, or as if her son were not on the verge of entering the shooting war.

Laura, sitting next to Jim on my right, was quiet, like Cynthia, and also ate very little. I could not help noticing the plain gold band on her finger, unaccompanied by anything resembling an engagement ring. She fingered it nervously with her thumb, until she noticed me watching. The three women brought home to me for the first time what war must mean to the thousands and millions of mothers, wives, and fiancées left behind. As we were waiting for dessert, even Mrs. Freeman fell silent, and I noticed her fumbling for Dave's hand under the table.

Then lunch was over and it was time to make preparations for getting under way. I had not had an opportunity to speak to Laura except to extend the usual wishes for future happiness. Keith, Hugh, and I went topside to set things in motion, while Tom, Jim, and Dave took the opportunity to show their guests through the ship. A small crowd had gathered on the dock and I noticed many of our men there also bidding their last good-byes. Some of the women were unashamedly sobbing, and there were many long embraces. A hard lump rose in my throat as I watched.

At 2:00 P.M., Hugh Adams, who had the duty, directed that all guests please leave the ship. A few minutes later the last few had struggled up from below and crossed the gangway to the dock. Last were Mrs. Freeman, Laura, and Cynthia Schultz. We stood at the head of the gangway for a few moments speaking our formal good-byes.

Mrs. Freeman reached out a gloved hand. "Captain," she said, "take good care of your ship—and bring my boy back safe." Her eyes gave her away. Though there was not the suspicion of a tremor in her voice, the grip she gave me carried much more than a casual feeling with it.

Cynthia Schultz now pressed my hand in her turn, kissed Tom tenderly, murmured something I could not hear, and was gone.

Laura was last. The perfunctory pressure of her hand and the deep misery in her eyes spoke volumes of feeling I would never be able to appreciate. How she must hate me! She turned to Jim, hid her face against him for a moment. He clasped her tightly to him, kissed her longingly. Her lips moved against his as she raised her face and leaned against him. The lump in my throat tightened till it hurt. I swallowed several times, finally turned away, struggling to retain my composure.

I had never wanted anything belonging to anyone else until that moment.

"Hugh," I said to Adams, "have the crew fall in at quarters."

After muster on deck abaft the bridge, I delivered a short speech to the effect that once we had left New London behind us we would be on our own. The sea was populated with enemy submarines who would like nothing better than a U. S. submarine's scalp to hang on their belts. We had a long trip ahead of us, I told them, and constant alertness would be our only assurance of safety. I finished my speech simply with the words, "Leave your quarters. Man your stations for getting under way," and walked forward.

Just forward of the bridge, waiting for me to finish, stood Admiral Smathers and Captain Blunt. On the dock near the gangway were the skippers of the two boats next in line behind *Walrus,* soon to leave for the Pacific themselves, and Stocker Kane and his wife, Harriet—unwillingly known as "Hurry"—a pretty, sandy-haired girl, almost as tall as he, which didn't, after all, make her very tall. Behind them a throng of relatives and well-wishers stood watching, waiting for us to get under way.

Admiral Smathers gripped my hand. "Good luck, Richardson, have a good trip. Watch out for German submarines." My old commanding officer gave me a firm clasp, "Good hunting, Rich, I'll be seeing you out there soon, I hope."

The other two skippers reached across the gangway, shook hands, murmured their best wishes. Stocker stood on the dock with "Hurry." He slipped his arm around her waist, hugged her to him.

"Congratulations, old-timer! I wish I could be going with you, but I'll be only a few weeks behind."

I hadn't heard about this, and looked at him with a question in my eyes.

He went on to explain. "I got my orders day before yesterday to the *Nerka* at Mare Island. I'm flying there tomorrow. It will take you so long to go through the canal that I might be in Pearl Harbor nearly as soon as you."

Stocker's wife hugged his arm to her. "Isn't that wonderful,

Rich?" she said. "I'll be leaving too in just a few days. Ever since you got the *Walrus* Stocker's been just itching for his chance."

Deep in her eyes a shadow belied her cheery voice. Two people this much in love shouldn't have to face war, I thought.

But of course it was no different for them than it was for everyone in *Walrus'* crew, except that our time was at hand.

A main engine roared into life, throwing a cloud of water and smoke out of the exhaust port and under the dock opposite. Two or three people standing nearby hastily backed clear of the spray. Then an engine on the other side thundered its defiance.

I saluted gravely as Smathers and Blunt stepped over the gangway. As I did so two more engines simultaneously bellowed their sixteen-cylinder starting song.

Hugh was now up on the bridge. "Single up," he shouted.

Our four lines were swiftly reduced from three strands to one each as the bights were taken aboard. The skippers of the other two boats stepped up on the gangway, briefly reached out to shake hands with me. "Good hunting, Rich—good luck." They drew back.

"Take in the gangway!" shouted Hugh.

Stocker and the two other skippers, disdaining to wait for the regular dock crew, grasped the gangway themselves and dragged it away from the ship.

I turned and mounted to the bridge.

"The ship is ready to get under way, Captain," said Hugh.

"Very well," acknowledging his salute. "Take her out on time." It was then within a minute of 2:30 P.M. As Hugh waited, I spoke quietly to Jim.

"Have you had the ship searched for stowaways?"

"Nobody I know would be wanting to make this trip with us, Captain. Anyway, I had Kohler go through the ship. We have no unauthorized people aboard, sir."

I nodded. It was hardly conceivable that anyone would want

to stow away, but it had happened to a Mare Island boat several weeks ago.

"Take in Two and Three!" Hugh was shouting to the men forward and aft of the bridge. "Stand by to answer bells," he said to the conning tower. A moment later, "Take in Four!" Number Four line came snaking in. "Starboard back two thirds! Left full rudder!"

We slowly began to gather sternway. Hugh stood on the side of the bridge looking carefully at the dock and our motion alongside of it and at the Number One line taut to the cleat at its head.

"Slack One," Hugh said to Quin, standing with the ubiquitous telephone headset under the overhang of the bridge.

Quin spoke into the mouthpiece. Number One line sagged.

"Take in One," said Hugh. Quin spoke again. Number One line came aboard.

Adams reached for a toggle handle nearby, tugged on it. A piercing foghorn blast roared out from beneath the bridge. He held the toggle for several seconds then released it; the foghorn stopped abruptly.

A shrill whistle. Rubinoffski standing in the after part of the cigarette deck had a policeman's whistle clenched in his teeth. The colors, which had been flying from the flagstaff on our stern, were taken down by one of our men who had been standing there waiting for the signal. Likewise, up forward the Union Jack was taken down and furled. Simultaneously, Rubinoffski reached down beside him, grasped a short flagstaff with a flag rolled around it, jammed it into a socket at the end of the cigarette deck bulwark, unrolled it to the breeze.

Walrus backed nicely out into the Thames River, twisted to align herself with the channel, and started downstream. We were on our way to war at last; down the familiar, often traveled river; through the railroad bridge and the highway bridge which, side by side, had to open simultaneously for us; past the Electric

Boat Company where *Walrus* had been conceived and born, and where the hulls of her sisters were taking shape; past the baroque old Griswold Hotel with its green-stained shutters and Victorian façade; past Southwest Ledge and New London Light; through the Race—that narrow channel between the eastern and western parts of Long Island Sound; past Cerebus Shoal buoy. Finally, late in the afternoon, with Montauk Point abeam to starboard, we set our course due south.

The manner in which we would make the southward passage from New London had been a matter of considerable thought and discussion. For the sake of a fast passage we would run all the way on the surface, except for occasional short dives for drills and once a day to check our computed trim. The big worry was the possibility of encountering a German submarine on patrol off our East Coast. We were a new ship, in transit, more vulnerable than any surface vessel. A submarine has so little buoyancy reserve on the surface—none at all submerged, of course—that it can never hope to survive a torpedo hit. But the main thing was that we were new, untried, and inexperienced; true, we had trained faithfully, but any German we might meet would have the inestimable advantage of weeks of constant alertness off a hostile shore, perhaps the knowledge that he had already been tried in the crucible of war, certainly the superior position of being at leisure on a station through which we would have to pass hurriedly.

For maximum concealment at night the ship was kept completely blacked out topside. Our running lights had not only been turned out but entirely disconnected, their glass lenses removed. The exterior of the ship was a dull black all over, including the once-bright brass capstans and other stray bits of shiny metal which, by the slightest reflection from moon or stars, might betray us. The only light permitted topside was a tiny red one in the gyro compass repeater for the Officer of the Deck, and the dim glow—also red—which came out of the open hatch at his feet.

Our topside watch consisted of four lookouts, one assigned to each of four sectors around the ship; the Quartermaster of the Watch, who normally stood on the after part of the bridge; and, of course, the Officer of the Deck. All six bridge watchers were equipped with binoculars. Instructions to all six were to use them constantly and to maintain the utmost vigilance for low-lying, dark hulls and suspicious streaks in the water which might be made by torpedoes. Of course we zigzagged, and, knowing that the best defense of a lone ship on the high seas is speed, we held our four sixteen-cylinder Winton diesel engines at maximum sustained power.

Only a few hours away from the safety and comfort of New London, everything now seemed entirely unreal. It was hard to believe that we had progressed so quickly from safety into mortal danger.

The first night out was uneventful, but I could not sleep. Ceaselessly I roamed the ship from forward torpedo room to after torpedo room, telling people off watch to be sure to get plenty of rest against the time when they would be needed, assuring myself that all was well with those who actually were on watch. Jim, I saw, was doing likewise. Evidently he could not sleep either, and by the time morning came we had succeeded in exhausting ourselves. It was a good thing the German submarine happened not to choose our first night at sea, or the day following, to make his attempt upon us.

Having had access to some of the reports of German submarine exploits in the Atlantic, we were well aware of the danger they presented. They had been built for service in the narrower ocean, had a shorter cruising-range requirement, and were consequently smaller than our boats, lay lower in the water, and were harder to see. The German Type-VII boat, apparently their favorite for the transocean patrols, was hardly half the size of *Walrus*. But it had nearly equal speed and packed an equally lethal wallop, torpedo for torpedo—though, of course, less than half the total war load we could carry.

It was no doubt one of these which attacked us in the early morning of our third night out of New London. We were still running south, zigzagging and making full speed. Tom Schultz had the watch on the bridge and I had just stepped below for a few minutes. It was a dark night, without a moon. We were in the Gulf Stream and the weather was clear, still, warm, and muggy, with myriads of stars studding a pitch-black sky. A moderately heavy sea was running from astern and what wind there was was also from the north. The four exhaust plumes, two from either side, appeared to rise almost straight up, and the moist, incenselike odor of diesel fumes pervaded the bridge. The motion of the ship was gentle—a slight pitch and an occasional deep roll as a quartering sea came in.

My nightly peregrinations had taken the form of periodic inspections below decks, with the rest of the time on the bridge ready for whatever action circumstances might bring forth. I had already made two such inspections and had barely reached the control room on my third descent when suddenly that sort of sixth sense which somehow grows within all ship captains twanged a warning note to my brain. Perhaps it was that the rudder went to full right and remained there, not easing off shortly as the zigzag plan would normally have required. It might have been the change from "full" speed to "flank," although it was my later impression that Tom had not yet called for more speed. At any rate, I had leaped to the conning tower and was halfway through it when the collision alarm sounded.

There is nothing more eerie at sea on a black, unfriendly night than to have the collision alarm sound unexpectedly. Somewhere out in the dark someone is trying to put the finger on you. He has seen you first—may already have killed you, only you don't know it yet. The collision alarm, in a vessel at war, is like a ship screaming in fright.

I don't consciously remember pulling myself up to the bridge, but I was there beside Tom before the alarm had stopped ringing, just before the hatch to the bridge went closed. Below decks the watertight doors were banging shut—and everyone below knew this time it was no drill. It was like one fairly drawn-out simultaneous bang. The collision alarm could not have been silent for more than fifteen seconds before a rapid voice on the bridge speaker announced, "Ship rigged for collision!"

Tom pointed off on our port beam. "There he is," he whispered. "He was broad on the bow when I saw him!"

I raised my binoculars still hung around my neck, looked long and hard in the direction Tom pointed—nothing. Even though the control room had been "redded" out—that is, darkened, with only dim red lights for visibility—I had reduced my night vision by going there, even if for only a second.

"I can't see him, Tom." For no particular reason I also whispered.

"I can all right! Can't see much of him though. We are fine on his bow."

I was subconsciously swinging my binoculars aft, trying to keep in the same line of vision as *Walrus* turned under us.

"Put our stern right on him, Tom," I said.

"Aye, aye, sir!"

I kept trying to see and suddenly there he was, surprisingly near, and surprisingly small. A little gray boat plunging deep in the sea; a square shadowy conning tower rising amidships. About the size of the *S-16*, I would have guessed, although it was hard to compare.

"Wonder if he's seen us?" I muttered. "No telling that . . ."

"God!" Tom grasped my arm so hard it hurt. He pointed to the water alongside and to starboard. Not fifty feet away a white streak suddenly appeared on the surface of the water parallel to our course. Swiftly it came alongside and passed ahead. I leaped to the other side of the bridge, leaped back again.

"Do you see any more?"

Tom did not answer.

I ran to the other side once again, looked once more. There came a scream from the forward starboard lookout.

"Torpedo wake!" he yelled.

Startled, I looked up, followed his outstretched arm with my eyes. It was the wake Tom and I had just seen.

"Torpedo!" The after starboard lookout was screaming, too, pointing farther aft. I swung around quickly, hoping my night vision was coming back. Nothing there. Merely the waves and wind slicks on the water.

I had been unconscious of the weather, except for its slight oppressiveness. Now suddenly it intruded itself upon my mind. The sea was neither calm nor rough but in that betwixt-and-between condition that is hard on small vessels and not even an annoyance to large ones. The wind, because of our radical course change, now came from our starboard bow, sweeping across our decks and whistling in our ears. The ship now rolled slowly and heavily, farther to port than to starboard, and occasional seas swept over our after deck. It was dark—a good night for murder. I looked back at the German submarine. She was still there, closer, if anything.

"What do you think, Tom?" I tried to speak calmly, but my voice must have betrayed the racing beat of my heart. "Do you think he is chasing us?"

Tom might have been about to answer when there came a loud cry from the port after lookout.

"TORPEDO, PORT QUARTER!"

This time there was no doubt. Another torpedo coming up on the other side. Close.

"Right full rudder!" shouted Tom.

"Belay that!" I screamed, right on his heels. The bridge rudder angle indicator wavered, then remained as it was.

"Tom," I said savagely, "nothing doing. That's what he wants us to do. As soon as we are broadside to him . . ." I let that thought finish itself.

"Sorry, skipper," Tom muttered.

Seconds ticked by. Tom spoke again: "Maybe if we manned the gun and opened fire . . ."

"No. Too risky down there on deck." Then I had an idea, pressed the bridge speaker button. "Control," I called, "load and fire three green flares." Perhaps if the flares went up close alongside the German, or overhead, the glare might blind him to our position or scare him or otherwise dissuade his pursuit.

The torpedo coming up on the port side looked even closer than the first one, but, since we were stern to, it had to run parallel to us.

"Lookouts," I shouted. "The only torpedoes that can hurt us are the ones that come right up the stern. Keep a sharp lookout."

I had not given much thought to how they would be able to distinguish a torpedo wake in the wash of our propellers but perhaps they might, especially from the advantage of their height. Another idea struck me.

"Tom, I'm going up on top of the periscope shears. Tell control not to raise either of the periscopes. Listen for me from there."

I climbed swiftly up to the top of the periscope supports. Three successive pops of high-pressure air came from somewhere below as I climbed up, and when I reached there Tom called up, "Captain, three green flares away." Swinging my leg over the top of the steel towerlike structure I bestrode the top of the periscope shears like a man backward on horseback. Just in front of me was the bronze-lined bearing for the after periscope and immediately behind me was the round hole through which the forward periscope would pass.

Should the control room by accident raise either periscope I would find myself in a most uncomfortable position, if not indeed impaled by the blunt end of the instrument. In my exposed perch the wind whistled and tore at my clothes, and I was flung from side to side as the ship pitched and rolled. I grasped the periscope supports with my knees. Back aft four plumes of exhaust smoke spewed forth with a shower of spray, spattering water over our deck and onto the heaving black sea which would periodically rise up to submerge them.

I raised my binoculars. There he was, all right. I could see more of him from my high location. No doubt he was chasing us but we were making full speed and were fresh out of dry dock. We should be able to outrun him, although so far there seemed to be little indication that we were doing so.

Less than a mile away, nearer to fifteen hundred yards, the sharp-angled gray shape, low, broad, and sinister, plunged along in our wake throwing a cloud of spray and spume to either side. I could only see his deck in flashes as he plowed along, but the squat, square structure of his conning tower remained visible all the time.

The main thing, of course, was the possibility of more torpedoes and I searched the water between us. Running directly away from the German we presented a very difficult target. Nevertheless there was always the possibility that a lucky shot might come our way. Two he had already fired, if one discounted the possibility of others we had not seen. He would not be likely to waste more without a better chance of a hit. Conceivably we could fire one at him, though with no greater chance. It looked like a stalemate. The German was hanging on, hoping, no doubt, that we might make a false move. If we were to submerge he could be practically on top of us for an easy shot during the minute it would take us to get under. If we turned either way and presented our broadside, a torpedo would be coming instantly. Time crawled painfully while I clung with one hand and both legs to my precarious perch. The wind seemed laden with salty moisture and my dampened shirt clung around my ribs. My right hand ached from holding up the binoculars and my left one was numb from holding onto the ship. *Walrus* swayed drunkenly from side to side, reaching me now far over to starboard, now even farther over the water to port.

More time dragged on. Surely a minute must have passed since Tom gave me the word that the flares had been fired! It was supposed to take them one minute to function after being ejected—surely they all could not have failed to function—and then I saw it: a brilliant green star burst directly above and in front of the German submarine, lighting up the surrounding water and reflecting the gray sides of the German boat with an almost dead-white color. The flare descended slowly, brilliant beyond all measure. Then there were two of them, and before the first flare had touched the water the third had exploded in the air so that three brilliantly lighted green stars in echelon formation were suspended above the enemy submarine.

I had thought of turning away or diving, or both, when our flares went off, but neither action was necessary. I could see the enemy boat clearly, every detail etched sharply against the black water, and as I watched she seemed to slow down; then her bow dipped and she was no longer there.

I climbed down to the bridge again, rejoining Tom.

"We'll keep going on this course for at least an hour," I said, "then turn south again. He can't catch us submerged."

Then the reaction set in and I found my hands shaking.

CHAPTER 6

OUR VIGILANCE WAS INTENSIFIED
by our escape from the German submarine, and for a time our
lookouts thought they saw torpedo wakes or enemy submarines
in every whitecap. But aside from several false alarms during
the next day and night, the rest of our trip was uneventful and
two mornings later we sighted the high tree-covered slopes of
Santo Domingo rising majestically above the horizon. Some distance to the left, lower-lying and not yet in sight, lay the shores
of Puerto Rico. Mona Passage, the waterway between, was re-
puted to be a favorite hunting ground for German submarines;
logically enough: a large percentage of the traffic to and from
the Caribbean Sea had to funnel through it. I could visualize

two or three wary U-boats lurking at periscope depth in the approaches. The bottom of the ocean on both sides, Caribbean and Atlantic, was already littered with the shattered hulls of our merchant vessels.

We went to the last notch of our speed, "All ahead flank," on the annunciators—the throttles jammed wide open—till the pitometer log dial in the conning tower registered twenty and a half knots. And as we neared the passage we stopped zigzagging and arrowed for it to get through as rapidly as possible.

Perhaps our stratagem was successful, perhaps it made no difference. Perhaps there were no German submarines there. At at any rate, hugging the shores of the one-time Pearl of the Antilles, we roared into the deep blue, transparent Caribbean Sea, the storied highway of the Spanish Plate Fleet, and of Drake, and Morgan—and Captain Blood.

The Caribbean Sea is one of the loveliest bodies of water in the world. It is warm, usually calm and peaceful, always beautiful—seldom roiled by bad weather, but able to produce, almost in minutes, the most violent and unpredictable hurricanes. Thus far in the war it had already proved a profitable operating area for German submarines. Somewhere, probably in one of the briefings just before leaving New London, I remembered having read a description of a proposal to convert it into an Allied lake. All the entrances—Yucatan Channel, Mona Passage, Windward Passage—on down through the Lesser Antilles to Trinidad and the coast of South America, were to be closed off by nets, mine fields, and heavily armed patrols. A mammoth project, but the destruction the Germans had already wreaked during half a year of war in its freely accessible waters was also mammoth.

It took us two days to drive across its broad expanse. Two days during which we doubled the lookout watch on the bridge and kept all watertight doors continuously closed—not dogged, but latched shut, ready for instant dogging down. Nor were there any complaints from the crew at this temporarily increased watch load or the inconvenience caused by latching shut the five-hundred-pound doors.

A period of even higher tension came as we neared Cristobal, the harbor on the Caribbean Side of the Panama Canal, where, if anywhere, German submarines would be concentrated—but where also our defense forces were massed in strength. A long-range, two-engine flying boat first spotted us. A little later another joined and we were continuously under air coverage for the last hundred miles of our approach. A few miles outside the harbor an escort vessel, a converted yacht similar to the *Vixen* but smaller, came out to meet us, flashing a signal searchlight insistently from the bridge. We had the recognition answer ready, flashed it in our turn.

"MIKE SPEED FOURTEEN," spelled out Rubinoffski, as another series of flashes came from the yacht. "What shall I tell him, sir?"

I paused for a moment, trying to think just how to word it. "Send him 'MIKE SPEED TWENTY REQUEST PERMISSION TO PROCEED AHEAD OF YOU.'"

The signal searchlight clattered as Rubinoffski banged away on the shutter handle. As the answering message came back, Rubinoffski shouted the words one by one.

"HELL YES THIS OLD TUB WAS BUILT FOR SEX NOT SPEED." Rubinoffski didn't get the ninth word, had to have it repeated twice more, by which time everyone on the bridge had recognized the letters with loud delight.

"Maybe that's the yacht I heard about a little while ago," Jim commented.

"Which one's that?" I said, inspecting her through my binoculars. "She's a mighty neat-looking craft, I'd say."

"Neat is right. The story is that a little while after the Navy took her over they found that if you pushed the right button the bulkhead between the skipper's and Exec's staterooms turned out to be an electrically operated sliding door."

The spectacle of a pajama-clad skipper confronting his

startled half-undressed Exec was too much for my straight face and I joined the guffaw of laughter.

"Send him 'THANK YOU,' " I called to Rubinoffski as soon as I managed to regain my composure. "Jim," turning to him, "lay us a zigzag course for the harbor entrance."

As Jim disappeared below I took another good look at our escort. Here and there streaks of black paint showed through the coat of wartime gray. Although salt spray encrusted her sides and delicate yacht fittings and she looked considerably the worse for wear, there was no doubt she once had been a trim and lovely yacht.

We passed fairly close aboard without slackening our pace. I watched her until the wash of our screws set her rocking in our wake, then turned to search for the passage through the Cristobal breakwater to the sheltered waters beyond.

Going through the Panama Canal is a thrilling and never-to-be-forgotten experience, even to those who have done it many times. The great locks, one thousand feet long and one hundred ten feet wide, were planned to take the largest ship anyone might conceivably want to build. Now streaked with moss and green with slime on their inner sides, they still performed the function perfectly—a testimony to the competence of the Army Engineers who built them. That only recently had any vessels tested their size was a testimony also to the vision of their designers.

It was still early on the morning of June sixth that we passed into the breakwater at Cristobal, there to be met by a message directing us to proceed to the entrance of the Panama Canal and make transit that same day. There was something in the wind. No one seemed to know what it was. It was not exactly hushed expectancy or worry, more an attitude of waiting for news. Our pilot, whom we queried as soon as he came aboard, knew nothing at all. Dave Freeman searched the schedule sheets, but beyond discovery of an unusually large group of messages all in the same code—which *Walrus* had not been is-sued—he could furnish no enlightenment.

It took us most of the day to travel the forty miles of canal from Atlantic to Pacific. When we got there we were met on the dock by the Commanding Officer of the Naval Station, an-other old-time submariner, now a Captain, U. S. Navy, but still known as Sammy Sams. His car was waiting, and he whisked me off in it to his office.

Once there, he closed the door carefully. "Rich," he said, "have you heard the news from the Pacific?"

"No, sir."

"It's a battle. Biggest one yet."

"Where?" I asked.

"Midway. The Japs are trying to capture it."

"Capture it? Not just attack it?"

"Nope, they're going to move in this time. They muffed their chance at Pearl Harbor. They could have taken Hawaii with a battalion, then, or Midway with a couple of boatloads of sea-men. This time they are coming for keeps."

"What are the latest reports? How's it coming out?"

"The whole Jap Navy," said Captain Sams, waving at a map of Japan on the wall behind him, "has been steaming across the Pacific loaded for bear. They attacked Midway yesterday, and it has been a hell of a fight. Our forces are badly outnumbered. I wonder how Nimitz scraped together enough carriers and air-planes to stand up to them."

"I guess it was not so much a question of 'how' as 'have to,' " I ventured.

"Have to, is right," Captain Sams exploded. "If those mon-keys ever get a base in Midway we might as well kiss Pearl Har-bor good-by."

We talked on for some time, and it was with an enlarged ap-preciation of the supremely critical nature of the Pacific opera-tion that I journeyed back to my ship. As I approached the dock where I had left *Walrus* I had a moment of panic. She was not in sight! I had visions of some catastrophe for a split second before I realized that in the interval I had been gone the tide had fallen several feet, concealing her hull from me.

It was a welcome relief to stretch our legs ashore after a week at sea, but Captain Sams didn't give us much time—only what remained of the day of our arrival in fact, and then solely for the purpose of using it to unload our cargo of "war shots" and take aboard exercise torpedoes. Next morning we were under way again, bound for what he called his "refresher training area," Las Perlas Islands, not far offshore. Not many submarines had yet come through his station, the Captain said, but he intended to help us make the most of the few days allotted before we were to start for Pearl Harbor. From somewhere he had collected a motley fleet of boats—they could hardly be classed as "ships"—to be used in "convoys" as targets, and for three days he kept us at it day and night, making us get under way as dawn flooded the anchorage and keeping us at approach work until long after dark.

For three days we fired torpedo after torpedo—the same ones over and over again because Captain Sams had only a dozen exercise torpedoes in his entire base and we had ten of them. We would fire a torpedo; then we would surface, pursue it, lift it aboard with our torpedo loading equipment, slide it down the torpedo loading hatch into one of the torpedo rooms, overhaul it, clean it up, refuel it, refill the exercise head with water, test all mechanisms; then we would load it in a torpedo tube and fire again. With six torpedoes in the forward torpedo room and four in the after torpedo room, there were always a couple under overhaul while the others were being fired. At the end of our first day our torpedomen simply curled up on the deck or on their zippered, waterproof mattress covers and went to sleep, oily, greasy, filthy, and exhausted. The rest of us were not far behind.

Sammy Sams drove all of us relentlessly, cajoling, wheedling, threatening, and promising. It was soon apparent that his target fleet either idolized him or was petrified with fear of him, for every morning they got under way before us in order to be ready for the first approach in plenty of time, and they always gave us the favored position, winding up at quitting time much farther away from the anchorage than *Walrus*.

At the end of the third day Sammy Sams declared our refresher training over, and invited everyone in the ship except the duty section to what he announced was a Hawaiian *luau*. There was no roast pig, no poi, nor any octopus, but we had fish and shrimp and other sea food delicacies, and the *pièce de résistance* was roast beef. Toward midnight the old submariner rapped for quiet and made us a speech.

"You men are men, not kids, even though some of you are still pretty young. This is the biggest opportunity you will ever have to repay to the United States some of the debt you owe for having been born there. The enemy is vicious and treacherous, but the important thing is that he is also very able—don't ever forget that. That's why, so far, he has had us back on our heels. There aren't enough of us and what we've been able to accomplish hasn't been nearly enough. He is equal to us in equipment and in the bravery of his soldiers and sailors, but the one thing he doesn't have, and never will have, is the tremendous staying power of America." He went on for some minutes, sometimes eloquent, sometimes bone dry. It didn't take me long to sense that he was trying to tell us why we were in a war and pass along to us something of his own philosophy about it.

His ending was simple. "I know you know this will be a tough war. I know you realize that *Walrus* may never come back and that maybe some of you men won't come back either, and if that's what it comes to for you—if I can leave you with one thought, one bit of comfort, it's this: It's worth it. It's what America expects of all of us." He sat down. There was silence for a second, then our men were on their feet with a roar, led by Kohler who was clapping like a man inspired. I saw a suspicion of moisture in the old man's eyes, and here again, as in the case of Captain Blunt, the thought sprang into my mind— here was an old submariner who had given his all to the cause of submarines, who, at the moment of their greatest trial, when all the teachings of his younger days were being brought to bear, found himself passed by, too old to participate. A little wistfully, these older men—men like Captain Blunt, Admiral Smathers, and Sammy Sams—were doing their best to support us younger ones who would have the duty, or privilege, of carrying on for them.

Next morning we got under way for Pearl Harbor with Captain Sams on the dock bidding us good-by. As we made our way into the broad expanse of the Bay of Panama and pointed *Walrus'* prow south to clear Punta Mala, the right-hand promontory, I could not help thinking that, though angry German submarines prowled the seas within fifty miles of us, except for the remote possibility of a Japanese submarine at this great distance we here in the Pacific might as well be a million miles away from danger. Here our danger was ahead in the home waters of the land of the Rising Sun, our next destination but one.

As night came I wrote in the Captain's Night Order Book: "Course 200. Transiting Gulf of Panama en route Pearl Harbor. Cruising on three engines 80-90; making about 14 knots, zigzagging. The ship is rigged for dive and darkened. Call me if other ships or land are sighted. Punta Mala is ahead and to starboard. Maintain a steady watch on air search-radar and carry out all instructions in the front of this book." Then I signed my name, went below, and had the first good night's sleep under way I had had since leaving the *Octopus,* fifteen months before.

Our trip across the Pacific was actually a little boring. We devoted a part of each day to fire-control and emergency drills and we permitted members of the crew in small groups to come on the bridge to sunbathe. The ocean was beautiful, the water sparkling, and the weather balmy as we forged steadily westward—west by north, actually, once we had doubled Punta Mala. Our progress was measured only by the steady change in our clocks as we kept up with the various time zones through which we passed. It was a peaceful, pleasant trip, marred only by the thought that at the other end lay war.

And then one morning, as Jim had predicted from his star sights of the previous evening, the headlands of Oahu hove in sight. We had been given a rendezvous position with explicit instructions regarding it, and we were there at the point of daybreak. Barely visible over the southwest horizon was the familiar volcanic outline of Diamond Head and, sure enough, here came a patrol plane to see if we were on schedule.

The approach to Pearl Harbor was in some respects a repetition of our approach to the Panama Canal with one exception—there was no levity. A PC boat, a steel-hulled submarine chaser expressly built for the purpose, came boiling up from the south to meet us, flashed us the recognition signal, and a curt "FOLLOW ME." We swung in astern and, still zigzagging, the two of us raced for Pearl Harbor.

We skirted close under Diamond Head, ran down past Waikiki Beach where through our binoculars we could see figures lying on the sand or playing in the surf. Well could I remember the few times I had been able to spend a week end off the *Octopus* here on this beach, or night-clubbing at one of the beautiful hotels lining it. In those days Waikiki was the height of fashionable play and only the wealthiest could afford to go there. A Navy Lieutenant's pay would last for only one or two evenings.

Alongside the white, square Moana was the Royal Hawaiian Hotel, gleaming purple-pink in the mid-morning sun, standing on the water's edge as though growing from the sea. A little to the left, and beyond, rose the rooftops of the city of Honolulu, with the Aloha Tower prominent along the waterline. Backdrop to all this were the mountains of Oahu, green and verdant, covered with sugar cane, pineapple, and other exotic semitropical plants. It was from here that the Jap planes attacking Pearl Harbor had swept down—over the mountains and through the mountain passes—on our unsuspecting fleet at Pearl Harbor. There had even been, so the story went, wide swaths cut through the sugar-cane fields pointing in the direction of Pearl Harbor, and we had heard stories of clandestine radio stations hidden in the hills, broadcasting vital information to the enemy.

As we neared the Pearl Harbor Channel entrance, naval activity increased rapidly about us. On the horizon we could see the tops of two new fleet destroyers evidently on anti-sub patrol. Closer in, another destroyer, an old "four-piper" like the *Semmes*, cruised about aimlessly. Passing out between the entrance buoys as we neared them was a gray-painted tug, a mine sweeper, with signal flags flying from her yardarm, and several hundred yards astern a float bobbed through the water carrying a small flag signifying the end of her tow. And the closer we approached to the entrance buoys, the more aircraft there were flying about.

"They're sure putting on a show, aren't they, skipper?" said Jim, standing alongside me on our gently heaving bridge.

"Show is right," I returned, "only I don't think this is just for appearances."

"Guess you're right. Wonder if the Japs have any submarines out here? Maybe we can find out when we get in."

I felt a pang of nostalgia as I swept the countryside with my binoculars, picked out the channel buoys, and surveyed the way into the harbor. It all seemed so much as I had remembered. We had operated from Pearl Harbor for months, and I had taken my turn as Duty Officer, getting the ship to sea and bringing her back again, so many times that I knew the harbor by heart. It was here that we had brought *Octopus* in that day the *Yorktown* had rammed us. It was through these buoys that I had taken her out for my qualification for command trials. On the day before I was detached and sent to *S-16* I had done the same—and now, only a year and a few months later, I was back again, now in command of a newer, finer version of the *Octopus,* a ship not even thought of then, and the *Octopus* and all my shipmates were gone beyond recall, numbered among the first sacrifices our submarine force had laid on the altar of war.

There was something unreal about the scene near the harbor entrance. It was so much the same and yet so vastly different. The urgency of our escort—the determined manner in which the planes overhead flew their search orbits—bespoke an entirely different atmosphere. I wondered what we would see after we reached the harbor itself.

Dave Freeman, Officer of the Deck, was standing alongside me. "Permission to station the maneuvering watch and enter the harbor, Captain?"

"Permission granted," I returned. The feeling of unreality was growing. Dave bent his head under the bridge coaming and shouted at the open hatch at his feet: "Station the maneuvering watch! Line handlers stay below." Then a few minutes later, after taking a good look through his binoculars, "Right ten degrees rudder! All ahead standard!" I could feel the rudder take hold gently and ease the ship around into the channel. The black left-hand buoy at the channel entrance swam into my field of view. The forceful beat of our engines back aft subsided just a trifle, and there was a different motion to the ship as the seas caught her from another direction.

It still seemed unreal, too familiar; even the corkscrewlike motion of the ship, as Oregon fought to keep her on her new course, was exactly as I had expected. The unprotected channel entrance, at right angles to the line of the shore, permitted seas to sweep right across it, resulting at times in a peculiar heave to the ship and difficult steering. Once we were free of the ocean effects, however, and inside the sheltered headlands of the harbor itself, the channel was as smooth as a millpond. With her speed reduced, *Walrus* forged steadily onward past Hospital

Point, around the next bend to the left, then to the right, and suddenly I gasped. Nostalgia vanished, never to return.

There indeed were the old familiar landmarks: The Navy Yard with its huge cranes, Ford Island in the center of the harbor, ten-ten dock—so named for its length of one thousand and ten feet—extending rectangularly into the water and blocking view of the submarine piers beyond. And there were the dry docks and tanks and buildings as I had known them. But my brain encompassed none of these.

The stench of crude oil was everywhere. It struck my nostrils almost with physical pain. The shoreline, wherever it could be seen, was black; filthy; and the water was likewise filthy, with here and there a coagulated streak of black grease clinging like relaxed death to bits of oily debris.

But the worst was alongside Ford Island, to port as we came through, and it slowly unfolded itself as America's one-time battle line came into view. I had been prepared, but not enough. The pictures had showed a lot, but they could never show the hopeless, horrible desolation and destruction, the smashing, in an instant, of years of tradition and growth. *California's* cage masts had seemed canted a bit peculiarly when we first caught sight of them, now we could see why. Her bow was under water. Only a few feet of her stern were exposed. Clustered about her were boats, a small tug or two, and there was considerable activity going on alongside. Repair work evidently. Astern of her lay the bulging side and bottom of a great ship with one huge propeller sticking out of the water. I knew from pictures that this was *Oklahoma.* Some kind of a structure had been erected on her slanting belly and a few men seemed to be working around with hoses and other paraphernalia. I could see one large hole in the heavy plates, and remembered what we had heard about men trapped inside.

A little distance away from *Oklahoma* another shattered, sunken hulk showed its gaunt sides: *West Virginia,* once the pride of the fleet; winner of the Marjorie Sterrett trophy for excellence in battle practice more times than any other, and the Iron Man trophy for athletics likewise. A grimy, dirty waterline, now high out of water, showed how far she had sunk. She was obviously now afloat again, but horribly mangled. We could see some of the shattered side, gaping above the cofferdam built around it.

Abaft *West Virginia,* a single tripod mast stood in the water. Below it a silent gun turret, water lapping in the gun ports and around the muzzles of the huge rifles. Nothing forward except a confused, jumbled mass of rusty junk. A flag floated from the gaff of the tripod mast, symbol that the United States Navy would never surrender. *Arizona's* forward magazines blown up by the uncannily accurate Jap bombing, nothing left of her except her iron will, she could still serve as a reminder of the sacrifice war had demanded on its first day, and the huge reckoning we would someday exact in return.

Dave Freeman by this time had given permission to open deck hatches and some of the crew had come topside to get our mooring lines ready. But no one touched a line. All stood staring in awe at the spectacle of destruction. Here and there I could see some of them pointing. Perhaps they recognized something, a ship they had once served in—some recognizable bit among the twisted, shattered remains. We had been forewarned of this and yet the full realization of what the Japs had done to us that day last December had not struck home until now. Except for a few commands given by Dave as he conned us through the harbor, not a word was spoken for several minutes on *Walrus'* bridge. This was death, unvarnished. This was the holocaust; this the destiny of three thousand U. S. sailors and officers.

Jim broke the silence. "Good lord!" pointing to the *California.* "I heard she was not seriously damaged."

"Depends on what you figure is serious, I guess," I answered. "It looks pretty serious to me all right."

"Serious! Hell, I think she's sunk!"

"We'll get her back up and in commission." I was repeating

what I had been told in the briefing before leaving New London.

"Maybe so." Jim's voice was dubious. "What about that one?" He pointed to the *Oklahoma*. "I suppose she's not very badly damaged either?"

I felt myself distinctly on the defensive. The newspaper accounts we had read and the official briefings I had received were all to the effect that the *Oklahoma* also would be returned to service.

"Well," I said, "we'll turn her right side up again, clean the mud off . . ." I paused, realizing how ridiculous I was sounding. Jim looked at me with a strange expression, exhibiting puzzlement, amazement, and disbelief all at the same time. Then the corners of his mouth quivered and he almost laughed. He pointed to the *Arizona*.

"Nothing wrong with her either, much. Just no hull!"

The comment was so spontaneous, comical, and so true that I would have laughed myself, except that it contradicted all the feelings of the past few moments. These ships had been the Navy's backbone for twenty years. As a boy I had had pictures of all of them posted on the walls of my room. Someday, I had dreamed, I would be Captain of one of them. Now here they lay shattered, twisted, destroyed. Powerless to have defended themselves, powerless now, even to take revenge.

Dave Freeman had been tending to his business of conning us through the channel. The submarine base commenced to come into view as we reached the end of ten-ten dock, alongside of which was visible the side of another rolled-over sunken ship. This would be the *Oglala*, an old ex-mine layer in use as Service Force Flagship, which, according to unofficial reports, had simply died of fright. She had been touched by neither bomb nor torpedo, but her seams had opened up from the concussions nearby.

Up ahead something was going on at the submarine base, and the strains of loud band music claimed our attention. As the submarine base docks came into view suddenly my heart leaped—for there, with nearly every detail unutterably familiar, lay the *Octopus,* half out of a slip—with flags flying and people standing all about her decks.

She looked different, worn, and yet terribly the same. The cigarette deck bulwark was gone and there was no plating around her periscope shears. Their steel foundation structure stood naked, like bare bones. But I would have recognized her anywhere, and at the same time I cursed myself for being a sentimental fool. Of course it could not be *Octopus.* It must be her sister, the *Tarpon.* We slowed down and waited while she backed clear, turned, and squared away past us in the opposite direction. Through my binoculars I looked over the faces on her bridge. There, sure enough, stood *Tarpon's* skipper, easygoing old Jim Tattnall, who had been on my Qualification Board. He was wearing a cap with scrambled eggs on the visor, something I had not seen him in before, signifying his promotion to the rank of Commander. I grabbed a megaphone and yelled across the intervening water.

"Where are you going, Jim?" He cupped his hands, shouted back:

"Back where you came from! San Francisco!" He answered my upraised arm with a wave of his own as the two ships passed. He had not recognized me, didn't realize *Walrus* had come from New London instead of Mare Island, but that made little difference. The *Tarpon* had been brought back from the Southwest Pacific, was en route to Mare Island for a well-deserved overhaul. It would be a rest for her crew and a surcease from anxiety. *Octopus,* long ago, had received her surcease from travail in a very different way.

So might *Walrus,* for that matter, except that we didn't know what our fate would be yet. I nodded to Dave, and a few minutes later we gently nosed into the same pier which *Tarpon* had just vacated. The band greeted us with several well-known compositions, conspicuous by its absence, however, being "California, Here I Come!" a loud rendition of which we had heard a few minutes before.

A delegation met us as we put our lines over: Admiral Small, ComSubPac, followed by several other officers, one or two of whom I recognized. We shook hands. Then came two dungaree-clad men bearing a huge sack of mail. This was pounced upon by Quin and dragged forward where he was immediately surrounded by a crowd of eager *Walrus* sailors. Next over the gangway came two five-gallon tins of ice cream, well frosted on the outside, and finally a crate of choice red apples. Russo was topside in a moment at Dave's quick summons, but he was too late to save the apples from the eager hands which had already removed nearly all. The ice cream, however, he pre-empted and carried, grinning, down below.

Admiral Small was speaking. "Richardson," he said, "we're short of boats as you know and we've got to get you on the firing line as soon as possible. How soon can you go to sea?"

"Right away, sir," I answered, "we have a full load of torpedoes, but we'll need to refuel and reprovision."

"The E&R shop can handle any outstanding repairs."

The Engineering and Repair Officer was one of those whom I had recognized from my times as Engineering Officer on the *Octopus.*

"We're in pretty good shape material-wise," I began.

"Good," said the Admiral, "all we'll need to give you then is a quick going-over. We want to take all your torpedoes out and check them, and we have a few pieces of equipment to install in the ship. Then you will have a one-week training period before you go."

"We don't need any training, Admiral; we're all set," I protested.

"Oh, yes, you do, Richardson. The training you've had has been all to peacetime standards. I know how it is in New London. It's my responsibility to make sure every boat is up to scratch before it leaves here. Besides we want to give you an SJ-radar.

"What's that, sir?"

"The radar you have is only the SD-type, designed for aircraft search. This is for surface search and it will increase your effectiveness at night. After you get it, you'll have to learn how to use it. That's another reason for the training period."

I nodded, and he changed the subject.

"Would you care to show me through, Richardson? I want to see what your boat looks like down below."

The Admiral was an enthusiastic visitor as I took him through the ship. As I pointed out several of her internal features, he compared them to older installations of the same type and commented upon the improvement. He was especially pleased with our control room and conning tower, and spoke favorably of our two engine rooms and the four great sixteen-cylinder diesels installed there.

He also insisted on meeting each of the officers and as many of the enlisted men as he could. Then he was off, and as I saluted him over the gangway a horde of workers, inspectors, and checkers descended upon us.

Pearl Harbor, or at least the submarine base in it, was really well organized, I reflected a few hours later. A crew was already on the bridge installing the new radar; two cranes were on the dock hauling out our torpedoes from both ends at the same time as rapidly as our men could get them ready. Another group had summarily confiscated both of our 30-caliber machine guns, replacing them with four 50-caliber models, and a gang of welders was going about the ship installing mounts for them. To my consternation I discovered another crew of men happily cutting away the bulwark around our cigarette deck and two more had climbed on top of the bridge and were removing the plating on the sides of the periscope supports. At this I registered a protest.

"What's the idea!" I asked my friend, Eddie Holt, the E&R Officer.

"Relax, Rich," he said. "Admiral's orders." He went on: "We're trying to cut the silhouette down as much as possible. Every boat that comes in here from the States has got too much stuff on her and looks bigger than the one before, and he's out to cut it down so you can get away with night surface attacks without being seen. Say," here Eddie's eyes widened, "weren't you the boat that was shot at by the German sub a while ago?"

I nodded. We had, of course, reported the incident by dispatch immediately.

"W-e-l-l, I should think you'd have had all this extra superstructure off here before this. He nearly had you, you know. The way I heard it, you didn't even see him until he fired the torpedo at you."

"That's about right," I admitted.

"We've found that pulling off the plating around the periscope shears lets enough light through that they can't be seen on the horizon. The difference is even more noticeable at night. That's why we're taking off your cigarette deck bulwarks—you don't need them. We'll give you lifelines to lean against."

Three days we were alongside the dock at Pearl Harbor, during which the welding smoke, the babble of workers, and the clatter of air-operated chipping hammers never left us. I had thought the workmen at Electric Boat were fast, but these, every one an enlisted man in the Navy, were faster. Furthermore, time apparently meant nothing to them. They worked as if their lives depended upon it, and more than one man I saw remained aboard for twenty-four consecutive hours, working almost continually. Russo, I found, was responsible for some of this. He and his assistants always seemed to be cooking something. There was a never-ending stream of sandwiches, bowls of soup, cookies, and the like coming out of his galley. I noticed also a few private little repairs and improvements being accomplished under his direct supervision, and, having had some experience in the ways of the American sailor, said nothing. No doubt we had paid for them with a couple of extra sandwiches or perhaps a surreptitious midnight steak.

Toward the end of our third day alongside, exercise torpedoes once again arrived. Next day we took a cut-down *Walrus* to sea for our first day of training.

It was a repetition of our time at Balboa except that we had farther to go to reach our target area, and there was plenty of help to retrieve torpedoes. We got under way before daybreak and returned after dark. Three nights we remained at sea all night—for a convoy was arriving from San Francisco and an opportunity to practice a convoy attack was too good to miss.

The radar, although it did not work consistently and gave us some other incidental troubles, proved to be an invaluable instrument in making a form of attack I had never thought of before. The Germans, it seemed, had done most of their destruction at night without bothering to dive. By staying on the surface they had greater mobility than the slow, closely bunched ships in the convoys, and they would race about at high speed, firing their torpedoes when opportunities best presented themselves. Apparently because they lay so much lower in the water than their huge targets, they were practically never sighted. Admiral Small believed we should adopt the same tactics, and had been pushing for a radar which could assist us. The Germans, of course, had used no radar, but our convoys were so large that they hardly needed one. The Japanese, on the other hand, had small convoys, and a "fire-control" radar, as he termed the SJ, would be invaluable.

Finally our week's training was over. It had been an exhausting period. *Walrus* lay quietly alongside the dock at the submarine base and the torpedo trucks began returning our original load of torpedoes to us after overhaul by the Submarine Base torpedo shop. Apparently the Admiral had not been entirely satisfied with the performance of torpedoes in recent months and had directed that every torpedo brought in by a submarine from the States, as well as those he had in his stockpile, should be overhauled and checked before being issued for war patrol.

Fuel we took on from a connection right in the dock, and then came trucks bringing provisions. Every nook and cranny in the ship was crammed with food. I had a couple of extra lockers in my room, a single, relatively commodious room compared to the one I had shared with Jim in the *S-16*, with floor space nearly four feet by five feet and a desk all to myself. There was more space than I would be able to use; so Russo crammed several cases of canned food—can by can—into the unused spaces.

Other empty corners throughout the ship were packed in the same way. Up forward on both sides of the torpedo tubes there developed a large space, not very accessible, but ideally suited for stowage of food in cans. In the corners of the control room and behind the engines in the engine room were other such spaces. The regular dry provision storeroom and the refrigerator space, of course, were crammed to overflowing. Under Russo's ingenious supervision veritable mountains of canned food disappeared below, and Russo proudly reported that he had even stocked the storeroom in accordance with the menus. When I looked in I knew what he meant.

He had crammed the shelves and the spaces between the shelves and then he had started stacking things on the floor. Finally food had been piled up right to the access hatch in the control room deck. It wouldn't do in such circumstances, according to Russo, to put all the beans in one place and all the potatoes in another, because if we did we would be eating beans for a week before getting to the potatoes and eating potatoes for two weeks before we got to the canned soup.

It was the day before we were to get under way for patrol that we had what appeared to be a serious casualty. Jim and I were relaxing over a cup of coffee in the wardroom when a piercing scream came from aft. With one motion we leaped to our feet and raced down the narrow passageway to the control room. Jim got there first. I was just behind him. The place was filled with choking, black smoke. Kohler was already there and Larto arrived from the conning tower at about the same time as we.

"Fire in the control room!" bellowed Jim.

Without saying a word Kohler reached up alongside the ladder to the conning tower, pulled the general alarm. Then he grabbed the announcing system microphone. "Fire in the control room!" he shouted.

I could hear the word "Fire" reverberating throughout the ship. The smoke was coming out of the forward distribution panel, in the forward starboard corner of the control room near the door through which Jim and I had just entered. Larto darted forward.

"Excuse me, Captain," he muttered, pushing me back at the same time. He reached down, grabbed a switch near the floor, pulled it. There was a loud electric "snap" and the smoke commenced to subside.

Sitting on the floor, staring in disbelief at his right arm, was one of Russo's "mess cooks," a young, red-haired sailor known as "Lobo" Smith. I looked, too, and nearly retched. The arm was charred black. Great lumps of what had once been flesh hung on it. I was surprised Lobo was still conscious. It must have been excruciatingly painful—or completely numb with shock.

Groups of men came pouring into the control room carrying various pieces of fire-fighting equipment. Jim waved them all aside. "Fire's out," he said.

Russo showed up from aft. "What's the matter with Lobo?" he began.

John Larto turned on him furiously. "You dumb bastard, who told him to stow anything behind the power panel? Look at him!" Larto indicated the hapless Lobo's right arm.

Russo stepped forward suddenly and, before anyone could stop him, gripped his assistant by the injured arm, commenced to strip off the charred flesh. There beneath it was Lobo's arm perfectly good and sound, though minus its usual crop of red hair.

"You jerk, Lobo," he said, "don't you have no more sense than to store powdered milk over there?"

So saying, Russo pulled the shaking Lobo to his feet, still gripping the supposedly injured arm. "Listen, I told ya before, PORT corner, not STARBOARD! Don't ya know which is PORT and which is STARBOARD on a ship?"

By this time all the charred "flesh" had been knocked off Lobo's arm. Russo indicated the switchboard, looked at the electrician, who nodded. He reached behind the panel and pulled forth the remains of a can with a blue paper wrapper labeled "KLIM." The edges were seared and melted; the contents, once a white powder, had bubbled up with the flame into large black globules. Covering and sticking to Smith's arm, this was what had given us the impression of charred flesh.

"I thought you was going to qualify in submarines, Lobo," Russo said roughly. "You get everybody mad at you and you'll be mess-cooking all your life—you'll never qualify. Now you pull all this powdered milk out of here and stick it where I told you to and then you go get a rag and clean up the back of this here auxiliary power panel."

Larto grinned and nodded, and Lobo began to reach with trepidation toward the power panel. Tom Schultz, who had meanwhile arrived, and Jim were by this time grinning at each other, and Kohler and Larto broke into guffaws.

"G'wan, Lobo," said Kohler, "it won't bite you."

"Look out, Lobo," offered Quin, "it might burn off your other arm or maybe your head this time."

Lobo looked appealingly at me. After his experience he was obviously in deathly fear of the power panel. He had piled up cans of dried milk behind it until one of them had made contact with a copper bus bar. The resulting flash of fire had scared the wits out of him, not to mention the reaction at seeing his arm apparently burned off to the shoulder. I couldn't help chuckling a little despite his discomfort and terror.

"Go ahead," I told him, "there's no more juice on the board. Larto's cut it off."

Larto grinned a large, even-toothed smile, nodded to the frightened Lobo.

"She's all right now, Lobo. I'll just sit and watch it while you clean it up so you don't make no more mistakes."

That ended the incident and the crowd gradually drifted away, but for the next two hours we were aware of a running fire of sarcastic comment from Larto as he grimly supervised poor Lobo Smith's labors behind the once spotless electrical distribution board.

The next morning I presented myself in the Admiral's office. "Come in, Richardson," said the Admiral. He led me into a room where a curtain had been pulled back to disclose a wall map of the Pacific. Various areas were outlined around the coast of Japan and elsewhere. Thumbtacked in some of them were paper submarine silhouettes, each bearing the name of a vessel. "Here's your area, Richardson," he said, indicating a spot off the eastern coast of Japan. "This is AREA SEVEN. You have one good harbor entrance here—Bungo Suido—leading into the Inland Sea of Japan between the islands of Kyushu, Honshu, and Shikoku. There will be a lot of coastwise traffic and perhaps some ocean traffic in and out of the Bungo. Here is your Operation Order." He handed me a freshly made-up pamphlet. "Take a look at it now and take a good look at this chart. Maybe you'll want to study it a while and then we can talk further. You may not discuss it with anyone else until you're under way—not even your Exec."

And so a few hours later I stood on *Walrus'* forecastle as preparations for getting under way were being completed. The Admiral, as evidently was his custom, had come down to see us off and there was a small group of officers and enlisted men on the dock in addition to the line-handling crew and the band that we'd first seen on our arrival.

"You'll go via Midway Island," the Admiral had said. "We've put a little mail aboard you for them. When you get to your area take it easy at first and explore the place. We've only had four other submarines bring us reports from there, and we want to get the lay of the land. Note particularly the traffic routes, what kind of ships seem to be using the Bungo Suido, whether there are any patterns of behavior, that is, whether they travel by night or day, morning or evening, zigzagging, in convoy, or whatever. We would like you to try that night surface technique, also."

Then the Admiral became grave. "The last boat to come back from your area went close inshore after a few days and was badly depth-charged. He thinks the Japs knew he was there the whole time. Anyway, he didn't have much luck and brought all his torpedoes back. Remember, Richardson, you have a submarine here. Don't let them detect you. Your mission is to inflict as much damage as you can on the enemy, not to get spotted or attacked yourself."

The band was playing as the Admiral said his good-byes. "Oh, by the way," he said, as he turned to go back ashore, "a couple of old friends of yours are due in here soon. Captain Blunt is coming in to be my Chief of Staff and the *Nerka* will be here in two weeks from Mare Island. Aren't you a friend of her skipper, Kane?"

"Yes, sir," I said. This indeed was news. Stocker Kane, I might not see, because he would be gone on patrol long before *Walrus* was due back in Pearl Harbor. Blunt, however, would be there to welcome us back from our first patrol. "I'll be looking forward to seeing them, Admiral," I said. "Give them my best." I answered his salute to the colors as he walked across the gangway. Reaching the other side, he turned.

"Good hunting, Richardson," he called. "It's open season on monkeys."

Some wag had cooked up what he called a hunting license on monkeys and a copy of it was on my desk below.

The gangway was pulled ashore. I waved to Jim on the bridge and could hear the deeper note as our diesels commenced to deliver power. Slowly we backed away from the dock and I waved one last time to the Admiral and his staff. The band continued playing until we were out of sight.

CHAPTER 7

OUR FIRST NIGHT OUT GAVE US
fair warning that this trip would not be a repetition of our voyage from Balboa to Pearl. I had just written the night orders and had gone below for a couple of hours' sleep, after which I would relieve Jim of the "on-call duty," as we termed our agreement to alternate wakefulness. On my bunk fully clothed, not having even bothered to remove my shoes, I could feel myself slipping rapidly into slumber when there came a faraway call.

"Captain to the bridge!" I jerked into alertness, still not sure I had heard it. Running footsteps came from the control room and Lobo Smith, standing messenger watch, thrust his disheveled head past the curtain which I had drawn across the entrance to my room.

"Captain, wake up!" he shouted. "Captain to the bridge!"

I jumped out of my bunk, thrust past Smith, dashed down the passageway into the control room, up the ladder, and was on the bridge within seconds.

"What is it?"

Jim was already there, standing beside Hugh Adams.

"There's a ship out there, Captain," Hugh said, pointing to our port beam.

It was a sticky, black night. I could barely see Jim and Hugh's shadowy forms. My binoculars revealed nothing.

"What kind of a ship, Hugh?"

"Can't tell, sir—low to the water—fairly small, I think, not too far away!"

"I saw him too for a minute, sir," said Jim. "That's about right, I think."

"Could you tell which way he was going?" I asked.

"No, sir," both answered at once. "Looked like nearly broadside to," Jim added.

I leaned toward the hatch. "Conning tower," I called, "tell Mr. Freeman to come to the foot of the hatch.

"I don't remember anything in our Operation Order about any friendly ships in this area," I muttered. "We were supposed to be informed."

"Do you think it might be a Jap?" Jim broke in.

"No telling." I picked up my binoculars, searched the port beam again. There was nothing to be seen.

"Hugh, has the SJ radar picked him up?"

"No, sir," Adams answered. "I had it searching over there but no luck."

"Radar's either not working or he's too far away," I mused, still trying to see the other ship.

"Can you still see him?" I asked.

"Not right now," Jim began.

"There he is," Hugh broke in, "Broad on the beam!"

"Well, there's no point in giving him our broadside to look at. Put our stern to him, Hugh," I ordered.

Walrus swung steadily to the right until our stern was pointed in the direction of the other ship.

Dave Freeman was at the foot of the hatch to the conning tower. "Did you want me, sir?"

"Yes, Dave. Break out our Operation Order and also go through your latest dispatches. See if there is anything in there about a friendly ship northwest of Oahu. We are a little more than a hundred miles away, I guess. If you don't find anything, draft a message to ComSubPac saying that we have contacted an unidentified ship out here. Get Rubinoffski to give you our position coordinates."

"Aye, aye, sir!" He disappeared.

My eyes were getting slightly more accustomed to the darkness and I could see the horizon. Jim and Hugh on the bridge were more distinct now, but still I could not see the other ship.

Jim spoke. "Skipper, maybe we are running away from him. If it's a Jap—it would be a sub, wouldn't it? Couldn't it be one still on patrol after the Battle of Midway?"

"Could be," I said. "It would be a pretty long patrol, though." Then to Adams: "Hugh, cut in the other two engines, and slow down to one-third speed. We don't want to get too far away from him, but I want all the engines ready."

Adams leaned toward the conning tower hatch without responding.

"Answer bells on four main engines," he ordered. "All ahead one third."

We had been proceeding on only two engines, the other two lying idle. Within seconds of Hugh's command there came a sound of machinery revolving as air was admitted to turn over one of the engines, then a *klunk* as the hydraulically operated exhaust valve was opened. The triumphant belch of our third diesel engine added its note to those of the other two. A second later the process was repeated, and four engines settled down to a quiet idling rumble.

About this time I caught my first glimpse of the other vessel. A low-lying ship, broadside to us, barely distinguishable against the horizon and perhaps half as far away—three miles.

"He hasn't seen us, sir," Jim muttered. "He'd have turned one way or the other."

This seemed plausible.

"I'll bet this is a Jap submarine. He'd sure be a feather in our cap, wouldn't he, skipper!"

"He would be, if he turned out to be a Jap," I said. "If only we could be sure."

Hugh picked up the ship's blinker tube which was part of our night bridge equipment, peered over Jim's shoulder to read the chalked recognition signal marked on the black surface of the bridge windshield.

"TVU," he said. "Shall I make it, Captain?" Hugh aimed the blinker tube at the other ship.

"God, no!" Jim almost shouted, "if it's a Jap that will alert him!"

"That's right, Hugh," I said. "We should not try the recognition signal on him unless ready to shoot torpedoes instantly if he doesn't come back with the right answer. That's the way to handle it."

"I didn't think of that," Hugh mumbled sheepishly, as he carefully put the blinker tube down again.

The outline of the other ship was becoming less distinct. I was about to make mention of the fact when Jim spoke again.

"Looks to me that we are farther away than before, Captain."

I agreed. "Hugh, turn around and head for him. Use a little speed to get around and then slow down again."

Walrus was swinging to the left as Dave Freeman spoke up from the hatch below.

"Captain," he called. I came forward, bent over attentively.

"What did you find out?"

"Nothing, sir. There isn't supposed to be any ship anywhere around here except us—and there's nothing in the skeds about one. I made up a message." He read from a paper in his hand, aiming a tiny red flashlight beam at it. "URGENT FOR COMSUBPAC X SMALL VESSEL SIGHTED NORTHWEST OAHU ONE THREE ZERO MILES X COURSE THREE ZERO ZERO X SPEED ONE TWO."

"How did you dope that out?"

"Rubinoffski said it would be a good guess—about the same as ours was."

That seemed reasonable. "Go on," I said.

"REQUEST CONFIRMATION NO FRIENDLY VESSELS THIS VICINITY X WALRUS SENDS X URGENT FOR COMSUBPAC X."

"Good. How long will it take you to code that and send it out?"

"I woke up Keith to help, Captain. He's setting up the code now. We'll have it ready in about fifteen minutes and maybe have it off in fifteen minutes after that."

"That's a long time to wait, Dave. Do it as fast as you can."

Freeman dashed below. I stood up, again scanning the sea and horizon dead ahead. The indistinct outline of the other ship was a little closer now, still broadside, without any sign of having detected us.

"Jim," I said, "this may well be a Jap sub. We'll track it until we get an answer to our message. Then if it is, we'll go in and shoot him!"

"Why not get closer and see? If it is a Jap we can let him have it right away."

"We can't take a chance on its being friendly, Jim. If it's one of our own, a PC boat for instance, he might open fire on us."

Jim was not convinced. I had never seen him like this. The anticipation of combat had made a different person of him. He was all eagerness: "We've got the drop on him. We can go in . . ." he began, but I shook my head, and his face fell. He swallowed his disappointment with a strange look, quickly masked.

"Aye, aye, sir. Do you want to go to battle stations now?"

It seemed a bit premature, but it was best to be safe.

"Yes," I said. "We had better."

The possibility of combat had started a nervous tingling in my backbone, too.

"I'll have to go below to sound the general alarm, sir. Shall I stay at my station in the conning tower?"

"Yes, Jim, go ahead. I've got the picture up here."

Jim departed and in seconds the sound of the general alarm could be heard. This was the first time it had been sounded in earnest and the response in *Walrus* was electric. Within thirty seconds Jim's voice rang out on the ship's announcing system.

"The ship is at battle stations, Captain," he said. The blast of his voice on the bridge loud-speaker startled me. I was almost afraid it would reach across the intervening two or three miles of water and alert the enemy, if such indeed he was.

By this time the other ship had drawn a little to the right. We changed our course to the right accordingly. In a few minutes there came a call from the conning tower:

"Radar contact, bearing three-five-zero."

"Range?" I called down the hatch.

"Three-five-double-oh," came the prompt answer. "A small pip, sir."

"Jim," I called, "start tracking the target!"

The SJ radar was mounted at the top of a shaft secured to the forward part of the periscope supports, extending down into the upper part of the conning tower. It was thus right behind the Officer of the Deck's normal station, and it was possible to tell something about how the radar was working merely by reaching behind or leaning back against it. It had almost become instinctive to put my hand on it, when a bearing and range were being taken, to satisfy myself that Jim in the conning tower was indeed getting the information needed for coordination of the approach party. It was apparent that he was. In a few minutes Jim called up from below.

"Target course two-nine-zero. Speed ten. Recommend our course two-seven-zero, speed fifteen, to close in."

"We can't close until we get the answer to our message, Jim. Give me a course and speed just to stay in contact."

"Two-nine-zero. Speed ten!" There was a note of harshness in his voice, the barest suggestion of disaffection, as though his mask had slipped for an instant and been immediately replaced. Something I couldn't fathom had shown through.

The nights off Hawaii are beautiful. It rains frequently, but between the rains one has clear, star-studded skies and friendly seas. This was such a night. It was warm, humid, and dark, and *Walrus* rolled easily in the long ocean swells. As we increased speed our bow dipped into the successive seas and we felt a slight breeze on our faces. Back aft four clouds of vapor drifted gently away in the breeze and spatterings of water from the exhaust fell on the deck. Such a night was more fit for cruising in a sailboat or dancing on the deck of an ocean liner than for sudden death. I was struck by the similarity—in reverse—with the situation the German had caught us in, halfway from New London to the Panama Canal. Except that he knew beyond question we were an enemy, while here we were not so sure.

The two vessels, pursuer and pursued, ran steadily to the northwest. We, waiting for the all-important answer from Pearl Harbor; they, unconscious of their danger. Finally, after nearly an hour, it came. Dave read it to me from the conning tower.

"URGENT FOR WALRUS X NO FRIENDLY VESSELS YOUR VICINITY X TAKE IMMEDIATE ACTION X COMSUBPAC SENDS X"

Now that the moment for attack had come I felt myself a little weak in the knees as I gave the necessary orders.

"All ahead full! Come left to two-six-zero! Stand by forward!"

— 163

The song of our engines back aft lifted in frequency. Their power roar came clearly to our ears. The breeze of our passage, increasing in intensity, began plucking at our hair, searching the gaps in our shirts. It felt wet and clammy. I was sweating, and an alien unwelcome thought had intruded: Could there be a rebuke, implied or intended, in the message from Com-SubPac?

Walrus swung to the left, steadied on the new course, and the enemy vessel began to grow rapidly larger. I placed my binoculars into the bracket on top of the Target Bearing Transmitter, or TBT, a waterproof instrument by which target bearings could be transmitted to the TDC in the conning tower.

"Stand by forward," I repeated. Late or not, if we sank the enemy sub—for such it must be—any disapproval of our cautious attitude up to this point would be forgotten.

Back came Jim's voice: "Standing by forward, sir. Outer doors are open!"

"We will shoot a salvo of three," I said into the speaker at my side. "What's the range now?"

"Range two-five-double-oh! . . . Torpedo run three thousand!"

It was then that I realized we had made a serious error. In our anxiety to determine whether this was an enemy ship—and avoid being detected in the meantime—we had neglected to get into a proper firing position. One of the very first rules of submarine approaches, a cardinal principle, something I had known, had had drilled into me for years. When being approached from astern, the target's speed lengthens the distance a torpedo has to travel, and the submarine must consequently fire from closer range than it might otherwise choose. Likewise, a longer-than-usual range is possible if the torpedo is fired from well forward of the target's beam, but it is harder to hit by consequence of the sharp angle. The best position, considering the angle of hitting with the torpedo, or "torpedo track angle," is such that the torpedo intersects the target at ninety degrees. In the situation *Walrus* was in, to get a decent torpedo run of approximately fifteen hundred yards we would have to shoot from a range of about one thousand yards, and the torpedo track angle would be obtuse—in from astern after a stern chase—the least desirable situation of all.

My mind went through the calculations again. Barring a radical course change to the right, hardly to be expected, there was no hope for improving our firing position. If we turned away now for another attempt a little later, we would only expose our broadside to the enemy and almost certainly cause him to see us. No; we had already cast the die. Poorly situated though we were, we had to go through with the attack on the lines already begun. We were essentially bows on to him, too close to turn, so close that our detection sooner or later was a certainty. All we could do was to shoot soon enough, get our torpedoes on their way before the Jap lookouts spotted the telltale bow wave and bows-on silhouette on their starboard quarter.

"What's the range now?"

"Two-two-double-oh. Torpedo run two-five-double-oh."

Perhaps we could compromise a little—shoot from fifteen hundred yards and accept a torpedo run of two thousand. This would be better than getting so close—one thousand yards—as to be in danger of being spotted.

Another minute. "Range!" I called.

"Two-oh-double-oh," came the answer.

I had been watching the other ship through my binoculars. She was a submarine all right, with that ungainly, broken silhouette which could only spell Japanese. Jim had been right from the beginning. We need not have waited for a reply to our message. Had we only approached close enough we could have identified her by sight. No other ship but a Jap sub of the large ocean-cruiser I-class would look like this. She was a big ship, bigger than the *Walrus,* and not nearly so trim. I was about to ask for another range—it would have been the last one—when I realized she must have seen us. We were already abaft her

— 165

beam, but even as I watched, her length shortened still further. I found myself looking at her stern.

"We're all ready below, Captain," from Jim. "Shoot any time, sir!"

Heavy with disappointment, I had to give him the answer. "Don't shoot, Jim. Belay everything. Angle on the bow is now one-eight-zero."

The enemy submarine was harder to see, end on—just the silhouetted cut-up shape of her conning tower and bridge structure as she mounted the succeeding seas ahead, its reduction almost out of sight as she pitched into the hollows—and then I was looking only at the ocean. The gray-black silhouette had not remounted the next slow swell.

Hugh Adams noticed it a moment later. "He's gone, Captain! He must have dived!"

"That's right, Hugh" I said, still looking. *Walrus* ran on nearly half a minute before I caught on, and my hair lifted along the back of my neck. "Right full rudder!" I shouted into the conning tower. "All ahead flank!"

The rudder went over to full right, the diesels roared as the annunciators went all the way up against the stops, and our stern commenced to scud across the undulating Pacific swells. *Walrus* heeled to port, driving the port-side engine mufflers under water. They spluttered and splashed—threw a shower of spray into the air.

"What's the matter, Captain?" asked Hugh Adams.

Furious at the trap, I snarled back at him. "Why do you think he dived? He's ready for us now. He hopes we'll keep coming."

Adams stared, wide-eyed. "You mean . . ."

"Precisely!" I spat the word out. "He's looking at us this very minute. He's probably turned around and headed our way. We were almost close enough to shoot, remember, and so is he." I felt myself trembling with the reaction. From being the pursuer we had suddenly been converted into the pursued, and I

— 166

had blundered right into it. If only we had carried out Jim's original impulse, gotten close enough to attack immediately, we might have carried off a quick surprise.

Now, only failure! The Jap had been more alert than we. He had seen us soon enough, at sufficiently long range, turned immediately and dived, thus instantly taking the initiative right out of our hands.

We steadied *Walrus* on course northeast, almost directly away from where our attack had gone awry, ran on a good hour before daring to turn again toward the west. I felt sick at heart. It had been my first view of the enemy, and our first brush was hardly a drawn battle.

And, of course, there was the question of what to tell Com-SubPac.

Three days later we entered Midway Lagoon. We fueled ship, topping off our fuel tanks once more after the twelve-hundred-mile trip from Pearl Harbor, and we delivered an even dozen sacks of mail to the eager Midway population. When we departed that same day I had also made my first acquaintance with the large, foolish-looking "gooney birds" for which Midway had already become well known. The Laysan albatross, as the gooney bird is ornithologically called, is a most graceful, lovely bird at sea or in the air, but on land it is an ungainly, clumsy creature, the butt of jokes and the product of ninety per cent of the entertainment on Midway. This was the albatross which the Ancient Mariner had shot, I reflected, but it wasn't until we had left Midway over the horizon and one of them came gliding effortlessly in the ocean breezes, swooping and spiraling above us, circling ahead and astern, all without the slightest movement of its wings, that I could really understand the reverence in which the mariners of the old days held them.

Now began *Walrus'* first war patrol in earnest. It would take us twelve more days to reach Japan according to Jim's calculations, based upon running most of the distance upon the surface and spending the last few days en route submerged during daylight. We had approximately sixty full days at sea—two months—to look forward to.

We passed through the Nanpo Shoto submerged on the ninth day, within sight of Sofu Gan, or Lot's Wife—a desolate rock rising straight out of the sea—and at approximately noon of the twelfth day the hazy outline of the coast of Kyushu could be seen dead ahead through the periscope, bearing due west.

We had yet to see an enemy plane, ship, or other kind of enemy activity since the submarine off Oahu. Somehow, I think, we had expected to find AREA SEVEN teeming with ships, criss-crossing, going in all directions, but such was not the case. By the time the evening twilight had drawn to a close and it was nearly time to surface for the night, the coast of Japan was plainly in sight, low-lying on the western horizon. I had already come to the conclusion that the Japanese were aware of the possibility of American submarines off their coast, and were holding their ships in port.

We began to make preparation for surfacing. We would not, of course, come up until it was dark enough to do so with minimum danger of being seen by any Japanese aviator, fisherman, or other craft which might happen to be in the vicinity. At the same time, the sooner we came up the better horizon would there be for Jim to get his evening star sights. It was important to have our position accurate, after having been unable to navigate for fifteen hours or so, and it was also important to get our battery charge started as soon as possible in case it would be needed later. And finally, during a long day submerged, a crew of seventy men and six officers—seventy-six human machines breathing oxygen and exhaling carbon dioxide—could greatly reduce the livability of the atmosphere inside the ship. True, we carried carbon dioxide absorbent, hermetically sealed in shiny, metal canisters, and we carried oxygen in bottles for air revitalization, but these were needed for emergencies.

The resolution of the conflicting requirements was to juggle the various pros and cons and to surface as soon as possible. Today, our first day within sight of the Japanese coast, we waited a few minutes longer before surfacing, and when we finally started up nothing more could be seen through the periscope. I had donned red goggles twenty minutes before and was standing underneath the hatch leading to the bridge as I told Rubinoffski to sound three blasts on the diving alarm. The third blast of the klaxon horn had not yet died away when I felt the jolt of high-pressure air blasting into our ballast tanks, blowing water out. *Walrus* gave a convulsive shudder, inclined upward by the bow, and in a few moments we could hear the splashing and gurgling of water draining off the bridge.

Keith Leone was handling the surfacing procedure from the control room and now he commenced to shout depths up to me. "Four-oh feet," he sang out. "Three-five feet—three-oh feet."

"Crack the hatch," I said to Rubinoffski.

The Quartermaster leaped two steps up the bridge ladder, rapidly undogged the hatch hand wheel. Air commenced to blow out through the slightly open hatch rim and a few drops of water splattered in.

"Pressure one-half inch," came up from Keith.

This meant that our barometer indicated one-half inch more pressure inside the ship than had been the case on diving. Barring great atmospheric fluctuation "topside," this would be approximately the pressure differential existing now.

"Two-six feet, sir. Holding steady," from Keith again.

"Open the hatch." I was right behind Rubinoffski as he completed undogging the hatch and snapped open the safety latch. The heavy bronze hatch cover, counterbalanced by a large coil spring, flung itself open with a huge rush of air as Rubinoffski released the latch, banging the side of the bridge and latching itself open with a loud bell-like thud. The two of us, carrying binoculars, were on the bridge less than a second later. By prearrangement Rubinoffski ran aft to survey the after one hundred and eighty degrees sector, while I concentrated on the forward half of the ocean.

Slowly, intently, I scanned the horizon; then the water between us and the rapidly fading demarcation between sea and sky; then the sky above, where a few stars glittered stonily from between the clouds. I heard Rubinoffski report, "All clear aft." "All clear forward," I muttered, half to myself, then raising my voice, "Open the main induction; lookouts to the bridge. Start the low-pressure blow." The main-induction valve, just below the cigarette deck, opened with a thump. Four lookouts, all previously prepared with adequate clothing to stand watch up in the wind-and-rain-swept periscope shears, and having become at least partially night adapted by wearing red goggles for some time beforehand, came dashing up on the bridge and took their places. Immediately behind them came Keith, similarly attired, and then Oregon, who, as Quartermaster of the Watch, went back aft to relieve Rubinoffski.

"Ready to relieve you, Captain," said Keith after a few minutes, making a hand motion that might have passed for a salute.

I gave him the customary turnover: course, speed, and the various other details of the watch. As I did so an almost human screech came from below decks. One would have said that a wild animal was being tortured and was in mortal pain; its cry of agony—an undulating, wavering, high-pitched scream, piercing through the bowels of the ship. "There goes the turbo blow," I said. "Run it for five minutes. That will be plenty."

Walrus rode sluggishly on the nearly smooth sea. Her decks were almost awash and little ripples of water splashed in her superstructure above her pressure hull. Now as the turbo blow commenced to force large quantities of air into the ballast tanks—at just sufficient pressure to expel the water, thus saving our precious high-pressure air, *Walrus* slowly began to lift herself to a more seaworthy altitude. To bring the ship to the fully surfaced condition would require approximately fifteen minutes. Five minutes would get her high enough for the slow patrolling we proposed.

"Permission to come on the bridge." This was Jim. Keith had not yet relieved me so I still had the deck.

"Come on up," I said. Jim moved aft to our bulwarkless cigarette deck, joined Rubinoffski in whispered consultation. The latter pointed skyward in several directions, and in a moment Jim was shooting the stars with the sextant he had brought with him.

"Permission to start a battery charge." This was relayed up the conning tower hatch by the messenger stationed there.

"Permission granted," I called back. This also was part of our surfacing routine. A main engine snorted and then another, and I could hear them loaded down as the life-giving amperes began to be forced back from their generators into our battery.

"Permission to dump garbage?"

"Granted," I said again. Up came Russo and two mess cooks, lugging three large gunny sacks containing the day's accumulation of trash and garbage, each one of them weighted with crushed tin cans, broken or discarded tools, even a stone or two from the supply Russo had brought aboard. The sacks were unceremoniously pitched over into the water, floated aft as they slowly became waterlogged.

We'll proceed in toward the coast at slow speed, Keith," I said, "until Jim gets his fix. Be alert for aircraft or Jap vessels."

Keith nodded. "I relieve you, sir," he said. I moved back to the after part of the cigarette deck, leaned thoughtfully against the wire cable which had replaced our bulwarks. We had achieved our destination. We had come over eight thousand miles to war and a few miles ahead of us lay one of the main islands of Japan—southernmost Kyushu.

Kyushu is separated from the islands to the north and east, Honshu and Shikoku, by the Japanese Inland Sea. From the Pacific side there are two entrances to this confined body of water: the Bungo Suido between Kyushu and Shikoku and the Kii Suido between Shikoku and Honshu. Since the earliest times Japan's Inland Sea has been one of the island empire's main traffic arteries between the home islands and, of course, during the war it constituted a huge sheltered harbor in which their whole battle fleet could hold maneuvers if desired.

AREA SEVEN included the eastern coast of Kyushu, beginning with the Bungo Suido on the north and extending down almost to the southern tip of the island. Our instructions were to examine the area; determine what, if anything, were the Japanese traffic patterns; estimate how often the Bungo Suido was used, whether naval units were in the habit of using that entrance. And our mission was also to sink any and all Japanese vessels we might encounter—and avoid being detected, attacked, or sunk ourselves.

We were still headed west. Up ahead, no longer in sight, was Kyushu. I stared unseeingly in that direction, then took my binoculars and made a slow sweep all the way around the horizon. It felt good to be topside, to draw in clean, wholesome air instead of the torpid atmosphere we had been breathing. My greedy senses drank in the freedom of the ocean.

There was a musty tinge to the air, an odor of wet, burned sandalwood, of unwashed foreign bodies. A seaman, near shore, can always smell the shore—it is the smell landsmen identify as the "smell of the sea." But it is not noticeable at sea—only close to shore—and it pervaded my consciousness this night. All night long we cruised aimlessly about, seeing nothing, never losing the smell of Japan. By morning we had approached close enough to Kyushu to take up a patrol station about ten miles offshore where we hoped some unwary vessel might blunder into our path, and where the first of a series of observation posts on the Bungo Suido could logically be set up.

Jim and I had studied the chart. Inshore lay a bank of moderately shallow water, hardly deep enough to shelter us in the event of a counterattack. Jim had argued for going in closer, saying that coastwise Japanese shipping would run in as shallow water as possible. I demurred, pointing out that we had the dual responsibility of watching the Bungo as well, and that we could always go closer inshore after a merchant vessel if necessary. The spot we finally selected was intended to satisfy both objectives, though Jim never did express final satisfaction.

We were finishing an austere lunch when the control room messenger appeared. "Captain," he said, "you're wanted in the conning tower. Mr. Adams says there's smoke." I dashed down the passageway, hearing the last words of his hastily muttered message over my shoulder as I ran. In a moment Hugh turned over the periscope to me. Sure enough, a thin column of smoke could be seen close inshore northwestward. I watched it carefully to see which way it was going, finally accepted the fact that it was heading away. The smoke gradually became less distinct, faded out in the distance.

Twice more we sighted smoke that day, once more to the northwest and once to the southwest. In all three cases the ships were going away, not toward; and it would have been fruitless to have pursued them.

"Do you think they are slipping by us close inshore?" Jim asked me. I shrugged. There was no way of telling. "Maybe if we went in closer, close enough to see the coast distinctly . . ."

"Too shallow," I said, but the eagerness I had noted during the fruitless attempt on the Jap submarine was now dancing in Jim's eyes, showing through the considered awareness I had become accustomed to.

"Look, skipper, why don't we go in here?" He indicated a spot on the coast where the extent of shallow water was much less than elsewhere. "They couldn't get by without our seeing them if we went in here."

To fall in with his suggestion would have meant giving up our watch position on the Bungo Suido. The position we had chosen permitted us to cover one segment of the probable traffic lines from there. Several days in this position and several days in each of three others would, we had figured, give us some idea of traffic patterns.

"Jim, we've only been here one day. Keep your shirt on," I said in small exasperation. "We've got twenty-nine days more in the area." But Jim persisted, pointing out eagerly the configuration of the coastline and the depths of water here and there to bolster his argument. On our area chart he had drawn the approximate location of the three ships we had sighted.

"Look, Captain," he said, "we already know they are going here," indicating with his finger. "We know they are running close inshore. Our main mission is to sink them. After we knock off a couple . . ." We might have argued longer had not the musical notes of the general alarm interrupted us. Startled, I jerked up, caught Jim's eye and then with one move we raced to the conning tower.

"Bong, bong, bong, bong, bong"—the doorbell chimes were still pealing out as, breathlessly, I confronted Dave Freeman. Already the reduction of oxygen was becoming noticeable.

"A ship, sir, coming this way—a big ship." The periscope was down, evidently having just been lowered. I grasped the pickle, squeezed it as Dave spoke, started it up again. In a moment I was looking through it. There in the distance, exactly like our practice approaches in New London, were the masts, stack, and bridge structure of a large vessel. I could hear the warming-up notes of the TDC. Keith was ready for business.

"Bearing—Mark! Down periscope!"

"Three-two-eight," read Dave from the azimuth ring.

Keith furiously spun one of the handles. "Angle on the bow?"

"Starboard ten."

"Estimated range?" I had not tried to get a range.

The ship was still well hull down, only her upper works showing. "Give it fifteen thousand yards," I said.

Jim had extracted the Is-Was from its stowage, was rotating the dials. Rubinoffski, garbed in his underwear with hastily thrown-on shoes and carrying his trousers, came clattering up the ladder. Off watch, he had been caught in his bunk by the call to quarters. Freeman relinquished the pickle to him, dashed below, bound for his own station. The Quartermaster hastily thrust his bony legs into his dungarees, managed to get them hooked at the top in time to grasp the periscope control button and raise it at my order. I spun the periscope around quickly, lowered it. "Nothing else in sight," I said, motioning for it to come up again. Another look, this time carefully at the sky. Clear, a few clouds, not much cover for aircraft, no airplanes in sight. Down went the periscope again. I looked around, looked at Jim. He nodded briefly.

"Conning tower manned, sir." Quin was listening on his headset, nodded also. The periscope started up with my thumb motion.

"Observation," I snapped.

"Ship is at battle stations," rapidly called out Quin.

I rose with the periscope. "Bearing—Mark!"

"Three-three-nine and a half!"

"Use forty feet. Range—Mark!"

Rubinoffski fumbled with the range dial lining up the pointers.

"One-four-oh-double-oh!" The 'scope dropped away.

"Angle on the bow still the same. Starboard ten." Keith was spinning his TDC cranks with both hands.

"Any other ships in sight, Captain?" This was Jim. "No," I said, "No escorts."

"I have the dive, Captain, depth sixty feet." Tom had climbed up two or three rungs of the ladder to the control room, had his head at the deck level.

"Very well." I turned to Keith. "What's the course to close the track with about a thirty-degree angle?" Keith looked at his dials for a moment. "We're on it now, sir. Recommend no change. What kind of a ship is it, Captain?"

Jim had finished orienting the Is-Was, now crowded between

Hugh Adams at the plotting table and Keith at the TDC. He looked at me with that same look of anticipated pleasure, that eagerness for combat that I had recently noticed. "Can't tell yet. Buff superstructure, black stack, two masts. Some kind of a cargo vessel."

"Is he smoking?"

"No—no smoke at all."

"New ship then. Anyway, in good shape."

I nodded.

Up forward of the periscope hoist motors was the underwater sound receiver and control equipment for the sound heads under our bow. I leaned over alongside the earphoned sonar operator. His pointer was going around steadily and slowly. He shook his head at my inquiring glance. I indicated the area on our starboard bow as the place for him to concentrate on, stepped back to the periscope, motioned with my thumbs.

"Zig to his right," I called. The angle on the bow had changed, was now port twenty degrees, and I could see more of the enemy ship, a large new-type freighter. As I turned the periscope something else caught my eye—a discontinuity in the horizon—another mast. It would indeed have been highly improbable that a large, valuable freighter should be coming out of port unescorted. I looked closely on the other side, then back again. There were two small masts, one on either side, both apparently abeam or a little distance astern. This would not be as easy an approach as I had for a short time been hoping. "He has two escorts, Jim," I said.

"What kind?"

"Can't tell yet. They're a lot smaller and I can't see them." Quin was watching me. He picked up the telephone mouthpiece, spoke into it briefly. I could visualize everyone in the ship getting the word: "The skipper sees two destroyers up there!"

"Jim," I said, "have the ship rigged for depth charge. Shortly before we fire we will go to silent running also."

"Right," said Jim, as he squeezed by me to relay the necessary instructions to Quin.

Several observations later the situation had developed more clearly. Our target was a single large merchantman with cargo hatches forward and aft and four large goal-post type derricks. She had a single low, fat stack rising out of an amidships deckhouse evidently fitted for passenger accommodations. The ship had obviously come out of Bungo Suido and was headed south, perhaps bound for Guam or Saipan, making respectable speed and escorted by three old type destroyers. One escort rode on either beam of the target and the third one, which I had not seen until some time later, was following astern. I could feel *Walrus* tense up as the target drew steadily near her. He was zigzagging, presenting first one side and then the other. We were right on his base course and had only to maneuver for a shot as he went by. I could feel myself tense up as well, as the crucial moment approached.

We closed off the ventilation system, the air-conditioning machinery, and all other equipment not absolutely essential to the progress of the business at hand. The sweat spurted out of my pores, ran saltily down my cheeks and into the corners of my mouth. I ran my hands ceaselessly through my moist hair, wiped them off on my trousers. Hugh Adams was bothered by sweat dropping off the end of his nose onto his carefully laid-out plot.

Through the periscope I could see the whole ship now, even her red waterline heaving in and out of the sea. I had directed Tom to run several feet deeper to reduce the amount of periscope exposed, leaving me just enough height to make observations between passing waves. The range had closed to about two miles when the target made another zig.

"Angle on the bow—starboard thirty-five," I sang out, as the periscope descended. "Keith, what's the distance to the track?"

"Two thousand yards, Captain."

"Torpedo run?"

"Two-seven-double-oh." Jim, detailed to the angle solver on firing, relayed this one for me.

"Are we ready to shoot, Jim?" Jim glanced upward at his check-off list. My eyes followed his. Every item on it but one had been neatly checked off in grease pencil. "We're ready to shoot, Captain, except that outer doors are still closed."

According to the Pearl Harbor submarine base our torpedoes were prone to flood if left exposed in the torpedo tubes with the outer doors open for too long a period. It was advisable not to open them until just before firing. I turned to Quin. "Open the outer doors forward."

"Open the outer doors forward," he echoed into his telephone transmitter. Up forward at the command the torpedomen would speedily crank open the heavy bronze torpedo tube muzzle doors. This was the last act in the preparation of torpedoes for firing.

I nodded for the periscope, crouched before it till it came up, rode it to its full extension, spun it around, lowered it. "We're inside the screen," I said. "The near escort will pass astern, well clear." I failed to mention that the rear escort, a few hundred yards astern of the target, would by no means pass clear. Within minutes after firing, he would be upon us. No point in alerting or worrying our crew at this stage over something that could not be helped.

"We'll give him three torpedoes on a ninety track, or as near to it as we can!"

"Ninety track. Three fish spread!" echoed Jim.

"The next observation will be a shooting observation! Stand by forward!" My mind racing, I studied the slowly moving dials on the face of the TDC. We could already shoot at any time. It was only a matter of waiting until the situation was most favorable. The "correct solution light," a red F, was glowing brightly on the face of the angle-solver sector of the TDC. The "torpedo run" was well within maximum range of the torpedo. It would only be a few seconds longer.

I could feel the taut expectancy of the ship—this was to be our first kill. In the forward part of the conning tower O'Brien, the sonarman, had put the propeller beats on the loud-speaker. We could hear the "chug-a-chug, chug-a-chug, chug-a-chug, chug-a-chug," as the enemy's screws came closer and closer. Less distinct was the lighter, high-pitched beat of the nearest escort. "Thum, thum, thum, thum." The sonarman switched from one to the other, kept them both coming in. It looked about time.

"This is a shooting observation," I said again. "Up periscope!" The periscope handles met my outstretched hands. I snapped them down, put my eye to the eye guard. "No change," I said. "Bearing—Mark!"

"Three-three-six."

"Range"—I turned the range knob—"Mark!"

"One-eight-five-oh."

"Shoot," I said, snapping the handles up as the signal for the periscope to start down. Quin had turned around facing the firing panel, had turned the switch of Number One torpedo tube to "On."

"Fire!" shouted Jim. Quin leaned on the firing key. *Walrus* shuddered. Over the sonar loud-speaker I could hear the torpedo whine out of the tube. Jim made an adjustment to the face of the angle solver with his right hand, held a stop watch in his left, watched it intently. "Fire Two!" he shouted. Quin leaned on the firing key a second time.

Another adjustment by Jim, then "Fire Three!" and *Walrus* jerked for the third time. I motioned for the periscope again, took a quick look. Our torpedoes were running nicely.

"Torpedo run?" I called out, as the periscope was on the way down.

"One-six-five-oh." A quick calculation. A little over one minute to go. Up went the periscope again. I spun it around, dipped it, raised it again. One escort was passing astern. I hadn't given him much of an inspection before—he was an old type destroyer, *Momo* class as nearly as I could tell, with a well-deck forward of the bridge, and two stacks far apart. The periscope dipped again and then went back up to the target. All still serene.

"How long?"

"Thirty seconds to go." I swung around once more, then back to the target, just in time to catch sight of a white-clad figure racing out to the side of his bridge. Then a stream of vapor shot from his stack, evidently his whistle. Too late, however. There was now no chance of avoiding our torpedoes unless they were improperly aimed. I swung the periscope all the way around. The destroyer which had just crossed our stern was heeling over radically away from us, starting to turn toward with hard-over rudder. A quick look on our port beam. The rear-most destroyer was coming directly at us, showing white water all along his waterline.

There was no time to linger. "Take her down!" I shouted. There would still be a few seconds before the periscope went under, time, perhaps to see the torpedoes strike home.

I started to swing back toward the target, suddenly received a sharp blow on my head as the periscope yoke collar unexpectedly descended upon it. I reeled backward, momentarily stunned, looked up to see Rubinoffski's consternation. He was squeezing the pickle, and the periscope base with the rubber eye-pieces had already dropped out of sight into the periscope well. I could hear the rush of air in the control room as negative-tank flood valve was opened and Kohler yanked the tank vent. Negative would take in approximately nine tons of water, well forward of amidships, thus helping us to start down. I could feel *Walrus'* deck tilt forward gently. I rubbed my aching skull, opened my mouth to curse at Rubinoffski, but never got the words out. Suddenly there was a tremendous, stupifying roar.

Whrang-g-g. Our hull resounded like a tuning fork. The sensation could be likened to being inside a wash boiler and having a giant beat on the outside with a sledge hammer. My ears rang. Jim was shouting. "We've hit him! It's a hit!" He slapped me on the back. "You did it, skipper. You sunk the son-of-a-bitch!" Then he turned to Keith, pounded him on the back also.

"How about the other two fish?" I asked him.

Jim looked at his stop watch, shook his head regretfully. "No luck there . . ." As he spoke, there came clearly a tinny, high-pitched *Pwhyunng*. I glanced, startled. "That was timed for the third torpedo," Jim said, punching the winding stem of his watch, showing me its face.

Walrus' deck was tilted down even farther by now and she was clawing for the depths.

"What do you think that noise could have been?" I asked. Keith answered: "Gosh, I don't know. Maybe an air flash—have you ever heard an air flash explode, Captain?" Jim and I both shook our heads. I would have discussed it more but a shout from O'Brien started a whole new train of thought.

"He's starting a run on us!" I leaped to his side, grabbed the extra pair of earphones. The enemy destroyer's "pings" could clearly be heard, sounding just like our own destroyers'. They were coming in rapidly, too, and I could hear the "thum, thum, thum," of his propeller beats. The sonarman put his left hand on the gain control, ready to tune down the volume when the depth charges went off. I could see it shaking as he touched the knob.

"WHAM . . . WHAM . . . WHAM." The giant alongside us cut loose with three violent blows from his sledge hammer. *Walrus* quivered and shook. Dust rose from the equipment and the deck. A piece of cork bounced from nowhere, made a peculiar "plop" as it landed on Adams' chart table.

I became aware of a new sound, a click which seemed to precede each depth charge. "CLICK, WHAM . . . CLICK, WHAM . . ." two more depth charges. Then there was a prolonged swishing of water as though someone were hosing our side with a fire hose. The propeller beat, reduced in volume because of our having lowered the gain, suddenly dropped in frequency. O'Brien glanced up briefly. "He's passed overhead. That's 'Down Doppler.'" It was similar to the drop in pitch of a train going by at high speed.

"Maybe they'll go away now." This was Jim's voice. It did seem possible, for the destroyer's beat kept on without slackening or other change, toward the general direction of southeast.

"Search all around," I directed O'Brien. Obediently, he did so, holding the control handle over and causing the sound-head pointer to travel a complete circle. I still had the earphones on and something, a discontinuity in the sound as he went by it—some impulse—caused me to ask him to turn back to the northwest sector.

There it was again. A slight increase in noise level. Nothing specific, no propeller beat, just an increased sound from that bearing. *Walrus* reached her maximum designed depth and now we slowed to minimum speed in accordance with our silent-running routine. We should be difficult for someone else to hear, and, conversely, could hear better ourselves. But the noise, if such it really was, could not be resolved into identifiable components. I motioned with my finger all around the dial. Obediently O'Brien set his equipment in motion. The propeller beats of the *Momo*-class destroyer which had depth-charged us were still to be heard, more faintly than before but on the same general bearing. He was going away. There was no question of it. I could see O'Brien listen intently in its direction. Finally he looked up, uncovered one ear. "Captain," he said, "there are at least two ships over there. Two sets of high-speed propellers. Maybe more."

Jim had approached unnoticed. "Good," he said, "they've gone off."

"I'm not so sure," I muttered, half to myself. "This noise level . . ." I motioned to O'Brien, who went past the new sector again. When the sound head moved past the bearing rapidly there was no question about the increase in noise level, but when we turned directly on the bearing it was impossible to make anything out, or even to distinguish any difference.

Jim listened with me for some minutes. "What do you think it is?" he finally whispered.

"Don't know. Never heard anything like this before."

"Could it be the ship we sank?"

"Maybe."

"Maybe we should come up and take a look through the periscope."

For several more minutes we waited. Nothing more could be heard from the direction in which our *Momo*-class destroyer had disappeared. Nothing more could be heard in any direction, in fact, but the feeling of uneasiness persisted; the noise, if such it could be called, had not changed. If anything, it was a bit weaker. *Walrus* stealthily slipped through the depths, every nerve taut, unable to see, not sure of what she heard. I ordered a course change, to put the area of high-sound level nearly astern—not exactly, so as not to mask it with the quiet swishing of our own propellers.

More time passed. It was over an hour since we had fired our torpedoes. Gradually our guard relaxed. To relieve the oppressive heat and humidity I permitted the ventilation system and air-conditioning machinery to be started. It was quiet all around the sonar dial, except for our port quarter, where the faint noise level persisted.

"If there's anything up there, it's the ship we just sank! Maybe that's the sinking ship we're hearing!" Jim's sustained excitement was infectious. I could sense the approval of everyone in the conning tower. Every eye turned upon me.

Jim spoke again, eagerness flashing from every facial expression. "God, skipper! If we hurry we might be able to see him sink! We don't have to surface—just get up to periscope depth!"

The moment, after our moments of tension, was one of anticlimax. We had fired our torpedoes, heard what we had assumed was an explosion of one of them, plus another peculiar low-order explosion, and had withstood our first depth-charging. Besides, we had heard the screw noises of several ships departing from the scene of the attack, among them at least one positively identified as a destroyer. I was eager also to see the results of our first encounter with the enemy—and so I allowed myself to be convinced.

"Control! Six-four feet! Bring her up flat!" I leaned over the control-room hatch, called the order down to Tom, whose head I could see just below.

"Six-four feet, aye, aye!" Tom acknowledged, looking up. "Request more speed!"

"Nothing doing, old man," I responded, squatting on my haunches to speak to him more easily. "Bring her up easy. We've plenty of time." If Jim's evaluation was correct, there was nothing to worry about up above; there would be no reason why we should not come up with normal procedure, letting Tom have a bit more speed for better control. But more speed would mean more noise also, and more disturbance in the water. Some subconscious caution held me back, caused me to direct that the remaining torpedoes loaded forward be made ready for instant firing, though later examination of the events of the next few moments could furnish no clue as to why.

Gently *Walrus* inclined gently upward. With no more than minimum speed, it would take her a long time to plane up to periscope depth. After several minutes had passed we had only covered half the distance, and I could feel the impatience around me. As we passed the hundred-foot-depth mark the angle of inclination decreased still more; Tom was obeying my dictum to "bring her up flat." Two more minutes passed. The ship was at seventy feet, with zero inclination. Having no speed for control submerged, Tom was afraid to come right up to sixty-four feet for fear that some unexpected variation in water density or temperature might cause us to broach.

Slowly, *Walrus* swam up the few remaining feet. I now regretted not having authorized more speed, for at sixty-nine feet we were still totally blind, the periscopes still four feet short of reaching the surface. I nevertheless ordered one of our two 'scopes raised.

When it was "two-blocked"—all the way up—we were passing sixty-seven feet, and through it I could see, just overhead as though it were actually only a couple of feet above, the ripply surface of the ocean. Only two feet—as good as two hundred. As I waited, the wavy surface—which looked exactly as I had seen it many times, looking down from above—grew nearer, then farther, then nearer, as the Pacific swells passed over.

"What's the bearing of the noise now?" I spoke without taking my eyes from the periscope.

"It's shifted to the port bow, Captain!" Jim's voice.

"Put me on it!" I felt someone's hands laid on mine, felt the pressure. The periscope was twisted some considerable distance to the left, and I followed docilely.

Suddenly I was conscious of a flash of brilliant light; then it was gone, and the light through the periscope was darker than it had been before. In the split-second interval I had seen blue sky and clouds. I realized I had turned the elevation control to full elevation, was looking nearly straight up, had missed the precious chance to garner a quick look on the port bow. Hastily I turned it down to the horizontal, determined not to miss the next chance.

The periscope popped out again, for a longer interval, in the hollow of a long swell. It was possible to see only a few feet, and only for a moment at that, until the wave in front of me engulfed the periscope eye-piece. Then we were out again, in the trough of the next wave. I caught a glimpse of masts above the crest of the wave in the direction in which I was looking, but nothing more. They seemed fairly close, but the momentary impression was too fleeting to make much out about them.

I waited another second or two—I would be able to see in a moment—the periscope popped out again: there was a wave in front of it, beyond which I could see the upper section of a mast. It might be the mast of our target at some little distance away, perhaps a thousand yards, or it might be the mast of another ship considerably closer. I tried to flip the periscope handle to the low-power position, found that it was already in low power.

The wave in front of me receded, the periscope eye-piece topping it easily, and the source of the masts came clearly—and suddenly—to view.

It was a Japanese destroyer, broadside to us, and it was close, very close, nearly alongside in fact.

I snapped the handle into the high-power position, felt myself catapulted almost into his bridge. There were white-clad figures all about his topsides. A quick glimpse of activity, several arms pointed our way—we could not have been more than two hundred yards from him—a hustle on the bridge, someone battling the wheel, someone else doing something to an instrument which could have only been annunciators.

There was no time to do anything. No time to do anything at all except try to get away. We were caught—caught fair!

"FIRE!" I shouted. I banged the periscope handles up. My hair felt as though it were standing on end. The flesh crawled around my belly. "Down periscope! *Take her down! Take her down fast!*"

"What is it? What's the matter?" shouted Jim. Involuntarily my voice had risen in pitch, and my fright must have been evident. So was Jim's. Keith, Rubinoffski, and Oregon, at the wheel, likewise turned their startled faces toward me.

"Take her down! *Take her down fast! All ahead emergency! Left full rudder!*" The urgency in my voice brought instant obedience: Oregon heaved mightily on the steering wheel, whipped both annunciators all the way to the right, banged them three times against the stops. A whoosh of released air welled up from the control room, where Tom's action in flooding negative tank had probably been equally instinctive. Through it all I felt—sensed would be more accurate —three solid jerks in *Walrus'* tough frame as three torpedoes went on their sudden way.

We could practically feel the bow and stern planes bite into the water. The increased thrust of our screws heaved us forward and downward, but the movement of two thousand tons of steel is a slow, ponderous process.

"What is it, Captain? For God's sake, tell us what's the matter!" Jim was nearly beside himself.

"Destroyer! Waiting for us! Not over two hundred yards away! He'll be on us in seconds!"

"Do you think they saw us?"

"You're Goddam right they saw us! The people on the bridge were pointing at us!" I swore without even thinking about it or meaning to. "There were at least fifty men all over his topsides on special lookout watch, and they looked as though they all—every one of them—had a big pair of binoculars!"

"Is he headed for us?"

"Hell yes! We were so close I could even see them put the rudder over and ring up full speed!"

Careless of how it might sound, I had almost been shouting. Now I recollected myself, turned to Quin, "Rig ship for depth charge! Rig ship for silent running!" The yeoman's eyes were huge as he repeated the orders over the telephone. They flickered to the conning-tower depth gauge. It read sixty-five feet. It was hardly moving.

The sounds of slamming of watertight doors and bulkhead ventilation valves came clearly into the conning tower. No need to be careful about noise right now! Our straining propellers were making more than enough anyway, and besides, our torpedoes would give us away for sure—draw an arrow to our position at the apex of their wakes. No more ventilation. The conning tower again grew stifling and humid, but no one noticed. I crossed back to the sonar gear, picked up the extra set of headphones.

"Where is he?" O'Brien indicated the pointer in the sonar dial, nearly dead ahead, moving from port bow to starboard. Our rudder was still at full left, and *Walrus* was now swinging rapidly. Turning toward had been the instinctive thing to do, and also evidently the best maneuver in the emergency. We would let her turn a bit longer, then straighten out.

"What's our depth?" I looked at Jim. "Passing eighty feet!" His face worked as he spoke, and he tapped the glass face of the gauge to make sure it was not stuck. It had only been about twenty seconds since we had started down, hardly time for *Walrus* to have gained much depth yet. We had achieved a small down angle, however, should begin to go deep rapidly now.

I put on the earphones, immediately became conscious of the high-speed screws of our enemy, and his rapid, steady pinging. Gone also, now, was any attempt to quietness or concealment on his part. The screws were becoming rapidly louder. The pings were continuous, steady, practically without interval. He was well on our starboard bow, coming in at high speed, perhaps hoping to ram.

"Rudder amidships!" Our compass card slowed its spin, steadied. This would increase our speed across the enemy track, tend to make him shoot his depth charges astern. Perhaps our torpedoes would prevent him from attacking immediately, possibly one might even, by great good fortune, hit him.

Forlorn hope! The whole inside of the submarine was resounding with the enemy destroyer's propeller beats. The pings of his echo-ranging apparatus were fast, short, continuous, implacable. I could hear the echoes rap off our hull almost as soon as transmitted, could even hear a double echo—the return bounce off him. We had reached ninety feet when the destroyer's roar attained an excruciating, violent crescendo of sound, and coherent thinking became frozen. He could not have been more than thirty feet away from where I was standing, dead overhead, roaring like an express train. My brain throbbed in the furious convulsion of noise. There was a screaming of tortured gears, the whine of high-speed turbines, the spitting, churning, tearing fury of his propellers, the blast of water—all combined into a frenzied, desperate, sudden drive to send us forever into the black depths of the sea.

"Here we are!" I remember thinking. "Here comes the granddaddy of all depth-chargings!" *Walrus* moved bodily in the water as the destroyer passed overhead. We could feel his initial pressure wave, and we also knew, by the abrupt change in the pitch of the noise, the exact instant he passed over. Just before he did so, the bearing from which the sound had been coming in widened until it encompassed the entire three hundred sixty degrees around us. Ninety-one feet the depth gauges said. It was time—it was time—here it comes—

WHAM! A prolonged, crushing, catastrophic roar! The lights went out. I was thrown to the deck, grasped the periscope hoist wires with both hands. They were tingling, alive. The deck plates were rattling likewise. There was someone lying on the deck beneath me—as I felt for him, amid the convulsive shudders of *Walrus'* great steel fabric, my feet were jerked out from under me and I was flung bodily on top of him. He felt wet, warm-wet, and he didn't move.

Scrambling to my feet, I realized the motion of the ship had changed. We were on the surface. The ship still had a large angle down by the bow, but our rocking and pitching could only be the result of being on the surface in the wash of the vessel that had just passed overhead. No doubt our stern was well out, high in view—a beautiful target. I was still holding to the periscope wires, and to my horror I saw light at the bottom of the periscope well! Then the explanation occurred: the top of the periscope, though housed, was also out of water, and light naturally streamed out of the other end. To confirm it I reached for the other 'scope, looked down into the well, saw light there also.

Still black as ink in the conning tower. On rig for depth charge the hatch between us and the control room had been dogged down, and there was no communication except by telephone—useless at the moment, of course. The whole interior of the submarine was a huge, sounding cavern, reverberating and reflecting the uproar. If only we could see!

"Turn on the emergency lights!" I shouted. I might as well have whispered. The emergency lights should have come on. Standard practice called for them to be turned on automatically —by anyone—if the main lighting went out.

No need to look at the depth gauge anyway. "All ahead emergency!" I had already ordered emergency speed, subconsciously wanted to reinforce the order after the attack. In the shattering uproar I bellowed as loud as I could. Quin might hear me, might be able to get through to the maneuvering room, or Oregon, at the other end of the conning tower, could ring for flank speed again three times. They were probably having a pretty bad time back aft, but "emergency ahead," under the circumstances existing, would cause Larto to open the main motor rheostats as far as they would go, put everything the battery could give into the propellers.

The noise was subsiding a little. I had no knowledge of how many depth charges had gone off, perhaps a dozen all almost simultaneously, and there was no telling, yet, whether *Walrus* had survived. The conning tower, we knew, was still whole. With all hatches and ventilation valves shut tightly, there could be no telltale increase in air pressure as water came rushing into another compartment. Since our stern was on the surface, a hole there might give no indication at all, or merely a loss in what slightly elevated pressure *Walrus'* atmosphere might already have. We'd find out soon enough as we drove her down.

The destroyer's rush had carried him well past. I could hear his screws again—now on our port quarter. He had passed directly overhead. Our only hope was that the depth charges had been set too deeply, that, although blown to the surface, we were not seriously damaged—but there was no time to think about damage already received. Four-inch shells would be whizzing our way within seconds. We had to get back under immediately!

There was an emergency light switch near the ladder to the bridge. I collected myself, gropingly reached for it, fumbled a moment, turned it. Dim lights came on at either end of the conning tower.

The conning tower looked as if a cyclone had struck it. Hugh Adams' chart table, shaken loose from its mountings, had fallen to the floor. Hugh himself lay still on the deck. Evidently he had been the one I had stumbled over. Keith was still at his station, frantically gripping the handles of the TDC and bracing himself with his foot on the corner of the angle solver. Jim was standing shakily beside him, white as a sheet, but apparently unhurt. But these were not the important ones at the moment. Oregon was still at his steering wheel, and there seemed to be no damage in his locality. Quin was sitting on the deck holding his left arm. There was an ugly gash in it from which blood was dripping onto his trousers. He seemed otherwise in condition to be of assistance, however.

"Quin!" I roared. "All ahead emergency!"

Painfully the yeoman reached up with his uninjured arm, gave the order into the telephone mouthpiece. Fastened to the side of the conning tower beneath the firing panel was the hand telephone for routine communication throughout the ship. I reached for it, pressed the button. "Control!" The response was immediate.

"Control; aye, aye!" It was Tom Schultz himself on the other end, and I could remember the instant feeling of relief to discover that at least part of the ship was still functioning.

"We're broached, Tom. Can you get her down?"

"Trying, sir!"

"Have you got your vents open?" Possibly some of the gases from the underwater explosions could have come up into our ballast tanks and now, having broached, we would be bound to have air in some of them.

"Yes, sir," Tom replied again.

"We're going ahead emergency speed. Drive her as deep as you can. Get on over to twenty degrees angle if you have to," I told him. The order was superfluous, since Tom knew very well the seriousness of our situation, and the ship had already attained an angle of fifteen degrees down by the bow. The slanting deck was becoming difficult to stand on.

There was nothing further I could do and no reason to hold up the telephone from other use by talking myself. I listened, however, and within a few seconds was rewarded by hearing the reports of the various compartments. All had taken some damage from the knocking about, but none, apparently, was in serious trouble except the after torpedo room. The voice from there said simply, "We have a fire back here."

"Can you handle it?" I snapped.

"Yes, sir, we're handling it." I relaxed. We couldn't go to fire quarters. The men back aft had either to get the fire out by themselves or abandon the compartment. The main problem was getting *Walrus* into the safe haven of the deep depths.

The motion of the ship felt different—less jerky. I looked at the depth gauge. We were under again! The deck tilted down even more; I had to put my left arm around a periscope barrel to retain my balance. The bubble inclinometer, similar to a curved carpenter's level, mounted beneath the depth gauge, showed eighteen degrees inclination down by the bow—more than *Walrus* had ever experienced before, or I either, even counting in *S-16* and her Polish crew. I hoped we could take it, mentally resolved to drill at steeper-than-usual angles if we ever got the chance.

Quin was struggling to his feet, still clutching his injured arm.

"Test depth, Captain?" he said through strained, bloodless lips.

This was from Tom. Our decision, made some time ago, was automatically to go to full-test submergence in situations like this. Tom would not have had to ask, unless he anticipated possibly exceeding it.

Our hull, we knew, had a large safety factor of strength. This was, if there ever was to be, the time we had to use some of it. The answer I gave Quin brought a startled look to his face before he relayed it.

Down *Walrus* plunged, the depth-gauge needle spinning rapidly. The conning-tower gauge went only to one hundred fifty feet. When it reached one hundred forty I reached over and closed the valve in the waterline for fear of breaking the delicate mechanism. We could hear the rushing sound of water streaming past us. The power we were putting into our propellers was beginning to take effect.

"Two hundred feet!" said Quin. Our down angle remained rock-steady.

"Two hundred fifty feet!" The angle was still steady. Tom was really carrying out instructions. Finally he began to ease her off, until, without slackening speed, the ship became nearly level. Her whole frame now shook and trembled as she tore through the water. Something carried away topside and I heard a rattling, banging noise for a moment. Then it stopped.

I bent over the sound receiver. O'Brien looked up, shook his head. He could hear nothing at this speed. I waited a few moments. We would run on like this for a couple of minutes, I thought, then slow down and try to creep away . . .

WHAM! Another depth charge.

WHAM! . . . WHAM! . . . WHAM! . . . Three more. Compared to our initiation these were nothing to worry about, but they did disturb the water again. Maybe, added to what had gone before, they gave us the chance we needed.

"Right full rudder!" I called to Oregon. He put his full strength into turning the wheel and the ship leaned slightly to starboard, opposite to her list during a surface turn. The gyro compass card began to spin rapidly.

"All ahead one third." This would quiet our thrashing propellers. With the speed we had already built up, the ship would coast a good distance. I picked up the telephone again.

"Tom," I called.

"Yes?"

"I didn't hear you blow negative. Is it blown?"

"It's blown!"

"Good! I want to slow down now, to as slow and quiet as you can run. We'll stay at this depth, and run as silently as we can. With the start we've had and the uproar in the water back there, this may be our chance!"

A submarine's natural habitat is the deep, silent depths of the sea. The deeper she can go, the safer she is, and with the comfortable shelter of hundreds of feet of ocean overhead the submariner can relax. Deep in the sea there is no motion, no sound, save that put there by the insane humors of man. The slow, smooth stirring of the deep ocean currents, the high-frequency snapping or popping of ocean life, even the occasional snort or burble of a porpoise are all in low key, subdued, responsive to the primordial quietness of the deep. Of life there is, of course, plenty, and of death too, for neither are strange to the ocean. But even life and death, though violent, make little or no noise in the deep sea.

So is it with the submarine, forced, for survival, to join those elemental children of nature who seek, always, for quietness. Noise means death. Quietness, in the primeval jungle of the sea, is next to slowness or stock-stillness, as a means of remaining alive. And deep in the black depths, where live only those deep-sea denizens who never see the light of the day, who never approach the surface, and for whom in reality, it does not exist, *Walrus* sought her succor. Deep below the surface, at the absolute limit of her designed depth, her sturdy hull strained and bowed under the unaccustomed compression, her steel ribs standing rigid against the fierce, implacable squeeze of millions of tons of sea water, inescapable, unyielding, *Walrus* struggled for her life. Her propellers were barely turning over, her sea valves and hull fittings were tightly shut against the deadly pressure, and no noise—no noise at all—could she make.

On the surface we could hear the sound of our adversary's screws moving about from one side to another as if with a definite plan, as if trying to cover all the possible areas we might be. But there were no more depth charges, and after a while the screws themselves quieted down, and all we could hear was the same sibilant hum, the area of higher—but undistinguishable—noise level, which had presaged the destroyer's attack upon us.

But *Walrus* was not to be fooled a second time. We remained at silent running and maximum depth the rest of the day, and it was long into the evening before we secured from depth-charge stations. The Jap destroyer apparently became satisfied with the evidence of our destruction, for he never did resume the attack. Gradually his betraying noise faded from our sonar equipment. We did not, however, trust ourselves to come back to periscope depth until long after sundown, and we did not surface until nearly midnight.

Our first day in the war zone had been long, hard, and nearly disastrous.

We took stock of our damage topside and below. Examination of the attack periscope showed the top glass cracked and the tube flooded; no hope for it. Our SJ radar, inefficient though it had been, had been a comfort in that no surface craft could get any closer than a couple of miles without alerting us. Now it, too, was gone. We had another periscope, slightly larger in diameter at the top than the attack periscope, but we had no other surface radar. Both losses were serious.

Superficial damage topside there was aplenty. All our radio antennae were gone and so were the stanchions to which they had been secured. There was a large hole in our main deck forward—approximately twenty square feet of wooden slats missing—testimony to the force and nearness of at least one depth charge. Our superstructure held a few dents, inconsequential, of course, and the three-inch gun on the main deck must have had a depth charge go off right on top of it, for the telescopic sights for both pointer and trainer were gone.

Below in the innards of the ship our four most important items of equipment were fortunately entirely undamaged. Our propellers and propeller shafts, which might have been bent or distorted by the force of the explosions were, so far as careful inspection could tell, perfectly sound. The main engines had suffered no damage whatever; the battery seemed all right, althought it indicated a very low resistance to ground and had a few cracked cell tops. A hot soldering iron drawn across the cracks, melting and resealing the mastic, and a thorough washing down with fresh water afterward, brought the insulation readings—our main concern—up again. And lastly, our torpedo tubes seemed to have apparently suffered no damage. But quite a few other items had been put out of action for the rest of the patrol. The fire in the after torpedo room had been in the stern plane motor, ruining it. Until we returned to port our stern planes would have to be operated by hand power—not an easy task. The trim pump, cracked right across the heavy steel housing and knocked off its foundation, was beyond repair; we would have to cross-connect the drain pump to the trim line and make shift with it as well as we might. One air compressor was also cracked across one of its foundation frames and could not be used. The other was still intact; if we were careful it would provide us with enough compressed air to remain operational.

There were also several persons slightly injured, among them Quin and Hugh Adams, and we had one case of smoke inhalation from the after torpedo room. None of the injuries was serious, however, and all the men were soon back to duty. And after thoroughly looking the ship over, it was apparent we could stay on patrol.

During the remainder of that first night, from midnight to dawn, we worked feverishly against time to get things back in shape enough for *Walrus* to dive. The radar and the stern plane motor were probably our two most serious losses, and we wasted hours on both of them before admitting defeat.

But the ship as a whole was undamaged. We searched for evidence of cracks in her hull or dents where a too-close depth charge might have caved in her skin. There were none of any kind, despite plenty of mute evidence of the closeness of the explosions. I wrote in our patrol report:

Thorough inspection of the vessel indicates no further structural damage. The hull appears to have stood up very well. Our fervent thanks to the workers at Electric Boat who built this wonderful ship for us.

I meant every word of it.

It took us four days of steady labor, working submerged all day long, surfacing at night for battery charging and accomplishment of such topside repairs as were necessary. One immediate problem was the fact that all radio antennae had been swept clean off the ship. Before we could communicate with our home base we would have to get up some kind of jury rig. The lifeline around the cigarette deck was commandeered, as well as a few sections from one of the torpedo-loading tools and a spare hatch lanyard which we happened to have, and under Kohler's direct supervision—he being the only man aboard who had ever done any wire-splicing—a short, patched antenna wire was spliced together. During our second night of repairs we got it up and were able to receive messages, but it was apparent that we would not be able to send any until much closer to Pearl Harbor.

We had moved into a far corner of AREA SEVEN during the critical period of making repairs, and had seen no vessel of any kind, for which, under the circumstances, we were thankful. Finally on the fourth day, weary from our almost incessant labors but well recovered, we stood back in toward the Bungo Suido, stationing ourselves in the second of the four positions we had selected for surveillance of that harbor. For a week more we remained in essentially the same locality, sighting nothing. Jim and I renewed our argument.

"Let's get in to the coast, skipper," he pleaded. "We know they're going by close inshore. It is quite possible that that Jap destroyer did not report us as a sure kill, and, if not, that could be their reason for not sending any more ships out this way."

Finally I gave in, and we proceeded cautiously to a place Jim had picked some distance south of the Bungo, where coastwise traffic would have to make a jog to seaward to double a projecting point of land.

Our first day there also was fruitless, except for a number of fishing boats, which we kept clear of. On the second a small freighter hove in sight, chuffing a large cloud of dirty smoke from her single tall stack. Jim bared his teeth with a curious grimace when I described the target to him.

"Let me see, skipper," he begged. I stepped aside out of the periscope circle, motioning to him to take a look. I watched his face carefully as the base of the periscope came up and he put his eye to the eye guard.

"Bearing—Mark!" he said. "Range—Mark! Down 'scope!"

Rubinoffski dutifully read off the data, and Keith checked to see if it agreed with what the TDC generated. Jim grinned as he turned to me—a hard, tight grin.

"This fellow's our meat." His eyes were dancing as he reached for the Is-Was.

Our spot had been well chosen; the hapless vessel blundered into our trap and was saluted with a salvo of three torpedoes, one of which struck home. It was the first time I had ever seen a ship sink.

To my surprise there was something of sadness and grace about the submissive way the clumsy old freighter bowed her angular head under the waves, put her dirty stern to the sky and gently slid under. Several lifeboats, some debris, and half a dozen bobbing heads remained behind, and as we moved clear the men in the lifeboats were busy hauling the survivors aboard. Only a few miles from shore, they would be safe by nightfall.

It was several days more before we sighted another vessel; it went by too rapidly and was too far out of range. Then a week passed and we saw another lone ship. As before we worked into position, fired a three-fish salvo. The torpedoes ran perfectly, as far as we could see, and the target saw their wakes only a split second before they got there. We saw the streak of vapor from his funnel, although to whom he might have been signaling was hard to determine—and, for some unaccountable reason, the torpedoes missed.

Unexplained misses had been the subjects of some heated arguments among submarine skippers. Torpedoes which seemed to run in all respects exactly as they should, somehow frequently failed to hit the target. There were complaints that they were not running straight; that the gyros were not steering them correctly; that the TDC's were inaccurate; or that perhaps enemy vessels were not making the speed we thought they were. Another school of thought maintained the torpedoes were running below the targets; that Jap ships had been built with shallow draft for this very purpose. I had heard stories of torpedoes being set to run at two feet below the surface and still passing beneath a destroyer. It was hardly conceivable that such could be the case, but these were the facts and now *Walrus* had a case of her own to add.

— 199

Perhaps it was the cumulative reports of our activities in AREA SEVEN or perhaps the report of our near-hit by the last ship we attacked. At any rate, search as we might, we saw no more Japanese vessels, and during the latter part of August we passed through the Nanpo Shoto, heading eastward en route to base. "Base" in this case turned out to be Midway Island, and loud were the groans of disappointment from the crew when the location of our refit was announced.

CHAPTER 8

MIDWAY, ALTHOUGH LISTED AS one of the Hawaiian Island chain, is actually a coral reef containing two small islands, the larger of which is also known as Midway. Its chief inhabitants, until the Navy came along, were hundreds of thousands of gooney birds. People who had to spend time on Midway were known for their perverse refusal to appreciate the beauties of nature to which they were being exposed. After a man had been a while on Midway, the story goes, he both thought and acted like a gooney bird.

But we were to be spared this after all. Two days out of Midway, as flights of the albatross circled lazily about overhead, orders arrived directing us to stop only long enough to pick up our mail, which had already been forwarded there, and continue on to Pearl. Our consumption of fresh water for bathing purposes instantly tripled.

As we entered Pearl Harbor I looked over the scene with interest. Battleship row was minus one battleship: *West Virginia* had at last been towed away for repair. *California* would be next. I searched the Navy Yard as we passed it. At the far end, next to an empty dry dock, looming among the forest of cranes in all her battered majesty, bulked the unmistakable silhouette of a carrier. I gasped. She could only be the *Enterprise*. Her presence in Pearl Harbor must be a huge secret. *Saratoga,* I knew, was undergoing repair in Puget Sound. *Lexington, Wasp, Yorktown,* and *Hornet* had all been sunk in action. The Big E was our last effective flattop.

We put into the same dock from which we had set forth, almost exactly two months before, and this time the crowd and the band and the welcoming committee were all for us. Among the throng I soon spotted Admiral Small and Captain Blunt, watching us gravely as Jim warped us alongside. Nearly everyone looked at our battle scars with awe, but my old skipper gave me only a few moments to get used to their questioning glances. "Rich," he said almost as soon as we had shaken hands, "where's your patrol report?"

"Down below, Commodore—I mean, Captain," I said, clumsily retracting the courtesy title which had gone with his old job. "It's ready for the mimeograph machines."

"Give it to me right away, will you? I'll read it right off the stencil, if your Yeoman didn't put a carbon back-up in his mill."

I sent Dave for the stencils. Blunt took the parcel and turned immediately to leave the ship. "Rich, we're very interested in the dispatch you sent after you got near enough to Midway to transmit. I can see why you weren't able to before." There was something like respect in his rasping voice. "I want to talk to you right away. Come up to my office in the administration building as soon as you can."

The Admiral approached, with Eddie Holt behind him. "Congratulations again, Rich," said ComSubPac. "You took quite a beating out there. I'm surprised you were able to remain on station. I want you and Blunt to get together immediately. Maybe he'll bring you in to see me later, and anyway, we'll see you at dinner tonight in my quarters at Makalapa." He saluted and followed Captain Blunt over the side.

Eddie lingered behind. "Did anybody tell you you're going into dry dock, Rich?" he asked.

"Nope. When?"

"Right now. They're waiting on you. Maybe you saw the empty dock as you stood in. Dry docks around here don't stay empty for long."

"You mean, next door to the *Enter*——"

"Shhh!" Eddie looked startled. "Can that! Don't breathe that name around here! Better get the word to your crew, too, if you noticed her as you came in. She's Top Secret, and red hot. But that's where you're going, all right! We want you to get over there right now, before sending anybody off the ship or anything. You can do all you have to do after you get there. We promised you'd be out in three days, just long enough for a quick bottom job. We'll inspect you for underwater damage, too!"

"Dammit, Eddie, Old Man Blunt wants me. How'm I going to do both?"

"That's your problem, Rich. But if you don't get this beat-up bucket of yours into that dry dock in an hour, they're coming after me with a club. I had to swear upon my sacred honor and put up my wife's virtue as security that I'd have you there. We have a hell of a time getting dry-dock space, you know. You'd think we were in a different Navy. You gotta go!"

Eddie Holt's urgency was not to be denied, and there was a

way out. I had been turning it over in my mind for some days, and though my hand was forced, in a way, this was as good a time as any to spring it. "Jim," I said, "I've got business with the Chief of Staff. Get the ship under way and put her in the dry dock. I'll meet you over there."

Jim's face showed astonishment for a moment, then lighted as he realized that I meant it. A few minutes later I stood on the dock and watched *Walrus* get under way. It was the first time she had moved anywhere without me—even though someone else might have been doing the actual maneuvering, giving the orders, I was there, on the bridge, ready to jump in and take over if an emergency developed. I had become used to the idea that she could not move without me, and I was suddenly conscious of the most peculiar feeling, an indescribable sort of premonition, as she backed slowly away.

Premonition or not, *Walrus* seemed under excellent control as she maneuvered in the harbor channel. I watched her from the dock until she went out of sight, then turned away, and a few minutes later I was walking up the steps to ComSubPac's headquarters and opened the door marked "Chief of Staff."

"Lieutenant Commander Richardson," I said to the neatly dressed Yeoman seated at the desk.

"Yes, sir?" he began, "may I help you?" Then he leaped to his feet. "Oh, you're the Captain of the *Walrus!* The Chief of Staff is waiting for you." He led me through the next door into the inner office. "Commanding Officer, *Walrus,*" he announced.

I knew Captain Blunt well enough to skip the formalities. "Have you a pair of binoculars handy, sir?" I asked him. "I'd like to look out of your window for a minute to see how Jim's doing."

"Here!" Blunt opened a drawer in his desk. "What's up?" He grinned when I told him.

"That's an old submarine trick, Rich," he said. "Every skipper comes to it some time." He winked. "You know, things move pretty fast during war, and the tension of war patrol is just about the best test of a man's qualifications there is. I don't think there'll be any more Qualification for Command boards—at least, for the duration."

"You mean, it's up to me entirely?" I asked him.

"Yes. If you say your Exec is qualified for command of a submarine, we'll take your word for it and make the necessary notifications. All you have to do is write us a letter to make it official." He sucked his pipe.

"I'd like to recommend Jim, then," I said without hesitation. "He's had the seasoning he needed, and he'll make an outstanding skipper."

"Write a letter to ComSubPac and it's done!" Blunt stood beside me, watching *Walrus* move out past the tug berths and round the tip of ten-ten dock. She was making slow speed, staying under good control. Only the show-off goes racing around a crowded harbor with a big ship. If you have to cut loose, the time and place is at sea, where it might make the difference between victory and defeat. Blunt nodded in approbation as *Walrus* went out of our sight, then swung to me.

"Rich," he said, sucking on the inevitable unlighted pipe, "I suppose you're wondering why we changed your orders and had you come here for refit instead of Midway."

"I thought perhaps it was the dry-docking," I suggested.

"Partly, but that's not the main reason. I want to talk to you about that destroyer which depth-charged you—you stated in your dispatch and patrol report both that you got a close look at him before he worked you over. What was he like?"

I moved to the edge of my chair. "I got only the most fleeting look at him—well-deck forward, two fat stacks close together, bridge rounded in front with portholes in it."

"Not *Momo* class?"

"All three had a section cut out of the forecastle to form a well-deck—I was pretty sure the first two were of the small *Momo* class, though we never were very close to either of them. This one was probably the stern-most escort, and he was somewhat different, bigger, I thought."

Captain Blunt made notes with a pencil as I spoke. "What about his tactics? Anything odd or strange about them?"

"Only that he was waiting for us when we came up. He must have silenced his machinery, because we couldn't hear anything until after he saw us."

Blunt looked grave. "This is important, Rich. Are you sure he was not running machinery until after he sighted you? Could you have been below a temperature layer or some other unusual water stratum which could have prevented you from hearing him?"

"Nothing that we had any evidence of, Captain. Besides, we didn't hear him after we had practically reached periscope depth, either. And our sonarman swears he heard him start his engines."

Blunt made more notes. "This is extremely significant. You should have mentioned this in your report. What else?"

Slightly on the defensive because of the vague accusation of his last comment, I wracked my brains to find further details. "Well," I finally said, "there were at least fifty men on lookout watch with binoculars——"

"Wait a minute!" Old Blunt was writing rapidly. "Fifty men, all with binoculars? You did say something about there being an unusually large number of lookouts."

"They were all over his decks. A dozen on the wings of the bridge, a large group on the forecastle, more clustered around his stacks on a sort of deckhouse amidships, and still more around a searchlight platform, or whatever it was, back aft."

"All with glasses, you say?" still writing on the scratch pad. "It's most unusual for a ship that size to carry that many binoculars."

"Yes, so far as I could see." I was still wondering what the cause was for the particular interest in our first depth-charging, although, granted, it had been a terrifying experience.

"Anything else? You said you were close enough to see clearly on to the bridge. Did you get a look at anyone special on the bridge? Were there any white men there?—or anywhere?"

I stared at him. "No, sir. I got a quick look at a lot of people, but they were all Japanese."

"Rich, needless to say, you'll keep all this to yourself. It's probably no surprise to you that we and the British are carefully monitoring German broadcasts. Day before yesterday the British picked up one in which the German people were told that their great allies in the Far East had just sunk the second American submarine in two weeks, south of the Bungo Suido, and that this should be taken as evidence of the effectiveness of the cooperation already existing between the two countries. We were wondering whether you might have seen any German officers on Pete's bridge."

"Pete's bridge?"

"Bungo Pete's. That's who you ran into for your first brush with the enemy, Rich. You're luckier than you have any idea of. Exactly a week before you entered AREA SEVEN, the *Needle-fish* was due out of there. We never heard from her."

The *Needlefish!* Roy Savage's boat, the one to which he had received orders immediately after Jim's qualification fiasco!

"It's a tough war, Rich. Savage was a fine skipper, and the *Needlefish* was a fine submarine. She was one of the new Mare Island boats, and her first two patrols were outstanding."

"You don't know what happened to Roy?"

"Not a thing, until this dispatch from Washington relaying the dope from the German broadcast monitors. Bits of wood and other debris came to the surface in both cases, and in the second case the submarine attempted to surface and surrender, but couldn't make it." Blunt looked quizzically at me, and suddenly I realized what I had been slow to catch on about.

"You mean, we're the other boat!"

"Right, Rich. Not only that, they know it was the *Walrus.* Bungo always seems to know the name of his victims. He knew he had sunk the *Needlefish,* too." He chewed reflectively on his pipe. "It's of course vital to us to find out whether or not the Germans are actively helping the Japs with their antisubmarine campaign. God knows they've had their chance to learn which techniques of ours are the most damaging."

I nodded with dawning comprehension. "Who's in AREA SEVEN right now?"

"Your old side-kick, Stocker Kane!"

"Is he all right?" I couldn't help the question; it slipped out without conscious volition.

"So far as we know he is. He got a ship the first week he was in there, and one other since, I think. We're going to pull him out in a couple of days and shift him to Australia."

Mentally I crossed my fingers. "Will we be going back to AREA SEVEN again after he leaves?"

"Nope. If Bungo Pete is that good, it's time we let him waste some energy just looking for a while. We haven't enough submarines to cover all the areas yet anyhow."

Some time later a jeep swung me into the Pearl Harbor Navy Yard. It was some little distance, around an arm of the bay, and on down to the far end of the yard to where *Walrus* presumably was already settled down on the dry-dock keel blocks. We could see the *Enterprise,* also in dry dock, in the one next to ours. I looked her over with interest as we approached. This was the only carrier left in commission in the U. S. Navy, not counting *Saratoga,* laid up in the Bremerton Navy Yard with a hole in her side, and *Ranger,* still, for some reason, held back from the fighting zone. New carriers were coming, true, but none of them had yet hit the Pacific.

Enterprise, Yorktown, and the new *Hornet* had won the Battle of Midway against startling odds, and *Enterprise* was now the only one left.

"The Japs would give a lot to know your whereabouts, old girl," I thought as I looked her over. "You're supposed to be in the South Pacific." The situation down there, according to the newspapers and radio broadcasts, was just about a stand-off, with two big Jap carriers to our one, neither side anxious to risk an all-out fight. Little did they know the true facts! We dared not risk a fight, for we certainly could not afford to lose the Big E, as she was affectionately known. The enemy, on the other hand, had already felt her sting, and knew that she could easily take care of both of theirs if they took their fingers off them.

But *Enterprise* needed replenishment and repairs, just like any other ship. Hence, no doubt, her presence here in Pearl. Equally certain, she would depart unannounced, at full speed, probably in the dead of night so that concealed watchers from the hills of Hawaii or skulking Japanese submarines would not see her.

My mind drifted thus, watching her bulk grow as the jeep approached. There must have been a thousand men crowded all over her topsides, probably an equal number below decks, all engaged in different tasks, all working like men possessed. Every man of her crew and every man in the Navy Yard must realize what this ship meant to the United States at this particular instant of time. I was daydreaming, looking at her long gray side, when I saw a large puff of smoke spew up from the dry dock amidships.

Everything stood still for a second. I failed to comprehend the significance of it until another puff of smoke joined the first, and then a black cloud commenced to boil out of the dock around the carrier's underbody, racing up, partly obscuring her side and reaching high—in a few seconds—into the heavens.

"Driver! She's on fire!" I was sitting in the front seat, alongside the sailor-driver loaned to me by the ComSubPac motor pool, but I shouted nevertheless. He didn't answer, merely pressed the accelerator to the floor.

"Forget the *Walrus!* Take me over there!" I yelled.

This time he answered. "Aye, aye, sir." We stared, with horror in our faces, at the impending catastrophe.

The road along which we were gunning the jeep did not permit us to approach the dry dock directly. We had to run until we were dead ahead of the carrier, her bow pointed right at us—zero angle on the bow, in submarine parlance—before we could turn in, bumping and swaying on the unpaved road, hanging on to the car for all we were worth. Once I nearly flew out of it, clutched the windshield and roof bar grimly to save myself.

The *Enterprise* had gone to fire quarters. Streaming all over her topsides like thousands of ants, uncoiling hoses, bringing fire buckets, carrying fire extinguishers, her crew had gone into action like the veterans they were. A veritable army raced across the gangway and plunged down into the smoke and gloom now shrouding her bottom.

"Other side!" I snapped. The jeep driver had made as if to head for the gangway. There were ample men there to do what could be done. On the other side, however, the starboard side, there was no gangway, and so far as I could see, no one fighting the fire.

We had approached close enough to see fairly well into the dry dock. I saw a tongue of flame shoot out through the smoke, licking the smoothly rounded side of the ship. Swiftly it scorched its way upward. The black paint of her bottom peeled, hung in shreds, and vanished as the fire hit it. Within seconds the flame had reached gray paint and was mounting the side, up above the waterline.

Hanging over the bow of the flight deck in a boatswain's chair was a man with what looked like a pot of paint hooked to the side of the seat. The fire had developed so swiftly that he still held the paint brush in his hand, and as I looked a section of the fire seemed to leap through the air and seize the rope on which the chair hung. The speeding jeep's motor was loud, the roar of the fire and the shrill cries of the fire fighters louder still, yet I almost could hear the poor fellow's scream of terror.

On the flight deck someone began to haul up the line. The ridiculous, dumpy, gesticulating figure advanced by short jerks, a few feet at a time. The tongue of flame had disappeared, but a thin wisp of smoke issued from the rope near where it divided into two strands to form a bridle for the boatswain's chair. The paint brush was now gone, the paint pot wobbled spasmodically with the successive heaves from the man on the flight deck. I could visualize the latter's yells for assistance, his desperate single-handed try to beat the insidious corrosion of the smoldering hemp.

The helpless figure in the chair at the end of the line waved his arms more rapidly, more frantically, and suddenly the jerky motion of the line ceased, and he rose smoothly, quickly, speedily. Evidently three or four other men had tailed on to the line and had run away with it. Eager hands stretched forth over the edge of the flight deck—but first the damaged section of the line would have to run across the deck edge . . .

The jeep had straightened out, was proceeding down the starboard side of the ship by this time, but I turned half-around, craned my neck to see the finish of the drama: "Stop!" I shouted. "Stop! You can't make it! Pass him the good part of the line to grab hold of!"

Startled, the driver of the jeep slammed the brakes, skidded to a stop, and killed the engine. I lurched against the dash, leaped out of it. He followed, and the hasty indrawn breath over my shoulder told me that he too had taken in the danger. Even as we watched, the action reached its climax. The still-smoking section of rope passed over the deck edge, still under heavy strain from the sailors sprinting down the deck with it, and parted. The man in the sling had just reached the edge of the flight deck—I could have sworn at least one of the several pairs of hands reaching for him through the lifelines touched his own outstretched ones—and, clutching, clawed empty air.

For a long moment the tableau remained static; the man in the sling, the broken end of the line to it flipped into the air, the unseen men reaching for him. Then, swiftly, with terrible certitude, the doomed figure plunged downward. The arms and legs remained rigid, fixed in the pattern they had last assumed. There was no point in struggling more, and he knew it, but there wasn't time, nor awareness, to assume a more dignified posture. There was time only to scream, to expend all his breath in a last hopeless denial of what was happening to him, to scream a piercing, shrieking terror all the way down until his slowly revolving body, still tangled in the boatswain's chair which had trapped him, vanished into the smoke which mercifully shrouded the concrete floor of the dry dock.

This time I heard it, all the way, including the sloppy splash which put a period to it.

Shaken, I turned away and nearly stumbled over my jeep driver. He was doubled over, retching.

A quick look at the carrier—just in time to see a flash of flame under her bottom. There was no one anywhere around on this side. *Enterprise* was concentrating her fire fighting on the other, the port side. No doubt the fire was worse there, but it was bad here, too. Down at the bay end of the dock was a small structure, perhaps a fire house of some kind. "Come on!" I yelled, smacking the vomiting sailor on the rump.

Without really thinking about it, I hoped the unceremonious salutation would help him get over his sickness. It did. Wiping his lips with his white jumper sleeve, he jumped back into the jeep while I duplicated the move on the other side. We covered the three hundred yards to the little building in nothing flat. We were in luck; it was not a fire house, but an emergency dock pumping station, nearly as good. The door was locked, but the jeep's bumper took care of that. Madly we began to unreel hose. It was a monumental task for two men to get the equipment laid out, let alone start the pumping engine, and I had not really made any thoughtful plan of action. All I was conscious of was that the cloud of smoke was reaching ever higher into the sky, and that I could not only see fire but also feel the heat of it along the side of the threatened ship.

One end of the hose, the suction end, would have to go into the water of the harbor—just beyond the dry-dock gate would be the closest place. But the pumper had been made to pump the dock dry in emergency, not take a suction from outside it, and the suction hose was too short. It reached no closer than five feet of the water. I stood there wondering what to do next, when I felt an authoritative hand take it from me, and a familiar voice say, "Here, Captain, let's hook this to it!"

The voice was Kohler's, and I was never so glad to see anyone in my life. He carried another section of hose over his shoulder and several odd-shaped metal fittings in his hands. One of them spanned the joint between the two dissimilar hoses, and in about two minutes we had a suction line of beautifully scrubbed white hose drinking thirstily of the filthy, oily waters of the harbor.

I hadn't given thought, either, as to how the suction got started, but it was explained when we arrived back at the pumping station, for there stood Tom Schultz with Wilson, his leading Motor Machinist's Mate. The pump was churning up at a great rate, and more familiar faces were manning the nozzle, jumping down into the smoke of the dry dock, carrying tools, axes, carbon dioxide, fire extinguishers, and seemingly dozens of other pieces of paraphernalia. I lost myself in the mad swirl of events. Things happened in a kaleidoscopic sequence, and there is only one firm recollection of the remainder of that afternoon—the moment we could find no more fire to fight.

Jim was a sight, when I finally got a chance to talk calmly with him. He was splattered with black oil and completely soaked with dirty water. His trousers up to his knees were covered with black ooze from the bottom of the dock, and his shoes were filthy. I was not much better off. The fresh khakis we had put on only a few hours ago, in preparation for our return from patrol—how long ago that now seemed!—were completely ruined.

"Some day, eh Jim? Thank God you were able to get off the ship when you did!"

Jim grinned. "We had a hell of a time. The crane operator was going to leave us right then and there, with our big gangway in mid-air when the fire broke out. It took some quick talking to make him take the time to set it in place for us."

"How did you do it?"

"I let myself down into the dock with a rope, once *Walrus* was down solid on the blocks, and swam ashore." The light was dancing again in Jim's eyes, and he slammed his right fist into the palm of his left hand. I noticed the knuckles were bruised.

Following my look, Jim chuckled again. "He did take a little persuasion, but it was worth it. First time I've ever poked a guy that high in the air!"

"Good Lord, Jim! You didn't climb up into his cab—?" I let the sentence die. Jim grinned again by way of answer.

We were approaching the heavy steel-and-wood gangway which spanned the distance from the side of our dry dock to *Walrus'* deck. A group of our crew was already gathered there, and more were straggling in. I used the opportunity to tell Jim of my interview with Captain Blunt and of his own impending qualification for command of submarines.

It was quite a long gangway, and *Walrus* lay propped upright many feet below us. "You'll have to draft the letter," I was finishing, "that can be your initiation to one of the more prosaic problems of command." My gaze wandered to our ship, resting sedately in the now-pumped-out dry dock. There was no one to be seen on her decks. She was bare, deserted. Not even a gangway watch.

"Jim!" I ejaculated, as I took it in, "didn't you leave a duty section aboard?"

— 214

"No, sir!" He looked me evenly in the eye. "I pulled them all off, every one! Right now there's not a soul down there!"

"You know what the Navy regulations say about that?"

"You're Goddamed right I do! We were on the keel blocks and shored up. That part was done. This was an emergency—that carrier is the most important ship in the Navy, right now, and I don't give a hoot in hell what the regulations say, and you can forget the qualification, too!" The defiant look had come back. He put his hands on his hips, waiting.

"Jim," I said honestly, "you're absolutely right. I'd have done the same thing." I didn't know whether I could have or not, but there was no question that the Navy could much better spare both me and the *Walrus* than it could the *Enterprise*. Considering the stakes at issue, the personal risk to myself as Commanding Officer—or to Jim, since he had, in an unofficial way, temporarily relieved me—was as nothing compared to the larger importance of preserving our only effective aircraft carrier.

I grinned at him. "But now that the fire's out, let's get a watch section down in the ship before somebody comes and starts asking a lot of embarrassing questions."

Jim grinned back. "Roger!" he said.

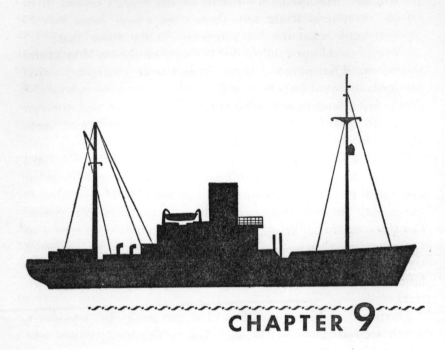

CHAPTER 9

THE SYSTEM EVOLVED BY COM-
SubPac gave us two weeks of freedom in the Royal Hawaiian
Hotel. A "relief crew," complete with skipper—my old friend
Eddie Holt—who came with orders detaching me temporarily
so that not even legal responsibility for *Walrus* remained, took
over the ship in its entirety. They would see to the completion of our outstanding work items, clean the ship thoroughly
after the refit, stand all necessary watches, and turn *Walrus*
back to us as good as new. In the meantime, for two weeks the
whole gang of us, crew and officers alike, were billeted in lux-
ury and had nothing to do except lie on the sand or sample the
other pleasures of Waikiki Beach.

Jim and I, as skipper and Exec, drew a corner suite with a sitting room between our two bedrooms. The place was nicely furnished, though it was apparent that some of the more delicate furnishings had been removed. Still tacked to the inside of the door was a card giving the prewar rates. Our suite, we immediately noticed, had gone for seventy-five dollars a day. We had been assessed a payment, ostensibly for linen, of one dollar per day each. Our crew, billeted in another wing, got theirs for twenty-five cents a day.

A long, soaking hot bath felt wonderful, after our workout in the fire, and so did the stacks of personal mail which had arrived for everyone. I had several from my mother telling of the doings of the little town in which I had spent my boyhood and of the difficulties of the ration system. There was a note from Stocker Kane, hoping we would meet somewhere in the Pacific, written just before departing on his first patrol; and Hurry, his wife, had also written.

Hurry Kane's letter was chatty and friendly. She occupied herself with war work, had joined the "Gray Ladies," took a turn at serving out coffee and doughnuts at the San Francisco USO, rolled bandages three days a week, and in general kept as busy as she could. She made no mention of her loneliness for Stocker, but it was there between the lines—the very fact that she had written to me at all, for the first time after our years of closer-than-average acquaintance, showed that.

The thing which most excited my interest was a paragraph halfway through her letter. "I saw quite a bit of Laura Bledsoe after you all left New London," she wrote. "Poor girl, having Jim go off to war so soon after they were married was pretty rough on her. She stayed on in the Mohican Hotel for several days—just didn't seem to know what to do with herself. When she came over to the apartment to help me pack and follow Stocker—that was only the next week—I really felt sorry for her. You men will never be able to understand how it feels to be left behind."

I debated whether to mention the passage in Hurry's letter to Jim. There was no reason why I should not, I thought, picking it up. I crossed the sitting room, pushed open the door to Jim's room, found him sitting half-naked on his bed, smoking a cigarette, with mail strewn all around him. He had received much more than I, and among the pile were many in identical blue envelopes. "How's Laura?" I asked him.

"Fine. She's back at her job in New Haven." Jim stretched his arms, stubbed his cigarette, and flopped back into the pillow. Most of his mail, including several of the blue envelopes, was still unopened and, carelessly pitched on the bed, was now crumpled beneath him. "What's that you've got there?" He wasn't interested, merely making conversation.

"I just heard from Stocker Kane," I side-stepped with a half-truth. "He might go to Australia, you know."

"The lucky stiff! One of my buddies from sub school is down there on the staff. He says there are twice as many women as men around, and they're all starved for affection. He's doing his best to help them out, and it keeps him pretty busy." Jim stretched his arms to either side again, looked up at the ceiling. "Let's us try to get sent down there, too, skipper. He can't handle all of that stuff by himself."

"There are probably twice as many women trying to stay out of your friend's reach as there are cooperating with his campaign to keep them from being affection-starved," I growled. I stuffed the letter into a pants pocket.

The Royal Hawaiian was wonderful. Three free meals a day, hours of lying in the sun, surf-boarding, playing billiards, wandering around the streets of Waikiki—it was the ideal life, a wonderful rest. After twenty-four hours of it we were bored stiff.

I took to spending hours in the submarine base, watching the operations board, reading the dispatches as they came in, wandering around the *Walrus,* and watching the progress of the work on her—much to the annoyance of Eddie Holt, who as Relief Commanding Officer was serving his apprenticeship for his own command. I had wondered why it was that there were so many people always out to welcome every submarine in from patrol or from the States, and likewise to see them off. After I had met my third I ceased to wonder.

Jim's reaction was nearly the same as mine, except that I did not see him much around the submarine base. He took to disappearing for long periods "in town," as he put it. And the rest of our crew went their own ways, each according to his own instincts and desires. Hugh and Keith, lively young fellows that they were, quickly found friends among the families still living in their homes in the Moano Valley, Waikiki proper, or elsewhere in the vicinity. And nearly every time I happened to be in town I would run into a *Walrus* sailor or sailors—sometimes in pairs, more frequently accompanied by a heavily tanned Hawaiian belle.

Despite the fact that he and I shared a suite, I practically never saw Jim at all during the last week of our "recuperation period." But the mystery was explained when the submarine base threw one of its monthly dances on the BOQ terrace, and Jim showed up with a girl whom he introduced as Joan Lastrada.

She was dark, with masses of black hair, deeply tanned, and very slender. Her face was rather too thin, I thought, giving her full sensual lips an almost outsized appearance. The dance was one of those difficult affairs where there are at least ten men to every woman, and it was hard to get away from the determined stag line. I cut in on Jim once myself, nearly gasped aloud when Joan stepped into my arms from Jim's reluctantly released embrace.

It was not only her lips that were sensual, I decided, after someone else had taken her away. She was sensual all over. Jim gave her new partner less than half a dozen steps before he claimed her back, and then he led her into a corner as far removed from the stag line as possible. But keeping Joan undiscovered must have been about as hard to do as keeping a gold mine under wraps, and the determined stags, conspicuously Keith and Hugh, gave him no peace. Half an hour before the party had been scheduled to break up, I realized Jim and Joan were no longer there.

Walrus was not quite the same when we moved back aboard —more of the bridge superstructure had been removed and a 20-millimeter gun had been installed at either end of it. The Admiral was of the opinion that we should be able to take care of ourselves in case we ran into one of the wooden armed sampans which had been appearing in ever-increasing numbers around the home-island waters of Japan. Some of the boats had been replacing their three-inch antiaircraft deck gun with a broadside four-inch or five-inch also.

Our Operation Order this time directed *Walrus* to proceed to Dutch Harbor for briefing, and thence to Kiska, which was to be our patrol area. The Japs had landed at Kiska and Attu and attacked Dutch Harbor at the same time as they had made their attempt on Midway. There were those who even claimed that the Midway attack was a feint, and that the real objective of the enemy the whole while had been to gain a foothold in the Aleutians. This was a bit hard to believe, considering the size of the fleet he had sent to take Midway, but the theory sounded plausible to some.

The evening before *Walrus* got under way, I had dinner again with Captain Blunt and the Admiral in the latter's quarters in Makalapa, as the Navy housing area was termed. Several other officers were also present, two of them skippers of boats just in from Australia. The talk was desultory, mainly anecdotal, but through it all ran a grim undercurrent. The United States, recognizing Germany as the principal menace, was indeed devoting its strength and resources to the ETO, just as President Roosevelt had said we would. We in the Pacific would have to wait our turn as patiently as we might. It was a hard outlook to be in sympathy with.

Things were rough indeed in Australia, according to the skippers just back from there. There was hardly a family but had one or more male members already in the war against the Axis before the Japanese struck. Now they felt defenseless, exposed, ripe for the plucking should the enemy make a determined effort. Our own Guadalcanal invasion, and the campaign in the Solomons, were their only hopes of staving off an invasion. From their point of view the Japanese had so far shown themselves invincible and were only a few miles away in Malaya, Sumatra, Java, and New Guinea.

It was with thoughtful concentration that I attacked the Operation Order next day, as Diamond Head faded over the horizon. The Japanese had landed on Kiska, and were presumably preparing for further conquests in the Aleutian area. Their supplies were undoubtedly being brought in by submarine and transport, though so far little was known about the size of this traffic. Our job would be to reconnoiter, report any suspicious or unusual movements—any movements of the enemy at all, in fact—and, of course, try to intercept as much of the supply traffic into and out of Kiska as we could.

The Operation Order went on to caution us that United States·fleet units also were operating in those waters, and that Japanese fleet units might well be expected. We were to attack immediately any unidentified war vessels encountered, having due care to the possibility of their being friendly and the necessity for adequate recognition signals. We would be informed, so the order said, of the proximity of any friendly vessels or planes.

It didn't seem to be a very satisfactory system to me, and still didn't after we had arrived at Dutch Harbor with the *Walrus*, and had our briefing as promised in the Operation Order. The idea of operating in the close proximity of our own forces, worrying—in addition to the normal quota of worry about the intentions and movements of the enemy—over what our own ships were doing, where they were going, and above all, whether they would be able to recognize us as friendly, was not too pleasing. We had all read entirely too many treatises about the manner of treating suspected submarine contacts: Full-scale all-out attack instantly, no waiting around. Said the doctrine, "The only good submarine is a dead one." Fine and dandy— but what if it had been on your side?

I need not have worried. The thirty days we spent patrolling off Kiska amounted to the most wasted month any submarine spent during the whole war. The weather was lousy; no other adjective could describe it. It was cold, freezing or nearly so, always rough except when very close into land, overcast, foggy or misty almost all of the time—and not once during the whole period did we sight an enemy ship.

Once our surface forces planned an assault, and a bombardment was carried out for several hours. We had hoped that some Japanese action might have been forthcoming as a result, that perhaps some ship might have attempted to escape or enter the harbor. And for a time, as we read the operation dispatches received, it appeared that we might be stationed in a position where such vessels would be forced to pass near enough to give us a chance for an attack. We had grown rusty in our attack procedure—tempers had flared over trifles, our daily drills had been performed perfunctorily; try as Jim and Keith might, they could not evoke interest in them, and my efforts along the same line produced little better result. Now, with the prospect of action to relieve the deadly boredom, we all took on a new incentive. For a week we drilled with a will, spent longer than usual at some of the operations which required polishing, overhauled the torpedoes once more, specially, so that there would be no hitches on their account, and then the whole thing, so far as we were concerned, fell apart into little useless pieces.

It must have been one of the last preparatory dispatches of

the operation, and Dave and Hugh's initial eagerness to decode it gave way, less than halfway through, to disgust. When finally typed in the smooth the message said:

WALRUS PROCEED TO POINT ONE HUNDRED MILES DUE SOUTH OF SOUTH-WEST CORNER KISKA RPT ONE HUNDRED MILES DUE SOUTH OF SOUTH-WEST CORNER KISKA X REMAIN ON SURFACE X FRIENDLY FORCES RE-QUIRE YOUR SERVICES NAVIGATION MARKER X DURING AND AFTER ASSAULT BE PREPARED TO VECTOR IN AND ASSIST SURVIVORS DAMAGED AIRCRAFT.

We didn't even have the satisfaction of seeing any of our surface units, the cruisers and old battleships, sweep by en route to the bombardment. It was nice weather, for Kiska, with visibility about five miles, and we knew when the task force went by because they told us by radio. But as far as seeing anything was concerned, the day was exactly like all the others we had spent in the area.

Jim's suggestion was probably about right: Our task-force commander, worried over the possibility of enemy submarines, must have insisted that the only U. S. submarine in the vicinity be withdrawn. If any submarines were to be detected, he didn't want to have to worry over recognition procedures before permitting his destroyers to do their stuff.

We went through the motions of the remainder of our time on station without further incident. Tempers grew short again, harsh words were exchanged and apologized for, and Russo wore himself out trying to inject a little variety in our monotonous existence. After a full month cruising aimlessly around Kiska, our radio brought not the release we had anticipated but a directive to remain for three days longer pending the arrival of the submarine sent from Pearl Harbor to relieve us.

Our relief was to be the *Cuttlefish,* one of the first fleet boats, antedating even the *Shark* and *Tarpon,* and notable primarily for her slow speed. The three extra days of waiting seemed particularly long to live through, and I remember strongly resenting the fact that we had to wait while she touched at Dutch Harbor for a briefing, just as we had. During the third day we edged over to the limit of our area, the closest point toward Pearl, and waited impatiently. When the notification arrived that *Cuttlefish* had at last arrived off Kiska, we were, within minutes, going south at full speed.

But the patrol had one good thing to be said for it: Almost from our departure from Pearl, I realized that Jim had changed at last. He seemed entirely his old relaxed self, and his support during the trying thirty days of inactivity off Kiska was heartening. I could sense it—almost touch the difference—and that contemplative awareness was gone.

This time there was no avoiding Midway. All of us could testify, after three weeks among the sand dunes, that even the gooney birds looked human.

As we completed the refit and prepared for our third patrol, new faces for the first time began to appear among our crew. A rotation policy had been set up whereby certain numbers of every crew were to be left ashore after each war patrol, with the looked-for result that the entire crew of men and officers would have been rotated after a reasonable number of patrol runs. Lobo Smith was gone, and so was Wilson, our Chief in Charge of the engine rooms. Tom had protested at losing his right bower, as he put it, but the needs of new construction back in the States took priority. A first-class Motor Machinist's Mate named Kiser was promoted into Wilson's shoes and Jim, after some inquiry, found the means to make him a Chief Petty Officer so that he could have the added rank and prestige to go with his new responsibilities.

Our officer complement remained the same, however, except that a new Ensign was ordered to us—and everybody except Jim and me received a promotion. Tom became a full Lieutenant; so did Keith. Hugh and Dave found their names in a promotion AlNav to the rank of Lieutenant, Junior Grade. Our new wardroom occupant was Jerry Cohen, fresh out of the submarine school and as green as grass. Though he had been sent to us for training—so said the ComSubPac Personnel Officer—it was obvious that he had to have a job and a battle station, and that some revision in our setup was therefore necessary.

Jim, Keith, and Tom, of course, stayed in their departments as before. Jerry Cohen, a short, slightly built lad, became assistant to Keith in the gunnery and torpedo department and took over Dave Freeman's chores with the commissary department. He also relieved Hugh on the navigational plot in the conning tower at battle stations, freeing that young man for direct help to Tom Schultz during such times.

We had two days of training, "refresher training" it was called—and then for two days more we loaded, fueled, and provisioned the ship. On the eighteenth day after arriving at Midway from our second war patrol, *Walrus* got under way for her third, bound this time for Palau and the area between it and New Guinea. As a matter of curiosity I had looked into the situation off the Bungo Suido, partly to see what Stocker had run into while there, and had found ample evidence of Bungo Pete's continuing effectiveness. The *Nerka,* somehow, had not met with him at all. Perhaps he had been otherwise occupied or under overhaul. But the next submarine in AREA SEVEN had been horribly knocked about and had to return to Midway for emergency repairs. And *Turbot,* the next one after that, had not been heard from for a long time and became one day overdue from patrol at the time of our own departure from Midway.

After the Aleutians, Palau was a pleasure cruise, warm and balmy, most of the nights star-lighted, the sea smooth. Except for one thing: where our Aleutian patrol had been notable for lack of activity, Palau gave us all we could handle, and then some, nor did it wait for our arrival.

We ran all the way to Palau on the surface, except for one

day spent submerged in the vicinity of Guam so as not to be detected by planes flying patrol from there. We crossed our area boundary at midnight, were speeding southwest in hopes of getting in sight of the main island, Babelthuap, before submerging for the day, when Jim called me to the bridge. I was up there within seconds. He had slowed down and we were swinging to the northward.

"There's a ship, Captain!" He pointed to the southern horizon. I had taken the precaution of keeping red goggles on whenever I went below at night, even when lying down for a few minutes' doze on my bunk. Hence I could see the object he was pointing out almost right away. It was a small vessel, short and stubby, with a lot of top hamper and a single tall, thin stack. A small freighter, alone and unprotected.

"Call the crew to battle stations torpedo, Jim," I ordered. He dashed below eagerly. A second later the musical chimes of the general alarm rang forth, and the scurrying of feet told me that *Walrus* was girding her loins for action. Tom came to the bridge, relieved Keith of the deck; the latter ran below to his TDC. On night surface action Tom had nothing to do unless we dived, hence we had decided that he would relieve whoever happened to have deck at the time, and back me up on the bridge as QOD.

This indeed seemed a good opportunity to try the night surface attack technique. Our SJ radar had been worked over and much improved during our last refit, and a talk-back circuit had been rigged up between the conning tower and the bridge so that I no longer had the nuisance of trying to shout down through the open hatch or of relaying orders and information by messenger or through the bridge speaker. Word would come up from Jim via the general announcing speaker, as before. In a moment it blared:

"Bridge, conn testing!" I picked up my mike: "Loud and clear, conn; how me?"

Jim's steady voice came back in reply: "I hear you the same!"

— 226

A few seconds later Jim again: "Bridge, the ship is at battle stations. No range yet to the target."

We were still too far for radar to get a return echo from the target. "Give him eight thousand yards," I called back. "Angle on the bow looks like starboard—about broadside—give him starboard ninety! Stand by for a TBT bearing." So saying, I jammed my binoculars into their socket on top of the instrument, twisted it around until the other ship loomed in the center of their field, and pressed the button. In the conning tower the relative bearing would appear on a dial repeater near the TDC, could be set into it exactly as a periscope bearing might. Similarly, Jerry Cohen would set it up on his plotting sheet.

Without radar ranges, a few bearings alone would give us an idea of the enemy's course and speed. If two of them could be paralleled by accurate ranges, we would have a definite solution, the essential information necessary for accurately angling our torpedoes.

The objective, of course, was to get the enemy's course and speed quickly, run in close and finish him off before he spotted the submarine or had other opportunity for escape. We were still making slow progress on our new course, to the north. To get a radar range it would be necessary to approach a little closer. "Jim, I'm going to change course toward the target to get within radar range," I called down, and directed Oregon to put the rudder full left, calling for more speed as I did so.

Snorting from her four aroused diesels, *Walrus* wheeled in the smooth water toward the enemy ship and began to close the range at an oblique angle.

"Radar contact!" The speaker blared beside me. Then Jim's steady voice. "We have him on the radar, Captain. Range six thousand. Give us a bearing!"

I went through the business of transmitting a TBT bearing below. Approximately a minute later I did the same thing again. In the conning tower they would get a range at the same instant, and the resulting plot would give us enemy course and speed, which was all we needed to know.

It was time to sheer out again, run on up ahead, attain our firing position, and get ready to let go our salvo; but this was where the roof caved in on us. I was looking at the target through my binoculars, had him clearly in my field of view, when suddenly his whole side erupted into light. At least four simultaneous flashes—two amidships, one on the bow and one on the stern. Seconds later there came a tearing whistle close overhead. As if by magic, four white blossoms appeared in the water, two alongside to starboard, one just astern, one a few feet ahead and to port. Foaming water deluged our forecastle. We had been trapped, as neatly as you please, and by the oldest trick in the book.

I fumbled frantically for the bridge diving alarm, pressed it hard, twice. "Clear the bridge!" I yelled. "Take her down!" Our vents popped, almost simultaneously. Air whistled out of them, casting thin geysers of vapor up through our deck slats. Our four lookouts tumbled down from their perches up on the shears and scuttled for the hatch, Tom right behind them. Our bow planes up forward, normally housed against the side of the ship while on the surface, began to turn out and down into the "rigged out" position for submerged operation.

I swung back to the enemy, just in time to catch the second salvo—a bit more ragged than the first. Four more white blossoms in the black ocean, no closer than before, thank God! He had some kind of salvo-fire system, and was no doubt firing as fast as he could reload his guns—in a way a fortunate circumstance for us. Also, I noticed, his length had decreased and he was stubbier than ever. Obviously he had turned toward, was racing for us as fast as his engines would drive him.

Our deck dipped, went under. I was the last man left on the bridge. Time for one last look—a third salvo coming—not at all together this time. The night was ripped again—once—twice—three times . . . "BLWHRURANGGG!" I saw nothing but stars and bright flashes. A hit! We had been hit! There was no other conscious thought. I was knocked against the side of the bridge, felt, rather than saw the open hatch to the conning tower yawning at my feet, Rubinoffski standing in the middle of the hole with the bronze lanyard gripped in his hand, the sea rushing up the side of the conning tower, gurgling and splashing. I lurched to it, sort of half-stumbled into the Quartermaster's arms, felt myself unceremoniously pushed aside and down as, intent upon only one thing, Rubinoffski jerked the hatch lid down with one hand, spun the dogging hand wheel with the other. Not a drop of water came in, but it could not have been far behind.

I would have landed head first on the deck at the foot of the ladder had not a couple of pairs of hands gathered me in on the way down. "Skipper, are you all right? What happened?" asked a faraway familiar voice—Jim's.

I felt shaken, though otherwise all right. "We're hit!" I gasped. "Check——" That was as far as I got. Jim whirled, dropping me none too gently, shouted down the hatch to Tom.

"Surface the boat! Blow everything!" He snatched the telephone hand set from its stowage, slammed it to his face. "Silence all along the line," he rasped. "We've been hit by gunfire! All compartments report!"

There was silence, too. All you could hear was the sound of the vents going closed again—at least they apparently still worked—and the high-pressure air whistling into the ballast tanks. In a moment I could feel the down angle begin to stabilize. It had been increasing rapidly, now it remained steady, but in a second or two it would start decreasing and we would shoot to the surface.

But what would we do then? We'd stand no chance against the gun power of our adversary. Even if our pressure hull had been pierced, we'd be better off trying to control the flooding and stay submerged—of course, it all depended on how big the hole was. I could feel my wits returning, pulled myself to-

— 229

gether, stood up. Jim spoke rapidly, covering the mouthpiece of the phone as he did. "Don't worry, skipper. Blowing is just precautionary. If the hole is too big to stay down, at least we'll have started the boat on the way back up. If it's just a small one——"

He broke off, listening. "Make your reports in order, from forward aft, unless you're flooding!" he snarled into the phone. He listened another second or two. It could not have been more than thirty seconds all told since the hatch was shut behind me. With our emergency dive, however, *Walrus* had built up a terrific downward momentum. She was already well past periscope depth, with the down angle barely starting to come off.

"Tom! Open your vents and resume the dive!" Jim bellowed the order down the hatch. "Take her on down—there's no water coming in!"

Tom was quick to countermand his instructions of less than half a minute before. The vents banged open once more, and the high-pressure blowing stopped. Now I could hear the roar of the erstwhile trapped air streaming out of the suddenly vented ballast tanks, and the bow and stern plane motors groaned as they reversed the planes once more.

"Conn!" It was Tom's voice, up the hatch. "Conn, aye, aye!" Jim answered him.

"Conn, I blew both safety and negative! Permission to vent them!"

"Granted!" shouted Jim. You couldn't tell that safety tank vent had been added to the others releasing air, but you certainly could tell negative, because it could only be vented into the ship, not overboard like the others. Having been blown dry at a deeper than usual depth, it had much higher air pressure than usual in it, and the resulting instantaneous increase in internal atmospheric pressure within the ship was distinctly unpleasant. Not that we minded it.

Our momentum problem was now in the other direction. We had actually started *Walrus* on the way back up, even though the down angle of the dive had never come to the horizontal.

All of our initial downward momentum, upon which the ship depended to get into the depths rapidly, had been lost. Now we would have to drive her forcibly down again, and in the meantime our friend with the surprise broadside battery would be coming with a bone in his teeth. He would have a beautiful marker as to where we were and the direction we were going—in the huge froth of air bubbles he would find.

One way to fix that. "Left full rudder!" I said to Oregon. At least we could turn toward him, perhaps surprise him by getting under him and away before he looked for us, certainly make his job a little harder.

O'Brien pursed his lips and shook his head. No chance for him with the uproar going on. I slung the extra pair of sonar earphones around my neck, leaned over for a look at the depth gauge. Eighty feet, just beginning to increase slowly! The inclinometer mounted below it showed twelve degrees down angle. Maybe that would be enough.

I felt a hand reaching for me. O'Brien. He pointed to his sound receiver. Red flashes. I put the phones over my ears, heard the pinging. No doubt this chap carried depth charges and knew how to use them.

One hundred feet. We were going down faster but I could hear screws now, fairly high-speed ones, not slow, chunking merchant propellers. Jim was silent, looking at me. I nodded gravely. "We're in for a depth-charge session. Better get set for it!"

As Jim gave the necessary orders I concentrated on listening. We slowed down to creeping speed as we approached our depth, got there in plenty of time after all, and sat there cursing the very name of this Jap who had so messed up our entry into his area. Of all things to fall for—a "Q-ship!" I winced at the thought.

He was pretty good, too, with his depth charges. WHAM! . . . WHAM! . . . WHAM! . . . WHAM! Four good ones, shaking up our guts, making the insides of the ship ring. I felt a little weak in the knees. WHAM, WHAM, WHAM, WHAM, *WHAMWHAM-WHAMWHAMWHAM*. He *was* good. Wiping the moist palms of my hands frequently on my trouser thighs, I tried to figure out his maneuvers, outguess him as he crisscrossed overhead. He was nearly as good as Bungo Pete—might well qualify as his little brother. He had not been able to catch us quite so near to the surface as Bungo had, but he was doing well nevertheless. And, of course, it takes only one depth charge to finish you, if it's close enough.

For hours *Walrus* crept along at deep submergence, while our enemy battered at her tough hide with depth charges. Hours during which we twisted and turned, listened to his propellers —a destroyer's high-pitched "Thum, thum, thum, thum, thum," twin screws, rather than the slower and more sedate chugging of the single merchant propeller this type of ship should have had. Try as we would we could not shake him. His horrible resounding pings came steadily through our earphones, kept the dial of the sonar receiver flickering with red flashes. First he would come along one side, pinging coldly and steadily, evaluating; then he would cross over, either ahead or astern, do the same thing from the other side. When finally satisfied he would pass overhead—or nearly so—and drop.

Just a few at a time, not many, aimed as accurately as he could. We would listen to the Q-ship's propellers, try to determine when he was starting a run for real, when only to change position. Then, at the proper psychological moment, we would put our rudder over, speed up, or slow down a little, try to make him miss. "WHAM! WHAM! WHAM! WHAM! WHAM! Successively louder, then diminishing again as he straddled us with his patterns. We got so we instinctively knew when the closest charge in any given pattern was due, and would cringe inwardly until we had felt it and survived. We were up against a professional and everyone in the ship knew it. We went about our duties with parted lips and staring eyes, and the peculiar parched-skin condition, contrasting strangely with the continual sweating of my palms and the general high humidity inside the ship, was not entirely due to loss of body fluid.

Give him credit for putting us *hors de combat,* for it was long after daybreak before we got clear of him and were able to come back to periscope depth, there to wait until night before surfacing. There might be a plane waiting to pounce on us, we reasoned, or some damage which, having once surfaced, might prevent our diving again upon necessity.

Before we finally got *Walrus* to the surface, a match would not stay lighted, nor would a cigarette burn. The slightest exertion brought the sensation of being badly out of breath, and a dull lassitude settled over all of us which took a determined effort to fight off. The first few breaths of cool, fragrant night air fixed that, however, and we turned to with interest to see what our topsides looked like.

The shell, probably about four inches in size, had struck the after part of the bridge and exploded, tearing off a chunk of the cigarette deck and wrecking the 20-millimeter gun. Several pieces of light plating hung loosely, but the structure beneath, our main induction valve and the associated piping, was unscathed.

It was good that we had not surfaced prematurely, however, or been forced to dive before making a thorough inspection and removing the damaged plating. Once we had opened the main induction valve, a jagged section of steel framing hanging loosely nearby in all probability would have jammed it open. It was over an hour before Tom pronounced us ready to submerge again. And we had to prohibit use of the cigarette deck for the remainder of our time on patrol.

Two nights later it was our turn. We sighted a cloud of black smoke against the eastern horizon, shortly before moonrise, and took off after it. A couple of hours later the smoke had turned into two ships proceeding in company, about a mile apart. This time the radar produced a range of four miles as its initial offering, showing that it was working better, or that the ships were bigger, or both. We tracked them for a short time, got their course and speed—twelve knots, due north, zigzagging. There was no escort.

We chose a position ahead of the two ships and slightly on their starboard bow, waited for the next zig. As soon as it came, our own rudder went over too, and the increased power song of the diesels back aft sounded choked off as the heel-to-starboard drove two of their mufflers underwater. It was, as usual, clear, calm, and warm. Stars twinkled overhead, millions of them. The moon was now well up, its glow reflecting off the somber black sides of our targets. The horizon to the north was blackest, which was where we were coming from. But visibility all around was entirely too good to take any chances. We had to come in fast and get it over with.

We kept our bow turned exactly on the leading ship, changing course to keep it so as he came into torpedo range, and we increased our speed to "full"—not everything wide open, but close to it. We would shoot three torpedoes at the first ship, three at the second, and save the four in our stern tubes for whatever might develop during the ensuing confusion while we retired.

Swiftly the three ships approached each other. We, the hunter, already carrying a scar where their protectors had drawn first blood; they, the hunted, trapped in their turn. Swiftly we drew closer, rapidly they grew larger in my binoculars. I could feel my pulse racing, my nerves tightening up. We were fully committed now—they were as big and broad as a barn, bigger than a barn. I could see them clearly: standard merchant types, not very different from the Q-ship of two nights ago; every detail etched itself in my mind. Just a little closer—get in close, so close you can't miss—here's the leading ship, old-style tall-stack freighter making lots of smoke . . . he's nearly broadside to, now—*surely* they can see us . . .

"Range!"

"One-five-double-oh!" Fifteen hundred yards. I had my binoculars in the TBT bracket, was holding a dead bead on the vertical stack, had been for several long seconds.

"Shoot!"

"Fire!" I could hear Jim's bellow from the conning tower, and the sea was calm enough to let me feel the slight jolt as the fish went out. Three jolts. Three fish. Their white streaks stretched relentlessly, reaching for the first target.

"Shift targets!" I swung the TBT to the rear-most vessel.

"Shifting targets, aye, aye!" I could picture Keith setting in the new bearing, turning the crank as fast as the cramped space would permit his arm and hand to move. Since course and speed were the same as for the first target, he needed to change only bearing and range. "Set!" came from Jim.

But we were not set at all. The second ship was too far away, too far astern of the leading one. "Left full rudder!" I shouted the command down the hatch to the helmsman and into the mike at the same time. We swung rapidly to the left, leaving our torpedo tracks running on to their destiny in a long, thin fan. There were about thirty seconds more to wait.

"Rudder amidships!" as our swing approached the best attack course for the new target. "Steady as you go!"

"Steady as she goes!" echoed Oregon up the hatch. He put the rudder a little right to stop the swing, caught it, centered the wheel. "Steady on two-two-eight!"

"Let her go two-three-oh!"

"Two-three-oh, aye, aye!"

At a sharp angle we raced toward the second ship. It was so far behind that our attainment of a perfect firing position for the first had brought us much too fine on the bow of the second. But there was nothing to do but ride it on through.

I was suddenly conscious of the breeze whistling in my ears and the swish of the water as we tore through it. *Walrus* pitched gently. Far up ahead she drove her snout down toward a small roller, stopped before she got under it, lifted her bow again with a gentle, tantalizing withdrawal, lowered it softly once more.

The slats of her wooden deck were clearly outlined by the white water washing over our pressure hull, several feet below, alternately black, solid-looking, the next moment ephemeral, etched black-on-white in delicate detail, every fore-and-aft plank precisely lined out, each thin steel crossbeam an interlocked solidity which had neither depth nor length. The pulsing roar of the diesel exhaust was the pounding beat of my heart as, rolling just a little from side to side, we careened onward.

This was infinitely more dangerous than the attack on the first ship. All this one had to do was turn only a little toward us, only thirty or forty degrees, and we would be in a bad way. It would be bow to bow, then, and we would have to expose our own broadside to sheer off.

"A light!" Tom Schultz and the starboard lookout were both shouting, pointing to the first ship. We were broadside to broadside, just past each other on opposite courses. There was a light on his deck, about the size of a flashlight, pointed over the side. I looked hard—our torpedoes should have reached there— sure enough, there were their wakes. Three up to it, one only going on beyond. As I looked I could see some kind of disturbance in the water, as if something were thrashing alongside. Another flashlight joined the first, and then a clearly visible cloud of steam issued from the forward edge of his stack. A moment later we heard the whistle.

I cursed aloud. *Damn* the torpedoes! Damn them and their designers to bloody hell forever! Why couldn't they build an efficient torpedo? Why did we have to carry the thing all the way into enemy waters to prove it wouldn't work! A consuming fury possessed me.

"Jim," I said bitterly into the mike, "we got two hits; good shooting. None of them exploded."

An answering whistle from the other ship, our present target, and now the situation was critical indeed. I watched him narrowly, suddenly tense. With our ineffective torpedoes, if he should see us, turn toward to ram us . . .

But he didn't. He turned away, presented a perfect target, and we fired everything left in the forward tubes at him. It looked as if all three hit, and at least one exploded—right under his stack. His steel hull folded up like paper, bow and stern rising high, center going under water, stack still vertical in the middle, rising now out of roiled-up water.

We put our rudder left again, then right and circled by him. I called Jim and Keith up to see and together the four of us stared at what we had done. He was gone beyond help, no doubt of that, even if help could have reached him. As we looked, the broad V became sharper. The sides rose, became more vertical, then folded up completely together, forecastle to poop deck with the stack crushed between, and sank from sight. The bow half was several feet shorter than the stern half, and the last thing we could see as the wreck took its final dive was the big bronze propeller, framed in the rudder bearings, still spinning slowly.

Seconds later a heavy explosion came resounding through the water.

"What's that?" cried Tom.

"Dunno," muttered Jim. "Maybe it's his boilers letting go when the cold water reached them."

"The boilers should already have been flooded, from where we hit him," I ventured. "Maybe it's some compartment collapsing from the increased pressure."

"Not with all that noise!" Jim looked incredulous. "That was an explosion!"

"Maybe an explosion inward. Ever blow up a paper bag and pop it?" But we were arguing from ignorance, and more important matters needed our attention. A muffled reverberation from somewhere ahead called them to mind. Gunfire.

"That's the other ship!" Jim spoke before anyone else. "He went off to the northeast!"

It made sense that he should carry a gun, but under the circumstances it might have been smarter of him not to have fired it. Jim and Keith raced below again, the former to plot our interception course, the latter to superintend reloading and checking of torpedoes forward.

We made a long run of it, keeping well out of sight of the fleeing ship, closing in only occasionally for a radar check of his latest position, guiding ourselves by the sporadic booming of the gun on his forecastle or stern. The moon having risen higher, it was now even brighter than before, shedding an all-pervading radiance which, to our night-adapted eyes, seemed as bright as day. Since the target had been alerted and would doubtless observe maximum precautions, these two factors combined appeared to rule out any chance of our getting close enough on the surface to make an attack. It would have to be done submerged.

After three hours of chase, having attained a satisfactory position on the fleeing freighter's bow, *Walrus* quietly slipped beneath the waves. We had obtained a fair solution of the zigzag plan, now much more radical than the previous one, and needed only the last-minute refinements. One thing we had decided, however, based on the five hits we had obtained on the two ships previously and the single explosion resulting: We would make sure of him this time. We would shoot four torpedoes, all aimed to hit, and we would hold the two left forward as well as the four aft in reserve for a quick second salvo if the first also proved a dud.

The night was dark enough to make one thing unnecessary—raising and lowering the periscope for frenetic moments of observation. I kept it up, its tip only a few feet above the waves, and waited for the zigzagging freighter to cross our bow. It was just as Captain Blunt had said, a long time ago: "After you get in front of him, anyone ought to be able to hit the target. The problem is getting in front."

We had gotten in front, and we bided our time until his zigzag threw him right across our bow. We had opened the outer doors on only four torpedo tubes—at the last possible moment—

"Shoot!" I said, watching the huge bulk of the ship glide past.

"Fire!" Jim. "One's fired, sir!" Quin. I could feel the torpedo going out. Someone was counting out the seconds. Up to ten. I shifted the periscope cross hair from the target's stack to his forecastle.

"Shoot!" I said again.

"Fire!"

"Two's away, sir!" Periscope wire now on the stern, bisecting the deckhouse there. "Shoot!" The jolt of the third fish —cross hair on the stack for the last one. "Shoot!" Four white streaks in the water, only a thousand yards, half a mile, to go. The first one looked like a sure bull's-eye, right under the stack. The white streak of bubbles, clearly visible against the gray-black of the uneasy sea, drew unerringly to the point, got there. I could see the white froth where the side of the ship intersected it, held my breath for a frozen second, let it out with a sigh. This was exactly the way it had looked during all these many years of training in Long Island Sound or off Pearl Harbor. This would have been scored a bull's-eye all right; the torpedo would have been recorded as passing exactly where aimed, under the target. There was no difference, and I could feel the unreal "time reversed upon itself" sensation, which I had experienced upon entering Pearl Harbor, lying dormant, just under the surface.

"Time for Number Two fish, skipper." Jim spoke quietly, into my ear. I swung the 'scope slightly.

White froth at the bow also. Plus something else. A splash—a small geyser of water and spray rose halfway to the target's deck. Something had exploded, not the warhead, however, or at least only a small fraction of the TNT supposed to be inside it. Seconds later we heard the sound of it, clearly audible in the conning tower. *"Pwhuuung"*—the same sound we had heard some months before in AREA SEVEN.

"Jim," I said furiously, "Make a note in the log. Low-order explosion. Possibly air flask!"

"Aye, aye, sir! Time for the third torpedo, skipper."

This one would be aft. I swung the 'scope to the right, caught the torpedo wake going into the rudder and propeller declivity in the counter stern. This time it exploded; there was a flash of light from right out of the water, accompanied by a cloud of white spray, so fine that it resembled steam. The freighter shuddered under the impact. The stern was partially obscured by the cloud of mist, though there was no high-rising column of water such as some of the patrol reports had described. I had an instantaneous impression of great force being contained within the sides of the ship, almost as though the stern itself had been beaten in.

"*WHRANNGG!*" There was no mistaking this noise. It was a combination explosion, unlike a depth charge, for it included the smashed sheet-metal sound of crushed and crumpled steel.

"It's a hit! We've hit him!" Jim's excitement was plain to hear. I braced myself for the blow over my shoulders. It did not come, however; instead there was Jim's voice again: "Can I have a look, sir?"

"Wait a minute," I growled. "How about the fourth fish?"

"Time right now—mark!"

It should go right into the area under the stack, like the first one. I looked for the wake, found it. It terminated just forward of the stack, between the stack and the bridge structure. It, too, looked exactly like a drill torpedo, set to run under.

But it made no difference, for as I watched in astonishment the bow of the ship suddenly swooped into the air. The stern had already disappeared under water, and the weight of the submerged portion had lifted the bow of the freighter right out of the water. It could not have taken ten more seconds before the ship was vertical, straight up and down. She had gone so fast that I was certain I could still see some forward momentum to the up-and-down hulk. Things—gear, debris of all kinds —fell from the bridge into the sea in a cascade of junk. At least two items were human, and they moved as they fell.

"Let me see, *please!*" Jim was beside himself with eagerness, almost pushing against me.

"Here!" I relinquished the periscope.

"Stand by to surface—Surface!" I shouted. The whistle of air, the upward heave of *Walrus'* hull, and she started up.

A shout from Jim. "She's sinking! God—look at her go!" Keith had slipped away from his TDC, was standing alongside Jim. With the conning tower darkened for better periscope visibility I could not see his expression, but his very stance communicated eagerness to see, too.

I gave Jim a gentle shove. "Here, let Keith look too."

"She's going fast!" Keith spoke rapidly, echoing Jim. Suddenly he jerked back, grabbed Quin by the arm, propelled him to the periscope. "Take a look, quick!" The Yeoman jammed his face to the eye-piece. Keith gave him a few seconds, pushed him away, turned the instrument over to Rubinoffski who was hovering eagerly nearby. Jerry Cohen was next, and even O'Brien, the sonarman, received a split-second glimpse.

In the meantime the familiar sounds of coming to the surface could be heard, and finally the voice of the Diving Officer started shouting out the depths from his control-room depth gauges. "Twenty-six and holding!" He called at last.

"Open the hatch!" I rasped at Rubinoffski. Instantly he whirled the hatch hand wheel, snapped the latch back with almost the same motion. The heavy bronze hatch slammed out of his hands, crashed against the side of the bridge. Released air inside the boat howled out—firing four torpedoes builds up a not-inconsiderable air pressure—and the Quartermaster was lifted bodily off his feet and began to sail up the open hatch. Years ago the old *Salmon* had lost a man overboard in just this manner. It was at night, too, and they had never found him. I barely managed to grasp Rubinoffski around one ankle as he went by, hung on for dear life with my other hand and my own toes hooked under the ladder rungs. Bits of debris, dirt, cork chunks from behind some of our instruments, pieces of paper, and even someone's carelessly stowed white hat went shooting by past us, and then the storm of wind subsided. We leaped up the remaining ladder rungs, got our binoculars to our eyes within seconds.

There was nothing to be seen. Fearful that I had somehow gotten disoriented, I swung the glasses all around through a full circle, but there was still nothing.

"Nothing in sight, Captain! I can't see him, sir!" It was less than two minutes of the time that our torpedo had struck.

Our lookouts boiled up to the bridge, followed by Tom and Jim. "Where is he? Where is that son-of-a-bitch?" The excitement of battle was in Jim's voice. I tried to make my own calm and dispassionate:

"Gone, Jim. He's already sunk!"

Jim was bubbling over. "How about that!" he shouted, pacing around the confines of the undamaged part of our bridge, staring over our port bow, which was the last observed bearing of the vanished ship.

A cry from the port forward lookout. "Something in the water, sir!" He pointed.

In the intermittent hollows of the shallow sea could be seen several dark masses clustered together. Wreckage, perhaps a boat or raft or two. "Where are they?" Jim rushed forward, aimed his own glasses briefly in the indicated direction, dashed below. In a moment he had reappeared with a bandolier of ammunition slung around his shoulder and one of the ship's two Browning automatic rifles clutched in his hands. "Just in case we need it," he explained carefully. He drew one of the previously prepared twenty-cartridge clips from the bandolier, fitted it to the magazine of the gun.

Walrus wallowed in the ocean, making barely steerageway, the turbo-blowers just beginning their whining lift to seaworthiness. A few hundred yards away the group of wreckage could now be more clearly seen, still black and essentially formless. One boat, maybe another, were distinguishable. I thought I could make out movement in the Stygian mass and Jim, Tom, and I leveled our glasses at it.

Afterward I found it hard to explain why we did not leave forthwith, for there was no advantage to be gained from looking over the unhappy victims of our success, only possibly trouble if one of them happened to have a gun and in defiance chose to use it. Nor was it chivalry, for we could not help them, and they were certainly close enough to Palau to make their way there without excessive difficulty. It must have been a subconscious force within us, some insatiable need or curiosity or motive of vengeance.

"Left full rudder," I ordered. With our slow speed this would put us a little closer. Two boats now could be made out clearly, plus some dark objects which were most probably life rafts, and miscellaneous pieces of floating debris.

"Rudder amidships!" I could hear the groan of the hydraulic mechanism. From the pump room beneath the control room came the thump as the hydraulic accumulator replenished itself and cut off, and the screaming of the blowers welled out of the hatch in a never-ceasing wail. We coasted gently closer. Now people could be distinguished in the life rafts, sitting motionless, crouched over, faces turned toward us. There were many bobbing heads still in the water, hanging on to a barrel or hatch cover, or to the ropes lining the sides of the rafts. In the lifeboats no one could be seen, though the dark interior seemed to be solid with a crawling, jostling life-movement.

A wave of passion shook me. This filthy, spineless, crawling thing was the enemy! This, the perpetrator of the Pearl Harbor crime! This the killer of innocent women and children in the Chinese war, and now again in the Philippines! I could feel the savage lust for revenge. I had never hated the Japanese so much as now—now that I could kill them, crush them, smash them to small bits, ram their fragile boats with my ship, grind them beneath her ribs of steel . . .

"Yaaaah! You Jap bastards! How do you like it now! Go back

and tell your —ing emperor and his buddy Tojo about this!" Jim cupped his hands, was screaming at the top of his lungs in the general direction of the enemy survivor group as they slowly came alongside.

There was no movement, no answering hail, no indication of having heard, much less understood. Suddenly Jim reached for the automatic rifle, really a portable machine gun, raised it to his shoulder before anyone could stop him. He pulled back the bolt, aimed into the middle of the nearest lifeboat. I reached him just in time, grabbed the gun. His face was livid. "Stop it, Jim!" I hissed savagely into his face. "Stop it, or so help me I'll ——" I never did know what I'd have said, for Jim, breathing hard, released his grip on the gun.

"Thanks, skipper," he whispered after several deeply drawn breaths, "I must have flipped my lid—I'm sorry! I-I-I don't know what came over me—" his voice trailed off.

I could sense the revulsion of feeling taking possession of him, and felt the same within myself, as the boatloads and raft-loads drifted past. Stricken faces stared at us or turned away to hide from us. The pathetic figures huddled together—not for warmth, for it was warm enough, but for fear of us. To them, probably only simple merchant seamen, we must have seemed malevolent, inscrutable, the perpetrators of all that was evil. It was a wonder, in fact, that there were so many of them. Their ship had sunk so rapidly that there could hardly have been time even to get topside after the explosion of the torpedo.

Tom put it into words: "They must have been sitting in the boats and rafts waiting for us to attack that ship!"

There could be no other answer. Furthermore, the lifeboats must have simply floated off as the decks went under—certainly they could not have used davits and lowering gear. The sinking of their consort, and the previous unsuccessful attack in which two dud torpedoes had already hit their ship, had no doubt provided ample incentive for all hands to get into the boats. Even so, those on the forecastle of the ship must have had a bad time of it, for any boats or rafts located there must have been hurled over a hundred feet into the water!

It was, Jim estimated, about one hundred and fifty miles to the nearest island of the Palau group, Babelthuap. The kindest thing we could do for the survivors was to leave them alone and to depart the scene before some hothead in their group unlimbered a gun he might happen to have carried with him. We headed northward, doubled around to the southwest after losing sight of them.

Palau is a most frustrating area to try to patrol with a single submarine. In the first place, there are two entrances to the main ship harbor of the archipelago, one on either side of the island chain, and keeping a watch on either one is a full-time job for one boat. If a ship is attacked near either entrance, or if presence of a submarine is known or suspected, it is a simple matter merely to use the other one until the scare dies away. Under the circumstances we felt as if the enemy retained the initiative.

Certainly, our first two days in the area were not characteristic of the remainder. We went for a week without sighting another ship. Then it was a huge, new tanker making high speed. We pulled out all the stops, ran our battery almost flat, never got within shooting distance. We tried patrolling on the surface, out of sight of land, changing our locale radically whenever there appeared the possibility of our having been detected by a plane. Days went by in which we slowly wandered about in an oily, flat sea. The oppressive heat of the sun beat down upon us until our bridge watchers, at least, gave the lie to the theory that all submariners looked pale and wan when they got back from patrol. But we saw no enemy ships.

We had already decided to head back to close-in submerged patrolling around the entrances to Palau harbor, when finally a convoy showed up. Four ships, this time, and we sighted them shortly after daybreak on a calm, clear, hot day without a vestige of cloud, hint of rain, or shadow of a breeze.

Two *Chidori*-class small destroyers or large submarine-chasers, depending on how you wanted to look at them, furnished the escort group. We ran up a periscope, maintained a watch on the enemy ships through it, and ran on the surface at full power to get in front of them, so that we could submerge and lie in wait. They were zigzagging, which made it more difficult, and because of their high speed it took us all day. After we did dive, which was only an hour or so before sunset, the absolutely flat sea caused any kind of periscope exposure to take on the aspect of a severe risk of detection. And the two little *Chidoris* didn't make it easier, for in preparation for the inevitable depth-charging, turning off our ventilation shot the temperature within the sub to fantastic heights. One hundred thirty-seven degrees in the hot engine rooms and maneuvering room, someone reported.

The approach was routine, without incident. We got inside the escorts, fired three torpedoes at each of the two leading ships, were swinging to bring our stern tubes to bear, when all hell broke loose. The harbinger was O'Brien. He turned a pale face to me right after the sixth torpedo was sent on its way: "High-speed screws, running down our port side!"

I spun the periscope. Nothing. Putting it down, I grabbed for the extra earphones and heard it. No doubt about it; O'Brien was right. It sounded very much the same as one of our own torpedoes—the same high-pitched whine I had heard hundreds of times. It crossed our stern, came back up the starboard side, veered to the left as if to cross our bow. That was enough. My hair tingled as I thought of the secret magnetic exploder in the warheads of our torpedoes. No doubt that this was one of our fish, running awry, in circles. If it passed too close, or overhead . . .

"Take her down, Tom! All ahead emergency!" No time to wait to see the results of our other torpedoes. We'd be lucky to get out of this ourselves! *Walrus* clawed for the depths, the depth gauge slowly, ever so slowly, indicating safety gained.

The screws approached again, from the port side again. Didn't seem to be running down toward the stern this time, might curve away before getting to us, though—O'Brien's face looked positively pasty as he manipulated his control handle. "Coming right at us!" he whispered to me.

I nodded. It all depended if we could get deep enough in time. The screws became louder, still louder—and still on the same relative bearing. Probably the arc of the circle the misguided torpedo was making just happened to be such that it kept up with out increased speed.

"Right full rudder!" I said. I had refrained from giving the order until now for fear that the slowing effect of the rudder might also slow our dive to the shelter of deeper depths. Maybe now it would be all right. The depth gauge showed eighty feet. Still wearing the sonar phones, with the horrible little propellers beating into my ears, I looked about me. For several seconds I had forgotten the remainder of the conning tower party. They stood in hypnotic attention, riveted upon me. In his hand Jim held the stop watch with which he had intended to time the torpedo runs to the targets . . . I could see the slender hand moving around the dial. It was almost straight up toward the winding stem—one minute since we had fired.

Time, indeed, stood still. Every second was a heartbeat. I imagined I could hear the ticking of the stop watch—an impossibility because of the earphones and the fact that I was listening to the hypnotizing rhythm of our own juggernaut come back to seek us out. The high whine came closer, louder, still closer—sweat standing out on the face of O'Brien, cold sweat. Salt taste in my mouth; I licked the edges of my lips. They were dry and salty, too.

WHRAAANNGGG! The explosion seemed to burst my eardrums! The conning tower danced before my eyes. I felt myself flung bodily against the sonar receiver. *Walrus* lurched madly, her hull resounding, her deck plates drumming beneath our feet. Startled eyes looked widely at me, and at the familiar instruments about them. Jim's mouth moved. I couldn't hear him. I ripped off the earphones, still couldn't hear. There was a roaring in my ears. I cupped my hand behind them.

"What?" I said—or tried to say. My mouth made the motions, my vocal chords felt normal, though a bit dry, but I could hear nothing come out. I tried again. "What?" Then I realized I was deaf. O'Brien was holding his hands to his ears, rolling his head from side to side in helpless pain. He had forgotten to tune down his sonar receiver, and he and I had gotten the full force of the amplified explosion. No wonder I was deaf!

Jim's lips moved again, but this time he was addressing Quin. The Yeoman spoke into his telephones. "All compartments report," his lips seemed to form.

Before he could receive answers, three more explosions came in. "WHAM! . . . WHAM!" . . . a little wait, then "WHAM!" for a third time. These I could hear clearly, though they seemed not nearly so loud as the explosion just preceding. Three hits, they sounded like—ordinarily a cause for rejoicing, but hardly worth noticing for the moment. Quin was receiving his reports. My ears were recovering, for I heard his own: "All compartments report no damage, sir!"

We were still going deep, which it seemed appropriate to keep on doing until we arrived at deep submergence. Then we quieted everything down and waited for the depth charges. They came, too, but they couldn't compare in loudness with the near-hit of our own torpedo nor the workout from the Q-ship, and after several hours of evasion we slowly crept away.

We had no torpedoes left forward, and received orders the next night, as a consequence, to return to Midway again. Our time on station was nearly done anyway, but the orders to Midway were a big disappointment. It was unusual to send a ship there twice in succession. Many of the crew had had their hearts set on a trip south of the equator to Australia.

CHAPTER 10

OUR STAY IN MIDWAY WAS NO DIF-
ferent from the previous one, but the island itself had undergone considerable change since the last time any of us had seen
it. There was a big new pier constructed in the lagoon, and one
of our great seagoing submarine tenders, the *Sperry,* was
moored there to increase the refit capacity of the island base.
Instead of one submarine, there were four in various stages of
refit between patrols at the atoll, *Walrus* becoming the fifth.

There seemed to be at least twice as many men on the island
as before, twice as many planes, and four times as much work
being done. Midway did its best for us, receiving us with a brass
band when we warped alongside the *Sperry,* dumping a load of

mail on our decks, plus ice cream and a crate of fruit, and we were carted off almost immediately to the old Pan-American Hotel, now known as the Gooneyville Lodge, to begin our two weeks' rest and recuperation. During the ensuing time we did our best to avoid boredom. We threw a ship's party, complete with huge steaks and all the trimmings, and we organized fishing parties, baseball games, and other diversions.

Naturally, it was not enough, and no one pretended it was. More and more our crew spent their free time down in the ship, watching her get ready for our next run, and more and more we speculated where it would be. The only thing which could be counted to keep most of us away from the ship, for a time at least, was the receipt of mail, which arrived on the average of three times a week from Pearl. I never ceased to wonder at the efficiency of the San Francisco post office, which somehow always knew where to send mail so that it would be waiting for us when we arrived, and kept it coming until we had left. Then, apparently, the mail would be allowed to accumulate somewhere—probably in Pearl Harbor—until our next port of call.

Jim, as usual, received the lion's share of mail in our group, and somehow also seemed to be able to view it with greater detachment. For the rest of *Walrus'* crew, and for all of Midway, for that matter, arrival of the mail plane and the unavoidable, aggravating wait while the Midway mail clerks swiftly parceled out the different bags, had assumed the proportions of a ritual. The reception committee at the airfield, for instance, merely to see the mail plane arrive, grew so unwieldy that a notice over the signature of the Island Commander was issued requesting the practice be terminated and promising utmost dispatch in sorting and handling.

And, with little else to occupy their spare time, our crew became prolific letter writers. This added a burden to Hugh, Dave, and Jerry, who were required to censor every piece of outgoing mail. After giving them a hand once or twice, which all the officers did when the pile grew excessively large, I could readily understand their often-repeated reassurance to the crew that they did not remember what they had read. But I did carry away the impression that some of our letter writers were certainly unabashed, if not adept, at putting their thoughts and yearnings down on paper.

ComSubPac's endorsement to our patrol report, when at last it came in, was of course of consuming interest to Jim, Keith, and me. We were credited with two ships sunk and two probables, which was what we had expected, but the comment of most importance was the one which simply stated, "The reports of torpedo failure during this patrol are important additions to the growing body of evidence in this regard, and to the remedy of which active steps are in hand."

Two days later a bulky package labeled "Secret" arrived in the mail, addressed to "The Commanding Officer, USS *Walrus*." It was from ComSubPac and contained our Operation Order. We were to return to AREA SEVEN, the scene of our first patrol.

And three days after that, a newly painted *Walrus,* now gray instead of black, refitted, repaired, and cleaned up—and her bridge even more cut down than before—pointed her lean prow once again to the western sky. She was no longer the brand-new submarine we had brought out from New London the previous year. The miles she had steamed and the battles she had fought had taken their toll on her appearance. Over a hundred depth charges had left their marks, both internally and externally, as well as the chance hit by a Japanese shell. The changes brought about by time and use, the modifications required by ComSub-Pac, and our own realization of our needs to do the job—more plotting equipment, more bunks, more food stowage, a bigger crew—were equally marked.

Walrus' bridge was now a low, streamlined structure, with a bare steel skeleton bracing the periscope supports. It looked a little strange compared with the sleek, rounded bridges and elongated conical periscope shears of the newer subs beginning to arrive from the States, but it was roomier, and did the job as efficiently. Around the bridge were welded several foundations for 50-caliber machine guns, and on its forward and after parts we now carried two double 20-millimeter gun mounts, with watertight stowage alongside for the four guns when not needed.

On our main deck the torpedo reload equipment had been removed entirely. The large steel mast and boom originally stepped in the main deck forward had been demounted and left in Pearl. Our old three-inch antiaircraft gun which had been mounted aft of the bridge was gone. In its place, but mounted forward in the area of the torpedo loading mast, was a broadside-firing four-incher, exactly like the gun the old *S-16* had carried and very likely lifted from one of her sisters.

Down below, the interior of the ship looked somewhat different too. Much new equipment had been added, welded to the steel skin of the ship or bolted to the deck. The smooth cork lining of the interior of the pressure hull was now pocked with spots where it had to be removed for welding and had been less attractively patched. New instruments had been installed: An automatic plotter, which required two men to keep pointers matched with our course and speed, and forced us to move Jerry Cohen's plotting position down into the control room; a gadget which measured the temperature of the sea at different depths; an improved SJ radar, using much more power, and producing longer detection ranges; and more air-conditioning, required not only for the increased heat output of our new gear but also for the increased crew we carried as a partial consequence.

And as we got under way for the coast of Kyushu once more, changes again had been made in our crew. Fifteen men had to be left behind to fill the insatiable demands of new construction, and to provide continuity for the rotation program. Eighteen new hands, all graduates of the submarine school but otherwise entirely new to submarine duty, took their places.

The loss which affected the wardroom most was good old steady Tom Schultz, whose orders detaching him and ordering him to the submarine school as instructor had arrived in our first mail. Hugh Adams had moved into his shoes as Engineer, not without some trepidation, and two new Ensigns had reported aboard.

We held a special wake for Tom in Gooneyville Lodge, and he promised to look up our mothers, wives, and relatives back in the States. Not that any of the rest of us was married except Jim, who shook his head when Tom offered to carry any special trinket or message to Laura for him.

The crew also tried hard to show Tom how well he was liked, presenting him with a gold wrist watch they purchased at the Ship's Service, and Tom, in his turn, insisted upon personally handling all our lines from the dock when we got under way.

The changes left Keith, now a seasoned submariner and a full Lieutenant, the third officer in rank aboard, next after Jim. Hugh was fourth, and Dave Freeman, his junior by only a few numbers, fifth, now serving as Keith's understudy as well as Communications Officer. Jerry Cohen, keeping his job as Plotting Officer during battle stations, became Hugh's assistant in the engineering department. Our two new Ensigns, who were named Patrick Donnelly and Cecil Throop, would, like Jerry during the previous patrol, be given general assignments under instruction.

One disadvantage of this new setup, so far as I was concerned, was that I now had to share my room with someone, since *Walrus* was not fitted with the extra accommodations in the wardroom "country" that some of the later submarines carried. Throop, who drew the unpopular assignment of sleeping in the bunk newly installed above mine, proved to be a very sound sleeper, and a very loud one. As we made our way west, I began to wonder how long I would be able to stand it when the irregular hours on station began to take their toll.

One thing which it was unnecessary to burden the others with, at the moment at any rate, was the following special entry in the Operation Order pamphlet, which I pulled out before handing the pamphlet over to Jim to read:

> *Particular caution is enjoined with regard to an old destroyer of the* Akikaze *class operating out of the Bungo Suido. This vessel had been unusually successful in antisubmarine work, and prefers the astern position when escorting. You will under no circumstances seek combat with it except under conditions of special advantage.*

I read and reread the words. There must be some important reason behind them—and add to this the remembered conversation with Captain Blunt months before. Of specific information as to Bungo's activities I had heard very little, though there had been stories circulating about Bungo Pete and his abilities as a depth-charge launcher for some time. "He even seems to know the names of his victims," I remembered Captain Blunt saying.

The fact that we had been warned against him was understandable; the restriction not to attack him except under conditions of "special advantage" could only mean that we were to stay clear of him unless fate practically delivered him into our hands. But what were we to do if a convoy turned up with Bungo Pete as one of the escorts? For that matter, there was more than one *Akikaze*-class destroyer in the Jap Navy. How, then, to tell them apart? I studied her in the book of recognition photos until I could have recognized her, or one of her many sisters, through the periscope, from the bridge on a dark night, or anywhere else we might be likely to run into her. But if we ran into an *Akikaze,* it could be any one of fully thirty-four nearly identical tincans.

My final evaluation was the only one possible. Bungo had an *Akikaze,* he liked to escort from astern, and he operated in AREA SEVEN. Therefore we would avoid tangling with any destroyer of this type occupying such a position while convoying— at least of our own volition. But if he knew of our presence and general position, he would carry the fight to us anyhow, and in this case we might as well do as well as we could for ourselves if we got the chance.

Another portion of the Operation Order dealt with the possibility of encountering Japanese submarines, and this Jim, Keith, and I discussed at length. There were indications (unspecified) that Jap submersibles were being used for antisubmarine work, perhaps ordered out to wait for U. S. boats going or coming on patrol. We might therefore be apt to encounter one of them almost anywhere.

Daily drills en route to our operation areas had seemed a simple matter of keeping at the peak of training, and they had been an accepted part of our daily routine. Now, with the two special problems *Walrus* might run into, one of which only I knew about, I directed that the drills be doubled in frequency. We concentrated on two things: on detection and avoidance of an enemy submarine torpedo, calculating the quickest ways of dodging it in the various possible situations; and on swiftly changing fire-control problems, with emphasis on flexibility in setting the new data into the TDC and the angle solver and getting off an answering shot.

Most important from the self-protection angle, of course, were measures to avoid enemy torpedoes. First came the absolute imperativeness of seeing the torpedo as it came at us, or of spotting the enemy sub's periscope. To confound his approach, Jim and Rubinoffski cooked up a special zigzag plan of our own which consisted of steering either side of the base course line —never on it—and following an indefinite zigzag while so doing. Once taught to our helmsmen, the plan took care of itself. It sent us all over the ocean and we hoped it would force the enemy boat to use his periscope more often and thus increase our chances for spotting it. The need for alert lookouts we dinned into the ears of our new men, and our old ones too, with never-ceasing emphasis; it was up to them to see the telltale wake or periscope soon enough to enable something to be done about it. On that simple requirement our salvation depended.

Once sighted, we could turn forward or away, or even line up for a torpedo shot in return. Given enough time, we knew we could get clear.

All the way out to Kyushu we drilled on the possibilities, and when we got there we were as ready for them as we could be. Keith, already an expert on the TDC, became adept at switching his inputs virtually instantaneously at my snapped command. Jim, hovering as backer-up for both of us, found it possible to speed things up by making certain of the settings for him when he had both hands otherwise engaged. And I realized that in Jim one of the sub force's best TDC operators had never been developed, for it seemed to be nearly second nature to him.

We varied the procedure and the personnel, too, so that our abilities did not depend on who happened to be on watch when the emergency came. About the time we passed through the Nanpo Shoto our crew was so tuned to the problem that from a standing start, with only the cruising watch at their stations, we could get our torpedoes on their way within thirty seconds. Our battle-stations personnel could shoot a salvo at a destroyer going by at high speed, thirty knots, shift target to a submerged submarine at three knots on a different bearing, make the necessary changes in torpedo gyro angle, depth, setting, firing bearing, and get a second salvo of torpedoes on its way—all within ten seconds by stop watch.

Perhaps our great emphasis on preparation also led me to expect something out of the ordinary as soon as we entered AREA SEVEN, just as we had on our first patrol, so long ago. Subconsciously I had nerved myself to having a Jap sub fire at us somewhere during the trip across the Pacific, and to finding Bungo Pete waiting for us at the other end. Neither eventuality came to pass. The patrol began with the most prosaic of beginnings—a week on station, within close sight of land, without any sign whatsoever of enemy activity except for an occasional airplane, and numbers of small fishing smacks with groups of straw-hatted Japanese out for a day's fishing.

During the early part of our second week a big old-fashioned freighter, heavily laden, crawled up the coast pouring smoke from a large stack nearly as tall as his masts. He wasn't making much speed and disdained to zigzag, probably figuring he wasn't fast enough for it to do any good. There was plenty of time for both Jim and Keith to get a look at him before we sank him; he went down belching smoke and dirt. A great expanse of filthy water, studded with floating junk and debris of all kinds plus a number of round black objects which slowly clustered together, marked his grave.

Two days later we trapped another single ship not far from where we had sunk the first, this time shortly after we had surfaced for the night. The approach was entirely by radar, for it was so dark that we did not see the target until just before firing. He never knew what hit him, either. We fired three torpedoes at short range, and all three exploded with thunderous detonations, one forward, one amidships, one at the stern. The ship went down like a rock, still on an even keel, leaving at least three boatloads of survivors. They must have been living in the lifeboats!

This was when Jim had an idea and, acting upon it, we ran south at full speed the rest of the night, moved close in to the coast in a totally new spot by next morning. Two ships sunk in the same vicinity would be sure to bring trouble instead of more targets, as he put it, and if we could move closer to where our victims came from—they had both been heading north—we might nab one before he was diverted.

He was right, too, for the very next day a small tanker happened by. I told Jim that this was entirely his own ship, that he had found it, and that therefore he had the right to do it the necessary honors while I took over his job as backer-upper and general understudy.

Jim needed no urging or second suggestion. He grabbed the periscope eagerly, took over command as though born to it, and the conduct of the approach was beyond criticism. He even swung at the last minute to use the stern tubes instead of bow tubes, thus equalizing our torpedo expenditure; and there was that same unholy exhilaration in his face as he gave the final command, "Shoot!" I wished old Blunt could have seen it—in any event I would see that he heard about it.

The only criticism I might have made was that instead of lowering the periscope after firing and getting it back up in time to see his torpedoes hit, Jim left it up the whole time the torpedoes ran toward the target, and watched the doomed ship's hopeless last-minute efforts to evade with positive glee.

It took it twenty minutes to sink, with one torpedo amidships which blew part of his side off. Jim gave everyone in the conning tower and several from the control room a chance to get a look at the death agonies.

Three ships in four days, and not a depth charge in return! We felt pretty cocky as we stood out into the center of AREA SEVEN to let our "hot spots" cool off a little. We had not even experienced much trouble with our torpedoes, though one of the odd *"pwhyunng"* noises had been reported during each of the first and last attacks. After a day we moved into one of our old positions on an enemy probable course line drawn from the mouth of the Bungo Suido.

Another week went by. We changed our position several times, went close into the coast once more, then back out to the original position again, all to no avail. The Japanese were simply refusing to cooperate, we decided.

And then one night, after the surfaced routine for the night had become well established, Kohler rushed to the bridge hatch, called up to me: "Captain! They're calling us on the radio!"

There was something strange about this, I felt, as I hastily put on a pair of red goggles and climbed below. Kohler preceded me down the ladder, but he went right by the radio room, led me into the crew's mess compartment immediately aft of it. A crowd of our men were gathered around the entertainment radio mounted above one of the mess tables. Several were hastily clothed, some merely in their underwear, one man, I saw, half-shaven with lather drying on his face. Dave was there, looking grave, and so was Pat Donnelly. A woman's voice was coming over the loud-speaker.

". . . American submarine sailors," she was saying, "we regret to have to do this to you, but you have brought it upon yourselves. Japan did not make war upon you; you brought killing and wanton destruction to us. You have violated our waters, killed our toilers on the sea whose only crime is that they sought to travel our own home waters, which you have unjustly invaded. For this you have merited death, and death you shall have." Her voice lilting, she kept on: "While you are awaiting your last moments, perhaps this recording from home may make the thought of the future easier to face with equanimity." The melodious voice stopped and the strains of a popular dance tune filled the crowded compartment.

"Who the hell is that?" I interjected angrily.

Dave turned, seeing me for the first time. "Haven't you heard her before, Captain? The men call her 'Tokyo Rose.' "

Kohler nodded. "Yessir, we've had her on a couple of times before this. Usually she just plays music and hands out a load of baloney. Tonight, though, she was different."

"Dammit, Kohler!" I blazed, "I don't want anyone to listen to her again! I'll have the radio disconnected until we leave the area if you do!" Her words had been disturbing enough to me; who knew what their effect could be on some of our less experienced sailors?

"But she called us by name, Captain!"

"*What!*"

"That's what I tried to you tell you, sir! She was telling that to us—to the *Walrus!*"

— 259

Dave nodded. "I heard it too, sir. She said she had a special message for the crew of the U. S. submarine *Walrus*. She said she knew we were here, not far from the Bungo Suido, and that we had sunk some ships, but those were the last ones we'd ever sink." Several solemn faces nodded in corroboration.

The music stopped. "Men of the *Walrus*," the limpid voice said sweetly, "enjoy yourselves while you can, for eternity is a long, long time. Think of your loved ones, but don't bother to write because you'll never be able to mail the letters. Just think of all the thoughts they will be wasting on you, and the unanswered letters your wives and sweethearts will write—those who do think of you, and who do write!" She ended in a loud titter, almost a giggle. I had never heard anything quite so evil in my life.

"Turn that Goddamed radio off! Kohler, remember what I told you!" I stamped furiously away and climbed back on the bridge, more upset in mind than I could admit anyone to see. I needed to think.

No one on Midway—for that matter no one in the ship, either, except Jim—had known of our destination until after we had left the island out of sight. But somehow the Japanese propaganda ministry had full knowledge that *Walrus* was the submarine currently off Kyushu. Captain Blunt already had hinted that he was worried about some of the uncannily accurate information Bungo Pete seemed to possess; now I could see why. There could be only one explanation: espionage at Pearl Harbor!

For that matter, only Captain Blunt, ComSubPac himself, and one or two others on his staff knew where we had been sent, and even if others had guessed, how could they have predicted our movements so accurately? It had to be more specific than guesswork. No, unless some rational explanation presented itself, there must be a security leak back in Pearl. It was a horrid conclusion, yet inescapable. Then another thought presented itself: We had not yet gotten to the bottom of the torpedo troubles. Could there, somehow, be some connection? Could those, also, be the result of sabotage or espionage? I paced back and forth on the cigarette deck, puzzling over the few facts at my disposal, feeling the cool breeze of the night on my forehead, feeling anything but cool inside.

Despite premonitions I could not put down, nothing of note occurred the rest of the night, nor during the next day, but I had done some heavy thinking. When next we surfaced there was one significant change in our routine. Our garbage contained several carefully prepared scraps of paper bearing the name USS *Octopus,* some official in appearance, some apparently from personal mail. Quin, entering into the spirit of it, had even made, by hand, a very creditable reproduction of a large rubber stamp of the name. And all vestiges of the name *Walrus* had been carefully removed.

The garbage sacks were thrown overboard as usual, and as usual they floated aft into our wake, slowly becoming water-logged. As I had suspected, and found to be so upon investigation, some of them were not so well weighted as others. There was a good possibility that some of them might remain afloat for an appreciable time.

There was no longer a submarine in our navy named the *Octopus.* Choice of that name for our stratagem had been made for that reason, and out of pure sentiment. It was a good joke through the ship that the skipper had decided to change the name of *Walrus* to that of his first boat, the old *Octopus.*

And I told no one that my regular nightly visits to the radio room, which became a habit at about this time, were for the sole purpose of plugging a pair of earphones into the extra receiver and surreptitiously listening to Tokyo Rose's program.

She several times made me speechless with rage, but she never mentioned the *Octopus,* nor, for that matter, did she refer to the *Walrus* again. The whole thing began to look like a great waste of time and effort, for our men had to go over everything they put into the garbage very carefully, and every day Quin had to prepare more natural-looking paper with *Octopus* on it. But we kept it up during the rest of our time in the area.

There wasn't much time left, as a matter of fact. A few days more than a week, and our "bag" of three ships was beginning to look like the total for that patrol. The week passed. We sighted nothing but aircraft and a number of fishing boats. Then, only two nights before we were due to leave the area, the radar got a contact. It was a rough night, dark, overcast, raining intermittently, with a high, uneasy sea running. It was warm, too, unseasonably so, and the ship was bouncing uncomfortably with no regular pattern as we slowly cruised along, two engines droning electricity back into our battery.

"Radar contact!" O'Brien happened to have the radar watch, and it was his high-pitched voice which sounded the call to action. "Looks like a convoy!" he added.

"Man tracking stations!" responded Keith, muffled in oilskins on the forward part of the bridge. Pat Donnelly, standing watch with Keith as Assistant OOD, was aft on the cigarette deck, as was I. I was beside Keith in a second.

"What's the bearing?"

"I've got the rudder over. We'll have it dead astern in a minute!" A main engine belched and sputtered; then another, and we had four half-submerged exhaust ports blowing engine vapor, water, and a thin film of smoke alternately above and under the waves.

"True bearing is nearly due north, Captain!" Keith was doing my thinking for me. "We're steadying up on course south right now, still making one-third speed."

I went aft again, searching the ocean astern. Nothing could be seen through the binoculars, not even the faint lightening of the murk which would indicate where water and sky met to form the far-distant and unseen horizon. *Walrus* pitched erratically, and a sudden gust of warm wet wind whipped my sodden clothes around my body. I spread my feet apart and leaned into it with my knees slightly bent, adjusting to the jerky motion of the ship. Holding my binoculars to my eyes, I made a deliberate search all around the horizon, or where I imagined the horizon to be. Nearly completed, I was startled by a small black object which abruptly intruded into my field of view, relaxed as quickly. It was only the stern light fixture, mounted on top of our stern chock where, for over a year, it had been a useless appendage.

"Keith, have the radar search all around!" I called. It wouldn't do for us to become so interested in our contact that something else, an escort vessel perhaps, or some as-yet-undetected section of the convoy, could happen unexpectedly upon us.

"Nothing on the radar, sir! Just the original contact!" Keith had anticipated that, too. I moved back to the forward part of the bridge, almost collided with Hugh Adams, who chose that instant to come jumping out of the hatch. He was rubbing his eyes.

"Take me a few minutes to relieve you, Keith," he gasped. "I'm not night-adapted—I was sound asleep when you called tracking stations."

"I've been up here. I can see fine," I broke in. "Keith, I'll take over that part of it. You go below and take over the TDC so that Jim can organize the approach."

Both of them nodded gratefully, and delaying only long enough to make the turnover of essential details to Hugh, Keith swung himself below.

Jim's voice came over the announcing system: "Captain, it's a good-sized convoy. Looks like a dozen ships, maybe more. At least two of them are escorts—maybe more of them, too. Course one-six-zero, speed about ten!"

"Steer one-six-zero!" I told the helmsman. Not Oregon—he would not come on until battle stations was sounded. "All ahead two thirds." Then raising my voice, "Maneuvering, make turns for ten knots!" The conning-tower messenger would relay the word to the maneuvering room via telephone. In a moment

I could feel our speed pick up, a slightly more determined manner with which *Walrus* thrust her snout into the seas. Some of them began to come aboard over the bow, running aft on the deck, partially washing down through it, smothering our new four-inch gun and breaking in a shower of spray on the forward part of the bridge beneath the 20-millimeter gun platform.

We ran on thus for several more minutes. Jim's voice again: "Recommend course one-six-five, speed twelve."

I gave the necessary orders without comment. No doubt that was the convoy course and speed according to more extensive plotting data.

Several more minutes. "Captain, we've got eleven big ships, three or four smaller ones. Possibly one other astern, also small. They're zigzagging around base course one-six-five, speed fourteen knots, making good about twelve down the course line. We're almost dead ahead of them. Range to nearest ship, the leading escort, is ten thousand yards."

"What's the range to the stern escort?" These fellows had come out of the Bungo, all right, and that stern escort must be nobody else but Bungo Pete himself. At least he was keeping to Bungo's old favorite position, astern, the clean-up spot. Bungo would have figured that after an attack the submarine was most apt to wind up astern of the convoy, and out of torpedoes, too, until a reload could be effected. It was not a bad analysis. It would almost unquestionably be true for a submerged attack, very likely so for a surfaced one as well. Captain Blunt had wondered whether any German liaison officers might have been helping him—here I caught my breath as an idea rose, full blown, in my brain: Bungo might most likely be a Japanese submariner himself! He would be one of their old-timers, no doubt, working on the problem for all he was worth and making, thereby, his own contribution to the war effort of his country! Just as Captain Sammy Sams was doing in the role relegated to him!

As such he was doubly dangerous, though I couldn't hate him quite so much as before. And if this, indeed, was Bungo himself, cruising along in his *Akikaze*-class tincan behind the convoy, we were in for an interesting night of it.

"Range to stern escort—we can hardly make him out—he's fading in and out of the radar scope—about fifteen thousand yards." Jim fell silent for a minute. "Zig! The convoy has zigged to his left. Now on course one-three-zero!"

We followed suit. "Keep plotting and checking his zigs, Jim," I said. "When we get them down pat we'll start in." I began to weigh the various factors of the problem. Bungo was astern, and he was by far the most dangerous of the many destroyers and antisubmarine escorts. Instead of turning toward the rear of the convoy, which would be the natural thing to do after shooting our torpedoes, maybe we should turn back toward the head.

This would keep us clear of Bungo for a while. If we could count on a bit of confusion on the part of the Japs, perhaps overdependence on Bungo's sweeping-up operation, we might get away with it. One thing we would have to be careful to avoid, however, was the temptation to dive. If we dived, we became virtually stationary, and that was what Bungo Pete wanted us to do. Plodding along astern of the convoy, having had ample time to be fully alerted to our presence, he would be upon us immediately and subject us to another one of those silent, thorough, unhurried, and practically lethal creeping attacks, or perhaps something else, even better, which he might have thought of since. That, above everything, we had to keep away from.

"Another zig, right, this time! Course now one-six-five! Recommend increase speed to fourteen knots!"

"All ahead standard!" I ordered. "Sound the general alarm. Jim, will you come up to the bridge for a moment?"

"We're already practically at battle stations, skipper," said Jim a second later. The musical chimes were still sounding.

"Just a couple of men haven't taken over their regular battle stations yet." He looked at me questioningly.

"Jim," I told him, "I want to avoid tangling with that last ship. It's no doubt a tincan, and it might even be the one that nearly sank us on our first run here."

"How do you know that?"

"I'll tell you all about it later. Should have before this. Besides that, we mustn't dive unless it's absolutely an emergency. I want to try to stay on the surface, and if we have to we'll take our chances with any of the other escorts. But if they make us dive, that fellow astern will come on up and take over, and we can figure on having a hell of a time!"

My voice was clipped and short. Jim didn't bother to question further. "I've got it," he breathed.

"Just as soon as they zig once more and give us an angle on either bow, we'll swing with them and go on in. We'll need full power, so as to have plenty of speed for maneuvering if we get into a tight spot."

"Aye, aye, sir!" Jim disappeared.

"Hugh," I said, "did you get all that?"

"Yessir!" in a taut voice.

"We might be getting gunfire on the bridge. If I order everyone below, you go too. You can be the last one down, but if we have to dive, you're our last hope. We can't take a chance on your being knocked out."

"Yessir!" again.

"All right. Now, have all the bridge guns mounted. Get all the twenty millimeters up, with two extra men to man each mount, and all four of the bridge fifties. Get plenty of ammunition, too." Hugh leaned to the hatch to give the orders. "Bring up both BAR's also. You and I might as well have something to shoot too."

In a few moments a veritable arsenal was handed up the bridge hatch and the lookouts busied themselves setting the guns in place. The 20's, stowed in pressure-proof containers, had to be lifted out and placed in their mounts. The 50's came up from below, were set in their sockets, and the BAR's we leaned in an out-of-the-way corner. Near each gun we made a neat pile of extra ammunition, belts for the 50's, bandoliers of clips for the BAR's, and a half-dozen round magazines for each of the 20-millimeters. If we should have to dive it would all be lost, but that didn't matter.

Two of the extra men were detailed forward of the OOD's platform for the forward mount, the other two aft on the ciga-rette deck. The 50's could be handled by the lookouts, one to each, with Hugh and me helping with the ammunition belts and firing our own BAR's in between. Preparations were completed just about the time the enemy convoy zigged again.

"Zig, to his right! Angle on the bow, port thirty-five!" Jim's voice in the bridge speaker. It was time to make our move.

"Right full rudder! All ahead flank!" The diesels groaned with the suddenly increased load. Their exhaust spewed forth with doubled vigor. The ship leaned to port, the two port muf-flers choking and splashing, and our stern skidded across the sea, half under and half over the water. Big waves leaped high on to our decks, spraying great patterns of shredded white clouds to half-conceal our stern. A semitransparent mist rose over the deck, whipped by the wind into the cloud pouring out of the starboard muffler pipes, trailed off to starboard and aft, lying low in the tossing, dirty sea.

It was dark, lampblack dark. Only the faintest hint of gray above the water and in the sky. No telling where the horizon was—it all combined into the same dullness, the sea rising right up into the sky. It had stopped raining and the atmosphere felt oppressive, warm, humid. I could smell the odor of sweat mixed with salt spray.

A sea mounted our bow, came straight aft, smothered the gun, and broke in a tall shower at the base of the bridge. Hugh and I ducked, got only a bucketful or two on our backs. The two men standing by the forward 20 were drenched, water streaming down from their hair and off their faces.

"Come on back here!" I yelled. Gratefully they climbed over the bulwark separating us. "Stay here until you're needed," I told them.

"Bridge! Recommend course three-one-zero!" That was Jim. I cupped my hands over the bridge gyro repeater, took a careful look, had to wipe out the accumulation of water before I could read it. We were already nearing due west, two-seven-oh.

"Steady on three-one-zero!" I shouted down the hatch. The rudder began to come off, and *Walrus* straightened up.

Now her speed increased even more, and she pitched and bucked like a wild thing. The wind whistled in my hair, the salt droplets battered my face. No longer rising to the sea, she simply disregarded it, smashed through it. Great clouds of spray were thrown to either side, rising to bridge height as we raced by. Sea after sea rolled over her bullnose, pounded against our bridge front beneath the 20-millimeter gun with a repetitious, drumming hollowness, cast more spume and water into the air.

It started to rain again. The fresh water felt good, washing some of the salt from my face and out of my eyes. It and the spray were bad for the binoculars, though, for the droplets would mar our vision. "Hugh!" I said urgently, "Lens paper! Lots of it!"

Hugh handed me a wadded-up hunk, leaned to the hatch to call for more.

"Range!" I shouted into the mike.

"Five thousand, leading ship!"

"Where's the nearest tincan!"

"Four thousand, thirty degrees on our port bow!" answered Jim.

"How about the other one on this side?"

"Sixty-five hundred yards, sixty relative!"

Jim had gotten us into the best position possible. We were going in astern of the leading escort, which was maintaining station more or less dead ahead of the convoy, and were well clear and ahead of the port-flanking tincan.

"How much farther to go?"

"I figure to start shooting at two thousand. They're all pretty well bunched. We'll shoot a spread of six fish forward, then swing for the stern tubes, shoot them, and in the meantime reload the four torpedoes left forward. Then if we get a chance we can let go with those four. That will leave us only one fish, in the after torpedo room."

"Good," I said into the mike. "What's the range now?"

"Four thousand! We're all ready, except for opening the outer doors. We'll start opening them at three thousand yards!"

I felt curiously detached and emotionless. The die had been cast the moment I directed the rudder be put right. Now it was merely the matter of riding it on out to a finish. The reload would be a problem, because of the motion on the ship, and I was glad that back in New London Keith had insisted on the installation of special pad-eyes for extra securing tackle. We had also carried out special reload drill while on the surface, against just such an eventuality as was now before us.

The ship, of course, carried only twenty-four torpedoes in all, sixteen in the forward torpedo room and eight in the after room. Having attacked with three fish twice out of the forward tube nest and once out of the after nest, we had fifteen fish left: ten forward and five aft. It would be worthwhile to reload the four left after the first salvo forward and try to get them off, but hardly so for the single left aft.

"What's the range now?" I had been searching for the targets, was still unable to see them. We were racing to destroy some men and some ships I had never seen. Perhaps I never would see them—I could tell their approximate bearing by looking up at the angle swept by the parabolic radar reflector whenever, from the motion of the mast behind me, I knew it was taking a bearing. They had been slightly on the starboard bow; now the leading ship bore several degrees on the port bow.

"Three-three-double-oh! Recommend change course to two-nine-oh! We're starting to open outer doors now—with this speed it may take us a little time!"

The newer boats had hydraulically operated outer torpedo tube doors, but not *Walrus,* already outdated. Ours had to be cranked open by hand, one by one, against the water pressure built up by our speed.

"Left to two-nine-zero!"

The rudder indicator went left a little, came back to center. Oregon's voice: "Steady on two-nine-oh!"

Out of nothing they popped into view. "Targets!" I bawled. I flung my binoculars into the TBT bracket, twisted it violently both ways, taking it all in. A solid mass of ships, dead ahead and to starboard. Well to port, a single smaller vessel, the leading escort. No need to worry about him. To starboard, far to starboard, a single tiny shape—the port flanker. He would be a problem soon.

But the ships ahead—we couldn't miss! There must be three columns at least, solid black against a lowering grayness. Eleven ships in all, Jim had said.

"Range, Jim!" I said into the mike. "I've got the TBT on the leading ship—looks like a tanker!"

"Two-five-double-oh! Do you see the escorts, Captain?"

"I see them! We're all right! Keep the ranges coming!"

"Range, two-four-double-oh! Outer doors are open, sir! Two-three-double-oh! Two-two-double-oh! Taking a radar sweep—clear all around—Range two-one-double-oh!"

"TBT is on the leading ship, Jim," I said into the mike. "Angle on the bow is large, around port ninety."

Hanging on to *Walrus'* careening bridge, I kept my binoculars rigidly fixed on the leading ship. *Walrus* rolled spasmodically from side to side, pitched her bows under—her bows, where six bronze warheads needed only the word from me to send them on their deadly mission. A sea roared up to the bridge; instinctively I ducked. *Walrus* heaved and pounded. It had stopped raining. Somehow the sky looked just a bit less dark, the gray less pronounced. Our targets were outlined distinctly for me now. Two tankers in the near column. Maybe more beyond. A large freighter bringing up the rear of the nearest column. All big ships, big and fast.

"Two thousand yards!" Jim's voice carried a finality, a defiance to it.

I risked a quick glance to starboard—the port-flanking tincan was still clear, much nearer. We had a couple of minutes to go, to be deliberate with. Now that we had got there, as Captain Blunt used to say, TAKE YOUR TIME AND MAKE EVERY FISH COUNT!

"Stand by forward!" Into the mike. "I'm on the leading ship, Jim! Let me know as each one goes out!—Shoot!"

"Fire!" Jim had been holding the announcing system button down as he gave the command. I felt nothing. No jolt, no jerk as three thousand pounds, a ton and a half, was expelled.

"One's away," blared the bridge speaker. A pregnant pause. "Two's away!" More time. I took my glasses off the TBT, swung around to inspect the nearing destroyer. "Three's away!" Jim was shooting a spread, would need no further TBT bearings from me. "Four's away!" I looked forward, reaching out to see the white wakes, impossible in the heaving black water. "Five's away!" The oncoming tincan was looming larger all the time. Wonder if he's seen anything yet? "Number six away! All torpedoes expended forward! Range to target, one-three-double-oh!"

"Left full rudder!" I yelled the order. *Walrus* scudded around, the starboard mufflers roaring their choked protest.

"Recommend course zero-nine-zero!"

"No!" I shouted, then recollecting myself, grabbed the mike: "No good, Jim. Too close to the port-flanking tincan!" I tried to speak calmly. "How about one-seven-zero with a left ninety gyro for the stern tubes?"

"Roger!"

"Oregon, steady on one-seven-zero!" He had heard the colloquy with Jim, and the rudder had already eased a few degrees in anticipation. But, disciplined helmsman that he was, he had to have the order.

"Steady on one-seven-zero!" No question about Oregon's steering ability. He gently eased the rudder off and the ship lunged ahead, the lubber's line right on the marker.

I picked up the mike, ran to the after TBT, plugged it in. "Stand by aft! After TBT!" I said into the mike. I had to push Pat Donnelly aside to give me a clear shot for sighting.

The after bridge speaker: "Standing by aft! We're all set below, Captain! Range one-two-five-oh!"

"Shoot!" I had the TBT aimed right between the first and second ships of the near column, at another ship in the second column whose black silhouette completely filled the space between them.

"Seven's away! Eight's away!" Another look at the destroyer. We were running nearly right away from him, gaining, with our temporary speed advantage. "Nine away! Ten away! All torpedoes expended, Captain! We're reloading forward."

Ten torpedoes—we were lighter by better than thirty thousand pounds, and about seventy thousand dollars' worth of complicated mechanism was out there running in the ocean.

And we were in something of a box, too. Any change in course would increase the approaching destroyer's chances of catching us, make it easier for him to see us.

"Range to the near escort, dead astern!" I called the inquiry into the mike, leaning against the periscope supports with my feet braced in front of me. In this location I could not feel the radar mast rotate, but I could sense it going around, sweeping aft. *Walrus'* motion was no different on the new course. Seas were still sweeping her with regularity, leaping higher than her radio antenna stanchions—higher than a man's height—splattering all over the deck aft, sometimes virtually submerging it.

Steam, from our hot mufflers under the deck, boiled up through the wooden slats, drifted faintly away. It would be suicide to walk aft there.

"Range to escort, one-nine-double-oh!" He WAS close!

Something had happened in the direction of the convoy. I turned—a flash as though of light, but bigger than any light, and yellower. It lasted only a fraction of a second. Then another, and another! No sound—there couldn't be any sound, with all the natural noises of wind and sea going on. I looked harder. Could that be the suspicion of yet another flash in the second column? These were all torpedo hits, of that there could be no doubt, and probably from our bow salvo at that. Our stern shots would be a minute or so later getting there.

Back to the escort: "What's the range now?" He didn't look any different, but in the dim visibility it would be hard to tell anyhow. Still bows on, still coming, no indication of having seen anything out of the ordinary.

"Range to escort, one-nine-five-oh!" That was not good. We should be making twenty knots to his fourteen, should be pulling ahead faster than that.

Flash! Another hit! And then, flash-flash—two, almost together. Some notice at last from the convoy. Now it was evident that it was breaking up. Ships were turning every which way. Suddenly it was no longer an entity, a constant you could think of as a single thing; it had disintegrated, almost in an instant, into eleven different ships. It was as though they were being driven by some inner compulsion. Dark forms outlined against the slightly less dark sky seemed to be motivated by only one emotion, one heedless, reckless, awful necessity: to get away from the convoy center.

"Good God!" The outburst came without conscious volition. A violent cone of flame, white-hot with fringes of yellow and orange, screamed into the heavens! It towered over the convoy, towered over us too, cast everything into pitiless relief, turned the night into broad daylight!

— 273

In the insane light of the explosion the leading tanker was visible, broken in half, bow and stern floating idiotically with nothing between them. The second tanker seemed all right; so did the third ship in that column. The one which had blown up must have been one of those in the middle column. As I watched, fascinated, the masts of the freighter, last in the near column of ships, grew shorter, his stack disappeared—and I was looking at his bottom.

Then the noise of it reached us, a horrible, sudden, all-gone crash, a detonation of a million pounds of TNT, a complete, unutterable holocaust! It could only have been an ammunition ship. No wonder the ships of the convoy had been trying to get away!

"Captain! What is it!" Jim's voice on the bridge speaker.

"I'm OK—come on up here!" Jim arrived in time to see the second tanker burst into flames. His comment was identical to mine:

"Good God! Did we do that?"

"Yes, Jim." I silently pointed out the tincan on our tail. "He can't miss seeing us now, unless he's too interested in what's going on over there to tend to his business."

"We'll have to watch for our chance, now, old man." I said. "Most of those ships have escaped the blast, though we can probably scratch four of them. Get back on the radar and give me a picture of how it looks."

Jim ran down the hatch. His voice came in a couple of seconds: "Convoy has scattered. We have only nine pips on the scope left. One seems to have fallen behind"—that would be the capsized freighter—"they're really in a mess there, all right."

"What's the range to the tincan?"

"Near destroyer—one-seven-double-oh!"

He was closing to look us over. There was no doubt about it: we were in trouble. Normally we should dive. Only one other thing to do.

"Range to convoy?"

"Convoy—nearest ship one-five-double-oh. The rest on up to three-oh-double-oh!"

That settled it. The convoy had at least one fleeing ship nearer to us than the destroyer, coming in more or less on our beam. Presumably he would be jittery, scared, not, at all events, a ship-of-war.

"Right full rudder!" I ran back to the fore part of the bridge. "All right, boys! Man those guns!" They jumped to them with alacrity. "When we go by this ship, put everything you have into his bridge! Never mind anything else, just his bridge!"

I took a bearing, gave Oregon a course so as to pass starboard to starboard at about a quarter of a mile. This would put the Jap ship between us and the escort. As the rudder went over, Jim informed me that our torpedo reload had been completed. We were ready for business again, with four fish forward and one aft.

The range closed swiftly at our combined speeds. Larger and larger loomed the blunt, black bow of the ship. I don't think they even saw us. At point-blank range—it was more like four hundred than five hundred yards when we got abeam— we opened up with everything we had, swept his bridge. It was grim work holding the 20's on, especially for the two men forward who were half under water a good part of the time, but they kept to it. I could see the tracer bullets arching into the enemy's bridge area, disappearing into the square-windowed pilot-house, as we swept on.

I shot a quick glance across his stern. The pursuing destroyer had not changed course yet, was still heading more or less for the bow of the ship behind which we had disappeared. It was dark again, the flare of the explosion having gone, but the lights of two big fires in two of the convoy reflected from the hulls of both ships behind us. We, by contrast, must be in the shadow, unless unlucky enough to become silhouetted. The freighter we had raked wavered in his course. Perhaps we had gotten the steersman—he swung off to the left, toward the onrushing tincan, his swing increasing rapidly. The destroyer saw it too, put his rudder hard over, barely avoided colliding. This gave us an opening:

"Range to destroyer!" I yelled into the mike. "Stand by aft! Angle on the bow, starboard ninety!" It was greater, but he would surely turn again. "Shift to after TBT!" I ran aft, plugged in the mike.

"Range eight hundred!" said the speaker.

"Give him twenty knots!" I waited an age, it seemed to me. It could not have been more than ten seconds.

"Set!"

"Shoot!" I shouted. There was only one torpedo left aft, but it might do some good, if we had luck. I reached for the mike, tugged at it to unplug it, when the whole side of the destroyer blossomed in red and orange. Heedless, I ran forward as the tearing crack of several shells passed close overhead. There was a screaming of machine-gun bullets and several dull thuds, followed by the characteristic wavering whines of a ricochet or two. In the midst of this came the twin chatter of the after mount; Pat Donnelly and the two men detailed to the after 20-millimeter were holding it steady into the black hull of the destroyer.

And then, cataclysmically, a mushroom of white water burst in the middle of the other ship, hoisted him up amidships, his back broken, bow and stern sagging deep into the water. His guns stopped, except for one small one on the bridge which kept going for several seconds longer until the black ocean closed over it.

Up ahead, chaos. Two ships on fire, one black hull still not under, but bottom up, showing red in the flame. Other ships, one minus a stack, probably as a result of the explosion of the ammunition ship close aboard, cutting madly in all directions. Too close, now, to change course again. Keep going. Have to keep going. We aimed our course to go between the two burning ships. Just beyond we found another, all alone, making off to the west. We drew up alongside, less than a mile away, keeping out of the light of the fires. We turned toward.

Angle on the bow, port eighty, range fifteen hundred—Fire! Two fish. Two left. We put our rudder right, ran past him on the opposite course, saw both torpedoes hit, saw the splash as the air flasks of both blew up. I raved with impotent fury at the sight, forgetting that we should instead be thankful that the single torpedo we had fired aft, less than three minutes before, had functioned properly.

Nothing to do but come around again. We left the rudder full right, turned madly in a full circle, lined him up again—Fire! That did it. One torpedo hit and exploded and he sagged down by the bow. Maybe he'd sink, maybe not, but we had no more fish to make sure.

Another tearing, ripping noise overhead. Then another, and a third and fourth. Two ships shooting: Bungo, racing up from his position astern to join the fight, and someone else, either the starboard flanker or the lead escort. We were trapped—we'd have to dive. They were too far away for effective reply with our automatic small-caliber weapons, and there was no question of our trying our own four-inch gun in reply, even if we could stand on deck to use it.

"All hands below!" I yelled. Hugh wavered as the lookouts and Pat dashed past us. I motioned impatiently to the hatch. He dropped below.

"Rudder amidships—all ahead emergency!" I yelled to Oregon. I aimed for the narrow space between the two flaming ships again. If we could get between them once more—I knew there was no escort vessel on *that* side—that would force the two destroyers to slow down and maneuver to avoid their own ships. That might be our chance.

I pushed the bridge speaker button for the general announcing system: *"Maneuvering, give it everything you've got!"* They did, too. Clouds of blue-white smoke poured out of our exhaust. Our speed picked up perceptibly. *Walrus* arrowed for the hole, slipped through it, headed eastward at full speed, leaving the wrecked ships behind and a cloud of diesel smoke to obscure our passage. The two destroyers, shadowy figures at fairly long range, were cut off, had to shoot over them. Both were firing continuously, the one from the convoy's rear particularly well. From his position that must be Bungo, and he was using salvo fire with methodical precision. The shells were still tearing overhead, closer, if anything, than before, despite the obstruction in the range. One or two dropped close alongside, kicked up great spouts of water. No question about it. Old Bungo was a good naval officer and ran a taut, tough ship. His destroyer—*Akikaze* class, all right—was shooting at least two to the other's one, and accurately, despite the weather.

I picked up the mike. "They're going to have to slow down because what's left of their convoy is in the way," I said. "Take a sweep around with the radar . . ."

Another salvo from Bungo. I could see all four flashes from his guns. He would have to hold back on the next salvo or two, now, because of the ships in the way.

There was a blinding flash. The whole world turned kaleidoscopic. Stars and pinwheels and fireballs whirled about me, all emanating from a round, sunlike face emitting rays of white-hot fire—the face of Bungo Pete. He looked benign, friendly, despite the fireballs . . . surprisingly like Sammy Sams.

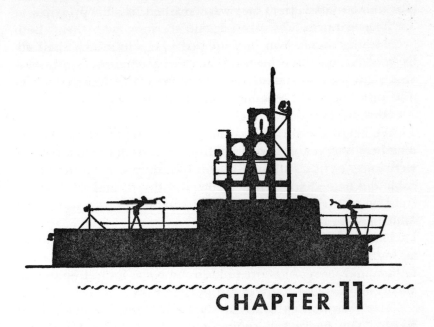

CHAPTER 11

THE WHEELS WERE STILL SPIN-
ning when I opened my eyes. I was lying in my own bunk, and
there was the smell of medicine all around. Cecil Throop's bunk
springs and mattress, which had been slung above mine, were
gone. Jim and Keith were standing beside my bunk, smiling
at me, bracing themselves against the gentle heave of the ship.

"What happened?" I managed to say. "What about Bungo . . . ?" I gripped the sides of the bunk, tried to raise myself. My whole right side shot excruciating pain through my
body.

"Take it easy, skipper, everything's fine. We're through the
Nanpo Shoto, and we're on our way back to Pearl Harbor. Right

now it's broad daylight and we're riding on the surface on three engines, making excellent time. Now that you're feeling better, everything's jake." Jim's face was wreathed in a happy grin.

"What happened?" I asked again.

"Nothing much. You just stopped a Jap four-inch shell all by yourself and have been out for three days, that's all. And your right leg's broken, so don't try to get up." I fumbled for it. The cast felt as if it occupied half the bunk.

"How did I get down here?"

"We heard the shell hit—you were talking on the mike, remember? And you were still holding the button down after you were knocked out. Rubinoffski and I found you lying there, out cold. We hauled you down below and dived, and we've been running ever since. We had to lay you out on the wardroom table to set your leg and sew you up."

"How badly hurt am I?" I knew part of the answer without asking. The strain of what little talking I had already done was telling, and it was an effort to keep my voice from dropping to a whisper. Jim and Keith began to edge for the door.

"The Pharmacist's Mate says you'll be fine, skipper," said Keith. "You had a bad concussion and a couple of bad cuts besides the break, but nothing that won't mend in time."

A wave of pain hit me as the two lifted the green curtain and passed out into the passageway. I tried to call out, but couldn't. The bulkheads receded, wobbled, blended into a dull ivory from their original white and gray. Someone came through the curtain—I hardly noticed the jab of the needle.

Despite Jim's and Keith's assurances, and the number of smiling well-wishers who came to see me during the latter stages of our trip, I was far from being in good shape when we put in to Pearl. I don't remember much of the first part of the trip, or whether anything out of the ordinary happened during it. Once in a while, it seemed to me, we dived—whether for drill or for real I could not tell, and cared less. Later on there was a discussion of having a plane meet us near Midway to take me off. I remember becoming violently upset at the idea, as well as the following suggestion, in a few days, that *Walrus* put in there to leave me. I became more lucid rapidly then and was able to think of some of the things lying ahead for all of us. One thing was obvious, though everyone avoided the subject until I brought it up. I was through as skipper of *Walrus*.

Two nice things happened before we got in to Pearl: A dispatch from ComSubPac, which Jim brought in with a smile shortly after I had regained my senses for the first time, and an AlNav a few days before our arrival.

The dispatch said:

FOR WALRUS X PASS TO YOUR FINE SKIPPER OUR HEARTFELT WISHES FOR HIS SPEEDY RECOVERY AND CONGRATULATIONS ON AN OUTSTANDING PATROL X COMSUBPAC SENDS X

The AlNav was a promotion announcement. Jim was made Lieutenant Commander. Hugh and Dave became Lieutenants, and Jerry Cohen a Lieutenant, Junior Grade.

There was another AlNav, which Jim showed me also. This one gave commanding officers of certain types of vessels, of which submarines were one, authority to promote deserving members of their crews. As a consequence, Jim prepared and I signed promotions for Quin, Oregon, Rubinoffski, Russo, and O'Brien. Kohler, Larto, and one or two others, already Chief Petty Officers, were at the top of the ladder and could not be promoted higher; so we did the next-best thing and sent papers recommending them for promotion to Warrant rank to the Bureau of Naval Personnel.

Once I was safely ensconced in the hospital at the Pearl Harbor Navy Yard, the events of the past few months seemed almost like a dream, and it took an effort to bring myself back to reality. To begin with, it was my shinbone or tibia, as the doctors called it, which had been broken, and it was decided that it was not healing properly. So the doctors broke it again and set some silver pegs into it—a most painful and inconvenient arrangement. It was hot in the hospital, and the Navy Yard noises were neither close enough to make out anything of interest from them, nor far enough away to be unbothersome. Most of the time I lay in a foggy stupor, hardly aware of what was going on around me. The only times I felt at all normal were when one of my shipmates of the *Walrus* or some other old friend dropped in—a courtesy difficult to find the time for in their busy lives.

There were, of course, a few items of urgent business to clear up. The most important was brought up by Captain Blunt within a few days. "Rich," he said, "you know we've got to find a new skipper for the *Walrus*." I had been expecting this one.

"Yes, sir." I had my own idea ready to spring when he gave me the opening.

"We've got two or three in mind. Since she's your ship I thought you might like to have something to say about it—unofficially, of course."

"Have you thought of giving her to Jim Bledsoe?"

"Why, no—he's pretty junior—um——" He sucked on the pipe. "Isn't Bledsoe the chap you weren't willing to turn the *S-16* over to?"

"He sure is, Captain, and you know why I couldn't do it. But listen to this." I told Captain Blunt how Jim had made an approach all by himself, swinging to shoot the stern tubes on his own initiative so as to equalize our expenditure of torpedoes, and I told him what a great fighting heart he had. I made quite a little speech out of it, winding up with the clincher that he already was skipper of *Walrus* in fact, having assumed command upon my incapacity, and that the morale of the ship would inevitably suffer if someone were put over him who did not have equal or greater experience in submarine combat.

Old Joe Blunt was impressed, I could see that. He pulled the pipe out of his mouth, palmed the bowl lovingly, slid it into his pocket. "We'll see what can be done about it, Rich," he said as he rose to go, and I knew I had won. At the door he paused. "We'll have to give Bledsoe a new Exec," he said. "Leone is good, but he's pretty junior too. Besides, the next patrol will be his fifth, and he ought to be coming off pretty soon for rotation."

One victory was all I could legitimately hope for, and I had to let that one drop. Keith was not at all disappointed, however, when I told him about it. He'd be tickled pink to be Jim's Number Three, he told me. Knowing him, I knew he would.

I had several long conversations with Jim before he took the *Walrus* to sea, and told him, among other things, everything I knew or guessed about Bungo Pete. In the process I described my fears that there might be some kind of security leak in our submarine command headquarters here in Pearl Harbor. Despite my good relations with Captain Blunt, I had not yet quite felt up to bringing that matter up with him, I told Jim, but would do so at the first opportunity.

Jim and Keith were the most faithful about coming to see me, though the rest of the crew and officers made honest efforts to come also. Shortly after they had returned from the Royal Hawaiian rest period, Kohler, Larto, and a group of others touched me deeply by bringing in a small metal model of *Walrus* which they had all had a hand in making. "She's made out of a CRS bolt," explained Kohler—CRS being the Navy equivalent of stainless steel and valuable for ships because of its noncorrosive properties. "Yah," grinned Larto, his magnificent teeth flashing, "they still wonder what happened to that main induction gag bolt."

"You guys ought to be in jail," I growled in an attempt to register anger I did not feel. "You'd steal your own grandmother blind!"

Russo had the answer for that one. "This ain't stealing, Captain. You're still in the Navy, ain't ya?"

Quin, more thoughtful, said, "We thought you'd like something to remember the *Walrus* by, Captain, and this seemed to be the best idea—it came off the ship, and we made it on a shaper in the sub base machine shop."

When they had trooped noisily out, a few minutes later, they had left not only the model of the *Walrus* but also a gaudy commercial "get well soon" card and a round-robin testimonial signed by every member of the crew to the same effect. And Russo, with considerable smirking and bashful hemming and hawing, hauled out his own personal offering which had been temporarily left in the hall: a huge cake covered with thick varicolored frosting and surmounted by a frosted submarine.

The day before their departure for patrol, all the wardroom came to see me, and I bade them good-by with a lump in my throat. As they filed out, Jim hung back. "Skipper," he began.

"Call me 'Rich,' " I said.

"OK, Rich then. I thought you'd be interested to know—we won't be coming back here for a while. We're going to Australia on this trip. Our patrol area is off Truk, the big Jap base down in the Carolines, and after we're relieved we'll head for Brisbane. We'll do the same thing in reverse on the way back." Jim grinned faintly.

"Why, you lucky dog, you," I said. "That's all you've been thinking of ever since the war started. How did you manage it?"

"Just kept talking it up. I guess they needed a volunteer about the time I got there, and so we got the nod."

"They say it's wonderful country and has wonderful people . . ."

"Especially the wonderful people," Jim agreed. The grin was a bit self-conscious as he said it.

Walrus had hardly been gone a day when Joe Blunt showed up suddenly, unannounced as before. I had already started to sink back into lethargy, hadn't even shaved that morning, and looked like hell in general, which is not the way for any junior to receive a senior, even if he is sick in bed. I pulled myself together.

"Rich, did you or Jim write this patrol report?"

"I did, most of it. I was keeping it up as we went along."

"Good. You mentioned that Tokyo Rose called the *Walrus* by name—did you hear her?"

"Yes, I sure did!"

"Well, as you know, we've been wondering where they got their dope. One other boat, before you, also heard Tokyo Rose call them by name, and of course old Bungo Pete apparently makes a point of showing us that he knows the names of all the boats which operate in AREA SEVEN. But this time something strange has happened. It's the first time he's missed like this, too. Another one of those intelligence reports I told you about arrived this morning, and it mentions the Japs as knowing *Walrus* had been in the area, but goes on to say that the old *Octopus* also made an attack on a convoy, and was sunk by shellfire from the destroyer *Akikaze*. Can you account for that?—What's so Goddamed funny!"

For I was laughing helplessly, pounding the bed in my mirth and relief, rolling my head from side to side with tears coming to my eyes: Gasping, I finally recovered myself sufficiently to tell him of my suspicions and of the garbage stunt. Old Blunt's eyes narrowed as I told him of my deductions regarding the security of ComSubPac, but when I told him about the *Octopus* and the garbage, he burst into a roar of laughter.

"Well, I'll be switched! So that's how Bungo gets his dope. The old son-of-a-bitch paws over our garbage! Why, he probably makes a business of picking it up!" Blunt joined in my renewed guffaws. "Wait until I tell the Admiral about this. This will relieve his mind greatly, and we'll pass it on to the boats. That wily old bastard doesn't miss a trick, does he!"

"Old bastard," I repeated. "Do you know who he is?"

"Sure, we know who he is! His name is Tateo Nakame, and

he's a Captain in the Japanese Navy. He was a submariner and was known for being a mean old cookie, too. I guess they had to be pretty hard-boiled in those days, but anyway, not many people liked him."

So my deduction had been right! "The *Akikaze,* is that his ship—is that the one which landed me here? Why did he quit chasing us, then?"

Blunt chuckled. "You guess. I've been guessing three hours trying to figure out this *Octopus* brainstorm of yours." He waited. "How many destroyers were there in that convoy?" he asked.

"Four, counting Bungo."

"Right, and you sank one of them. Then there were three."

"Yes."

"And how many submarines were there?"

"Only us."

"Guess again. There were two, the *Walrus* and the *Octopus.* From the hell you raised in that convoy he was certain there must have been two subs attacking. When he saw the shell explode on your bridge he figured he had done for one of them —especially when *Walrus* dived immediately afterward. All the rest of the night, and next day too, I think, he collected what was left of his outfit and waited for the other submarine to show up again." Old Blunt's grin threatened to split his face right in two. "This makes twice you've outsmarted him, Rich. He knows the *Walrus* by now, and unless I miss my guess by a mile he knows you also by name. He'd like nothing quite so much as to have your scalp to hang on his belt. He was a mean one in the Jap Navy, remember, and that was during peacetime."

"I'll remember," I promised. But a sickbed and a traction splint in the Pearl Harbor Navy Yard Hospital seemed a million miles away from Tateo Nakame and His Imperial Japanese Majesty's ship *Akikaze.*

Lying in the hospital, I lost all track of time. The hot days came and went. So did the nights. I got a few letters, finally got up the energy to answer them. Hurry Kane wrote me a nice long letter, wishing me quick recovery. She had heard from Stocker in Australia, and expected to get another series of letters any time now. Laura had written her from New Haven and was fine. A couple of newsy letters from Mother every month or so about finished it.

The weary days dragged on. It was a month before they would even let me sit in bed, another month before I could get out of it for any reason whatsoever. When I finally got so I could hobble around, life took on a little more interest. The big news was from Jim, or rather about him. He had entered Brisbane harbor flying a cockscomb of eight Jap flags, signifying eight ships sunk. The Admiral had finally allowed him six positives with two which had to be counted as only damaged, but that had not altered the impact of his arrival. He and every member of the *Walrus* crew had been lionized by the submariners and Brisbaners alike. Apparently all eight ships had been in a single convoy which he had chased halfway across the ocean and attacked repeatedly until he had wiped it out.

Jim, so the letter from Keith read, had been like a wild man, driving *Walrus* and himself relentlessly until all the enemy ships had been sunk. The more sedate official endorsement to his report of *Walrus'* fifth patrol said virtually the same thing in naval jargon: "This patrol must go down in submarine history as one of the most daringly conducted and persistently fought submarine actions of the war."

Jim, I knew, could now have anything in Australia for the asking.

The time finally came, nearly five months after my injury, when I was able to limp with a cane into Captain Blunt's office and ask for a job. I'd go crazy if he couldn't find something for me to do, I told him. He looked at me thoughtfully.

"You can't go to sea for a long time yet, Rich."

"I'll be ready sooner than you think!"

"Maybe so. But while you're waiting—um." He drummed the table. "Rich, there is one way you could be very useful indeed, though it might turn out to be pretty strenuous. But we need someone with your experience and interest."

"Try me," I begged. "What is it?"

"It's the torpedoes. What do you know about them?"

"They're lousy. Everyone knows that."

"You're not the only one who thinks so. Look at this!" Captain Blunt rose and opened a file-cabinet drawer. It was filled with papers. "This is only part of the file. Every paper here is someone's complaint or suggestion regarding our torpedoes."

"What are we doing about them, sir?"

"That's exactly it! Nothing! The Admiral has sent letter after letter to Washington about it. He's even made three trips back there to try to get some action. They say they're making a new exploder which will solve all the problems—and you know when they say we'll get it?" Blunt didn't wait for an answer. "Next year, maybe! Ha!" He pointed the stem of the pipe at me like a pistol. "They don't even know what's wrong with the fish!"

"Then why don't we tell them?"

"That's exactly what we're fixing to do. Admiral Small is about ready to blow his stack, but he wants the clincher first. He wants to take on the project of finding out what the matter is right here in the submarine base, where it can be done under his direct supervision. And he wants a Project Officer who feels the way he does. That is, mad as hell!"

I had never seen Blunt worked up like this. It must have been an extremely sore subject among the whole staff. "I'm your man," I said quickly. "Let me try the job. As a matter of fact, I've had some ideas." I really hadn't, not recently, at any rate, though there had been some at one time. "Look," I said, laying down the cane and getting to my feet. I wobbled across the room, turned and wobbled back. The weak leg throbbed. "See? I'll be giving back the cane in a couple of weeks!"

"You're a liar, Rich!" Blunt was grinning at me. "I've already asked the doctors about you and they say you won't be rid of it for a month. But if you want the job, I'll see if I can talk the Admiral into letting you have it."

I could have whooped for the sheer pleasure of it.

The very same day I sat down to read through the pile of stuff written about the torpedoes. It was immediately evident that someone had already done a pretty good job of sorting and classifying. In general the complaints which occurred most often could be classified as three: *Dud hits,* that is, torpedoes known to have hit the target but which failed to explode; *underruns:* torpedoes seen to pass harmlessly under the target; and *prematures:* explosions taking place before the fish reached the target.

The firing mechanism of the torpedo warhead contained a device—highly secret before the war—which was designed to cause detonation when passing into the magnetic field of a ship. Torpedoes passing under a target's keel should therefore explode somewhere beneath, with devastating results. Some of them did. Perhaps the port-flanking escort, which had chased us and had been broken in two with our last torpedo aft, had been a casualty of this type of explosion. And that also, of course, was why our circular torpedo during the patrol off Palau had gone off while passing overhead; and I remembered that it had actually made three passes at us before finally detonating. Clearly there was something highly erratic about the manner in which this part of the mechanism functioned. It could be blamed for nonexplosion of the underruns and the premature explosion of others.

Another section of the exploding mechanism was intended to cause the torpedo to go off upon hitting the side of a ship. One report in this part of the file was circled in red crayon and bore evidence of considerable handling. It detailed the experience of one skipper who happened to cripple and stop a large tanker on the open sea. There were no escorts, and no air cover, but he couldn't surface because the tanker had manned its guns. Conditions otherwise were ideal—weather sunny and calm. And he had sat there, firing torpedo after torpedo in single shots, as though he were shooting torpedo proving shots in Newport Harbor. And not one of them had gone off. He had fired fifteen all together, eight under the most ideal setup imaginable, and except for the initial salvo there was not the slightest question but that every torpedo hit the target. Yet the only detonation out of the whole bunch was one of the initial salvo which just happened to strike in the vicinity of the propellers.

And of the underruns themselves: why did torpedoes set to run at a depth of ten feet beneath the surface sometimes pass under ships which must draw twenty feet or more? One or two submarine skippers had theorized, early in the war, that Japanese vessels must have extraordinarily shallow draft, but this could not be the answer. I came upon reports of some experimental firings in Brisbane in which practice torpedoes were fired through nets. When the nets were hauled in it was found that the holes made by the torpedoes were considerably deeper than expected. A full report had been sent in to Washington, of course, but as yet nothing remedial had been done about it.

My interview with Admiral Small was nearly a repetition of the talk with his Chief of Staff. This was going to be his personal project, he told me. What he wanted me for was to be Project Officer, to follow through for him and render reports as to what had been discovered. One comment he made was to the effect that he was tired of sending torpedoes all the way to Japan to find out that they wouldn't work. "We'll try them out right here, with regulation warheads on them!" he said.

That was why, within a few days, I found myself poring over large-scale charts of the Hawaiian Islands, trying to select a spot for what the Admiral had in mind. With the topography of the Islands, the place was not difficult to find: a sheer rock cliff, with deep water right up to the rock. Plenty of room for a submarine to approach and fire into the rock, and for a torpedo to make a normal run without danger of hitting the bottom. A sandy bottom, to make later recovery of the torpedoes practicable.

And not long after—about two weeks, and I still needed the cane—I stood on the bridge of the *Skipjack* as she fired a deliberate salvo of warshots into the cliff. One out of four went off. The other three were duds. Then the divers went to work, and for the next several days there was the tedious job of looking over each fish to find out what had happened.

Similarly, we fired numbers of torpedoes down a torpedo range through a series of nets, marking and calibrating exactly at what depth each fish was actually running for each net position.

We built up great experience tabulations, based on the net shots and the explosion tests. To get more data for our tables, the sub base strung guy wires to a building, slid torpedo warheads down them—loaded with a mixture of sand and sawdust to the right weight, however, instead of TNT—to collide with a section of steel plate on the ground. We used several guy wires, so as to simulate various angles of impact, and the heights were carefully calibrated to produce the proper speeds.

The results of all our tests, when Admiral Small finally gave them his approval, were conclusive. The magnetic feature was so delicate and intricate—a marvel of design and ingenuity but totally undependable in service—that it might as well be forgotten. The mechanical part of the exploder, which should invariably go off upon impact, was also too delicate and at the same time too heavily constructed. Its inertia was so great that upon impact the firing pin, key to the whole thing, would be deformed or bent before it had a chance to do its job. And the torpedoes habitually ran as much as twenty feet deeper than they were supposed to. Like everything else about them, however, the depth was erratic; they wobbled down the course like a sine wave, alternately deep and shallow. It was just luck what part of the curve the target happened to be on.

The more we got into the problem, the madder everyone got.

Everything we had discovered should have been found out on the proof ranges long ago, before the war in most cases. The design failures should have been discovered by proper tests before the torpedoes ever got to the proof ranges. And there was no excuse for our not receiving the correct depth-running data, no more than for the refusal of the torpedo designers to accept, or at least investigate, our earlier findings that the torpedoes ran deeper than set. When the Admiral took off for Washington this time, he was loaded.

When he returned, not many days later, there was a glint of cold fury in his eyes. Captain Blunt and I met him at the airfield. By this time I had given back the cane, though the leg still bothered me. "They believe us at last," he growled, "but they're not doing a thing about it. The new exploder will be the answer to everything—when it's ready." He snorted. "Ready! Hell! Maybe next year, it might be ready! They haven't even built one yet!"

Blunt turned to me. "Tell him your idea, Rich," he commanded.

The idea was simply stated. "I've been looking over the exploder," I said, "and of course if we could make it work the way it ought to, that would be the best answer of all. It occurred to me that perhaps if we could rebuild the mechanical firing gadget with lighter parts and completely disconnect the magnetic part of the exploder, we might get acceptable results. As far as the depth settings on the torpedoes are concerned, which is an entirely separate problem, at least we know what's wrong and can make allowances for it."

Admiral Small's reaction was characteristic. "Hop to it, Rich!" was all he said, but I found doors opening for me wherever I went. More weeks of work followed, and I had the heady feeling that we were at last getting somewhere. Our research, if it could be called that, now had a definite goal: a firing-pin mechanism strong enough and light enough to complete the necessary motion upon impact with the target before the crushing force of the impact itself bent it all out of shape. We were work-ing with split seconds, and the answer, when it was finally found, was unbelievably simple. Airplane propellers had to be very light and very strong. We collected all the damaged propel-lers we could find and cut the required parts from the hard, light metal.

"Better use for a busted prop," the Army Major at Hickam Field told me, "could not be found anywhere!"

From then on the problem became one of production, for the Admiral insisted that he would hold a submarine back from patrol, if necessary, before letting her go without previously having seen to it that every exploder she carried in her torpe-does had the modification. Every available machine shop in the submarine base was pressed into service to make the new parts. A rigid inspection system was set up, too, for Admiral Small was adamant on this score.

The reports from the first few boats which took the modified exploders to sea were jubilant. Where previously torpedoes had been fired with the hope they would function properly if they hit, they were now fired with the certainty that they would. The only problem remaining was the only one we should have had to worry about from the beginning: hitting the target.

My duties were changed also, for with the final solution of the torpedo problem and the setting up of the production and inspection lines, there was nothing left for me to do. Blunt re-fused to give me another submarine; I would have to wait a while longer, he said, and I found myself detailed, instead, as Officer in Charge of the Attack Teacher.

This was virtually the same gadget which *Walrus'* crew had trained on during our precommissioning days in New London, with one difference: the trainees here would within weeks be doing it for real. Some days we were extra busy, and for weeks at a time I would have to allot appointments just as a doctor might, trying to give most to those who needed it most. And there were slack periods when nobody seemed to want our synthetic attack training. During those times, to keep the small crew of the Attack Teacher from growing stale and at the same time to keep my own hand in, I used to run off attacks on my own, sometimes taking the part of the submarine skipper, sometimes for variety that of the target. On these occasions it became a sort of no-holds-barred competition and our favorite cast of characters was to pit the destroyer against the submarine, one of each, with the destroyer, to make it even, aware of the sub's presence, though perhaps not exactly where. The Attack Teacher included a sonar-attack section also, so this was integrated into the game.

The men loved it; especially whenever one of them got me, as make-believe submarine skipper, into a box from which, try as I might, I could not escape. More than once my theoretical submarine was rammed by the destroyer; and much more frequently I was driven below periscope depth, after which the whole group would repair to the sonar rooms and with high hilarity try to knock me out with depth charges. Part of the time the submarine won the fight, too, and when it was my turn to shoot torpedoes at the destroyer, I always pretended, in my own mind at least, that I was shooting them at Bungo Pete.

Stocker Kane showed up with the *Nerka* shortly after I had taken over the Attack Teacher, and many pleasant hours of visiting with him in the Royal Hawaiian Hotel ensued before he set out for his next patrol. He had loved Australia. It was as he imagined America must have been a hundred years ago, he said.

He talked a lot about Hurry, too, and a little, not much, about Laura. "You know how you'll take a liking to someone," he said. "Laura and Hurry seemed to hit it off especially well, and they've been corresponding with each other ever since you all left New London. Hurry doesn't think she's happy, though. She's been trying to get Laura to come out and stay with her in San Francisco, so that she'll be there when they send the *Walrus* back for overhaul." He chuckled. "She says Jim doesn't write enough. Hurry's always looking around for someone to mother a little, not having any youngsters to keep her busy." The faintest suggestion of a shadow crossed his face.

"Maybe she's working on me, too," I said. I told him of the two letters she had written me.

"She told me she was going to. She thinks you ought to get married, Rich. Leave it to Hurry! She probably thinks you ought to have been the one to marry Laura, instead of Jim."

I managed to smooth my startled look into a grin.

This would be *Nerka's* sixth patrol, probably Stocker's last for a while. The rotation policy rarely permitted a skipper more than five patrols in succession. But *Nerka* would most probably be heading for Mare Island or Hunter's Point for a much-needed overhaul after her sixth, and no doubt ComSubPac was willing for Stocker to have the privilege of bringing her back.

Three weeks later I was, of course, on the dock when *Walrus* came in, having completed her seventh patrol on the way back from Australia. She was something to see as she came bravely around the point of ten-ten dock. From her bullnose to the top of the periscope supports was a perfect clothesline of small Japanese flags, each one representative of a ship she had sunk. She looked weather-beaten, tired, patches of rust showing here and there, though with no visible damage, but there was no denying a certain *élan* about her and about the sure manner in which Jim put her alongside the dock.

His fame had preceded him. He had made three patrols in and out of Australia instead of two. His second run had been better than the first, and on his third he had entered an enemy harbor, sunk two ships there and shelled a fortified island, exchanging fire for half an hour and escaping unscathed. He had sunk a Japanese cruiser near Palau, and he had put three torpedoes into one of the huge Jap battlewagons, a sixty-thousand-ton monster. A Japanese submarine had fired a torpedo at him; personally seeing it first himself, he had swung away to avoid the torpedo track, then fired two torpedoes out of his stern tubes back at the submerged Jap. A great explosion had announced his success, and all sorts of debris had come to the surface by way of proof. With only nine torpedoes left, three forward and six aft, he had engaged in a melee with a six-ship convoy during which he had actually backed into action at one point, and sank three more ships. Finally, with no torpedoes remaining, he had attacked one of the surviving freighters with the four-inch deck gun and every automatic weapon the ship possessed, silencing her defensive battery and sinking her—and still without receiving a scratch in return.

To cap it all, he picked up four prisoners and brought them back with him. The crowd which awaited *Walrus* was the biggest I had ever seen for any submarine. Jim looked wonderful; bronzed, alert, brimming with self-confidence. I shook hands with him right after the Admiral and Captain Blunt.

"Hi, Rich!" he said. "How's the leg?" Still holding my hand, he turned to Admiral Small. "Here's the man who's responsible for all I know about submarining, Admiral." He winked at me as the congratulations engulfed him.

Keith also looked tan and fit, as did Hugh, Dave and the rest, though I did not see Jerry Cohen. Leone's grip was hard and firm. "Hi, Captain! Glad to see you back on your feet! Guess I'll be joining you here for a while!"

"You being rotated?"

"Yep! They tried to make me get off in Australia, but I said nix to that. So this is my last trip in the old *Walrus*. Dave took leave in Brisbane during the sixth run, so now he will finally get his chance at the TDC."

"Good! You rate a rest, after seven runs—where's Jerry Cohen?"

"Oh!" Keith chuckled. "We've been calling him Cobber instead of the skipper. He stayed in Australia—liked it better than anybody, but by this time he's probably out on a patrol with one of the boats regularly based there."

Jim's Exec, a Lieutenant named Knobby Robertson whom

I had met when he reported aboard the *Walrus* after my injury, now approached. "Will we see you at the Royal tonight, Commander Richardson?"

"Oh, no," I demurred. "You fellows have a lot to talk over your first night in. I'll drop over later."

"No, sir. The Captain said he might not get a chance to ask you himself, and for me to make sure that you come!"

That night I realized finally that I had lost *Walrus* completely. There was a difference about my old comrades, a difference hard to put into words. They looked the same—they *were* the same—but the songs they sang, the stories they told, and the general tough, devil-may-care attitude about them were all new. Perhaps I was subconsciously disappointed to find such a radically complete change. I had almost forgotten that nearly a year had elapsed in the interim, that *Walrus* had made three more patrols, three hard-hitting, supremely successful patrols, since I had last seen them. They had gone on, had continued to pursue their destiny. It was I who had grown slack and soft.

The whisky flowed, more and more bottles were opened, and I felt myself drifting away from them, a little farther with each story retold. This was their party, their right to relax from tension, their given privilege—not mine. I wondered if Jim's request for my presence had only been politeness after all. He had become reeling drunk.

Finally I heaved myself to my feet, declined the proffered additional drink, made the excuse that I had work to do the next day.

"No, you don't! Not yet, skipper—I mean Rich!" Jim grabbed me around the neck, nearly fell, then steadied himself. "Listen. I got something I want to tell you. Been meaning to for a long time." He turned me half-around, fumbled on a nearby table, grasped a bottle by the neck, waved it at the others.

"See you all later, fellows! Here's the best skipper the old *Walrus* ever had, my old pal Rich, and we're going away to have a talk!" With that he pushed open the door into the adjoining room, kicked it shut behind us, sat, or rather flopped, on the bed. He held out the bottle.

"Pour a drink!"

"No, thanks. Don't you want to save this for later, Jim? I've got to go."

"Pour a drink, I said!" The bottle wavered in his hand. I took it, poured some in a glass in the bathroom, pretended to sip it.

"That's better. Lissen." Jim's eyes were bloodshot, bleary. His voice was loose, his face puffy. "I've been meaning to tell you this for a long time—took too much whisky so I could. Lissen. I'm a bastard."

"No, you're not, Jim. Quit it. We can talk tomorrow." I rose.

"Siddown! Gawdamit, Rich, the Captain of the *Walrus,* the best gawdam submarine in the Navy, wants to talk to ya."

I sat. There seemed nothing else to do.

"I've been doing some thinking. All during these last patrols. Not just last three. Before that. 'Member when you stopped my qualification on the old *S-16?* I swore then I would get even with you. I swore I'd make you regret the day you did that to me. I was gonna sabotage everything you tried to do. I was gonna mess you up so bad you'd wish you'd never seen me. Laura told me not to. Said she'd never marry me if I did that. Said the war would find you out for what you were. Said I should stick it with you for crew's sake."

I sat staring, embarrassed to hear him. I had realized that Jim must have told Laura something of our contretemps, but naturally I could not have supposed it had gone this far. Nor had I suspected that Jim's apparent friendliness had all been a sham. But I couldn't see what he was driving at now.

Jim upended the bottle, took a deep swig. "Siddown. I'm not finished yet. I pretended to like you, and went along with you and the *Walrus,* and all the time I hated your guts. I thought you were yellow for not tangling with that first Jap sub we saw, and I hated your guts all the way out to Japan. Then when ole Bungo Pete got after us I saw a real submarine skipper in action, and I realized it was you that saved us all. And gradually I came to know that you were a prince of a fellow and that I didn't know the first thing about being a skipper. When you gave me *Walrus* I found out."

"You're drunk, Jim. You don't have to tell me all this . . ."

"Down, I said. I'm still not through yet. Gotta get this thing off my chest. This is war—tough racket—maybe I'll get sunk nex' time—maybe you will. May never get another chance to talk."

He took another swig, wiped his mouth.

"So now I'm skipper of the *Walrus*. You gave her to me. I'd never have gotten her if you hadn't talked ole man Blunt into it. And I've had three patrols to learn what it's like to be all alone. There's nobody out there for the skipper to look to, tell him what to do . . . You know that? You're all alone. You got no buddies. You got friends—sure, everybody on the ship's your friend—but you got no buddies. Nobody to tell you what to do. You got to figure it all out yourself, 'cause you're all alone on your own. That's what you been trying to teach me, Rich, ole man. I want you to know that I think you're a great man. You're my best friend, an' you're wunnerful—an' I'm sorry I was such a bastard—an'—an' I already wrote to Laura and tole her so. . . . Tell her again too . . ."

The bottle slipped from his hands. He was swaying where he sat on the bed. His voice trailed off into an unintelligible mumble. I laid him back, pulled off his shoes, trousers, and shirt, threw a blanket over him. He wasn't quite gone yet. "Laura," he muttered, "Laura—she's a sweetheart. I'm a bastard—always was. Never should . . . never should . . ."

I quietly went out the door into the hall, turned out the light, and softly closed the door behind me. I felt sorry for him, and oddly at peace.

CHAPTER 12

DESPITE MY DESIRE TO SEE MORE
of my old shipmates, our paths for the next three weeks were
cast in dissimilar patterns. The three patrols they had made
"down under," and the taste of Australia in between, were
enough to set them apart, make them somehow different, from
the men I had known. And now that they were back again from
patrol, entitled to temporary freedom from care at the Royal
Hawaiian, there was a practical barrier too.

I caught a glimpse of Jim once, driving the station wagon
issued to *Walrus,* with the handsome, dark face of Joan
beside him. Neither of them saw me. She was sitting rather
away from the right-hand door, but even so the breeze through

the open window rippled her heavy black hair as she turned attentively in Jim's direction.

Keith I saw a couple of times. Being due for detachment upon *Walrus'* departure, he had been left in charge of her refit until the regular crew returned from their recuperation period. This gave us a few opportunities to renew old acquaintance-ship as we occasionally encountered each other around the submarine base, and I came to notice him more particularly than before.

He had changed mightily from the willing but inexperienced youth who had reported to the *S-16's* fitting out and precom-missioning office three years and some months ago. Tanned and fit, as most of us were who were fortunate enough to draw topside bridge watches, he was now poised, confident, sure of himself and his abilities. His wide-set eyes had turned a deep gray from their original pale blue—some of the color of the sea had seeped into them—and the set of his jaw betokened strength fired through experience. His once-boyish face was now a bit finely drawn, his hair bleached to a lighter shade by the sun and salt wind, his voice a perceptible amount deeper. He was the same old Keith, but a stronger, more vital one.

For that matter, Jim, too, had undergone changes. He was decisive, sure of himself, the old wayward immaturity long burned out of him. Probably all of us showed evidences of the passage of time and the effect of the hell of undersea combat.

There had been talk about sending the *Walrus* back to the States for overhaul, but it was eventually decided that she was in good enough condition to make one patrol before do-ing so. When the day came for her to depart, Keith and I were there to see her off. She looked beautiful in her coat of new gray paint, beautiful, lean, and deadly. The aura with which she had arrived was still there. Compared to some of the newer boats she might have an old-fashioned look about her, but neither could any of them boast her record of thirty-three ships sunk or damaged. It was hard to appreciate that she was only two years old—the *Octopus* had been still considered brand-new at the comparable time.

Next day Keith left for the States for a well-merited thirty days' leave, and I returned to my office, to the suddenly humdrum routine of the Attack Teacher. I could hardly sit still.

That afternoon I sought out the Chief of Staff. "Captain," I said without preamble, "when may I have another ship?"

He looked at me thoughtfully. "What's your hurry, Rich? Tired of the routine of Pearl Harbor?"

"Yes. I just saw Jim Bledsoe go out for his eighth consecutive patrol. I've only made four. I've got a few more than that left in me."

"Maybe we'll let you relieve Kane when he brings the *Nerka* back."

"That's no good, Captain. She'll be going back to Mare Island, and Stocker rates bringing her back. I've spent enough time on soft jobs. Besides, my leg is OK now."

"OK, Rich," Blunt surrendered gracefully. "I'll put your name back on the active list."

Back to the Attack Teacher. Back to making fifteen approaches a day, teaching doctrine to would-be dolphin-wearers, showing the latest tricks of the trade to skippers in for refresher, waiting for my ship to come in. The days passed, one upon another.

Three weeks later I was back to see Blunt. The boats had been going through Pearl steadily. Quite a few changes in skippers had been made, but always, it seemed, there was someone waiting to whom the available boat had already been assigned. I was ready to put up a beef, but he didn't give me a chance.

"Sit down, Rich. I was about to send for you." His voice was grim. "Do you know what day this is?"

"Yes, sir. Tuesday, the twenty-fifth."

"It's the day the *Nerka* was due back from patrol."

"*Was* due. What do you mean?" I half-rose again. Not Stocker Kane!

— 302

"Was due, Rich. We won't see her again." Blunt spoke gently, sorrowfully. "She was a grand ship, and had a grand crew. Kane was one of the best."

"What happened to her?" I cried. "Where did she go?"

For once the battered pipe lay unnoticed on the desk top. Blunt met my eyes steadily. "He was in AREA SEVEN. That makes six boats that have been lost there."

"*Six submarines* lost in AREA SEVEN?" I was incredulous. No one I knew had had any idea of this.

"Yes, six. The *Needlefish, Turbot, Awlfish, Lancetfish, Stingback,* and now the *Nerka.*"

"But, good Lord, Captain, the *Turbot* and *Awlfish* were lost en route to SouthWestPac in Australia! And I never heard of the *Stingback!*"

"Quite so. Naturally we didn't want to give Bungo any information as to how badly he was hurting us. Incidentally, he thinks he sank several others too, among them the *Octopus.* But I think he's taken the *Walrus* off his list; at least, he doesn't mention her any more. He got the *Turbot* last year and Eddie Holt in the *Awlfish* several months ago; we made out that they had been sent south, just to quiet the local rumor factories. *Stingback* was a brand-new submarine, built at Manitowoc, Wisconsin, but she had a veteran skipper and so we let her go in to SEVEN anyhow. She was the boat just before the *Nerka.* You were deep in the torpedo problem at the time, and I'm not surprised you don't remember her."

I couldn't believe it. Poor old Stocker Kane! Why, only a few weeks ago he and I had sat up into the wee hours in his room at the Royal Hawaiian chewing the rag over old times. And now he was dead! Poor Hurry! I wondered how she would get the news. "How did it happen—about the *Nerka,* I mean?"

"We don't really know anything, yet, Rich." The pipe went into Blunt's mouth at last. "He's only been overdue at our new base at Majuro for a few hours, but old Nakame has been claiming him for two weeks. And we've not had a message from him in that time."

"Did Bungo give any hint as to how he sank her?" I was holding a wake, but I couldn't help it.

"The old fellow is too smart for that. The only thing we know about him is that he is still apparently picking up garbage sacks, despite our caution to the boats about them, and is getting their names out of them. I guess it's pretty hard to keep all mention of your ship's name out of all your garbage."

I was counting on my fingers. "Good God, Captain! Out of the last six boats that have gone into AREA SEVEN, he's sunk three!"

"That's right. And of the last two, he's sunk both of them. And Jim Bledsoe is in there now."

My stomach felt suddenly all washed out. *"Walrus,"* I gasped. "Why did you send the *Walrus?* Jim's already made seven consecutive runs—the whole ship is tired. They deserve a rest! Not this! Why, this is suicide!"

"Easy, Rich." Blunt's eyes were steady, but his face looked old, troubled. "ComSubPac has orders to keep the Bungo Suido and Kii Suido under surveillance. Maybe the Jap fleet's in there—I don't know. Some day maybe Admiral Nimitz will let us know why. In the meantime, all we can do is put our best boats in there, let them know what they're up against, and try to prepare them the best we know how. Besides, at the time Jim left Stocker was doing fine. We had a message from him only the day before."

I told him I was sorry for my outburst. "But what can we do?" I anxiously asked him. "We've got to do something! We can't just let *Walrus* run into that kind of setup without some kind of action to help him!"

"We're doing all we can." Blunt fumbled in a pile of papers. "Here's what we sent him."

The message said:

URGENT FOR WALRUS X INDICATIONS EXTREMELY EFFECTIVE ANTISUB-
MARINE ACTIVITY VICINITY BUNGO SUIDO X TAKE MAXIMUM PRECAU-
TIONS THIS IS AN URGENT WARNING FROM COMSUBPAC.

Silently, I handed it back.

"The *Walrus* has been in the area nearly a week already, Rich, and he's sunk three ships. Two the first night, and one several days later. If there's anyone who can handle themselves in there, it's Jim Bledsoe and your old crew. But that's not why I wanted to see you. I think we've got a ship for you. That please you?"

Would it! In spite of the ominous shadow that lay on my mind, I started up eagerly at the news.

"The *Eel* is coming in from Balboa, and they think their skipper has pneumonia. We'll have to check the whole crew, of course, and may have to transfer some of them if they show signs of having contracted the disease. You can have her as soon as she gets in."

Eel was a brand-new Portsmouth-built boat, containing all the new and fancy gadgets which we in the old *Walrus* had wanted for so long, and improvised to get. She had a thicker skin and heavier frames, a narrower silhouette bows on, a larger conning tower with more gear in it and a smaller bridge, and the very latest in radar. In her engine rooms were four of the new ten-cylinder double-crankshaft Fairbanks-Morse diesels, rated at the same horsepower as the earlier nine-cylinder jobs and as the sixteens of the *Walrus,* but capable of considerably more. On deck she carried the same gun armament as *Walrus,* except for a new five-inch gun instead of our old S-boat four-incher. Altogether she was a wonderful command, a real dreamboat, except for one thing—she had no crew.

It turned out that the trouble with her skipper was diagnosed as tuberculosis, and every man in her whole complement had to be sent up for observation. The probability of any others having it, the submarine force doctor said, was not too

— 305

high, but they had been breathing the same air as their skipper for a long time, and in the confined quarters of a submarine—especially when submerged and recirculating the ventilation—the chances for wholesale exchange of germs could not help but be at their highest. The ship was thoroughly fumigated after the crew was taken off, and a crew of medical corpsmen went over her with disinfectant before anyone else was permitted to go aboard. When I got my new ship, that's exactly what I got—a ship. Bare.

Not that getting a crew assigned was difficult. With the normal rotation system in full swing, there were ample men with the necessary rates and skills to fill out several complete crews. And some of the old *Walrus* crew, who had been left behind when she last departed, had already had enough of the rotation and specially asked to be assigned to the *Eel*. Among these were Quin and Oregon, both now first-class Petty Officers with war experience which belied their youth.

My best piece of luck, however, was in getting Keith assigned also. He was due back anyway from leave in a few days, so I sent a telegram to his leave address asking him if he wanted the job of Executive Officer, and telling him to come back right away if he did. The answer came back next morning, and consisted of only one word: ENROUTE.

The rest of the officers were taken from the various relief crews which were the usual rotation assignments. I was careful to take only volunteers, however. A thin, nervous-looking Lieutenant named Buckley Williams came as Gunnery and Torpedo Officer, and another Lieutenant, Al Dugan, rather heavy-set and phlegmatic in appearance but already known for his sure touch on the dive, as Engineer and Diving Officer.

But merely having the personnel assigned is a very long way from having a fighting submarine, or a fighting anything else, for that matter. First we had to get things organized, lay out a Watch, Quarter and Station Bill, assign everyone in the crew a locker and a bunk, divide them into watch sections and into the various departments aboard a ship, lay out all their duties in accordance with what needed to be done as determined by the way the ship was built—and then begin the training.

Fortunately, having had the pick of the relief crews, *Eel's* new complement was basically all experienced. We were not, at least, required to take aboard a load of trainees in addition to the rest of our training problem. Though it was a back-breaking job, it turned out to be a fruitful one. I was amazed at the amount of progress that could be made in a day. As an Exec, Keith was a natural. In four days we had *Eel* at sea for her first dive, and in six we were shooting torpedoes. In two weeks I was beginning to wonder what area we would draw for our patrol.

The last week, our third, was spent merely polishing things up. We practiced the quick snap shot at an enemy submarine, taught all the officers, and the Quartermasters too, how to determine the quickest way to turn, how to line up the shot with sight of eye, what essential inputs the TDC had to have, and how to shoot. And we practiced how to shift instantly from one target to another, how to anticipate the enemy's next zig during the firing and how to correct for it. By the time I reported *Eel* to Captain Blunt as in all respects ready for a combat assignment, there was no doubt in my mind that this was the case.

He had to come out with us for a day's operations to see for himself, of course, and his comment before the day was half over was proof of his satisfaction. "You've got a beautiful ship here, Rich," he told me. And he told me where he planned to send us for our first patrol: AREA TWELVE, the Yellow Sea, between Kyushu and the mainland of China, all the way up to the Gulf of Pohai on the north.

It took quite a while to put *Eel* through all her paces, and it was long after dark before we finally put her back alongside the dock in the submarine base. As we came in, the ComSub-Pac Duty Officer and a car were waiting for Captain Blunt.

There was a whispered consultation. He turned back to me before stepping in: "Rich," he said, "after you get finished with the ship, come on up to my office, will you?" His face was grave. Something was wrong.

I turned a few details over to Keith, followed Blunt in a few minutes, a cold foreboding clutching at my heart. I knew what it was the moment I opened the door to his office. He was standing alone, looking out the window at the black waters of Pearl Harbor, the pipe in his mouth, hands clenched behind his back. He didn't turn when he heard the door open. "That you, Rich?" Upon my affirmative, he told me to sit down. Still he didn't turn. Just stood there. I stood also, waiting.

For about a minute he stood there, motionless. I could hear him breathing. His hands were working gently behind his back, massaging his fingers.

Then, without turning, he commenced to speak softly, almost tenderly. "There are some parts of that ocean out near Japan which are worth more than any material value can ever express. They are parts which are consecrated, for they are hallowed by our heroic dead. One day God, in His infinite wisdom, may let us see the reason why some men must die young that others may live to a useless old age—why men like me, who have never heard a shot or seen a torpedo fired in anger, must be the arbiter of life and death for younger and better men."

He paused, turned to face me. "Every grave on land and in that ocean is a tomb to an ideal. Some of the ideals are wrong, some right. But the graves are never wrong—they are monuments to the heroic men of either side who sleep there. For who has the right to say to the men who bear the brunt of the battle, 'This was wrong, this was worthless to die for?' Is not the warrior the purest and most heroic of all, because he dies for his beliefs? It is the men who send the warriors on their quests who must answer to that question."

He stopped.

"When did it happen?" I asked quietly.

"Maybe it hasn't happened!" he turned away again, almost fiercely. "This might just be their propaganda claim!"

"Jim was not due out till tomorrow, was he? Should we have heard from him?"

"Rich, we had him reporting weather every three days from his area. Our task forces need to know that weather data. It moves from west to east, you know. Three days ago he sent a message, giving the weather and telling us that his total bag for the patrol so far was then six ships. He had only four torpedoes left, all aft. Ordinarily we would have had him come back, but we have to keep a watch on the Bungo, and we have to have those weather reports. So we told him to stay till tomorrow, which is the day the *Tuna* is scheduled to move in there to relieve him. Bungo Pete claims to have sunk him the same night he sent his message. Another one was due this morning, but he made no transmission."

"Maybe he's only been damaged and his antenna or his radio are out of commission."

"Maybe so. Anyway, we can't send any more boats into SEVEN. You were right, it is suicide. I've already sent a message to the *Tuna* to stay clear, and the Admiral has an appointment with CinCPac in the morning to tell him the same. If only there were a way of eliminating that bastard Nakame! Until we do, I'm afraid we'll have to give up on this much of our assigned mission. The trouble is, of course, that once he realizes we're not going into the area around Bungo any more, he'll simply shift his own operating ground."

"Let me go into SEVEN! I can get him!" I spoke with a surge of confidence and rage. "I've been practicing for just this type of thing all during the past months at the Attack Trainer. Give us just a couple of days to get ready." I argued a long time, finally got down to pleading with the old man. At first he wouldn't hear of it, but the thought of the explanations the Admiral would have to make finally swung the tide in my favor. I was determined, reckless, in a mad fury. Bungo

Pete had to go! *Walrus* had outwitted him twice before, with a little luck. Now *Eel* would not only outwit him, but sink him—and we'd not need luck!

We got the base ordnance shop to give us a little high-priority emergency assistance: we designed some waterproof demolition charges which we could put into the garbage which would go off when the package was opened. We carried along a lot of old *Walrus* stationery and got some papers made up with rubber stamps and other markings, just as we had improvised for the *Octopus,* only using the name *Walrus.*

And we put aboard a full load of brand-new electric torpedoes, the wakeless kind.

When we finally shoved off, somehow it looked as though word of our mission might have leaked out. A great crowd of submariners gathered silently on the dock to see us off, and I could feel the cumulative force of their unspoken thought. The Admiral was there, of course, and so was Captain Blunt, and as we backed clear the band struck up "Sink 'Em All" which, by this time, had become a sort of submarine hymn.

Under the circumstances, it had a special meaning for us. They kept playing the same tune over and over until we had headed up beyond ten-ten dock, and the submarine piers had drifted beyond our sight.

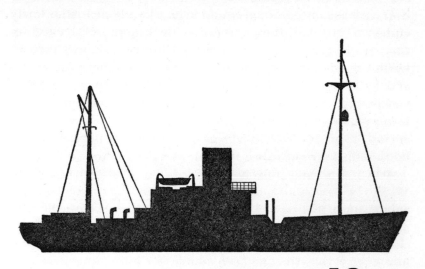

CHAPTER 13

The trip west made no conscious impression on my mind. We topped off fuel at Midway, got on our way again the same day, kept on going. The only thing I could think of was Bungo Pete, or to use his proper name, Captain Tateo Nakame, Imperial Japanese Navy. He was no doubt a Jap hero because of the number of U. S. subs he claimed to have destroyed. To Keith and me he was a devil, and needed to be destroyed in his turn.

War rarely generates personal animosities between members of the opposing forces, for it is too big for that. The hate is there, but it is a larger hatred, a hatred for everything the enemy stands for, for all of his professed ideals, for his very way of life. Individuals stand for nothing in this mammoth hate, and that is why friends—even members of the same family—can at times be on opposite sides, and why, after the fighting is over, it is possible to respect and even like the man who lately wished to kill you. Bungo, however, had done us personal injury, really many-fold times personal injury, and had thereby lost his anonymity. We had learned to know him by his works and by his name; it didn't seem in the least strange to Keith and me that this time, this once, we should be consumed with bitter personal enmity toward a certain personality among the enemy. That this individual was only doing his duty as he saw it, as he had a right to see it, made not the slightest difference.

And it was not entirely one-sided. For Nakame knew the *Walrus* by name too, and was doubtless gloating in his own turn over the fact that he had at last squared accounts with the submarine which had dared to outwit him twice, even though accidentally, and had sunk one of the destroyers working under him, even if that also had been a fluke. He might know my own name, just as I knew his—it could not have been too hard to discover.

It was with this thought in mind that Keith, Quin, and I worked out one of our ideas for the campaign against Bungo. We had previously prepared for it by bringing along stationery and other material originally belonging to the *Walrus*. All the way out to Kyushu, Quin worked an hour or two a day on the papers. We made certain that the name *Eel* would nowhere appear in our garbage sacks, but that the name *Walrus* would with normal frequency. And I wrote my own name in several normal places, as though on papers which had been spoiled or discarded for one reason or another and thrown away. In this way the *Walrus* would once again have escaped him. Keith and I were agreed that our personal revenge would take the form of robbing Bungo Pete of that satisfaction before destroying him.

And after his curiosity had been aroused by discovery that

the *Walrus* had returned to make depredations in the home waters of Japan, after he had had plenty of evidence and would be searching for the answer to the riddle, then we would put the demolition charges in the garbage sacks.

The explosives might not get him, probably would not, for he would have subordinates dig through the sodden sacks of putrefying garbage. But they would amount to a message he could not ignore.

Eel was a new submarine, with a new crew. This would ordinarily have been a disadvantage for the fight in which she was about to engage, but not in this instance. For every man in that crew was a veteran of submarine warfare, and she had come all this distance with one single mission. We worked her guts out all the way over. When she passed through the Bonins, or the Nanpo Shoto, *Eel* was superbly trained, better than she had been when Captain Blunt gave her his approval, better than *Walrus* had ever been. And her torpedoes, of course, had the latest modifications, our new exploder. Something *Walrus* had never had while I knew her.

It was with a sort of defiance our first night in AREA SEVEN, that I directed the cook to bring garbage topside and dump it. Twice before Keith and I had been here, but this time it was something special. We were beginning our mission of vengeance. *Walrus* had come back to haunt Bungo Pete and kill him if she could.

First it would be necessary to alert him, to cause him to come out after us. We wasted no time getting down to the southern and eastern portion of our area, near Toi Mistaki, where ships rounding Kyushu would have to make their course change to the north. Two nights and a day with nothing sighted, only the ubiquitous fishing boats, then a small tanker came by in the blackest part of the night. Our powerful radar picked him up two hours before we saw him. I held the new model TBT on his middle, thumbed the button in the handle of the built-in pressure-proof binoculars, felt two torpedoes start his way.

He was not a large ship, not worth more than two torpedoes. Both of them hit and both exploded, and when the spray-and-water column came back down, he was no longer there. Our first calling card.

But he had had no time to radio in the warning, could not have accomplished what we wanted. We waited a few days longer, found another ship, a little larger. Freighter, also new. Submerged periscope approach this time, two more torpedoes. It took him about fifteen minutes to go down.

That night, having first dropped our garbage near where the freighter had been sunk and near where analysis of non-arrival of the tanker might show it, too, had gone down, we put everything on the line and headed for the other end of AREA SEVEN, off the coast of Shikoku, between the Bungo and Kii Suidos.

Two days more, again with only fishing boats in sight, during which we were careful that trash and garbage was dumped in a specially weighted sack which sank immediately. We were submerged, close in to the coast, when we sighted masts. Two ships, hugging the coast. Then there was a third mast, a tincan, patrolling to seaward. Not Bungo, however. Smaller destroyer-type, probably sent out as a protective gesture now that another submarine was known to have entered the area. *Eel* maneuvered between the escort and his convoy. Four stern tubes at the tincan—close quarters, but there was time to get them off. He joined his ancestors in a cloud of mingled flame, smoke, and spray. Then for the two ships. Three at the leader—just as he was turning. One hit, enough. He sagged down by the bow, water coming over his forward cargo well.

In the meantime the second ship in the convoy, an old rusty freighter, had put his rudder hard over. There was only one way for him to go, however; back where he came from. He had to go toward the shoreline and back out again around a point of land, if he wanted to stay in shallow water. That was his mistake, one Bungo would never have let him make. He was not very fast. We didn't even have to pull much out of the battery to get across the mouth of the little bay in time. *Eel* was waiting for him quietly when he came out.

That night we made sure our garbage would not sink and threw over a couple of extra bags of it for good measure. Then we raced for the Bungo Suido.

We had left our calling cards liberally sprinkled on both sides of the entrance to the Inland Sea. Now it was time to play it slow and easy and to watch developments. The closer in we could get, the better. Bungo would no doubt expect us to stay well away.

For a day—three days and the nights between—nothing happened. Again we were making sure our garbage would sink without trace. And we allowed two old ships, proceeding alone, to enter the harbor unmolested.

"We'll let it jell for a while, Keith," I told him. "We've raised enough Cain around here. He'll come."

But he didn't. Keith put his finger on it the third day. We had the chart of the area out on the wardroom table, were studying it, as had become our habit in hope of ferreting out some clue to Bungo's operations.

"You know, skipper," he said, "this guy Nakame is no slouch. He's a very particular operator. Have you noticed that he hardly ever shows his hand until whatever boat is in this area has been here for a while? Maybe he even waits until the boat is low on torpedoes."

"That doesn't hold for our first patrol in the *Walrus*," I told him.

"No, sir, but it does for the rest of the cases. That must have been an accident. We'd only been in the area a few hours, and he couldn't have known we were there yet."

Looking back over the boats which had been lost, and the experiences of those, like *Walrus* on her fourth patrol, who had come through it, a certain pattern began to take shape. Stocker Kane and the *Nerka* had been in AREA SEVEN for three weeks before Bungo had got him. Jim likewise. So had we, on our fourth, before he came out.

Evidently he studied the tactics of his intended victim, waited methodically for them to become clear to him, then sallied forth to lay his trap for him. As Keith said, our first patrol had been an accident, in that the contact had been unexpected by Bungo as well as ourselves.

No doubt he searched the area of a contact or action—especially after he had depth-charged a submarine—for the telltale sacks of garbage, which might float around for several days, but if there were no submarine activity he would probably not bother.

Bungo would be puzzled at the apparent reappearance of *Walrus,* would remember that twice before he had thought he had sunk her, and twice before been fooled. Once he had even swallowed evidence of the existence of an entirely fictitious submarine. Furthermore, Jim's reputation had been made as a night fighter, on the surface, while every ship the pseudo-*Walrus*—ourselves—had sunk, with the exception of the first one, had been as a result of a submerged day attack. It was logical that Bungo would want to wait and evaluate for a while.

But how would he be getting information? We had seen no one enter or leave the Bungo, except the two freighters. It was possible, though hardly likely, that he had slipped by us to search for evidence . . .

"Of course!" I said aloud. "We missed one of the most obvious things!"

"What do you mean, Captain?" Keith looked puzzled.

"The fishing boats! Of course the fishing boats! They are his lookouts. Those are the people who find the sacks of garbage for him! No wonder we've not seen anything. They're probably just plain, simple, old Japanese fishermen, but he tells them where and when to look, and he sits back and analyzes the results!"

"Then you think he may be waiting for more garbage?"

"Nope! He's got that by now. But right now he doesn't know where we are. No point in just rushing out to where a ship was sunk—we'd be gone. He wants a contact of some other kind, one where there might be a chance of our sticking around for a while to give him time to come after us." An idea was growing. The fishing boats—there were quite a few around, and more up and down the coast, in both directions from the Bungo Suido.

"Keith," I said, "let's go find us a fisherman, hey?"

"Going to put a bomb in the garbage sacks and teach him a lesson?" Jim might have gone for that idea, but Keith, I could see, was a little dubious.

"Not quite. We're just going to let him find us!"

Keith relaxed in a wide grin as he got the point.

It was the next day, a bright mid-morning, before we found one. We had purposely moved a goodly distance away from the Bungo Suido. It was a regular wooden boat with a sort of platform on which a half-dozen straw-hatted figures sat cross-legged, tending fish lines and poles. The day was balmy, bright, and sunny, though in the eastern sky storm clouds were gathering.

"These fellows will want to be back home by nightfall, before the wind blows the sea up," I told Keith.

The *Eel* swam sibilantly toward the fishing boat, passed close alongside. Nothing disturbed the monumental calm of the wizened graybeards under the straw hats. I was looking right at them with the periscope, only a hundred yards away as we went by. We turned around, came back. Closer this time—about fifty yards abeam. Still no sign of having seen us.

"Keith," I muttered, as he took a look at them, "if this is the best kind of help Bungo has got, the old rascal is slipping badly."

Keith chuckled as he put the 'scope down. "Don't waste too much pity on him, skipper. Nobody ever tried to get discovered before. These guys have probably never seen a submarine in their lives, and never expect to."

"We'll fix that!" I crossed to the hatch, looked down to the top of Al Dugan's head. "Control, watch your depth. We're going to go right underneath this little guy!"

"Watch the depth, aye, aye!" Al leaned his head back, acknowledged the caution.

Eel turned around again. Instead of going right under, Keith suggested we pass within a very few yards. This would permit continual observation of the fishing boat, whereas passing right under would require dunking the 'scope. We must have been less than five yards away from the boat as we passed this time, and I was looking through the periscope in low power practically under one of the straw hats. Keith had the other 'scope up, was doing likewise.

He was an old Jap in the classical mold. A long gray beard, about twelve inches long, wispy, and doubtless silky to the touch, ended in a point on his chest. His face was leathery, seamed from years under the sun's unshaded rays. No telling his age. It could have been anywhere from fifty to eighty. His eyes were closed, or half-closed, and he was the picture of peace and contentment as he sat there, balanced bolt upright with his bare toes sticking up from behind bony knees.

The picture changed radically and suddenly when the old man opened his eyes. It must have been the noise of the water rippling past our extended periscopes, or perhaps the shadow of the most tremendous fish he had ever seen passing beneath him. Whatever the immediate cause, his peaceful contemplation was shattered beyond reclaim. His eyes grew as large as two butter plates, and his mouth, startlingly red, popped wide open. I could have sworn I heard him scream with terror—he jumped to his feet, forgetting the fishing pole he had been so blissfully tending, pointed frantically right at me.

The other five old men hopped up as if stung, crowded to his side, all six mouths wide open, an even dozen eyes staring with stupefied terror. They looked over into the water on both sides of their boat—no doubt our gray hull and black topsides could

— 318

plainly be seen down beneath them—gesticulated violently, pointing down, raised their hands to their heads, waved them around helplessly.

"No more fishing for those fellows for a while," Keith commented grimly. "Guess we taught them a lesson at that!"

"I hope they have a guilty conscience for helping old Bungo," I laughed. "Serves them right!"

Through our sonar equipment we could hear the high-pitched putter of a light gasoline engine. Our fishermen friends had started for home as fast as their little craft could carry them. We watched them fading out of sight toward the shore, in the meantime set our own course at best-sustained speed back toward the Bungo Suido.

"Let's see," mused Keith over the charts a few hours later. "Let's see. Give the six old men three hours to get home and another hour to get the news through—they'll have a phone somewhere in their village, don't you think? Old Bungo ought to be stirring his stumps some time this afternoon. Maybe he'll come on out tonight."

"That's the way I've got it figured, too, Keith," I answered. "He'll have us pegged for a day-submerged operator, so he'll plan on flushing us at night."

Buck Williams had been an interested listener. "Do you think maybe we might have overdone it?" he asked. Buck's apparent nervousness was just a mannerism, I had already decided. His brain was clicking all the time.

"Could be," I answered him. "But we've already used up fourteen torpedoes leaving our calling cards on Bungo Pete's doorstep, and we have only one full load left for our torpedo tubes. The best way would be to try to sink another ship, but then we'd have some dry tubes when we finally did meet up with the old rascal!"

Buck nodded, convinced. "I guess he'll be sufficiently sure of himself to come after us anyhow," he said.

"Well," responded Keith as he folded up the charts and

handed them to Oregon, "he surely knows we're around anyway, and has enough reason to wonder what is happening out here in his back yard. If he can, he'll be out tonight. Otherwise, tomorrow for sure. That's my guess!"

"Mine too! Bungo will have a pretty good idea of where to look for us tonight—at least he will think he has. And that's why we should get back as near to the Suido as we can tonight. Maybe we'll be on him before he suspects we're laying for him!"

All the rest of the day *Eel* raced for the entrance of the Bungo Suido, where we had been only the day before. It wasn't much of a race, as races go, for we had to balance our consumption of battery power against our speed and calculate carefully the degree to which it would be wise to allow it to be run down in prospect of the battle with Bungo Pete. We got in as close as we dared, right into the shallow water where the channel leading out of the Bungo Suido joined the open sea. It was dangerous because there was not enough water to go really deep—we'd hit bottom first—but it was the place to be if we hoped to nail Nakame before he realized what was going on. It presented our best chance.

As the last rays of the setting sun were cut off behind the hills of Kyushu, the clouds to the east had grown until they covered nearly the entire sky. Through the periscope we could see that a freshening wind had already built up. Choppy waves four to five feet in height were running in from the east, and it was apparent that the wind also was coming from that direction. Shortly before it was dark enough to surface, Keith sought me out in the conning tower where I had gone to get ready.

"It looks like a storm to me," he said. "We've had no radio warning of it, but all the signs are exactly like the description in Knight's *Seamanship*." He handed me the ship's copy of the classic, open to the chapter on hurricanes. The page showed diagrams depicting the behavior of storms in northern and southern latitudes.

I already had my red goggles on; so I didn't try to read the text. I had studied it all at the Naval Academy anyway. "I've been thinking the same," I told him. "With the weather coming in from the east, it looks as though the storm is to the south, and if it behaves the way storms are supposed to it will curve toward the east as it moves north. The storm center will pass just to the east of us, and this area will get a good lashing."

"When will it hit us?"

"Tonight—before morning, unless it goes erratic on us."

"Maybe that will foul up things for tonight!"

"It can't be helped, if it does. But old Bungo might think it will give him an advantage!" I had raised the periscope, was slowly swinging it around in a circle. It was growing dark rapidly.

"Five-eight feet!" I ordered. "Stand by to surface!" The waves were high enough that I would need the two extra feet for better visibility.

"Five-eight feet, aye, aye. Standing by!" Williams on the dive. He would have the first bridge watch, too. The whole ship was in a special state of superwatchfulness. Keith and I had both napped, or tried to, during the afternoon, and we had put out instructions to the crew to do likewise. Our electric torpedoes had been given a specially loving last-minute check, including a freshening battery charge. Tonight there would be special extra lookouts on, and one torpedo at each end of the ship was in readiness for instant firing, needing only to open the outer doors—hydraulically operated, hence the work of a second. *Eel* was as ready as we could make her.

I went around again, slowly. Something caught my eye to the northwest, in the direction of the Bungo Suido. Steady now—I fixed on it. "Keith. Mark this bearing!"

"Three-two-eight! What is it?"

"Dunno—ship, I think." I shifted the periscope from side to side ever so slightly. It was getting so dark it was hard to see. My eyes were not completely accommodated, for the red goggles are not one hundred per cent effective protection. It was growing darker faster than my eyes were accommodating themselves. But the object—ship, it must be—was getting nearer, too.

"Bearing—Mark!"

"Three-two-eight and a quarter—just a hair more than before!"

I spoke without taking my eyes away from the periscope eyepiece. "Keith, are all lights out in the conning tower and control room?"

"Yes, sir."

"Very well." I spoke distinctly, still looking. "Sound the general alarm!"

I could feel the bustle through the ship. Keyed up as we were, the tension mounted like steam in a boiler.

"What is it, Captain? Do you think it's Bungo himself—already?"

"Don't know, Keith," I admitted. "It doesn't look like a destroyer." We waited. Time had slowed down. This might be it, our big fight. No time to take a chance. Still getting darker, and the waves bigger. The ship drew closer.

"I can see him now. Big freighter. High, anyway—dark hull, no visible waterline—angle on the bow about starboard ten." I looked searchingly astern of him. Something was ringing a bell in my brain, something wrong with the setup, somehow . . .

"Control! Five-five feet." Three more feet of periscope out. Have to watch it—that's eleven feet of it exposed, although the size of the waves makes for some reduction. We're in good position to shoot him on this course, just as we are, if he doesn't suddenly zig. He hasn't zigged yet. Wish I could get rid of the feeling there's something wrong with this whole thing. It's too easy. I have a feeling we're looking right into a trap, just like that time off Palau . . .

Palau! The Q-ship! High out of water. Short and stubby, because floating high! No doubt loaded with cellulose, or balsawood, or Ping-pong balls! So she could not sink, of course, even with half her side blown open!

"Give him eighty feet, Oregon. Range—Mark!"

"Three-five-double-oh!"

"Angle on the bow starboard thirty! Mark the bearing!"

"Three-four-five!"

I could hear Buck Williams whirling the TDC cranks. "Set!" he said.

"Ready to shoot, Captain!" Keith. He had anticipated everything. All I had to do was give the word.

"We'll wait while the situation improves," I said. This smacked of something Bungo might pull. I kept looking for the destroyer, couldn't find him. But something else caught my eye, astern. Low and bulky. Not a tincan. My heart leaped into my throat—a submarine! Coming along astern of the Q-ship!

"Rig for silent running! Six-oh feet!" This would barely let me see over the tops of the waves, if I could see at all for long. I could feel sweat on my face around my eyes inside the rubber eye-guards, didn't dare take them away. "Boys, this is it! I think Bungo is on his way out to look for us!"

How fortunate it had been that we had come back so quickly, had taken station so close to the harbor exit, despite the shallow water!

We watched while the high, stubby Q-ship, for there could be no doubt of it now, went by. The submarine swept forward. Then I saw the tincan. A dull, dark shape on the far side of the sub, running about abeam of it.

This was a quandary. We might get the sub, but then Bungo would have us exactly where he would like to get us, submerged, in shallow water. And the Q-ship was no slouch at depth-charging, either. No doubt they'd work a coordinated attack on us.

"Range to sub—Mark!" Instinctively I spoke in a low key. Oregon read it right away. "Three-oh-double-oh!"

"We have the sub on sonar!" Keith murmured in my ear. "The bearing checks."

The sonarman's name was Stafford. An old-timer. He'd been around submarines for years. Suddenly I heard his voice, raised for me to hear him directly. "The submarine is diving!"

So this was the play! This was how they had gotten Stocker Kane and Jim! Slow-speed convoy of a single ship, escorted by a single destroyer, zigzagging radically and making slow speed so that the submerged submarine could keep up! *Walrus* and *Nerka* had probably come in on the surface, fired their torpedoes, and been fired on in their turn by the submarine! A very, very slick stunt indeed! If the Jap sub didn't get a shot off at first, he must have had plenty more chances while Jim and Stocker came back in for another try at the cellulose-loaded Q-ship! And I could imagine old Bungo watching it all in his tincan, playing the part of an unwary and incompetent escort but ready to mix it if he had to.

I could see the diminishing silhouette of the submarine, now, and seconds later couldn't see him at all. "Do you still have him on sonar?"

"Yes, sir. Coming in like a threshing machine!" Stafford turned the sonar to loud-speaker so that I could hear it, a pounding, thrashing, gurgling noise. "He's pumping and blowing at the same time, I think!"

"Keith," I said, speaking rapidly. "We've got to get the sub first! They won't expect us this close, probably won't settle down to a good sonar watch for a few minutes anyway. What range will he pass abeam?"

Buck answered. "Twelve hundred yards!"

"Good! We'll shoot him when he gets there! Figure him to be at periscope depth!"

On and on came the bearing of the Jap sub, slowly creeping up to where we had decided to shoot him. It was a perfect sonar approach, exactly like those we had practiced for years at New London and Pearl Harbor, and rarely used in the war. The only new twist—funny we had never thought of it—was that it was sub against sub.

"We'll shoot one mark-eighteen electric fish," I decided. "He'll probably not even hear it, and if it doesn't work we'll try another."

"He's approaching the firing bearing, Captain!" Keith's voice. I was still on the periscope, now staring at *Akikaze,* now the Q-ship, now making a sweep all around just in case Bungo might have other ships in his convoy.

"Shoot when he's on, Keith!" One advantage of firing with a ninety track as we were doing was that the range in that precise situation drops out of the problem. No matter how far the target is, or how close, your torpedo will hit, if aimed properly and if it runs long enough.

"Fire one," said Keith. The *Eel* jerked under me.

"One fired electrically," said Quin's familiar voice.

"Torpedo is running!" said Stafford. I could hear it, a high whine, not as loud as the old steam fish.

"How much longer, Keith!"

"Thirty-three seconds!"

I spun the 'scope around. "How long now?"

"—fifteen seconds—ten—five—NOW!"

Nothing. You could hear the ticking of the stop watch in Keith's hand. Then—BOOM! A loud roar filled the conning tower. I looked on the bearing, helped by Keith's hands on the periscope handles. A froth of white water, an angry spume flung into the air, followed by a mushroom of white. Nothing else.

Stafford was yelping. "He's sinking!" His voice raced excitedly on, much like a football-game announcer's: "Listen to the water pour in! Somewhere they've got a watertight door shut —there's another one slamming—his screws are slowing down —*listen to the water pour in!* I can hear things falling inside him! He must be standing right on end, straight up and down!"

We could all hear the grim cascade, the torrent of suddenly

— 325

released black water smashing through thin bulkheads, filling compartments with shocking speed, compressing the air with the frenzied pressure of the sea. Then another noise, crunching, rending. "He's hit bottom," announced Stafford.

"Any chance for them, Keith?" Williams turned serious eyes at the Exec.

"To escape from the sunken sub?" Keith snorted. "Not at the depth he's at, even though it feels pretty shallow when they're after you with depth charges. Besides, I don't think Jap subs carry escape gear."

"Right full rudder!" I called out. "All ahead standard! Keith, what was the enemy sub's course?"

"One-five-oh, Captain!"

"Steady on one-five-oh!"

I waited for Scott, the helmsman, to echo my commands before explaining. "Keith, what would you do if you were Bungo and you heard an explosion in the general vicinity of a submarine you were responsible for?"

"I'd go over and take a look!"

"And what would you expect to see?"

"Well, if I got too close to the submerged sub, he'd probably broach to show me where he is so that I'd not run over him— only this time torpedoes will come instead!" Keith's grim smile of anticipation was oddly reminiscent of Jim's.

"Very good. Only, it's not Bungo who's coming!"

"What do you mean?"

"The tincan just signaled with a small searchlight to the Q-ship, and he's started to turn around instead. So, as soon as we get turned around and squared away on the Jap course, we'll broach for the Q-ship. It's so dark that I can barely see him, and if we give him our bow while he's still fairly distant he'll not be able to tell it from the Jap sub's.

"Bungo will be watching, too. He'll see us broadside."

"Yes, but he's farther away, and we're about the same color as the Jap sub was. Besides, we want him to come our way, though we'd rather it be unsuspectingly—damn this periscope! It's fogging up. Give me some lens paper!"

A wad of paper was stuffed into my hand. Shutting my eyes, I swabbed at the glass, felt somebody wiping off my streaming face with a towel at the same time.

"Thanks!" I put my eyes back into the eye-guard.

"Skipper, how could the Japs figure on seeing OK at night when you can hardly make them out?"

"Their optical industry is excellent, Keith. I understand all their submarines have a very large and fine night 'scope."

"Steady on one-five-oh!" Scott brought us back to the problem at hand.

"Tell Al to blow bow buoyancy and stick our bow out," I told Keith. "Then flood negative and get us back down quick! We don't want to get the whole boat on the surface!"

Eel's hull shivered as the lifting strain of the bow tank came on. Al must have at the same time put full rise on the stern planes to hold the stern down, and we took a large angle up by the bow. I saw our bullnose come out, stay for a long instant, go back down in a smother of externally vented air. There was venting and blowing inside, too, as negative was first vented to flood it, then blown dry, then vented again to take the pressure off.

This evidently satisfied the Jap, for he turned away again, and in a few minutes went off at an angle from his original course.

"They're beginning the zigzag plan," I told Keith. "We'll watch our chance and nail Bungo as soon as we can!"

For two hours *Eel* plodded along in the steadily worsening weather with the two Japanese vessels weaving back and forth in front of us. Several chances presented themselves to shoot at the Q-ship, but that would have given the whole show away, and with the already seriously depleted condition of our battery we couldn't stand the all-out search and attack which would have then ensued. Bungo's role was to be a lackadaisical

— 327

escort vessel, to stay too far from the ship he was supposed to be protecting, thus to invite attack from the U. S. submarine for whom the trap had been laid—us.

We could hear him echo-ranging in the distance, patrolling station back and forth first on one flank, then on the other. If we left our sanctuary astern of the bait and were picked up on his sonar, he'd attack us anyway, and we'd be right where we didn't want to be.

"Keith," I muttered, wiping my face while Oregon cleaned off the periscope eye-piece for the umpteenth time, "this isn't any good. Bungo is never coming close enough for us to shoot him, and we sure can't keep this up all night!"

"Maybe we'd better do like the Arab and silently steal away, Captain. At least, we know there's no Jap submarine around to worry about. The only one Bungo would allow would be the one whose place we're taking."

So it was decided, and shortly before midnight, several miles astern of Bungo and his baited trap now short one important character—the *Eel* crept to the surface.

The instant we got on the surface it was evident that the storm was rapidly becoming worse. The barometer had fallen markedly, the wind was still from the east, and it was blowing hard. The sea Oregon estimated at force five on the Beaufort scale, which is a sailor's way of saying that it was a baby gale already. Not yet fully surfaced, the ship wallowed in the waves, every one of which rolled up on our water-level deck and splashed in great showers of spume and spray on the bridge. Several huge combers rolled black water right over the bulwarks. Keith and I, wearing hooded oilskins, were nevertheless instantly drenched, and we had to hang on firmly to the railing to keep our footing under the drunken rolling of the ship.

The wind shrieked around our ears, tore at our clothing, blew words right out of our mouths. We crouched under the forward overhang of the bridge to converse or give orders; I did not dare permit the lookouts to come up yet, nor to open the main induction, which would be the signal for the engines to begin pumping the vital electricity back into our battery. Opening the main induction at this point—the cigarette deck above it was in a sea of white froth and black water—would have flooded our main induction line all the way back to the engine-room valves. First we had to wait for the turbo-blowers to lift the ship into a condition of buoyancy sufficient to ride the waves. I couldn't hear them, but I could see the results of their work; and when I finally gave the order, four main engines burst out almost simultaneously.

We were frantic for battery power, so three of them went immediately to recharging the battery, leaving the fourth for propulsion. Rapidly the life-giving amperes flowed back into the "can," and with every ten minutes of recharge, especially at this early stage, when the battery, being nearly flat, was most receptive, we could count on an hour's submerged running.

The surfaced routine safely under way, Keith and I were able to hold a council of war and take stock of the situation. The SJ radar, a newer and more efficient model than the one we had been used to in *Walrus*, still held contact with the two Japanese ships. If we could keep contact until our battery was at least partially recharged, we decided, we might be able to return to the offensive.

I seized the chance to go through the ship, talk to the men at their stations, and tell them how matters stood. We had found out Bungo's secret, I told them, and now we were after Bungo Pete himself.

After three hours we were about as ready as we would ever be, Keith and I figured. It was a lot rougher, too. A full-fledged storm was upon us, with seas fifteen to twenty feet in height, perhaps fifty feet across. We had gone back to battle stations, were heading toward the enemy, when Keith called up from the conning tower. The bridge speaker blared something unintelligible in the noise of the sea, and I had to make him repeat it:

"Bridge! Bungo's gone over and joined the Q-ship! I think they've both reversed course!"

This could only mean that Captain Nakame had decided it was too rough to keep up the game, and was going to return to port. No doubt he was signaling for the submarine to surface. Getting no answer, there was an excellent chance he would realize that something was amiss.

"Keep watching them, Keith," I yelled in reply. "Try to keep oriented as to which one is Bungo!"

We built up to standard speed, fourteen knots. *Eel* smashed and bucked into the seas, quivering in every solid frame as the big ones came over the bow and crashed on the bridge. It was absolutely black. Blacker than I had ever seen it, a musty, smelly black, dirty and dank and malevolent. I could see perhaps five hundred yards, hardly more. The wind tore at my binoculars, ballooned out the back of my rain hood, beat at my face with the salt particles it whipped out of the ocean. I couldn't use both hands to hold the binoculars, had to keep one free to hang on with. The deck heaved and pounded under me, the water rising and draining away through the wooden slats.

"Bridge! Range to Bungo, four thousand! To the other one, five thousand! They're milling around—Bungo is dead ahead, the other on our starboard bow!"

"Bridge, aye, aye!" I answered him. "Let me know the range every five hundred yards!" We couldn't attack quite yet; not before the enemy settled down to a definite course. "All ahead one third," I ordered. This was easier. *Eel's* motion still resembled a bent corkscrew, but fewer seas came on the bridge.

"Bridge! We've got the sonar gear down, and he's calling on sonar!"

No need to wonder what this was for, or to whom addressed. "Let him call!" I answered.

"He's hove to, bridge! Range, three-five-double-oh!"

This might be our chance. With Bungo concentrating on trying to raise his several hours' dead consort, his lookouts might just happen to be less alert than they should, especially in the storm. "All ahead standard! What's the course to head for him!"

"Zero-zero-eight!"

"Steer zero-zero-eight!" I yelled to Scott through the hatch.

Again the pounding, battering. Our bow would rise to one sea, smash down on the next, and go completely under water, allowing the wave to roll aft, unimpeded, till it broke in fury over the bridge. Cascades of cold ocean rolled off me. The lookouts were likewise drenched and miserable. I sent my binoculars below—they were soaked and useless anyway—and used the built-in pressure-proof TBT binoculars. Mounted on gimbals and fitted with handles, they also gave me some measure of support, though because of their stiffness it was a bit awkward to use them for ordinary purposes.

"Range, three thousand!" The starboard lookout lurched against me. His binoculars were in worse shape than mine had been, I saw, and he was giving full time merely to hanging on anyway. In the shape he was in, he was more hazard than benefit.

"Lookouts below!" I said. That left Al Dugan and me the only ones on the bridge, and I called him up forward from the station he had been occupying on the after part.

"Range, two-five-double-oh! Still hove to, and we can still hear him pinging!"

There was a new note to the wind. A higher shriek; louder, too. Three seas in succession came over the bridge front, left us gasping. "Range, two thousand! No change—we're opening outer doors!"

"What speed we making?" I yelled into the bridge mike.

"Ten knots!"

Ten knots. It should be fourteen under ordinary conditions. About right for firing torpedoes in this kind of sea, however.

"How does he bear now!"

"Dead ahead—still dead in the water!"

Less than a mile away. I couldn't see a thing. Nervously, I

rubbed the front lens of the binoculars with lens paper. Al silently handed me a fresh sheet when I threw my sodden one away.

"Fifteen hundred yards! Shall I shoot on radar bearings?"

"No!" A subconscious need to see him. "Wait!" *Work like hell to get into position, then take your time! Don't waste time, but don't throw your one chance away, either!* First Blunt and later poor Jerry Watson, long gone with the old *Octopus,* had sung the same song to me. And I had repeated the same words to Jim Bledsoe in my turn.

Fiercely I searched the horizon. "Range one-three-five-oh!" came on the speaker, and that was just the moment I saw him at last. It was an *Akikaze*-class destroyer, all right, broadside on. Two fairly short stacks, medium close together, small bridge but rather high for its length, turtle-back forecastle with a gun on it, and a deep well between forecastle and bridge. He was making heavy weather of it, I instantly saw. The canvas over the well deck had been blown away, and part of the bridge canopy also. Water was streaming in sheets off his decks, pouring in great torrents off the forecastle down into the well deck.

I was taking all this in as I shouted into the bridge mike: "Target! Starboard ninety! TBT bearing!" I pressed the marker plunger down with my right thumb.

"Set!"

"Shoot!" The way the command "Fire!" came out almost before I finished saying "Shoot!" was the measure of the crew I had with me. Keith was holding the bridge speaker button down on purpose.

Four times more the command "Fire!" came on the speaker, and all five torpedoes we had remaining forward went on their way. I couldn't see their wakes, for they were electric, nor could I feel the familiar jerk to the hull of the ship because of the motion and noise already going on. But I did see one torpedo broach the surface momentarily, then dive back under and continue on its way, with a flick of instantly extinguished spray. It had come up exactly on a line between me and the destroyer's bridge.

But this was not the time to play the spectator. "Left full rudder!" I yelled down the hatch. *Akikaze's* lookouts would see us in a moment, if they had not already, and Bungo would certainly get some kind of a salvo off at us. That we could depend on. Heedless, too, I gave the order I had held back all this time because of the weather: "All ahead flank!"

Before the *Eel* could feel the effect of the increased power, and before she had turned more than a few degrees, there was a flash from Bungo, and the brief scream of a shell overhead, immediately swallowed up in the storm. Then another flash—no scream this time. You certainly had to hand it to him, under the circumstances, for even getting the guns going at all.

But those were all the shots he got a chance to pump out at us, for about this time the torpedoes got there. Two certainly hit; maybe more, but two were enough. I saw the spout of water forward, and *Akikaze's* bow disappeared, broken short right at the well. The other hit under the stacks, breaking his back, lifting the center of the ship for a moment and then dropping it, like a broken toy.

We really began to take it over the bridge then, but neither Al nor I would have cared if the waves had been periscope high. We slowed after a few minutes of it upon Keith's report that the Q-ship, the only one left by now on the radar, was not chasing us, but had instead gone over to the spot where *Akikaze* had last registered an echo on our radar scope, and hove to.

The radar had also some other pips, three tiny ones, which came in and out on the scope and which clustered around the Q-ship when it got there. Lifeboats, without question.

It would take a feat of seamanship for Bungo's consort to pick them up, though probably no more than Bungo himself had showed in getting them launched in the first place. I didn't doubt that he could do it, all right. A wave of hopelessness swept over me when I realized that barring his own demise, hardly to be planned on, Bungo would return to port, get another *Akikaze,* and go blithely back to the same old business as though nothing had happened.

If we could sink the Q-ship—but how? We had four torpedoes, all aft. None at all left forward. And he was loaded with cellulose or something else equally floatable.

I don't remember making any conscious decision about it. There didn't seem to be any decision to make. A red haze flooded my mind, and I ordered Scott to put the rudder over once more.

"Keith," I gritted, "come on up here!"

For several minutes we talked out our tactics of how to get the stern tubes to bear. The wind was howling and the seas were pounding and the water poured in buckets off us, streamed off Keith's face, off his nose, into his mouth every time he opened it. The same with me, but neither of us took any heed. We ducked those we could, turned our backs to those we saw coming, ignored the rest.

We decided the Q-ship would not expect us to come back. Doubtless he would realize that making a reload was virtually an impossibility unless we dived for it, which would take extra time, and he would hardly expect us to come back otherwise. He would think, at least, that he had time—and his attention would be entirely taken up with the problem of getting Bungo aboard. If we could hit him with all four fish, fairly high up on his side, the weather might well finish for us what we had started.

"Three thousand yards!" said Quin's voice on the conning-tower speaker. Keith swung his dripping form to the ladder, slipped for an instant on the slick hand rail, caught himself, and disappeared.

"He's not under way, bridge! Target speed is zero!" Keith was back in charge down below, on the speaker again.

I pressed the button on my mike, let the insane howl of the elements make the acknowledgment for me. We were coming in at standard speed again, with our four engines on the line just in case. As the stern heaved up to a wave I could see the tip ends of four big pipes pouring out their hydrantlike exhaust. Then a smother of angry water would cover everything, and the four mufflers would be drowned, spluttering feebly, sending up little splashes which the wind instantly whipped away. On this course, chosen to bring us in to windward—presumably the skipper of the Q-ship would elect to pick up the boats to leeward—we were coasting downwind. The bow lifted as a huge sea ran under us, dropping our stern precipitantly and then racing on out beyond our bullnose; black water, streaked with white, capped with a boiling, dirty-white crest. Our speed, which increased with a downhill sledding effect when the stern lifted, decreased abruptly when it turned into uphill. Al Dugan and I were alternately thrown backward against the periscope supports and forward against the bridge cowling—almost as though we were riding a balky horse in slow motion.

The bow disappeared in a welter of white foam as the succeeding wave came under and over our after parts. Nothing at all forward of the bridge, now. Nothing aft, either. Just buffeting, angry, noisy ocean. Our bridge was like a disembodied statue, the upper part of a submarine riding on an angry sea-cloud.

"Two thousand yards, bridge!" I would be able to see him soon. Al helped me wipe off the lens of the TBT binoculars. We did a thorough job before I put my eyes to it.

"Fifteen hundred!" Through the flying spume and blackness I could make out the outline of a ship, a tall, stubby ship. He was nearly broadside to and rolling violently in the furious sweep of the wind and sea; occasionally, as we neared, he steadied up for a moment under some vagary of the elements, perhaps a nullifying combination of them. These were the moments in which he would attempt to pick up Bungo and his men. Probably throw them ropes, haul them aboard one at a time. A fantastic attempt, but seamen had done more fantastic things—history is full of the tales. Normally our role would have been that of the helpful bystander, regardless of the nationality of the shipwrecked mariners. Shipwreck at sea has its own code, its own morality—a joined constant fight for life and survival against the implacable ocean, with its pitiless netherworld of death. But we were out of our normal role. There was a war, the basic immorality of which transcended temporarily the more lasting and better motives of peace. It was our job to try to prevent that rescue by sinking the rescuer.

"Twelve hundred yards!"

Of course, one did not have to think of it that way. We had the duty of sinking any Japanese ship we ran across, and this one was surely as much a ship-of-war as the biggest battleship or the fastest aircraft carrier. Furthermore, it was a menace to our side, particularly to my own special segment of our side. There never could be any argument, except on purely philosophical grounds, and war is the rejection of philosophy.

"One thousand yards!" This was the turning point we had decided on. We had to get close to give us the maneuvering room to turn around. They would find it hard to look into the scud upwind; we could reach one thousand yards from that direction with a fair degree of impunity. Even if they did see us, accurate gunfire from that pitching, rolling platform would be impossible. Only a real director system, with a gyroscopically controlled stabilized firing circuit, could handle these conditions. Of course, there was always the chance of a lucky shot . . .

"Right full rudder! Starboard stop! Starboard back full!" It would be a job even swinging into the wind. *Eel* started to swing nicely enough, got halfway around before the wind really hit her. I could feel the combined force of the wind and sea as our bow rose and exposed itself freely to the effects of both. We stopped dead, as though we had hit a wall of mush. The gyro-compass repeater indicated that we had actually swung back a few degrees.

"Port ahead emergency!" With both screws racing, she would have greater force to push her around. Now I regretted having reversed the starboard propeller, for doing so had killed our forward progress and removed much of the effect of the rudder. And besides this, our straining engines were having all their exhaust fumes blown right down on the enemy ship. A keen nose would detect the characteristic odor of diesels, might just have the flexibility to do something about it.

Still no good. We gained a little, then lost it as the bow came up again.

"Control!" I thumbed the button for the speaker, spoke into it. "Open bow buoyancy vent!" This would lessen the buoyancy of the bow, reduce the area the wind would have to work on. If we could only keep the bow from coming up at all!

"Al! Go on down to the control room." I had to cup my mouth and hold it close to his ear to make him get it all. "Secure the engines and shut the main induction. Put the battery on propulsion. When I give you the word, open the forward group vents, hold them open for three seconds, and then shut them again!" I gave him a shove toward the hatch.

On diving, bow buoyancy vent and all the main ballast tank vents are opened and left open until the ship goes under. The main ballast tanks are handled as two groups, a forward group and an after group, with a set of controls for each. Opening the forward group of vents for about three seconds would not permit all the air entrapped there to escape, but would vent off a large percentage of it. We would not dive because the after group would be still holding all its air in addition to what had not had a chance to whistle out of the forward group vents. But much of our buoyancy forward would be destroyed, and our bow would sink deeper in the water. This would reduce the sail effect of the forward section of the ship—probably eliminate it altogether because we would inevitably ride under all the seas instead of only some of them.

Shutting off the main engines and going to the battery was

— 337

merely precautionary, so that we could close the main induction valve under the cigarette deck. Otherwise we'd pull tons of water down the huge airpipe when the bridge went under.

I grabbed the mike. "Keith, raise the night periscope and see if you can make out the target!" One of the 'scopes had a slightly bigger light path than the other and hence the name "night periscope." If Keith could see the enemy vessel through it, perhaps it would do to take bearing to shoot the torpedoes with, and I could repair below and do it from the relative safety of the conning tower. I waited a few seconds.

"No luck, skipper. Can't see a thing!" This might be because watching the dials and instruments—especially the radar scope —had cost him his night vision. We couldn't wait, however.

"All right, Keith. Station somebody in the bridge hatch ready to shut it if necessary."

"Roger."

"Bridge!" Al Dugan, from the control room. "Ready below!" There was no more exhaust aft. I had not heard the main induction go shut, but it no doubt had.

My little microphone went only to the conning tower. I had to press the bridge speaker button firmly and yell into it to reach Al. "Control! Open and shut the forward group vents!"

Instantly white spray whirred out from between our slotted forward deck, was blown, just as instantly, to nothingness. I counted three to myself. The spray stopped at "four." Nothing happened at first. We heaved up as before to a passing sea, rolling far over to port, losing the few degrees of turn we had managed to accumulate during the past several seconds. Then we dropped, far down. The next sea swept across our deck as though there were no deck there, poured over the bridge side bulwarks, inundated the whole place, filled it with foam-topped green water.

Instinctively I had sought the leeward side, the port side. And just as the roar of the approaching wave heralded its closest

— 338

proximity, boiling up from beneath as well as overwhelming us from on top, I saw the hatch slam shut. Tons of water roared around me. Frantically I gripped the lookout guard rail, felt my feet swept from under me. Sick despair engulfed me. The bitter certainty filled my brain that with the lack of buoyancy forward and the heavy seas rushing at us we had driven completely under. If we did not come up soon I was done for, and Bungo Pete would have won again.

Somehow, buoyed up by the water, I managed to pull myself up a little higher on the lookout rail—my lungs felt as though they would burst if I couldn't get a breath of air—and then I was out of it. The water had rolled past and part of our bridge reappeared. The after TBT came up, mounted on its tripod legs, just abaft of the periscope shears. My mike was gone, lost, but there was a bridge speaker installed under the TBT. Floundering in the water, I struggled aft to it; standing hip-deep I put my eyes to the binoculars. It was blurred—I wiped it off with my fingers, sucking the salt from them first. Still blurred. There was a piece of lens paper in my pocket, somehow only damp, not dripping—wiped it off with that.

"Captain! Are you all right!"

The speaker startled me, booming right into my chest. I pushed the button, twice.

"That did it! We're coming around! I'll steady up on course zero-eight-zero and slow down—all we need is the bearings, skipper!"

The last words were engulfed in another deluge of water. This time I relaxed, twining my arms and legs into the TBT stanchions, waited for it to pass. Twice more the ocean buried me, welling up from beneath the deck and hurtling over the side at the same time, before the welcome voice of my Exec announced that the ship had reached the desired heading. There was now some protection from the bridge bulwarks and periscope supports behind me, as well from the fact that the seas in sweeping in from dead ahead could not pick up quite so much of solid substance through the submerged forepart of the ship.

I wiped off the TBT lenses again, squeezing water from the precious piece of lens paper to do it, sighted through. "Ready, Keith! Single shots! Don't shoot unless I'm holding down the button!" This was to take care of the possibility that I might be temporarily unable to aim. I turned the TBT slowly from side to side, centered the cross hair in the middle of the Q-ship's wildly tossing stack.

"Range, nine hundred! Can you see our stern, Captain? Give us a bearing of the stern light!"

I sighted on to the stern light, which Keith and I had long ago designated as the bore-sight target for the after TBT, just as the center of the bullnose was for the forward one. It was a good precaution in case the seas had done some sudden unsuspected violence to the precious instrument, took only a second. *When you get there, take your time!* I pushed the button on top of the right handle twice.

"OK! Give us the target for the first fish!" Another deluge of water, not so long, this time. I hardly felt it, got the TBT on as soon as my head came out, blurred or not, held the button down.

"One's away!" I let go the button. We'd watch to see where the fish would go, we had decided. Wipe off the lenses again.

BLAM! A stunning flash of light, followed by a solid explosion! Amazingly, I heard it, and almost immediately!

"Hit, skipper!" The speaker—how could Keith have heard, with the ship battened down as it was? Then the obvious explanation: the phenomenon had been noticed before; the sound had traveled four times as fast through the water as it could through air. Occasionally one torpedo would thus produce the sound of two explosions, if fired under conditions permitting the noise to be heard through both air and water.

The hit had been forward of the stack. I put the TBT cross-hair midway between the stack and the stern, thumbed the button again.

"Two's away!" This time I was under when the explosion came in. It shocked my eardrums. They were ringing when I came out again, just in time to see the column of water subsiding, falling on the ridiculous foreshortened stern.

One forward and one aft. Not bad. I aimed the third one at the stack once more.

"Three's away!" The wait again. This was getting to be the payoff. To be reasonably sure of the destruction of the Q-ship, we had to hit her with a lot of torpedoes—three anyway, preferably all four. A quick, secret flash of orange—gunfire! He had unlimbered one of his broadside guns, was shooting in our general direction! I didn't even hear the passage of the shell, wouldn't have cared if I had. This was the payoff, this the moment of revenge. This was getting even for the *Walrus*, and for Jim, Hugh, Dave, and the rest. And it was making it up also for Stocker Kane, who never would have any children to speak proudly of the father who gave his life for his country, and for Hurry Kane, and Laura, and the rest of the people whose lives had been shattered by this fool war. Roy Savage and *Needlefish*, too, gone these long years, rusting their bones somewhere not far from where we were at this very moment . . .

WHRRUMP! Number Three went home, right under the stack. The explosion flash of the shallow-running torpedo momentarily obliterated him from sight. The water spout came up—I thought the motion of the stack looked a little strange, different from the crazily tossing masts of the rest of the ship —when the white water deluged down, the smokestack was leaning drunkenly, slowly toppled forward. And there was something a bit different in the way he rolled, too. Slower, farther over each time a sea tossed him.

The fourth fish. Same place—where the stack had been. Hold the button down: "Four's away, skipper!"

Maybe we could have saved that one. The masts had not

come back from the last roll, were still leaning toward me. I thought I could see part of the deck, grayer than the black hull. There they go—back up again, slowly, however—no, just a wave rolling past. Down came the two masts, lower than ever toward the black, eager water, the deck now clearly visible as a gray slash at the top of the black outline.

Our fourth torpedo smashed squarely into it, right into the black spot in the center of the gray where the stack and central deckhouse had been.

Supplicatingly, as if tired of conflict and travail, the masts lay on the water. The hull separated into two parts, and I saw the outline of the bottoms of both, intermittently, as the seas raced upon them.

"Radar shows he's sinking, skipper! We're blowing up now!" The *Eel's* forward half-rose quickly; they were using high-pressure air instead of the low-pressure blowers. In a moment, it seemed, we were fully surfaced, and Keith and Al joined me. I pointed silently astern. There was the thump of the main induction beneath my feet.

"I ordered it opened, skipper," said Keith. "We'll be putting the engines on in a minute." We were all three looking aft when four exhaust plumes shot out, and the roar of our engines came faintly upwind to us. Al handed me a clean piece of lens paper, helped me do a thorough job on the TBT binoculars.

We could barely make out the low-lying hulks of the two halves of our antagonist, more by their dark red color than by their shapes. Every succeeding wave which tore down upon them buried them, and finally there came a time when we could see only one.

"What's the range, conn?" I called into the after speaker.

"Eight hundred yards, sir!" We had been drifting backward during the whole time of our attack. "We still have four pips on the radar, bridge!"

At this moment the second red blob failed to rematerialize.

A long instant we watched for it to rise into sight, finally knew it too had gone. "One pip's gone, bridge! Three left, coming in and out!"

"He doesn't know what he's talking about!" muttered Al.

"No, he's right. Those are the lifeboats!" Keith's voice was matter of fact.

Of course, the lifeboats. And Bungo was just the man to weather the storm in them, too. Less than fifty miles from shore, he'd be back in business with his crew of sonar and depth-charge experts within a week!

"Go below, both of you!" I spoke roughly, an unaccustomed dryness in my mouth.

"Why, what's the matter . . . ?" one look and Keith shut up. I waved him impatiently to the hatch.

"Right full rudder! All ahead flank!" This time there was no trouble turning, with the wind helping. And then it was pushing us, blowing at my back, the seas alternately lifting first stern, then bow, as they steam-rollered on by. Every time our bullnose lifted clear of the water it must have heaved twenty feet into the air, before the sea caught up with it.

I pushed the forward speaker button. "Radar! What's the bearing and distance to the nearest pip!"

"Three-zero-zero, one thousand!"

"Keep the ranges coming!" I shouted. Then to the helmsman: "Steer three-zero-zero!"

We came right a little. After a little I could see it, a little boat with oars out, tossed up against the sky. It was not so hard to see; dawn was breaking, I realized. A little to starboard.

"Steer three-zero-five!" That put it right ahead. On we came. Now they saw us, lay on their oars, looking. A row of faces staring out of hunched-over bodies, heads sunk between their shoulders. They had had a rough night, and a rougher morning. I gritted my teeth. "Steer three-zero-four!"

They suddenly realized their danger. Oars moved jerkily, frantically, not in unison. They had been in the "no-quarter" business too. They knew what was coming. We were right on them, towered above them, our huge bow raised high on a wave, poised in deadly, smashing promise, pitiless; the row of freeing ports at the base of bow buoyancy must have looked like foaming dragon's teeth. I looked the steersman right in the eye as he stood at his oar, dead ahead and far below—the wave passed. Our bow dropped like a guillotine.

The boat never even came up. One black round head swam by, looking up with horror-filled eyes, arms and fists raised out of the water, skidded down our rounded belly, vanished aft spinning in our wake. I steeled myself. This was how they had looked in *Walrus* when the unexpected fatal torpedo explosion had hit them. This was the look Jim had given to Rubinoffski, that Knobby Robertson had exchanged with Dave.

Push the button again. Go on with it! This is what you came out here to do! You have to kill Bungo and all of his crew! "Radar! Range and bearing to the nearest pip!"

"North! Six hundred!"

I could hardly talk. My voice suffocated in my chest. "Steer north!" I croaked.

"Skipper, may I come on the bridge?" Keith.

"No! Goddamit! Stay below!" The choked swear words came easily. "Keep the hell out of this!"

"What's the bearing now!"

"Three-five-nine!"

"Steer three-five-nine!" I could catch the note of disbelief in the helmsman's voice as he acknowledged. Scott had not divined my purpose the first time, but he knew now. The rules of discipline held firm, however, and the lubber's line settled one degree left of due north.

It was getting lighter, and I could see better all the time. I didn't feel the wind and spray on my face, or the pounding of the sea coming aboard over our exposed starboard beam. I aimed the juggernaught—myself—exactly at the center of the boat. As before, they watched at first in surprise, suddenly in terror, when they knew. They rowed better than the first boat, started to edge out of our way. I was ready.

"Left ten degrees rudder!" We curved left a little. "Amidships!"

We smote it amidships with our bullnose rising, smashed in the side, tumbled it over, rolled it down and out of sight under our keel. Some sticks of kindling came up in our wake, nothing that could be recognized as a boat.

"Radar, give me the bearing and range to the last pip!"

No answer. "Radar! Acknowledge!" The voice was weak, hesitant. "Nothing on the radar, sir!"

"You're lying!"

"Zero-six-three, one thousand!" Keith's voice, strong and dominant.

This time it was right into the teeth of the storm. Mindful of our former difficulty in turning, I gave no order to the screws, only to the rudder. I staggered back as the wind hit me over the edge of the cowling, had to duck periodically as the seas came aboard and broke with great sheets of solid black and gray water yards over my head. The boat came into sight at around eight hundred yards, a tiny dot in the water, an infinitesimal oasis in the great sea-desert. Rolling, pitching, staggering, like a drunken man, we headed for it. Five hundred yards. One hundred yards.

"Zing!" A rifle bullet. "Zing!" "Zing!" A sharp rap, as one hit the armored side plating at the front of the bridge, and the whine of a ricochet. Somebody was still fighting. Maybe he had seen us ride down the other boats. The boat turned bow on as the *Eel* approached, making the most difficult target it could. I aimed right for its stem, watching carefully. Our bullnose rose above it with the short, quick, choppy movement of a ship plunging into a sea, just grazed it on descending, had it a little on the port bow.

"Left full rudder!" I ducked at the same time as I gave the order, a split second before a bullet smashed into the TBT binoculars.

Peering over the bridge cowling, I saw our bow alongside, pushing the boat as we began our swing to port. They were fending us off with their oars. Once the bow came by, of course, our stern would swing wide and clear by many yards. I ducked again.

"Shift your rudder to full right!" Scott had not yet reached full left, reversed himself immediately. We bumped them again with our belly, sideswiping.

The man with the rifle had been standing in the stern, alongside the steering oarsman. I caught a quick glimpse of a short, fat fellow with an impassive moon face as the boat skidded by. He looked mean, hard, in the oily dead-pan way that only certain Orientals can. Then the exhaust of the two port engines poured into the boat. A sea lifted it, set it down on the turn of our tanks, cracking the ribs with a loud smash of splintered wood. It bounced off, half-capsizing, drifted aft into our wake, bilged and flooding.

I left the rudder at full right, and we came around in a circle. This time there was no avoiding us. The lifeboat was completely filled with water. The rifle pocked the front of our bridge before we hit.

Our stem knifed through the fragile sides as if they were match sticks. It split in half. A final shot cracked overhead. I saw the gun flying out into the water at the instant of the collision. There were bodies in the water on both sides as we hurtled past. One shook his fists at us, his mouth open in a scream no one could have heard, and tried to swim over to us. It was only a few feet, and he managed to put both hands on the smooth skin of our ballast tanks back near the stern. But the speed of the ship and the heaving of the ocean were too much for him, and I last saw him spinning in the wash as our flailing propellers sucked him down and under.

"All ahead one third!" I yelled down the hatch. Then in the speaker, "Radar! Are there any more pips on the scope!"

Keith answered, as before. "Nothing on the radar, Captain."

My hands were trembling. They wouldn't stop. My knees too. I felt as if I were about to fall over. I wrapped both arms around the shattered TBT, and deep, wracking sobs came boiling up out of the hard, twisted knot that was my belly.

CHAPTER 14

KEITH WROTE THE MESSAGE TO ComSubPac for me. I couldn't bring myself to think about it. To get old Nakame, I had murdered three lifeboat loads of helpless Japanese.

We sent:

FOR COMSUBPAC X SPECIAL MISSION SUCCESSFUL X SCRATCH BUNGO PERMANENTLY RPT PERMANENTLY X ALL TORPEDOES EXPENDED X EEL SENDS TO COMSUBPAC.

The answer which came in the next night was hardly the one we expected. Instead of sending us back to Pearl or Midway for a new load of torpedoes, or even requiring us to keep the

Bungo Suido under close surveillance for a while until someone could be sent out to relieve us, we were directed to proceed immediately to Guam, there to stand by for lifeguard duty during a series of air strikes. And there was no comment about our success. It was absurd to think that somehow ComSubPac had heard what the *Eel* had done, but there it was.

The news was greeted with a chorus of dismay from the crew, who had been eagerly anticipating an early return from patrol. Their reaction to the final combat, during which we had deliberately murdered a lot of unresisting shipwrecked Japanese, was curious. At first I sensed disbelief, disapproval. Eyes looked at me silently, thoughtfully. The men fell silent when I happened near. When I left I could hear conversation resumed, low-voiced, uneasy. They thought me a murderer, I knew. They would obey me, do my bidding quickly—more quickly then ever—but they would never think of me as other than a man who had killed my fellow man in cold blood. War or not, I had gone beyond the permissible limit.

Some of the officers also seemed to be affected, the only exception being Keith, who had not changed. But nobody seemed in the least unwilling to take the maximum advantage out of it, now that the loathsome deed was done.

As for myself, the longer I thought about it, the more I dwelt on it, the lower I felt. There was no answering the arguments. I had done what I had set out to do; I had destroyed Bungo Pete, and he deserved destroying, by our lights, for he had destroyed many of our fellows. But to do it I had crossed the boundary dividing the decent from the indecent; the thin line between the moral and immoral. I was a pariah, despised, an outcast. I would never be able to look a decent, untarnished man in the face again.

All the way south to Guam the lifeboats haunted me. I couldn't sleep, tossed fitfully, always the tortured faces in front of me, screaming when we drove past them the last time. I dreamed that I could understand Japanese, or that they had shouted in English, and I strained to catch their last words. Always they cast some foul curse upon me and the *Eel,* always prophesying doom, swearing ever-lasting revenge. I took to spending long solitary hours on the bridge, alone, standing at the after part of the cigarette deck, looking at the water rushing past, or sitting on my bunk staring at the green curtain closing off the entrance.

Keith tried unsuccessfully to snap me out of it. "Don't take it that way," he'd say. "We all did it together. I'd have done the same thing! We had to do it—Bungo would have been back there with all his crew of experts in a new tincan within a couple of weeks. Nobody's blaming you. The men are proud of you."

But it didn't do any good. I hardly glanced at the operation dispatches as they came in, made Keith do all the planning, see to all the preparations. Vaguely I knew that we were supposed to stay on the surface during the air strikes, and remain in a certain spot, where crippled planes could find us. The aviators would ditch their planes or parachute out as close to us as they could get, and it was up to us to get them aboard. We were to remain there three days, unless the objectives of the air strike were achieved sooner.

On the morning of the first day, flying our biggest American flag, we were on station. The dispatches had said that the Jap aircraft would have much too much to do to spend any time bothering about a little submarine wandering around on the surface thirty miles south of Guam, but it felt a bit risky at first. Then several flights of U.S. carrier-based planes appeared to the south, flew overhead en route to make their attack. We were too far to see the actual bombing runs but some of the dog-fights took place within our sight. And as the dispatches had said, none of the Jap planes took a second look at us.

We got no business the first day. So far as Keith or I could see from the bridge, every U. S. plane returned safely to its carrier, in the big task force over the horizon to the south. There were no distress calls on the special aircraft frequency we were guarding, though we did hear the fliers talking to each other.

As the second day wore on, it appeared likely that we'd have no business either. Our forces greatly outnumbered the enemy, and they were having a picnic. Mid-afternoon they started back, some of them flying low over us and waggling their wings. As I looked up at them, I wondered how it felt to fly in combat over the ocean, with no succor nearby in case of trouble, and thought I could sense, in some measure, the moral support given by our presence.

"Guess it's about over for today, too," said Keith. "Wonder if we can try to stay on the surface instead of diving like yesterday?" The day previous we had dived as soon as the last planes had gone back, in accordance with our instructions, but the air had seemed so empty and peaceful that after a time we wondered why we had bothered.

It was about this time that the bridge speaker blared forth: "Bridge! Radio thinks they can hear a distress message!"

"I'll go down and see, skipper!" With that, Keith slipped down the hatch. In a few minutes his voice came up the speaker:

"It's a little business for us after all, sir. I'm telling the rescue party to stand by!"

Six men had been selected for their general stamina and ability to swim, to help bring wounded or helpless airmen aboard. Buck Williams was in charge, and they were outfitted with heaving lines, knives, Mae West life preservers, and other pieces of paraphernalia.

Keith on the speaker again: "There are three men in the plane, all wounded. They're going to try to ditch near us. They say they have us in sight!"

Low to the water, just appearing over the northeast horizon, a plane appeared, flying one wing low. It approached, circled us once. I could see holes in the fuselage and wing. The plane went off in the distance, turned, began to drop slowly, tail down.

The pilot had evidently picked his heading so as to finish fairly near to us, and he did a nice job of letting his craft down into the water. It came in pretty fast, however, struck with a tremendous splash, bounced into the air, belly-flopped back in, and skidded to a stop.

Before it stopped moving we were under way heading for it, and several short minutes later we drew up alongside the two yellow life rafts that had miraculously appeared before the plane sank. Our rescue party was down on deck, looking very businesslike as they waited for the ship to approach closer to the rafts. One of them, Scott, held a heaving line coiled loosely in his hand, as though he were going to heave it to shore.

There was about fifteen yards' distance to the rafts when our headway petered out. We were anxious, of course, not to come up too fast and take a chance of upsetting them with our wash. Scott took two or three tentative swings with the heaving line, wound up, and let fly. The heave was a beauty—which was why he had been picked for this job—and the weighted end landed just beyond the nearest raft, trailing the line across it.

Through my binoculars I could see the single flier in the smaller of the two rubber boats grasp the line and painfully haul upon it. It was evident that it hurt him to move. I cupped my hands, yelled at him: "Make it fast! We'll pull you in!"

He made no acknowledgment, but I could see him pass the end of the line through one of the flaps of the boat and take a quick turn.

"OK, Scott. Pull them in easy," I called. Three or four sailors on deck grabbed the rope, pulled slowly and gently, and in a few seconds the first life raft was alongside, the other following at the end of a short line. Several men reached down to help the fliers aboard, but it was evident that they were badly hurt, not to say exhausted, and beyond doing anything more to help themselves. Feebly, the man in the nearest life raft reached up, finally lay back, and shook his head with a helpless grimace.

"Pull them up forward to the sea ladder," Keith called to Williams. Buckley and Scott ran forward, pulling the heaving line with them, lined the rubber boats up with the foot holes cut in the side of our superstructure, knotted the line around one of the forward cleats. Then they ran back to where Oregon, also in the party, was preparing to lower himself over the side. His feet had already reached the first rung when one of the lookouts on the platform above me shouted a frantic warning.

"PLANE! PLANE!"

Keith and I looked over our shoulders instinctively. It was there, all right, a big four-engine patrol boat. It was coming right at us, the four big propellers glinting in the sun, the straight-across Japanese wing a thin, horizontal line bisecting them.

"Clear the decks!" I yelled. I reached down, pulled the toggle handle—our air-operated foghorn blasted its warning. Then, "Clear the bridge!" Keith and the lookouts dashed below. The men down on deck came racing up. Oregon almost flew up from his barely over-the-side perch. When Williams, the last man off the deck, had almost reached the bridge level, I sounded the diving alarm.

"They'll be all right in the rafts—I told them we'd come right back up for them," Buck said, as he ran past me.

"You bet!" I thought, "and we'll surface under the plane and smash it to bits if it lands to capture them!"

Our vents were open, air whistling out of them, as I gave a last look around. The plane was a fair distance away; we'd get down in time. But as I looked forward my heart froze like a stone in my chest. The heaving line Scott had used was still fast to the starboard forward cleat, and our bow was already dipping toward the sea!

Instantaneously my mind encompassed the inevitables. Within seconds we would be submerged, dragging the line, and the two rubber boats, with us. The three fliers would be dumped into the water. In their condition their survival for even a few minutes was a foregone impossibility. Even if we did come back for them, all we would find would be bodies, half-chewed by fishes attracted by the blood.

It could not have taken me more than a third of a second to assess the grim results of our carelessness. My carelessness in allowing the line to be made fast to the ship, Buck's in not cutting it free during the half a dozen seconds he had waited for Oregon, down on deck. All of ours, for not having anticipated the possibility of this very situation days ago.

Keith's head was framed in the hatch. "Skipper!" he shouted.

"Take charge, Keith!" I yelled the words at him while running to the after part of the bridge where the rail was cut for access to the deck.

I leaped down, raced forward. The bow had just begun to dip when I got there, water barely sliding over the deck. Furiously I ripped at the heaving line. It was made fast in a hitch; no loop to pull to release it. I cursed aloud. No knife in my pocket! How could I have been so improvident? The cleat was well under now, my hands buried inches—a foot—under.

The water rose rapidly to my face, the current due to our increase in speed on diving tugging at my arms. Frantically I pulled. My feet slipped, and I plunged into the cool water, sitting down facing aft, legs on either side of the cleat. This kept me from slipping further, and I concentrated on the now-soaked knot while I held my breath and tried to hold myself against the rising panic. *"Take it easy, take your time; take it easy, take your time!"* I said it over and over to myself, as the rush of the water bent me over the cleat. My ears began to hurt. We must be pretty deep now. I pulled again, got my fingers under some part of it, yanked with both hands and what must have been superhuman force, felt the line come free and slip swiftly from my hands.

Painfully I braced back against the rush of water. I got both hands against the end of the cleat around which my legs were spread-eagled, pushed with everything I had. There was a terrific pain in my groin, paralyzing, digging deep into my insides. I doubled over, clutching my abdomen, felt the pain and me and the suffocating roaring in my ears chasing each other around and around and around.

I must have been out for a moment, for the next thing I remember was bright sunlight and the most exquisite, excruciating pain I have ever felt. I was floating in the water, one arm hooked in one of the life rafts, my head pillowed on the rubber inflated edge. Something was holding my arm, and a voice was saying something I couldn't understand. I shook my head, looked up. A deep gash of agony made me double up again.

The spasm passed, leaving a quick, throbbing ache, and I managed to raise my head. "Hang on!" the voice said. It was the flier who had caught the heaving line. He was holding on to my arm like grim death itself, his face contorted, bloodless. It was obviously he who had pulled me, somehow, half into the rubber raft and held me there while I regained my senses. It, too, in his condition, must have called for a nearly superhuman effort.

"I'm all right now," I managed to say, and made as if to struggle aboard. Waves of acute ache pervaded my entire abdominal section, and I had to stop. Resting for a moment and gasping with the pain, I tried it again, this time tumbled head first into the soft rubber bottom of the raft.

"Easy, fella, that's mah busted leg!" the flier said. I twisted around carefully. "Are you the skipper?" he asked in a different tone. I nodded, clutching my knees to my chest to ease the pain, cradling it.

"I don't know how you did it," the flier said. "When your boat started diving I saw the rope tied up yonder, and I just naturally figured we'd had it after all. Then you came flying out to ontie it—and then you-all went under, and the rope started to pull us over to it and we were about going under ourselves before you got it loose."

A shadow flitted across us. I looked up. "There's the son-of-a-bitch that brought us all the trouble," the flier said. It was the Jap flying boat, all right, flying low over the water to take a good look. It passed not far off, made a circle, passed again, then roared off to the north.

My ache subsided a little, and I straightened up gratefully. "The sub will stick around to get us," I told him. "They'll surface as soon as the plane goes out of sight for good."

"Hope that's pretty soon. My men are bad hit." He shifted to give me a little more room, winced with the silent hurt of it. The bottom of the rubber boat had a puddle of diluted blood in it.

I looked at the other boat. The two men were still, lying quietly within it, only their heads showing. Their boat bobbed helplessly in the vast lonely expanse of the ocean. The water, which had seemed virtually flat calm from *Eel's* bridge, seesawed the rafts uneasily.

"Are they unconscious?" I asked him.

"They weren't when they got in it. Maybe now they are."

In the distance the flying boat went out of sight. I tried to sit up straighter, to disregard the discomfort it brought. "Can you see the periscope of my sub?"

"Nope. Never seen one. What does it look like?"

"Like a broom handle, floating straight up and down," I said. "It ought to be around here somewhere."

Presently he nudged me. "There's a broom handle." I looked where he indicated, saw the *Eel's* periscope approaching. I waved violently, involuntarily rocking the boat, to show Keith that I was all right. The periscope began to rise higher. Keith was surfacing, or about to surface.

The flier nudged me again. "There's that Jap bastard again!" To the north, sure enough, the now-familiar outlines were all too evident, coming back. Heedless of my companion's protests, steeling myself against the waves of pain, I stood up, braced myself on his shoulders, pointed determinedly down. I made several violent hand signals, shook my head from one extreme to the other, pointed to the north. A bubble of white burst astern of the periscope, and its length began to decrease. I saw the quick glint of the eye-piece as it turned in the direction I had pointed, and sat down again, relieved. Keith would have the word now.

For about an hour *Eel's* periscope slowly cruised warily about, and for an hour the Jap flying boat flew back and forth, flying over the horizon, coming back almost overhead, then flying out of sight again. Each time it disappeared I thought it might stay away, and each time my hopes were dashed by its reappearance.

"How long can this kind of a plane stay in the air?" I asked of my companion.

"I sure don't know. A mighty long time, but it depends on when they took off." He grinned a pain-filled grin. "Now let me ask you a foolish one. How soon do you figure you can come up and get us aboard? I'm getting worried about those two fellas over in the other boat."

I shook my head dolefully. "I'm beginning to think those Japs know what's happened down here, and they're expecting the sub to come back. That's why they're flying back and forth." An idea struck me.

"Let's time the flights. Have you got a watch? Mine's stopped."

Silently he produced one and at my instruction timed the flights of the plane from just before it went out of sight until it arrived back in our vicinity. While he did so, I busied myself hauling in the heaving line and inspecting it carefully. It seemed in fair shape. Carefully I fashioned a slipknot in the unweighted end, tested the security of the knot by which it was fastened to our raft. Likewise, I checked the line leading to the other raft and shortened it as much as I could, bringing the other rubber boat tight up against ours.

The preparations, in our cramped situation, took quite a while. It hurt like hades to move, too. "How long?" I finally asked as the flying boat swung around at the completion of its second circuit.

"Ten minutes this last time, eight the time before. Takes three minutes to go out of sight."

"Good. Maybe eight minutes will be long enough." I didn't want to rise in the rubber raft yet, for fear the Jap aviators would see that something out of the ordinary was going on. Obviously they were playing the cat-and-mouse game, hoping Keith would swallow the bait and try to rescue us. *Eel,* in the meantime, was cruising around with only the minimum of periscope showing, keeping it alternately fixed on us and the flying boat, with occasional looks all around the horizon just in case. When the plane came close, Keith would dunk the 'scope and we would not see it again until after the plane had started back on another leg.

The flying boat was well on its way now. I motioned to Keith to come alongside, to cruise as close to us as he could. The periscope went up and down several times, and slowly it began to approach.

He was a little too cautious, no doubt for fear of hitting the rafts and dumping us all, but I was ready for that eventuality. Carrying the noose end of the heaving line, I slipped over the side and struggled through the water into his path. The 'scope came at me surprisingly fast—three knots or so is mighty fast to a man in the water—but I managed to grab hold and slip the loop over the end of it. As the periscope took it away I slid down the tautening line until I reached the raft again and remained there in the water, my arm looped over the thin, tight cord.

The other periscope came up, turned around, studied the

first one, rising and descending slowly to inspect the line where I had made it fast, then steadied on us. I made a staying motion with my hand, looked to the plane. It was approaching the horizon, not there yet. I watched it going over, waited a deliberate twenty seconds, made a violent upward motion.

Beneath us I could see the long hull of the *Eel*—black on top, gray on the sides. Because of the refraction of the water, I could see the gray sides as well, made a mental note to carry the black just a little farther down the next time we painted her. We were dragging along somewhere over the five-inch gun.

Nothing happened for a long time. I knew Keith would not delay, wondered what was taking so long, finally realized the deck was nearer. Suddenly the periscope with the line around its neck disappeared. Keith had lowered it. The other, now higher out of water, commenced to show the bright cylindrical section which went down inside the bearings, began also to lean back toward us.

"Here they come!" I said. *Eel* came with a rush. Water cascaded from her periscope supports and from the bridge, poured in torrents from her main decks. It was a good thing Keith had had the foresight to lower the periscope to which I had tied the heaving line; otherwise its length would have been insufficient to reach the deck, and we should have taken a nasty tumble. Hanging on to it as I was, I was able to touch the deck first with my feet and, gritting my teeth against the hurt of it, to some small degree guide the landing of the two rafts.

The second one almost landed on top of the gun, avoided it by inches as I strained in the tumultuous rush of water to pull them forward toward me. And then there was the bang of the hatch on the bridge, and Keith's voice yelling. Men raced from the cigarette deck, dived over the rail, jumped down recklessly. Eager hands grabbed all four of us, hustled us to the bridge, pitched us unceremoniously down into the conning tower, feet first or head first, whichever end got there first. It didn't matter, for there were plenty of people inside to help out. Through it all I was conscious of great haste. Finally the last injured man was passed down the hatch, followed by Keith and Buck Williams, and the hatch was slammed shut. Instantly the vents went open—I heard no two blasts or anything else on the diving alarm—and *Eel* began to slip beneath the waves.

"Buck," Keith said urgently, "did you get the line cut?"

"You bet I did, this time, and I punctured both rafts, too!" Williams looked a bit shamefaced.

"Al! Take her right on down! They're coming in as fast as they can! Rig for depth charge!"

I had to admire Keith's command of the situation. He had thought of cutting the two rafts free so that they would not trail behind on the line to betray us, and he had certainly organized the rescue party in jig time. Now he held firm command of the ship in what amounted to a serious emergency. He paid no attention to me or anyone of the raft party, was strictly business, at the moment anxiously watching the conning tower depth gauge.

"Seventy-five feet," he finally said. "I guess we're clear!"

WHAM! Good and close, too. The *Eel's* tough hide rang for several seconds, and dust raised here and there. Keith crossed to the phone, picked it up.

"All compartments report," he said. He listened for a moment, hung it up. "No damage, skipper," he said.

Then he faced me squarely, his eyes two deep wells of concern. "God, skipper! What a helluvan experience! How do you feel? Are you OK? Do you need anything?"

I was dripping wet and I ached all over, and the pain in my groin was still a dull, throbbing knife in my guts, but I had not felt so good in a week. There was nothing more I needed, I told him.

CHAPTER 15

So that's about the whole story. We made three more patrols in the *Eel* and sank several more Japanese ships in the first two—during the last one we didn't because there were none left to sink—and then the war ended and I had to fly here to Washington for a round of ceremonies I had never expected would happen to me. Keith is still with the ship in Pearl, and Admiral Small expects me back next week when he pins the Navy Cross on him. Everybody seems to have gone wild over our rescue of the three fliers. I've sat through half a dozen speeches about it, all embarrassingly overdone, and there's a stack of mail piling up on the ship and at home in the same vein. Personally, I could tell about one thing that was an awful lot tougher, but that's all in the past and best forgotten now.

I only had an hour in San Francisco waiting for my plane, so I had to call Hurry up instead of going to see her. Twice there was a busy signal, and I was beginning to fear I'd not get to talk to her at all, but I got a connection just as they announced the plane.

"Rich!" she breathed when I told her who it was. "Where are you? Can you come over?"

"Wish I could," I told her. "But my plane is supposed to take off right away. I'll see you on the way back from Washington."

"I'm so proud of you, Rich. I think it's just wonderful about your getting the Medal of Honor, I mean!"

"I've got to go to New London for a little while . . ."

"Good!" she exclaimed. "Maybe you can stop over in New Haven and see Laura. You know, she was out here for a whole month just a little while ago—just left, in fact. She's a dear. What a dreadful shame about Jim!"

It was typical of Hurry to think about Laura instead of about her own loss. Maybe she instinctively knew that was what I wanted to talk about. "How is she?" I asked.

"Oh, she's fine. She's been working too hard and is a little thin, but I think she's more beautiful than ever. She took it pretty hard about Jim, though, especially right after he was reported missing and some of those stories started to drift back. He should have written more often to her."

"I don't think anybody was able to write as often as he would have liked," I began, but Hurry interrupted me again. She was talking rapidly, as though racing against time to get it all in.

"No, Rich. Listen to me. Jim's been gone a year, now, and I know it's dreadful to speak ill of the dead, but Laura was miserable. His letters kept getting fewer and shorter and more distant. She wrote him long letters, several times a week, and the measly little notes she got back were downright inconsiderate. And then there were those rumors about Jim playing around. Rich, why don't you go and see her while you're in New London?"

I kept leading, because I had to find out. "You know how she feels about me, Hurry," I said.

Hurry's voice took on a tinge of friendly exasperation. "Rich, what do you think I'm trying to tell you? Jim wrote her one time that he had finally understood how right you were about that qualification business. Then when she stayed with me we had plenty of time to talk—that's when I found out most of this, though I suspected some of it already. I told Laura a lot of things that I had learned from Stocker, about how it was to be a skipper of a Navy ship, especially skipper of a submarine with the lives of all those men depending on you. I told her that Stocker had had to disqualify his Engineer Officer once, on the *R-12*, and the Squadron Commander spun him out of New London so fast that nobody knew he was gone until he had been transferred for several days . . ."

The loud-speaker near the phone booth blared the second warning for my plane. Hurry must have heard it too, for she practically stuttered out the last words in her rush to get them all in.

"Promise me you won't tell her, Rich. At least not until after. But go and see her. I've always wished she had met you before Jim. You're more her type. She was fascinated by Jim—who wouldn't be?—but you're the man she needs. And she's always liked you, Rich. Even when she seemed not to, she really did."

"Well, I . . ." I started to say, but the warning call came again.

"Go on! Please! Don't just stand there and argue. You've got to go and at least see her." Hurry hung up.

I had to run to catch the plane, but the call was worth it. Now I've got just an hour and a half to get my suitcase and climb aboard the train for New Haven. There'll be plenty of time for New London later. Right now I want to see Laura, just as soon as I can. The war is over. She needs me and I need her. For once there'll be plenty of time for everything.

End of transcription of tape recording #16MH, recorded by Commander E. J. Richardson, USN on 30 August 1945.

Transcribed on September 17, 1945, by Susan Cork, Y3c, USNR (W). Checked by Mary Kruschendorf, Y1c, USNR (W).

Submitted:

S. V. Matthews,
Captain, U. S. Navy